"Why did you call me here tonight?"

"You wanted to talk about the poisoning and the attack, yes I know." Harry rose from the table. "But your breasts are all but naked and you've sent the servants away. The *other* servants. Why do you really want me here?"

"I . . ." George felt her heart quicken.

"Because I'm not what you think I am," Harry said evenly as he advanced around the table toward her. "I'm not a servant to jump to your bidding and then lie down when you've done with me. I'm a man with blood in his veins. If you start something with me, don't expect me to turn into a lapdog, panting at your call." Harry seized her upper arms and drew her against his hard body.

He drew a finger slowly across the edge of her bodice, watching her reaction. She couldn't think while he touched her. He dipped two fingers below her bodice. She shuddered . . .

Praise for *The Raven Prince*

"4½ Stars! TOP PICK! With its delicious blend of fairy tale and reality *The Raven Prince* is refreshing, fast-paced, and sensual romance dishing up plenty of tempting thoughts of desire. You'll adore Hoyt's intelligent characters and their spicy dialogue as much as the heated love scenes."

—Kathe Robin, *Romantic Times BOOKclub Magazine*

"A spicy broth of pride, passion, and temptation."

—Connie Brockway, *USA Today* bestselling author

"A must read! A beautiful romance that will leave you breathless . . . make you laugh and yet make you cry . . . and will touch your heart and soul. Tissues are a definite must! Hoyt knows how to tug on your heartstrings! I can't wait to read more from this talented author."

—RomanceReaderAtHeart.com

"A delicious romance...I enjoyed it immensely!"

—Jane Feather, *New York Times* bestselling author

THE
LEOPARD
PRINCE

OTHER TITLES BY ELIZABETH HOYT

The Raven Prince

The Serpent Prince

THE
LEOPARD
PRINCE

ELIZABETH HOYT

FOREVER

NEW YORK   BOSTON

Copyright © 2007 by Nancy M. Finney
Excerpt from *The Serpent Prince* copyright © 2007
by Nancy M. Finney

All rights reserved. Except as permitted under the U.S. Copyright Act of 1976, no part of this publication may be reproduced, distributed, or transmitted in any form or by any means, or stored in a database or retrieval system, without the prior written permission of the publisher.

Forever is an imprint of Grand Central Publishing.
The Forever name and logo is a trademark of Hachette Book Group, Inc.

Cover design by Diane Luger
Cover illustration by Franco Accornero
Book design by Stratford Publishing Services

Forever
Hachette Book Group
237 Park Avenue
New York, NY 10169

Visit our Web site at www.HachetteBookGroup.com

Printed in the United States of America

First Printing: April 2007

10 9 8 7 6 5 4 3

For my sister, SUSAN.

No imaginary characters were hurt during the writing of this book.

Chapter One

After the carriage wreck and a bit before the horses ran away, Lady Georgina Maitland noticed that her land steward was a man. Well, that is to say, naturally she knew Harry Pye was a man. She wasn't under the delusion that he was a lion or an elephant or a whale, or indeed any other member of the animal kingdom—if one could call a whale an animal and not just a very big fish. What she meant was that his *male*ness had suddenly become very evident.

George knit her brow as she stood in the desolate high road leading to East Riding in Yorkshire. Around them, the gorse-covered hills rolled away into the gray horizon. Dark was rapidly falling, brought on early by the rainstorm. They could've been standing at the ends of the earth.

"Do you consider a whale to be an animal or a very big fish, Mr. Pye?" she shouted into the wind.

Harry Pye's shoulders bunched. They were covered only by a wet lawn shirt that clung to him in an aesthetically pleasing way. He'd previously discarded his coat and waistcoat to help John Coachman unhitch the horses from the overturned carriage.

"An animal, my lady." Mr. Pye's voice was, as always, even and deep with a sort of gravelly tone toward the bottom.

George had never heard him raise his voice or show passion in any way. Not when she'd insisted on accompanying him to her Yorkshire estate; not when the rain had started, slowing their travel to a crawl; not when the carriage had overturned twenty minutes ago.

How very irritating. "Do you think you will be able to right the carriage?" She pulled her soaked cloak up over her chin as she contemplated the remains of her vehicle. The door hung from one hinge, banging in the wind, two wheels were smashed, and the back axle had settled at an odd angle. It was a thoroughly idiotic question.

Mr. Pye didn't indicate by action or word that he was aware of the silliness of her query. "No, my lady."

George sighed.

Really, it was something of a miracle that they and the coachman hadn't been hurt or killed. The rain had made the roads slippery with mud, and as they had rounded the last curve, the carriage had started to slide. From inside, she and Mr. Pye had heard the coachman shouting as he tried to steady the vehicle. Harry Pye had leapt from his seat to hers, rather like a large cat. He'd braced himself against her before she could even utter a word. His warmth had surrounded her, and her nose, buried intimately in his shirt, had inhaled the scent of clean linen and male skin. By that time, the carriage had tilted, and it was obvious they were falling into the ditch.

Slowly, awfully, the contraption had tipped over with

a grinding crash. The horses had whinnied from the front, and the carriage had moaned as if protesting its fate. She'd clutched Mr. Pye's coat as her world upended, and Mr. Pye grunted in pain. Then they were still again. The vehicle had rested on its side, and Mr. Pye rested on her like a great warm blanket. Except Harry Pye was much firmer than any blanket she'd ever felt before.

He'd apologized most correctly, disentangled himself from her, and climbed up the seat to wrest open the door above them. He'd crawled through and then bodily pulled her out. George rubbed the wrist he'd gripped. He was disconcertingly strong—one would never know it to look at him. At one point, almost her entire weight had hung from his arm and she wasn't a petite woman.

The coachman gave a shout, which was snatched away by the wind, but it was enough to bring her back to the present. The mare he'd been unhitching was free.

"Ride her to the next town, Mr. Coachman, if you will," Harry Pye directed. "See if there is another carriage to send back. I'll remain here with her ladyship."

The coachman mounted the horse and waved before disappearing into the downpour.

"How far is the next town?" George asked.

"Ten or fifteen miles." He pulled a strap loose on one of the horses.

She studied him as he worked. Aside from the wet, Harry Pye didn't look any different than he had when they'd started out this morning from an inn in Lincoln. He was still a man of average height. Rather lean. His hair was brown—neither chestnut nor auburn, merely brown. He tied it back in a simple queue, not bothering to dress it with pomades or powder. And he wore brown: breeches, waistcoat, and coat, as if to camouflage himself. Only his eyes, a dark emerald green that sometimes flickered with what might be emotion, gave him any color.

"It's just that I'm rather cold," George muttered.

Mr. Pye looked up swiftly. His gaze darted to her hands, trembling at her throat, and then shifted to the hills behind her.

"I'm sorry, my lady. I should have noticed your chill earlier." He turned back to the frightened gelding he was trying to liberate. His hands must have been as numb as her own, but he labored steadily. "There's a shepherd's cottage not far from here. We can ride this horse and that one." He nodded at the horse next to the gelding. "The other is lame."

"Really? How can you tell?" She hadn't noticed the animal was hurt. All three of the remaining carriage horses shivered and rolled their eyes at the whistling of the wind. The horse he had indicated didn't look any more ragged than the rest.

"She's favoring her right foreleg." Mr. Pye grunted, and suddenly all three horses were free of the carriage, although they were still hitched together. "Whoa, there, sweetheart." He caught the lead horse and stroked it, his tanned right hand moving tenderly over the animal's neck. The two joints on his ring finger were missing.

She turned her head away to look at the hills. Servants—and really a land steward was just a superior sort of servant—should have no gender. Of course, one knew they were people with their own lives and all that, but it made things so much easier if one saw them as sexless. Like a chair. One wanted a chair to sit in when one was tired. No one ever thought about chairs much otherwise, and that was how it should be. How uncomfortable to go about wondering if the chair had noticed that one's nose was running, wishing to know what it was thinking, or seeing that the chair had rather beautiful eyes. Not that chairs had eyes, beautiful or otherwise, but men did.

And Harry Pye did.

George faced him again. "What will we do with the third horse?"

"We'll have to leave her here."

"In the rain?"

"Yes."

"That can't be good for her."

"No, my lady." Harry Pye's shoulders bunched again, a reaction that George found oddly fascinating. She wished she could make him do it more often.

"Perhaps we should take her with us?"

"Impossible, my lady."

"Are you sure?"

The shoulders tensed and Mr. Pye slowly turned his head. In the flash of lightning that lit up the road in that instant, she saw his green eyes gleam and a thrill ran up her spine. Then the following thunder crashed like the heralding of the apocalypse.

George flinched.

Harry Pye straightened.

And the horses bolted.

"OH, DEAR," SAID LADY GEORGINA, rain dripping from her narrow nose. "We seem to be in something of a fix."

Something of a fix indeed. More like well and truly buggered. Harry squinted up the road where the horses had disappeared, running as if the Devil himself were chasing them. There was no sign of the daft beasts. At the rate they'd been galloping, they wouldn't stop for half a mile or more. No use going after them in this downpour. He switched his gaze to his employer of less than six months. Lady Georgina's aristocratic lips were blue, and the fur trimming the hood of her cloak had turned into a sopping mess. She looked more like an urchin in tattered finery than the daughter of an earl.

What was she doing here?

If not for Lady Georgina, he would've ridden a horse from London to her estates in Yorkshire. He would've arrived a day ago at Woldsly Manor. Right now he would be enjoying a hot meal in front of the fire in his own cottage. Not freezing his baubles off, standing in the middle of the high road in the rain with the light fading fast. But on his last trip to London to report on her holdings, Lady Georgina had decided to travel with him back to Woldsly Manor. Which had meant taking the carriage, now lying in a heap of broken wood in the ditch.

Harry swallowed a sigh. "Can you walk, my lady?"

Lady Georgina widened eyes that were as blue as a thrush's egg. "Oh, yes. I've been doing it since I was eleven months old."

"Good." Harry shrugged on his waistcoat and coat, not bothering to button either. They were soaked through like the rest of him. He scrambled down the bank to retrieve the rugs from inside the carriage. Thankfully they were still dry. He rolled them together and snagged the still-lit carriage lantern; then he gripped Lady Georgina's elbow, just in case she was wrong and fell on her aristocratic little arse, and started trudging up the gorse-covered hill.

At first, he'd thought her urge to travel to Yorkshire a childish fancy. The lark of a woman who never worried where the meat on her table or the jewels at her throat came from. To his mind, those who didn't labor to make their living often had flighty ideas. But the more time he spent in her company, the more he began to doubt that she was such a woman. She said gormless things, true, but he'd seen almost at once that she did it for her own amusement. She was smarter than most society ladies. He had a feeling that Lady Georgina had a good reason for traveling with him to Yorkshire.

"Is it much farther?" The lady was panting, and her normally pale face sported two spots of red.

Harry scanned the sodden hills, looking for a landmark in the gloom. Was that twisted oak growing against an outcropping familiar? "Not far."

At least he hoped not. It had been years since he'd last ridden these hills, and he might've mistaken where the cottage lay. Or it might have tumbled down since he last saw it.

"I trust you are skilled at starting fires, Mr. P-pye." His name chattered on her lips.

She needed to get warm. If they didn't find the cottage soon, he'd have to make a shelter from the carriage robes. "Oh, yes. I've been doing it since I was four, my lady."

That earned him a cheeky grin. Their eyes met, and he wished—A sudden bolt of lightning interrupted his half-formed thought, and he saw a stone wall in the flash.

"There it is." *Thank God.*

The tiny cottage still stood at least. Four stone walls with a thatched roof black from age and the rain. He put his shoulder to the slick door, and after one or two shoves, it gave. Harry stumbled in and held the lantern high to illuminate the interior. Small shapes scurried into the shadows. He checked a shudder.

"Gah! It does smell." Lady Georgina walked in and waved her hand in front of her pink nose as if to shoo the stink of mildew.

He banged the door closed behind her. "I'm sorry, my lady."

"Why don't you just tell me to shut my mouth and be glad I'm out of the rain?" She smiled and pulled back her hood.

"I think not." Harry walked to the fireplace and found some half-burned logs. They were covered with cobwebs.

"Oh, come, Mr. Pye. You know you wish t-t-to." Her teeth still chattered.

Four rickety wooden chairs stood around a lopsided table. Harry placed the lantern on the table and picked up a chair. He swung it hard against the stone fireplace. It shattered, the back coming off and the seat splintering.

Behind him, Lady Georgina squeaked.

"No, I don't, my lady," he said.

"Truly?"

"Yes." He knelt and began placing small splinters of the chair against the charred logs.

"Very well. I suppose I must be nice, then." Harry heard her draw up a chair. "That looks very efficient, what you're doing there."

He touched the lantern flame to the slivers of wood. They lit and he added larger pieces of the chair, careful not to smother the flame.

"Mmm. It feels good." Her voice was throaty behind him.

For a moment Harry froze, thinking of what her words and tone might imply in a different context. Then he banished the thoughts and turned.

Lady Georgina held out her hands to the blaze. Her ginger

hair was drying into fine curls around her forehead, and her white skin glowed in the firelight. She was still shivering.

Harry cleared his throat. "I believe you should remove your wet gown and wrap the rugs about yourself." He strode over to the door where he'd dumped the carriage robes.

From behind him, he heard a breathless laugh. "I don't believe I have ever heard such an improper suggestion made so properly."

"I didn't mean to be improper, my lady." He handed her the robes. "I'm sorry if I offended." Briefly his eyes met hers, so blue and laughing; then he turned his back.

Behind him was a rustling. He tried to discipline his thoughts. He would not imagine her pale, naked shoulders above—

"You aren't improper, as well you know, Mr. Pye. Indeed, I'm beginning to think it would be impossible for you to be so."

If she only knew. He cleared his throat but made no comment. He forced himself to gaze around the little cottage. There was no kitchen dresser, only the table and chairs. A pity. His belly was empty.

The rustling by the fire ceased. "You may turn around now."

He braced himself before looking, but Lady Georgina was covered in furs. He was glad to see her lips were pinker.

She freed a naked arm from the bundle to point at a robe on the other side of the fireplace. "I've left one for you. I'm too comfortable to move, but I'll close my eyes and promise not to peek if you wish to disrobe as well."

Harry dragged his gaze away from the arm and met her clever blue eyes. "Thank you."

The arm disappeared. Lady Georgina smiled, and her eyelids fell.

For a moment Harry simply watched her. The reddish arcs of her eyelashes fluttered against her pale skin, and a smile hovered on her crooked mouth. Her nose was thin and overlong, the angles of her face a bit too sharp. When she stood, she almost equaled his own height. She wasn't a beautiful woman, but he found himself having to control his gaze when he was around her. Something about the twitching of her lips when she was about to taunt him. Or the way her eyebrows winged up her forehead when she smiled. His eyes were drawn to her face like iron filings near a lodestone.

He shucked his upper garments and drew the last robe around himself. "You may open your eyes now, my lady."

Her eyes popped open. "Good. And now we both look like Russians swathed for the Siberian winter. A pity we don't have a sleigh with bells as well." She smoothed the fur on her lap.

He nodded. The fire crackled in the silence as he tried to think of how else he could look after her. There was no food in the cottage; nothing to do but wait for dawn. How did the upper crust behave when they were in their palatial sitting rooms all alone?

Lady Georgina was plucking at her robe, but she suddenly clasped her hands together as if to still them. "Do you know any stories, Mr. Pye?"

"Stories, my lady?"

"Mmm. Stories. Fairy tales, actually. I collect them."

"Indeed." Harry was at a loss. The aristocracy's way of thinking was truly amazing sometimes. "How, may I ask, do you go about collecting them?"

"By inquiring." Was she having fun with him? "You'd be amazed at the stories people remember from their youth. Of course, old nursemaids and the like are the best sources. I believe I've asked every one of my acquaintances to introduce me to their old nurse. Is yours still alive?"

"I didn't have a nursemaid, my lady."

"Oh." Her cheeks reddened. "But someone—your mother?—must've told you fairy tales growing up."

He shifted to put another piece of the broken chair on the fire. "The only fairy tale I can remember is *Jack and the Beanstalk*."

Lady Georgina gave him a pitying look. "Can't you do better than that?"

"I'm afraid not." The other tales he knew weren't exactly fit for a lady's ears.

"Well, I heard a rather interesting one recently. From my cook's aunt when she came to visit Cook in London. Would you like me to tell it to you?"

No. The last thing he needed was to become any more intimate with his employer than the situation had already forced him to be. "Yes, my lady."

"Once upon a time, there was a great king and he had an enchanted leopard to serve him." She wiggled her rump on the chair. "I know what you're thinking, but that's not how it goes."

Harry blinked. "My lady?"

"No. The king dies right away, so he's not the hero." She looked expectantly at him.

"Ah." He couldn't think of anything else to say.

It seemed to do.

Lady Georgina nodded. "The leopard wore a sort of gold chain around its neck. It was enslaved, you see, but I don't know how that came about. Cook's aunt didn't say. Anyway, when the king was dying, he made the leopard promise to serve the *next* king, his son." She frowned. "Which doesn't seem very fair, somehow, does it? I mean, usually they free the faithful servant at that point." She shifted again on the wooden chair.

Harry cleared his throat. "Perhaps you would be more comfortable on the floor. Your cloak is drier. I could make a pallet."

She smiled blindingly at him. "What a good idea."

He spread out the cloak and rolled his own clothes to form a pillow.

Lady Georgina shuffled over in her robes and plopped down on the crude bed. "That's better. You might as well come lie down as well; we'll be here until morning, most likely."

Christ. "I don't think it advisable."

She looked down her narrow nose at him. "Mr. Pye, those chairs are hard. Please come lie on the rugs at least. I promise not to bite."

His jaw clenched, but he really had no choice. It was a veiled order. "Thank you, my lady."

Harry gingerly sat beside her—he'd be damned if he would lie down next to this woman, order or no—and left a space between their bodies. He wrapped his arms around his bent knees and tried not to notice her scent.

"You are stubborn, aren't you?" she muttered.

He looked at her.

She yawned. "Where was I? Oh, yes. So the first thing the young king does is to see a painting of a beautiful princess and fall in love with her. A courtier or a messenger or some such shows it to him, but that doesn't matter."

She yawned again, squeaking this time, and for some reason his prick responded to the sound. Or perhaps it was her scent, which reached his nose whether he wished it to or not. It reminded him of spices and exotic flowers.

"The princess has skin as white as snow, lips as red as rubies, hair as black as, oh, pitch or the like, et cetera, et cetera." Lady Georgina paused and stared into the fire.

He wondered if she was done and his torment over.

Then she sighed. "Have you ever noticed that these fairy-tale princes fall in love with beautiful princesses without knowing a thing about them? Ruby lips are all very well, but what if she laughs oddly or clicks her teeth when she eats?" She shrugged. "Of course, men in our times are just as apt to fall in love with glossy black curls, so I suppose I shouldn't quibble." Her eyes widened suddenly, and she turned her head to look at him. "No offense meant."

"None taken," Harry said gravely.

"Hmm." She seemed doubtful. "Anyway, he falls in love with this picture, and someone tells him that the princess's father is giving her to the man who can bring him the Golden Horse, which was presently in the possession of a terrible ogre. So"—Lady Georgina turned to face the fire and cradled her cheek in her hand—"he sends for the Leopard Prince and tells him to go out quick and fetch him the Golden Horse, and what do you think?"

"I don't know, my lady."

"The leopard turned into a man." She closed her eyes and murmured, "Imagine that. He was a man all along...."

Harry waited, but this time there was no more story. After a while he heard a soft snore.

He drew the robes up over her neck and tucked them

around her face. His fingers brushed against her cheek, and he paused, studying the contrast of their skin tones. His hand was dark against her skin, his fingers rough where she was soft and smooth. Slowly he stroked his thumb across the corner of her mouth. So warm. He almost recognized her scent, as if he'd inhaled it in another life or long ago. It made him ache.

If she were a different woman, if this were a different place, if he were a different man... Harry cut short the whisper in his mind and drew back his hand. He stretched out next to Lady Georgina, careful not to touch her. He stared at the ceiling and drove out all thought, all feeling. Then he closed his eyes, even though he knew it would be a long while before he slept.

HER NOSE TICKLED. GEORGE SWIPED at it and felt fur. Beside her, something rustled and then was still. She turned her head. Green eyes met her own, irritatingly alert for so early in the day.

"Good morning." Her words came out a frog's croak. She cleared her throat.

"Good morning, my lady." Mr. Pye's voice was smooth and dark, like hot chocolate. "If you'll excuse me."

He rose. The robe he clutched slid off one shoulder, revealing tanned skin before he righted it. Walking silently, he slipped out the door.

George scrunched her nose. Did nothing faze the man?

It suddenly occurred to her what he must be doing outside. Her bladder sent up an alarm. Hastily she struggled upright and pulled on her rumpled, still-damp dress, catching as many of the fastenings as she could. She couldn't reach all the hooks, and it must be gaping around her waist, but at least the garment wouldn't fall off. George put on her cloak to hide her back and then followed Mr. Pye outside. Black clouds hovered in the sky, threatening rain. Harry Pye was nowhere in sight. Looking around, she chose a dilapidated shed behind which to relieve herself and tramped around it.

When she came back from the shed, Mr. Pye was standing in front of the cottage buttoning his coat. He had retied his queue, but his clothes were wrinkled and his hair not as neat as usual. Thinking about what she must look like herself, George felt an uncharitable smirk of amusement. Even Harry Pye couldn't spend the night on the floor of a hut and not show the effects the next morning.

"When you are ready, my lady," he said, "I suggest we return to the highway. The coachman may be waiting for us there."

"Oh, I hope so."

They retraced their steps of the night before. In light and downhill, George was surprised to find it not such a great distance. Soon they topped the last hill and could see the road. It was empty, save for the carriage wreckage, even more pitiful in the light of day.

She heaved a sigh. "Well. I guess we'll just have to start walking, Mr. Pye."

"Yes, my lady."

They trudged up the road in silence. A nasty, damp mist hovered off the ground, smelling faintly of rot. It seeped beneath her gown and crept up her legs. George shuddered. She dearly wished for a cup of hot tea and perhaps a scone with honey and butter dripping off the sides. She almost moaned at the thought and then realized there was a rumbling coming from behind them.

Mr. Pye raised his arm to hail a farmer's wagon rounding the curve. "Hi! Stop! You there, we need a ride."

The farmer pulled his horse to a standstill. He tipped the brim of his hat back and stared. "Mr. Harry Pye, isn't it?"

Mr. Pye stiffened. "Yes, that's right. From the Woldsly estate."

The farmer spat into the road, narrowly missing Mr. Pye's boots.

"Lady Georgina Maitland needs a ride to Woldsly." Harry Pye's face did not change, but his voice had grown as chill as death. "It was her carriage you saw back there."

The farmer switched his gaze to George as if noticing her for the first time. "Aye, ma'am, I hope you weren't hurt in the wreck?"

"No." She smiled winningly. "But we do need a ride, if you don't mind."

"Glad to help. There be room in the back." The farmer aimed a dirty thumb over his shoulder at the wagon bed.

She thanked him and walked around the wagon. She hesitated as she eyed the height of the boards. They came to her collarbone.

Mr. Pye halted beside her. "With your permission." He hardly waited for her nod before grasping her about the waist and lifting her in.

"Thank you," George said breathlessly.

She watched as he placed his palms flat on the bed and vaulted in with catlike ease. The wagon jolted forward just as he cleared the boards, and he was thrown against the side.

"Are you all right?" She held out a hand.

Mr. Pye disregarded it and sat up. "Fine." He glanced at her. "My lady."

He said no more. George settled back and watched the countryside roll by. Gray-green fields with low stone walls emerged and then were hidden again by the eerie mist. After last night, she should've been glad for the ride, bumpy though it might be. But something about the farmer's hostility to Mr. Pye bothered her. It seemed personal.

They cleared a rise, and George idly watched a flock of sheep grazing on a nearby hillside. They stood like little statues, perhaps frozen by the mist. Only their heads moved as they cropped the gorse. A few were lying down. She frowned. The ones on the ground were very still. She leaned forward to see better and heard Harry Pye curse softly beside her.

The wagon jerked to a halt.

"What's the matter with those sheep?" George asked Mr. Pye.

But it was the farmer who answered, his voice grim. "They're dead."

Chapter Two

"George!" Lady Violet Maitland ran out Woldsly Manor's massive oak doors, ignoring the disapproving mutter of her companion, Miss Euphemia Hope.

Violet only just refrained from rolling her eyes. Euphie was an old pet, a short, apple-round woman with gray hair and mild eyes, but nearly everything Violet did made her mutter.

"Where've you been? We expected you days ago and..." She skidded to a stop on the gravel courtyard to stare at the man helping her sister from the strange carriage.

Mr. Pye looked up at her approach and nodded, his face as usual set in an expressionless mask. What was he doing traveling with George?

Violet narrowed her eyes at him.

"Hullo, Euphie," George said.

"Oh, my lady, we're so happy you've arrived," the companion gasped. "The weather has *not* been all one could wish for, and we have been quite *apprehensive* as to your safety."

George smiled in reply and wrapped her arms around Violet. "Hullo, darling."

Her sister's marmalade hair, several shades lighter than

Violet's own exuberantly flaming head, smelled of jasmine and tea, the most comforting scents in the world. Violet felt tears prickle her eyes.

"I'm sorry you were worried, but I don't think I'm so very late." George bussed her cheek and stepped away to look at her.

Violet turned hurriedly to inspect the carriage, a rather dilapidated old thing that didn't look a speck like George's. "What're you doing traveling about in that for?"

"Well, there lies a story." George pulled off her hood. Her coiffure was incredibly bad, even for George. "I'll tell you over tea. I'm just famished. We had only a few buns at the inn where we got the carriage." She looked at the steward and asked rather diffidently, "Would you like to join us, Mr. Pye?"

Violet held her breath. *Say no. Say no. Say no.*

"No, thank you, my lady." Mr. Pye bowed in a sinister fashion. "If you'll excuse me, there are some estate matters I should see to."

Violet expelled her breath in a whoosh of relief.

To her horror, George persisted. "Surely they can wait another half hour or so?" She smiled in her wonderful, wide-mouthed way.

Violet stared at her sister. What was she thinking?

"I'm afraid not," Mr. Pye replied.

"Oh, very well. I suppose it is why I employ you, after all." George sounded like a prig, but at least Mr. Pye was no longer coming to tea.

"I'm sorry, my lady." He bowed again, this time a little stiffly, and walked away.

Violet almost felt sorry for him—almost, but not quite. She hooked her arm through her sister's as they turned back toward Woldsly. The manor was hundreds of years old and sat in the landscape as if it had grown there, a natural feature of the surrounding hills. Green ivy scrambled up the four-story redbrick façade. The vines were trimmed back from around tall, mullioned windows. A multitude of chimneys climbed the manor's gabled roofs like so many hikers on a mountain. It was a welcoming house, perfectly suited to her sister's personality.

"Cook baked lemon curd tarts just this morning," Violet said as they climbed the wide front steps. "Euphie has been mooning over them ever since."

"Oh, no, my lady," the companion exclaimed behind them. "I don't believe I have really. Not over lemon tarts, anyway. When it comes to *mince* pie, I do admit a certain fondness, not altogether *genteel,* I fear."

"You are the very epitome of gentility, Euphie. We all strive to follow your example," George said.

The older woman preened like a gray bantam hen.

Violet felt a twinge of guilt for always being so exasperated with the silly dear. She made a solemn vow to try and be more kind to her in the future.

They entered the manor's huge double oak doors, where George nodded to Greaves, the butler. Light streamed in from the crescent window above the doors, illuminating the coffee-and-cream walls and the entry's old parquet floor.

"Have you found something to amuse yourself with at Woldsly?" George asked as they continued down the hall. "I confess, I was surprised when you said you wanted to rusticate here with just Euphie. It's a bit of a backwater for a fifteen-year-old. Although, of course, you are always welcome."

"I've been sketching," Violet replied, keeping her voice carefully light. "The views here are a change from Leicestershire. And M'man was becoming quite tiresome at home. She claims to have found a new tumor in her right leg and has brought in a Belgian quack who is dosing her on some awful stuff that smells like cooked cabbage." Violet exchanged a glance with George. "You know how she is."

"Yes, I do." George patted her arm.

Violet looked away, relieved she didn't have to explain further. Their mother had been predicting her own death since before Violet was born. Mostly the countess kept to her bed, attended by a patient maid. Every once in a while, however, M'man would become hysterical about some new symptom. When that happened, she nearly drove Violet mad.

They entered the rose morning room, and George pulled off her gloves. "Now, then, what was the purpose of that letter—"

"Hist!" Violet jerked her head toward Euphie, who was busy instructing the maid to bring tea.

George raised her brows but caught on quick enough, thank goodness. She pressed her lips together and threw the gloves on a table.

Violet said clearly, "You were going to tell us why you changed carriages."

"Oh, that." George wrinkled her nose. "My carriage slid off the road last night. Quite sensational, actually. And then what do you think?" She sat down on one of the saffron settees, propped an elbow on the back, and rested her head in her palm. "The horses ran away. Left Mr. Pye and me quite high and dry—only, we were sopping wet, of course. *And* in the middle of who knows where."

"Good G—" Violet caught Euphie's censorious eye and changed her exclamation midbreath. "Gracious! Whatever did you do?"

Several maids with laden tea trays trooped in at that moment, and George held up a hand, indicating to Violet that she'd continue after they laid the tea out. A moment later, Euphie poured her a dish of tea.

"Ahh." George sighed contentedly over her cup. "I think tea would cure the worst of mental ills if only applied in sufficient quantities."

Violet bounced impatiently in her seat until her sister took the hint.

"Yes, well, fortunately Mr. Pye knew of a nearby cottage." George shrugged. "So we spent the night."

"Oh, my lady! All alone and Mr. Pye not even married." The revelation that George had spent an entire night with a man appeared to shock Euphie more than the carriage accident itself. "I do not think, no, I do *not* think it could've been comfortable for you." She sat back and fanned her face, causing the puce ribbons on her cap to flutter.

Violet rolled her eyes. "He's only the *land* steward, Euphie. It isn't as if he's a gentleman from a good family. Besides," she said practically, "George is eight and twenty. She's too old to cause a scandal."

"Thank you, dear." George sounded rather dry.

"A scandal!" Euphie clutched her dish of tea. "I know you will have your little games, Lady Violet, but I do not think we should bandy the word *scandal* about so carelessly."

"No, no, of course not," George murmured soothingly while Violet barely refrained from rolling her eyes—*again*.

"All this excitement has wearied me, I fear." Euphie got

to her feet. "Will it put you out terribly if I have a small lie-down, Lady Violet?"

"No, of course not." Violet suppressed a grin. Every day after tea, regular as clockwork, Euphie found an excuse to have a small lie-down. She had counted on her companion's routine today as she had in the past.

The door shut behind Euphie, and George looked at Violet. "Well? Your letter was incredibly histrionic, dear. I believe you used the word *diabolical* twice, which seems improbable considering you summoned me to Yorkshire, usually a most undiabolical place. I do hope it's important. I had to refuse five invitations, including the Oswalt autumn masquerade, which had promised to be full of scandal this year."

"It is important." Violet leaned forward and whispered, "Someone is poisoning the sheep on Lord Granville's land!"

"Yes?" George raised her brows and took a bite from a tart.

Violet blew out an exasperated breath. "Yes! And the poisoner is from your estate. Maybe from Woldsly Manor itself."

"We did see some dead sheep by the road this morning."

"Aren't you concerned?" Violet jumped to her feet and paced in front of her sister. "The servants talk of nothing else. The local farmers are whispering about a witch, and Lord Granville has said you'll be liable if the poisoner is from this estate."

"Really?" George popped the rest of the tart into her mouth. "How does he know the sheep have been deliberately poisoned? Couldn't they just have eaten something bad for them? Or more likely died from disease?"

"The sheep died suddenly, all at once—"

"Disease, then."

"And cut poisonous plants were found by the bodies!"

George sat forward to pour herself a cup of tea. She looked a little amused. "But if no one knows who the poisoner is—they don't, do they?"

Violet shook her head.

"Then how do they know he is from the Woldsly estate?"

"Footprints!" Violet stopped, arms akimbo in front of her sister.

George quirked an eyebrow.

Violet leaned forward impatiently. "Before I wrote you, they found *ten* dead sheep on a Granville tenant farmer's field just over the stream dividing the estates. There were muddy footprints leading from the corpses to the bank of the stream—footprints that continued on the far side of the stream on *your* land."

"Hmm." George selected another tart. "That doesn't sound too damning. I mean, what's to keep someone from Lord Granville's land tramping into the stream and back again to make it look like he's coming from Woldsly?"

"*Geor*-rge." Violet sat down next to her sister. "No one on the Granville estate has a reason to poison the sheep. But someone from Woldsly does."

"Oh? Who?" George lifted the tart to her mouth.

"Harry Pye."

George froze with the tart still hovering near her lips. Violet smiled triumphantly. At last she'd gotten her sister's full attention.

George carefully set the tart back on her plate. "What possible motive could my steward have for killing Lord Granville's sheep?"

"Revenge." Violet nodded at George's incredulous look. "Mr. Pye bears a grudge for something that Lord Granville did in the past."

"What?"

Violet slumped on the settee. "I don't know," she admitted. "No one will tell me."

George started to laugh.

Violet crossed her arms. "But it must have been something terrible, mustn't it?" she asked over George's chortles. "For him to come back years later and enact his diabolical revenge?"

"Oh, sweetheart," George gasped. "The servants or whoever has been telling you these tales are bamming you. Can you really imagine Mr. Pye skulking around trying to feed sheep poisonous weeds?" She went off again into gales of laughter.

Violet poked the remaining lemon tart sulkily. Truly, the principal problem with older siblings was that they never took one seriously.

"I'M SORRY I WASN'T WITH YOU, my lady, when you had the accident," Tiggle puffed behind George the next morning. The lady's maid was fastening an interminable row of hooks on the sapphire sack dress George had chosen to wear.

"I don't know what you'd have done, except end up in the ditch with us," George addressed Tiggle over her shoulder. "Besides, I'm sure you enjoyed the visit with your parents."

"That I did, my lady."

George smiled. Tiggle had deserved an extra day off to spend with her family. And since her father was the proprietor of the Lincoln inn they'd stopped at on the way to Woldsly, it had seemed an opportune time to travel on and leave Tiggle to catch up in a day. But because of the accident, Tiggle hadn't arrived that much later than they had. Which was good, because George would've made a mare's nest out of dressing her own hair. Tiggle had the hands of an artist when it came to taming George's messy locks.

"It's just that I don't like to think of you alone with that Mr. Pye, my lady." Tiggle's voice was muffled.

"Whyever not? He was a perfect gentleman."

"I should hope so!" Tiggle sounded outraged. "Still. He's a bit of a cold fish, isn't he?" She gave a final tug and stepped back. "There. That's done."

"Thank you." George smoothed the front of her gown.

Tiggle had served her since before George had come out, so many years ago now. She had laced and unlaced what must be a thousand gowns and had lamented with George over the frizziness of her orangey-red hair. Tiggle's own hair was a smooth golden blond, the preferred color of all those fairy tales. Her eyes were blue, and her lips the requisite ruby red. Indeed, she was a very lovely woman. Were her life a fairy tale, George should be the goose girl and Tiggle the fairy princess.

She walked to her vanity table. "Why do you think Mr. Pye is a cold fish?" She opened her jewel box and began rummaging for the pearl drops.

"He never smiles, does he?" In the mirror, she could see Tiggle gathering her nightclothes. "And the way he watches a body. Makes me feel like I'm a cow he's sizing up, trying to reckon if I will calf well another season or if he should send me to the slaughterhouse." She held out the dress George had worn during the accident and examined it critically. "Still, there're plenty of lasses hereabouts who find him fetching."

"Oh?" George's voice came out a squeak. She stuck out her tongue to herself in the mirror.

Tiggle didn't look up as she frowned over a hole she'd found near the gown's hem. "Aye. The maids in the kitchen talk about his fine eyes and pretty bum."

"Tiggle!" George dropped her pearl earring. It rolled across the vanity's lacquered surface and came to a stop in a pile of ribbons.

"Oh!" Tiggle's hand flew to her mouth. "I'm sorry, my lady. I don't know what came over me to say that."

George couldn't help but giggle. "Is that what they talk about in the kitchen? Gentlemen's bottoms?"

Tiggle's face reddened, but her eyes twinkled. "Too much of the time, I'm afraid."

"Maybe I should visit the kitchen more often." George leaned forward to peer into the mirror as she put on an earring. "Several people, including Lady Violet, say they've heard rumors about Mr. Pye." She stepped back and turned her head from side to side to study the earrings. "Have you heard anything?"

"Rumors, my lady?" Tiggle slowly folded the gown. "I haven't been down to the kitchens yet this stay. But I did hear something while at my pa's. There was a farmer traveling through who lived on Granville land. Said as how the Woldsly steward was doing mischief. Hurting animals and playing pranks at the Granville stables." Tiggle met George's eyes in the mirror. "Is that what you mean, my lady?"

George took a breath and let it out slowly. "Yes, that's exactly what I mean."

*   *   *

THAT AFTERNOON, HARRY HUNCHED OVER his saddle in
the relentless drizzle. He'd expected to be summoned to
the manor almost from the moment they'd driven onto the
Woldsly estate. Surprisingly, it had taken a full day and
night for Lady Georgina to send for him. He nudged his
mare into a trot up the long, winding drive to Woldsly
Manor. Perhaps it was because she was a lady.

When he'd first learned that the owner of the multiple
estates he would be managing was a woman, he'd been
taken aback. A woman didn't usually own land by herself.
Normally, if she did have an estate, there was a man—a son
or husband or brother—in the background, the real power
in how the lands were run. But although Lady Georgina
had three brothers, it was the lady herself who was in control. And what was more, she'd come by the lands through
inheritance, not marriage. Lady Georgina had never wed.
An aunt had left everything to her and apparently stipu-
lated in the will that Lady Georgina would have the reins
of her holdings and their income.

Harry snorted. Plainly the old woman hadn't had much
use for men. Gravel crunched beneath the bay mare's
hooves as he entered the vast courtyard before Woldsly
Manor. He crossed to the stable yard, swung down from
his horse, and tossed the reins to a boy.

They dropped to the cobblestones.

The mare stepped back nervously, the reins trailing.
Harry stilled and raised his gaze to meet the eyes of the
stripling boy. The lad stared at him, chin up, shoulders
back. He looked like a young St. Stephan readying himself
for the arrows. When had his reputation gotten this bad?

"Pick them up," Harry said softly.

The boy wavered. The arrows were looking sharper than he'd expected.

"Now," Harry whispered. He turned on his heel, not bothering to see if the lad followed his order, and strode to the manor, leaping the steps two at a time to the front doors.

"Inform Lady Georgina Maitland that I am here," he said to Greaves. He thrust his tricorn into the hands of a footman and entered the library without waiting to be shown in.

Tall windows draped in moss-green velvet lined the far side of the room. Had the day been sunny, the windows would have bathed the library in light. But it wasn't sunny. The sun hadn't shone in this patch of Yorkshire for weeks.

Harry walked over and stared out the window. Rolling fields and pastures stretched as far as the eye could see, a patchwork quilt in green and brown. The drystone walls dividing the fields had stood for centuries before he was born and would stand for centuries after his bones had crumbled to dust. It was a beautiful landscape to his mind, one that made his heart tighten every time he saw it, but something was wrong. The fields should have been full of reapers and wagons, harvesting the hay and wheat. But the grain was too wet to harvest. If the rain didn't let up soon . . . He shook his head. The wheat would either rot in the field or they'd have to reap it damp. In which case it would rot in the barns.

He clenched his fist on the window frame. Did she even care what his dismissal would mean to this land?

Behind him, the door opened. "Mr. Pye, I think you must be one of those odious early risers."

He relaxed his fingers and turned around.

Lady Georgina strolled toward him in a dress a shade deeper than her blue eyes. "When I sent for you at nine this morning, Greaves looked at me like I was noddycock and informed me you would have left your cottage hours ago."

Harry bowed. "I'm sorry to have inconvenienced you, my lady."

"As well you should be." Lady Georgina sat on a black and green settee, leaning back casually, her blue skirts spread around her. "Greaves has a knack of making one feel like a babbling infant in leading strings." She shuddered. "I can't think how horrible it must be working as a footman under him. Aren't you going to sit?"

"If you wish, my lady." He chose an armchair. What was she about?

"I do wish." Behind her, the door opened again, and two maids entered bearing laden trays. "Not only that, but I'm afraid I'm going to insist upon you taking tea as well."

The maids arranged the teapot, cups, plates, and all the other confusing stuff of an aristocratic tea on a low table between them and left.

Lady Georgina lifted the silver teapot and poured. "Now, you will have to bear with me and try not to glower so menacingly." She waved aside his attempted apology. "*Do* you take sugar and cream?"

He nodded.

"Good. Plenty of both, then, for I'm sure you have a secret sweet tooth. *And* two slices of shortbread. You'll just have to shoulder it like a soldier." She offered the plate to him.

He met her eyes, oddly challenging. He hesitated a moment before taking the plate. For a fraction of a second, his fingers brushed hers, so soft and warm, and then he sat back. The shortbread was tender and flaky. He ate the first piece in two bites.

"There." She sighed and sank into the cushions with her own plate. "Now I know how Hannibal felt after having conquered the Alps."

He felt his mouth twitch as he watched her over the rim of his cup. The Alps would have sat up and begged had Lady Georgina marched toward them with an army of elephants. Her ginger hair was a halo around her face. She might've looked angelic if her eyes hadn't been so mischievous. She bit into a slice of shortbread, and it fell apart. She picked up a crumb from her plate and sucked it off her finger in a very unladylike way.

His balls tightened. *No.* Not for this woman.

He set down his teacup carefully. "Why did you wish to speak to me, my lady?"

"Well, this is rather awkward." She put her own cup down. "I'm afraid people have been telling tales about you." She held up one hand and began ticking off her fingers. "One of the footmen, the bootblack boy, four—no five—of the maids, my sister, Tiggle, and even Greaves. Would you believe it? I was a bit surprised. I never thought he'd unbend enough to gossip." She looked at him.

Harry looked back impassively.

"And everyone since only yesterday afternoon when we arrived." She'd run out of fingers and let her hand drop.

Harry said nothing. He felt a twisting in his chest, but that was bootless. Why should she be any different from everyone else?

"They all seem to be under the impression that you've been poisoning the neighbor's sheep with some kind of weed. Although"—her brow puckered—"why everyone should fly up into the boughs about sheep, even murdered sheep, I'm not quite sure."

Harry stared. Surely she jested? But then again, she was from the city. "Sheep are the backbone of this country, my lady."

"I know the farmers all raise them hereabouts." She peered at the cake tray, hand hovering above it, apparently choosing a sweet. "I'm sure people become quite fond of their livestock—"

"They aren't pets."

She looked up at his sharp tone, and her eyebrows drew together.

He was impertinent, he knew, but damn it, she needed to know. "They're life. Sheep are a man's meat and his clothes. The income to pay the landowner his due. The thing that keeps his family alive."

She stilled, her blue eyes solemn. He felt something light and frail connect himself and this woman, who was so far above his station. "The loss of an animal might mean no new dress for a man's wife. Maybe a shortage of sugar in the pantry. A couple of dead sheep could keep his children from winter shoes. For a farmer living lean"—he shrugged—"he might not make the rent, might have to kill the rest of his herd to feed his family."

Her eyes widened.

"That way lies ruin." Harry gripped the settee arm, trying to explain, trying to make her understand. "That way lies the poorhouse."

"Ah. So the thing is more serious than I knew." She sat back with a sigh. "It would appear I must act." She looked at him, it seemed, regretfully.

Here it was, finally. He braced himself.

The front doors slammed.

Lady Georgina cocked her head. "What...?"

Something crashed in the hall, and Harry leaped to his feet. Arguing voices and a scuffle were coming nearer. He placed himself between the door and Lady Georgina. His left hand drifted down to the top of his boot.

"I'll see her now, damn your eyes!" The door flew open, and a ruddy-faced man stormed in.

Greaves followed, panting, his wig crooked. "My lady, I am so sorry—"

"That's all right," Lady Georgina said. "You may leave us."

The butler looked like he wanted to protest, but he caught Harry's eye. "My lady." He bowed and shut the door.

The man wheeled and looked past Harry to Lady Georgina. "This cannot go on, ma'am! I have had enough. If you cannot control that bastard you employ, I will take matters into my own hands and have great pleasure in doing so."

He started forward, his heavy face flushed red against his white powdered wig, his hands balled threateningly at his sides. He looked almost exactly the same as he had that morning eighteen years ago. The heavy-lidded brown eyes were handsome even in age. He had the shoulders and arms of a strong man—thick, like a bull. The years had brought closer the gap in their heights, but Harry was still half a head shorter. And the sneer on the thick lips—yes, that was certainly unchanged. Harry would carry the memory of that sneer to his grave.

The man was abreast of him now, paying no attention to him, his gaze focused solely on Lady Georgina. Harry shot out his right hand, his arm a solid bar across the other man's path. The intruder made to barrel through the barrier, but Harry held firm.

"What th—" The man cut himself off and stared down at Harry's hand. His right hand.

The one with the missing finger.

Slowly, the other man raised his head and met Harry's eyes. Recognition flamed in his gaze.

Harry bared his teeth in a grin, though he had never felt less amused in his life. "Silas Granville." Deliberately he left off the title.

Silas stiffened. "Goddamn you to hell, Harry Pye."

Chapter Three

No wonder Harry Pye never smiled. The expression on his face at that moment was enough to scare little children into fits. George felt her heart sink. She'd rather hoped that all the gossip about Mr. Pye and Lord Granville was just that: stories made up to entertain bored country folk. But judging from the filthy looks the two men were exchanging, not only did they know each other, but they did indeed have a nasty past.

She sighed. This complicated matters.

"You cur! You dare show your face to me after the criminal damage you've done on my land?" Lord Granville shouted directly in Mr. Pye's face, spittle flying.

Harry Pye did not reply, but he had an incredibly irritating smirk on his lips. George winced. She could almost sympathize with Lord Granville.

"First the tricks in my stable—the cut halters, the ruined feed, the vandalized carriages." Lord Granville addressed George but never took his eyes from Mr. Pye. "Then sheep killing! My farmers have lost over fifteen good animals in the last fortnight alone. Twenty, before that. And all of it began when he returned to this district, employed by you, madam."

"He had excellent references," George muttered.

Lord Granville swung in her direction. She recoiled, but Mr. Pye moved smoothly with the larger man, keeping his shoulder always between them. His show of protectiveness only enraged Lord Granville further.

"Enough, I say. I demand you dismiss this… this scoundrel!" Lord Granville spat the word. "Blood always shows. Like his father before him, he's the lowest form of criminal."

George inhaled.

Mr. Pye didn't speak, but a soft noise came from between his drawn-back lips.

Good Lord, it sounded like a snarl. Hastily, she broke into speech. "Now, Lord Granville, I think you're being rather rash in your condemnation of Mr. Pye. After all, have you any reason to suppose it is my steward instead of someone else doing the damage?"

"Reason?" Lord Granville hissed the word. "Reason? Aye, I've got reason. Twenty years ago this man's father attacked me. Nearly killed me, he was so insane."

George lifted her eyebrows. She darted a look at Mr. Pye, but he'd controlled his face into its customary impassivity. "I don't see why—"

"He assaulted me as well." Lord Granville speared a finger at the land steward's chest. "Joined his father in trying to murder a peer of the realm."

"But"—she looked from one man to the other, the first the very embodiment of rage, the other showing no expression at all—"but he could hardly have been full grown twenty years ago. Wouldn't he be a boy of… of—"

"Twelve." Mr. Pye spoke for the first time since he'd uttered the other man's name. His voice was quiet, almost a whisper. "And it was eighteen years ago. Exactly."

"Twelve is plenty old enough to murder a man." Lord Granville batted aside the objection with the flat of his hand. "It's well known that the common rabble mature early—the better to breed more vermin. At twelve, he was as much a man as he is now."

George blinked at this outrageous statement, said with a perfectly straight face and apparently believed as fact by Lord Granville. She glanced again at Mr. Pye, but if anything, he appeared bored. Obviously, he'd heard this sentiment or ones very like it before. She wondered briefly how often he'd listened to such drivel in his childhood.

She shook her head. "Be that as it may, my lord, it does not sound as if you have concrete evidence of Mr. Pye's culpability now. And I really do feel—"

Lord Granville threw something down at her feet. "I have evidence." His smile was quite odious.

George frowned and looked at the thing by her embroidered shoe tip. It was a little wooden figure. She bent to pick it up, a small, treacle-colored figurine, no larger than the ball of her thumb. Its features were partially obscured by dried mud. She turned it over, rubbing the dirt off. A hedgehog carved in exquisite detail emerged. The artist had cleverly taken advantage of a dark spot in the wood to highlight the bristles on the tiny animal's back. How sweet! George smiled in delight.

Then she became aware of the silence in the room. She looked up and saw the dreadful stillness with which Mr. Pye stared at the carving in her hand. Dear Lord, surely he hadn't really—

"That, I think, is evidence enough," Lord Granville said.

"What—?"

"Ask him." Granville gestured at the hedgehog, and George instinctively closed her fingers as if to protect it. "Go on, ask him who made that."

She met Mr. Pye's eyes. Was there a flicker of regret in them?

"I did," he said.

George cradled the carving in her two hands and brought them to her breast. Her next question was inevitable. "And what does Mr. Pye's hedgehog have to do with your dead sheep?"

"It was found next to the body of a ram on my land." Lord Granville's eyes bore the unholy light of triumph. "Just this morning."

"I see."

"So you must dismiss Pye at the very least. I'll have the charges written up and a warrant for his arrest drawn. In the meantime, I'll take him into my custody. I am, after all, the magistrate in this area." Lord Granville was almost jovial in his victory. "Perhaps you can lend me a brace of strong footmen?"

"I don't think so." George shook her head thoughtfully. "No, I'm afraid that just won't do."

"Are you out of your mind, woman? I offer to solve the problem for you—" Lord Granville cut himself off impatiently. He marched to the door, waving his hand. "Fine. I'll just ride back to my estate and bring my own men to arrest the fellow."

"No, I think not," George said. "Mr. Pye is still in my employ. You must let me handle this matter as I see fit."

Lord Granville stopped and turned. "You're insane. I'll have this man by sundown. You have no right—"

"I have every right," George interrupted him. "This is

my steward, my house, my *land*. And you are not welcome upon it." Striding swiftly, she took both men by surprise, moving past them before they could object. She threw open the door and continued into the hall. "Greaves!"

The butler must have been hovering nearby because he appeared with amazing speed. He was accompanied by the two biggest footmen in her service.

"Lord Granville will be leaving now."

"Yes, my lady." Greaves, a perfect example of his kind, showed no satisfaction as he hurried forward to offer Lord Granville his hat and gloves, but his step was bouncier than usual.

"You'll regret this." Lord Granville shook his head slowly, heavily, like an enraged bull. "I'll make sure of it."

Mr. Pye was suddenly at George's side. She fancied she could feel his warmth even though he touched her not at all.

"The door is this way, my lord," Greaves said, and the footmen moved to flank Lord Granville.

She held her breath until the big oak doors banged shut. Then she blew it out. "Well. At least he is out of the manor."

Mr. Pye brushed past her.

"I haven't finished talking to you," George said, irritated. The man could at least thank her before leaving. "Where are you going?"

"I have some questions that need answering, my lady." He bowed briefly. "I promise to present myself to you by tomorrow morning. Anything you have to say to me can be said then."

And he was gone.

George slowly unclasped her fist and looked again at

the elfin hedgehog. "And what if what I have to say can't wait until tomorrow?"

GODDAMN HARRY PYE and that haughty bitch as well! Silas Granville kicked his black gelding into a gallop as he left the Woldsly Manor gates. The animal tried to shy at the sting of the spurs, but Silas was having none of it. He yanked viciously on the reins, driving the bit into the soft sides of the horse's mouth until the animal tasted the copper of its own blood. The gelding subsided.

To what end did Lady Georgina protect Harry Pye? It wouldn't be long before Silas returned, and when he did, he'd be sure to bring a small army. She wouldn't be able to prevent him from dragging Pye away.

The gelding hesitated at the ford in the stream that divided Granville land from the Woldsly estate. The stream was wide and shallow here. Silas spurred the horse, and it splashed into the water. Bright drops of blood swirled and mixed with the current and were swept away downstream. The hills rolled up from the stream, hiding the approach to Granville House. A man on foot, carrying baskets on a yoke across his shoulders, was in the lane. He scrambled to the side at the sound of the gelding's hoofbeats. As Silas rode by, the man doffed his cap. Silas didn't bother acknowledging him.

His family had held these lands since the time of the Tudors. Granvilles had married, begot, and died here. Some had been weak and some had been intemperate in drink or women, but that didn't matter. What mattered was the land. For the land was the foundation of their wealth and of their power—the foundation of *Silas's* power. No one—especially not a baseborn land steward—was going to endanger that foundation. Not while the blood still beat in his veins. The loss of monies from the dead sheep on his lands was minimal, but the loss of pride—of honor— was too great to bear. Silas would never forget the sheer insolence on Pye's young face nearly twenty years ago. Even as his finger was being cut off, the boy had stared him in the eye and sneered. Pye had never behaved as a peasant should. It was important that Silas make a show of punishing Harry Pye for his criminal affront.

The gelding turned in at the great stone gates, and Silas nudged the horse into another gallop. He topped a rise and Granville House appeared. Gray granite, four stories high, with wings that formed a square around an inner courtyard, Granville House loomed over the surrounding countryside. The building was imposing and stern, meant to signal *here is authority* to any who saw it.

Silas cantered to the front door. He pursed his lips in distaste as he saw the figure in crimson and silver on the steps.

"Thomas. You look like a sodomite in that rig." He dismounted and threw the reins to a stable hand. "How much did that garment set me back at the tailor's?"

"Hullo, Father." His eldest son's face blotched red. "It really wasn't all that dear." Thomas stared at the blood on the gelding's heaving sides. He licked his lips.

"Gad, you're blushing like a lass." Silas brushed past the boy. "Come and sup with me, Miss Nellie."

He smirked as his son hesitated behind him. The boy didn't have much choice, did he? Not unless he'd grown a set of bollocks overnight. Silas stomped into his dining room, perversely pleased to see that the table wasn't set.

"Where the hell's my dinner?"

Footmen jumped, maids scurried, and the butler bab-
bled out apologies. Too soon the table was ready and they
sat down to dine.

"Eat some of that." Silas pointed with a fork at the rare
meat, lying in a pool of blood on his son's plate. "Mayhap
you'll grow hair on your chest. Or elsewhere."

Thomas hazarded a half smile at Silas's baiting and
shrugged one shoulder nervously.

Jesus! How had he ever thought this boy's mother
would make a good breeder? His offspring, the fruit of
his loins—which he never doubted, because his late wife
hadn't the spirit to cuckold him—sat across from him and
poked at his meat. His son had inherited Silas's height
and brown eyes but that was all. His overlong nose, lip-
less mouth, and puling nature were all his mother's. Silas
snorted in disgust.

"Were you able to see Lady Georgina?" Thomas had
taken a bite of the beef and was chewing it as if he held
dung in his mouth.

"Oh, aye, I saw the arrogant bitch. Saw her in the
library at Woldsly. And Harry Pye, damn his green eyes."
He reached for a roll.

Thomas stopped chewing. "Harry Pye? The same
Harry Pye who used to live here? Not a different man with
the same name? Her steward, I mean."

"Aye her *steward*." Silas's voice rose on the last word
to a mincing falsetto. His son flushed again. "It's not like
I'm apt to forget those green eyes any time soon."

"I suppose not."

Silas looked hard at his son, his eyes narrowed.

"You'll have him arrested?" Thomas spoke quickly,
one shoulder up.

"As to that, I've run into a slight problem." Silas curled his upper lip. "Seems Lady Georgina doesn't want her steward arrested, stupid wench." He took another swig of ale. "Doesn't think the evidence is damning enough. Probably doesn't care one way or the other about dead livestock—*my* dead livestock—seeing as she's from London."

"The carved figurine didn't convince her?"

"No, it did not." Silas picked a bit of gristle from between his front teeth. "Ridiculous to let a woman have that much land, anyway. What's she want it for? Probably cares more for gloves and the latest dance in London than she does for her estate. The old woman should have left it to a man. Or made her get married so she'd have a husband to run it."

"Perhaps..." Thomas hesitated. "Perhaps I could talk to her?"

"You?" Silas flung back his head and laughed until he began to choke. Tears appeared in his eyes, and he had to take a drink.

Thomas was silent on the other side of the table.

Silas wiped his eyes. "It's not as if you have a way with the ladies, now, is it, Tommy, my boy? Not like your brother, Bennet. That lad had his first cream jug while still in the schoolroom."

Thomas's head was bowed. His shoulders twitched up and down.

"Have you ever even bedded a wench?" Silas asked softly. Slyly. "Ever felt soft, fat titties? Ever smelled the fishy odor of eager twat?" He leaned back, balancing his chair on two legs, and watched his son. "Ever plunged your pud into a willing woman and fucked her until she screamed?"

Thomas jerked. His fork slid off the table and rattled onto the floor.

Silas sat forward. The front legs of his chair came down with a thump. "I thought not."

Thomas stood so suddenly his chair crashed over. "Bennet isn't here, is he? And not likely to be here anytime soon."

Silas pursed his lips at that.

"I'm your oldest son. This will be my land someday. Let me try to talk to Lady Georgina."

"Why?" Silas cocked his head.

"You can go there and take Pye by force," Thomas said. "But it isn't likely to endear her to us. And while she's our neighbor, it behooves us to remain on good terms. He's only her steward. I can't believe she'd start a feud over the man."

"Aye. Well, I don't suppose you can make it any worse." Silas drained his ale and banged down his cup. "I'll give you a couple of days to try and talk sense into the woman."

"Thank you, Father."

Silas ignored his son's gratitude. "And when you fail, I'll break down the doors of Woldsly if I have to and drag Harry Pye out by his neck."

Harry shivered as he guided the bay mare up the track leading to his cottage. In his rush to question the Granville farmers this morning, he hadn't bothered to take a cloak. Now it was well after sundown, and the fall nights were chilly. Overhead, the leaves in the trees rattled in the wind.

He should've waited and let Lady Georgina say whatever she was going to say this morning. But the realization that someone was actively trying to implicate him in the sheep killings had spurred him from the room. What was happening? There had been vicious rumors for weeks that he was the killer. Gossip that had started almost from the moment the first dead sheep had been found a month ago. But Harry had brushed aside talk. A man couldn't be arrested for talk. Evidence was a different matter.

His cottage stood off the main drive to Woldsly Manor, built, God only knew why, in a little copse. Across the drive was the gatekeeper's cottage, a much bigger building. He could have turned the gatekeeper out and taken possession of the larger house when he had first came to Woldsly. A steward, after all, was higher in status than a mere gatekeeper. But the man had a wife and family, and, the smaller cottage was farther back from the drive and hidden in the trees. It had more privacy. And he was a man who treasured his privacy.

He swung down from the mare and led her to the tiny lean-to against the back of the cottage. Harry lit the lantern hanging inside the door and took off the horse's saddle and bridle. Weariness of body and spirit dragged at his limbs. But he carefully rubbed down the mare, watered her, and gave her an extra scoop of oats. His father had drummed into him at an early age the importance of taking care of one's animals.

With a final pat for the already dozing mare, he picked up the lantern and left the stable. He walked around the cottage on the well-worn path toward the door. As he neared the front door, his step faltered. A light flickered through his cottage window.

Harry put out his lantern. He backed into the underbrush beside the path and hunkered down to think. From the size of the light, it looked to be a single candle. It didn't move, so it probably stood on a table inside. Maybe Mrs. Burns had left the candle burning for him. The gate-keeper's wife sometimes came to clean and leave him a meal. But Mrs. Burns was a thrifty woman, and Harry doubted she would waste a candle—even a tallow candle like the ones he used—on an empty cottage.

Someone waited for him inside.

And wouldn't that be a surprise after arguing with Granville this morning? If they meant to jump him, surely they would've taken care to wait in darkness? After all, he hadn't suspected anything until he'd seen the light. Had his cottage been dark, he'd have gamboled up, as trusting as a newborn lamb. Harry gave a soft snort. So. They—whoever *they* were—were very assured, waiting for him in his own home. They figured that even with the light showing so plainly from his windows, he'd be stupid or brash enough to walk right in.

And maybe they were right.

Harry set the lantern down, took the knife from his boot, and rose silently from his crouch. He stole to the cottage wall. His left hand held the knife by his thigh. Quietly he skimmed along the stone wall until he was at the door. He grasped the door handle and pressed the latch slowly. He took a breath and flung open the door.

"Mr. Pye, I had begun to think you would never come home." Lady Georgina knelt by his fireplace, looking quite unperturbed by his sudden entrance. "I'm afraid I'm hopeless at lighting fires, otherwise I would've made some tea." She rose and dusted off her knees.

"My lady." He bent and brushed his left hand over the top of his boot, sheathing the knife. "Naturally I'm honored to have your company, but I'm also surprised. What are you doing in my cottage?" He shut the door behind him and walked to the fireplace, picking up the burning candle on the way.

She stepped aside as he crouched by the hearth. "I fear I detect some sarcasm in your tone."

"Do you?"

"Mmm. And I am at a loss to understand why. After all, it was you who walked away from me this morning."

The lady was peeved.

Harry's lips curved as he lit the already laid fire. "I apologize most humbly, my lady."

"Humph. A less humble man I have yet to meet." From the sound of her voice, she was wandering the room behind him.

What did she see? What did this little cottage look like to her? In his mind's eye, he reviewed the inside of his cottage: a wooden table and chairs, well made but hardly the cushioned luxury of the manor's sitting rooms. A desk where he kept the record books and ledgers of his job. A set of shelves with some coarse pottery dishes—two plates, two cups, a bowl, a teapot, forks and spoons, and an iron cooking pot. A door off to one side that was no doubt open, so she could see his narrow bed, the hooks that held his clothes, and the dresser with the earthenware washbasin and pitcher.

He stood and turned.

Lady Georgina was peering into his bedroom.

He sighed silently and walked to the table. On it sat a crock covered with a plate. He lifted the plate and looked inside the pot. Mutton stew left by Mrs. Burns, cold now, but welcome nonetheless.

He went back to the hearth to fill the iron kettle with water and swing it over the fire. "Do you mind if I eat, my lady? I haven't had my supper yet."

She turned and stared at him as though her mind has been elsewhere. "Please. Do go ahead. I wouldn't want you to accuse me of withholding food."

Harry sat at the table and spooned some of the stew onto a plate. Lady Georgina came and looked curiously at his supper and then moved to the fireplace.

He watched her as he ate.

She examined the animal carvings lining his mantel. "Did you make all these?" She gestured to a squirrel with a nut between its paws and glanced back at him.

"Yes."

"That's how Lord Granville knew you'd made the hedgehog. He'd seen your work before."

"Yes."

"But he hadn't seen *you,* at least not for a very long time." She pivoted fully to look at him.

A lifetime. Harry served himself some more stew. "No."

"So he hadn't seen your figurines for a very long time, either? In fact, not since you were a boy." She frowned, fingering the squirrel. "Because I don't care what Lord Granville says, twelve years old is still just a boy."

"Maybe." The kettle started steaming. Harry got up, took down the brown teapot from his cupboard, and put in four spoonfuls of tea. He grabbed a cloth to lift the kettle from the fire. Lady Georgina moved aside and watched as he poured the boiling water.

"Maybe what?" She knit her brow. "Which question were you really answering?"

Harry set the teapot on the table and looked over his shoulder at her. "Which were you really asking?" He sat down again. "My lady."

She blinked and seemed to consider. Then she replaced the squirrel and crossed to the shelves. She picked up the two cups and a packet of sugar and brought them back to the table. She sat down across from him and poured the tea.

Harry stilled.

Lady Georgina was fixing him his tea, in his own house, at his own table, just like a country woman would, tending to her man after he'd had a hard day of work. It didn't feel at all like this morning in her sitting room. Right now it felt wifely. Which was a daft thought because she was the daughter of an earl. Only she didn't look like a lady at the moment. Not when she was adding sugar to his cup and stirring it in for him. All she looked like was a woman—a very desirable woman.

Damn. Harry tried to will his cock back down, but that part of his body had never listened to reason. He tasted the tea and grimaced. Did other men get cockstands over a cup of tea?

"Too much sugar?" She looked worriedly at his cup.

The tea was rather sweet for his taste, but he wasn't about to say that. "It's fine, my lady. Thank you for pouring."

"You're welcome." She took a sip of her own tea. "Now, as to what I'm really asking. How exactly did you know Lord Granville in the past?"

Harry closed his eyes. He was too weary for this. "Does it matter, my lady? You'll be letting me go soon enough, anyway."

"Whatever gave you that idea?" Lady Georgina frowned. Then she caught his look. "You don't think that *I* believe you murdered those sheep, do you?" Her eyes widened. "You do."

She put her cup back on the table with a sharp click. Some of the tea sloshed over the edge. "I know that I don't always seem very serious, but please acquit me of being a complete nincompoop." She scowled at him as she stood, arms akimbo like a red-haired Boadicea. All she needed was a sword and chariot.

"Harry Pye, you no more poisoned those sheep than I did!"

Chapter Four

As grand gestures went, it rather flopped.

Mr. Pye quirked a single eyebrow upward. "Since it boggles the mind," he said in that awful, dry tone, "that you, my lady, would ever poison livestock, I must be innocent."

"Humph." Gathering her dignity about her, George marched to the fireplace and pretended interest in the figurines again. "You haven't yet answered my question. Don't think I didn't notice."

Normally this would be the point where she'd say something flippant and silly, but somehow she just couldn't with him. It was hard to put away the mask, but she didn't want to play the ninny with him. She wanted him to think better of her.

He looked so tired; the lines around his mouth had deepened and his hair was windblown. What had he been doing all afternoon to make him so exhausted? She hadn't missed the way he'd entered the cottage, suddenly and in a crouch, his green eyes defiant. He'd reminded her of a cornered feral cat. But then he'd straightened and shoved something in his boot and was once again her phlegmatic steward. She might have imagined the violence she'd seen in his eyes, but she didn't think so.

Harry Pye sighed and pushed away his plate. "My father's name was John Pye. He was Silas Granville's gamekeeper when I was a boy. We lived on Granville land, and I grew up there."

"Really?" George turned to him. "How did you go from being a gamekeeper's son to a land steward?"

He stiffened. "You have my references, my lady. I assure you—"

"No, no." She shook her head impatiently. "I wasn't maligning your credentials. I'm just curious. You must admit it's a bit of a leap. How did you do it?"

"Hard work, my lady." His shoulders were still bunched.

George raised her eyebrows and waited.

"I got work as a gamekeeper on a big estate when I was sixteen. The land steward there discovered I could read and write and do sums. He took me on as sort of an apprentice. When a position on a smaller, neighboring estate became open, he recommended me." He shrugged. "From there I worked my way up."

She tapped her fingers against the mantelpiece. There had to be more to the story than that. Few men of Mr. Pye's age managed estates as large as hers, and how had he gotten an education, anyway? But that matter could wait until later. She had more pressing questions at the moment. She picked up a rabbit and rubbed its smooth back.

"What happened when you were twelve?"

"My father had a falling out with Granville," Mr. Pye said.

"A falling out?" George replaced the rabbit and chose

an otter. Dozens of the little wood carvings crowded the mantelpiece, each in exquisite detail. Most were of wild animals, although she spied a shepherd's dog. They fascinated her. What kind of a man would carve such things? "Lord Granville said your father tried to kill him. That sounds like much more than a falling out."

"Da struck him. Merely that." He spoke slowly, as if choosing his words with care. "I sincerely doubt he meant to kill Granville."

"Why?" She placed the otter next to the rabbit and made a little circle with a turtle and a shrew. "Why did he attack his employer and lord?"

Silence.

George waited, but he didn't answer. She touched a stag, standing on three legs, the fourth lifted as if to flee. "And you? Did you mean to kill Lord Granville at the age of twelve?"

The silence stretched again, but finally Harry Pye spoke. "Yes."

She let her breath out slowly. A commoner, child or not, could be hung for trying to kill a peer. "What did Lord Granville do?"

"He had my father and me horsewhipped."

The words fell into the stillness like pebbles into a pond. Emotionless. Simple. They belied the violence a horsewhipping would do to a young boy's body. To his soul.

George closed her eyes. Oh, dear Lord. *Don't think of it. It's in the past. Deal with the present.* "So you do have a motive for killing the sheep on Lord Granville's land." She opened her eyes and focused on a badger.

"Yes, my lady, I do."

"And is this story common knowledge in the district?

Do others know you've such enmity for my neighbor?" She placed the badger in alliance with the stag. The little creature's head was lifted, teeth bared. It made a formidable foe.

"I didn't hide my past and who I was when I returned as the Woldsly steward." Mr. Pye rose and took the teapot to the door. He opened it and tossed the dregs into the bushes. "There are some who remember what happened eighteen years ago. It was a scandal at the time." The dry tone was back.

"Why did you return to this neighborhood?" she asked. Was he looking for revenge in some way? "It does seem a bit of a coincidence that you should be working on the estate neighboring the one you grew up on."

He hesitated with the teapot dangling from one hand. "No coincidence, my lady." He walked deliberately to the cupboard, his back to her. "I pursued this position as soon as it opened. As you said, I grew up here. It's my home."

"It had nothing to do with Lord Granville?"

"Well"—Mr. Pye looked at her over his shoulder, a devilish gleam in his green eyes—"it didn't hurt that Granville would be irked to see me here."

George felt her lips lift. "Does everyone know about your carvings?" She waved a hand at the menagerie.

He'd brought out a dishpan and soap, but he paused to glance at the animals lining the mantelpiece.

"Probably not. I'd only made a few carvings when I was a boy here." He shrugged and began washing the tea things. "Da was known for his whittling. He taught me."

She took a cloth from the shelf, picked up a teacup Mr. Pye had rinsed, and began drying it. He glanced sideways at her, and she thought she detected surprise. Good.

"Then whoever put the hedgehog by the dead sheep either knew you before or had been in this cottage since your residence."

He shook his head. "The only visitors I've had are Mr. Burns and his wife. I pay her a bit to tidy for me and make me a meal once in a while." He pointed his chin at the empty crock that had held his dinner.

George felt a rush of satisfaction. He'd not brought a woman here. But then she frowned. "Perhaps you confided in a woman you've been walking out with?"

She winced. Not the most subtle of inquiries. Good Lord, he must think her a widgeon. Blindly, she put out her hand for another teacup and collided with Harry Pye's hand, warm and slippery with soap. She looked up and met his emerald eyes.

"I haven't walked out with a lass. Not since entering your employ, my lady." He picked up the crock to wash it.

"Ah. Well. Good. That narrows it down a bit." Could she sound any more a ninny if she tried? "Then do you know who could have stolen the hedgehog? I presume it was taken from above your fireplace?"

He rinsed the crock and picked up the basin. Carrying it to the door, he threw out the washing water. He caught the open door. "Anyone could have taken it, my lady." He pointed to the door handle.

There was no lock.

"Oh," George muttered. "That *doesn't* narrow it down."

"No, my lady." He sauntered back to the table, the firelight illuminating one side of his face and throwing the other half into darkness. His lips curved. Did he think her funny?

"Where did you go this morning?" she asked.

"I went to question the farmers who found the dead sheep and my carving." He stopped only a foot away from her.

She could feel the warmth of his chest not quite touching hers. Was he staring at her mouth?

He was. "I wondered if one of them had left the hedgehog. But they were men I didn't know, and they seemed honest enough."

"I see." Her throat was dry. She swallowed. He was her steward, for goodness sake. What she was feeling wasn't at all proper. "Well." George folded the towel and put it away on the shelf. "We shall just have to do some more research tomorrow."

"*We*, my lady?"

"Yes. I shall accompany you."

"Just this morning Lord Granville threatened you." Harry Pye wasn't looking at her mouth anymore. In fact, he was frowning into her eyes.

George felt a twinge of disappointment. "You'll need my help."

"I've no need of your help, my lady. You shouldn't be gadding about the countryside while . . ." He trailed off as a thought struck him. "How did you come to my cottage?"

Oops. "I walked?"

"You . . . It's over a mile from here to Woldsly!" Mr. Pye stopped and breathed heavily in that way some men do when a female says something particularly foolish.

"Walking is good exercise," George explained kindly. "Besides, I was on my own land."

"Nevertheless, would you please promise me not to go strolling about on your own, my lady?" His lips tightened. "Until this is over with?"

"Very well, I promise to not go out alone." George smiled. "And in return, you can promise to take me on your investigations."

Harry Pye's eyes narrowed.

George drew herself up straight. "After all, I am your employer, Mr. Pye."

"Fine, my lady. I'll take you with me."

Not the most gracious acquiescence, but it would do.

"Good. We can start in the morning." George swung her cloak around her shoulders. "About nine, I think? We'll take my gig."

"As you wish, my lady." Mr. Pye advanced ahead of her to the cottage door. "I'll walk you back to Woldsly."

"No need. I asked that the carriage be brought round at nine. It should be here by now."

And indeed, when Mr. Pye swung wide the door, a footman was waiting discreetly by the path. Her steward eyed the man. He must have approved, for he nodded. "Good night, my lady."

"Until tomorrow morning." George drew the hood up over her hair. "Good night."

She walked to the footman and then glanced over her shoulder. Harry Pye stood in his doorway, silhouetted by the firelight behind him.

She couldn't read his expression.

"WHAT ARE YOU DOING up so early?" Violet stared at her sister, already dressed and hurrying down the stairs at— she stepped backward into her room to check the clock— eight in the morning.

"Oh, hullo, dear." George did a little half-whirl on the stairs, peering up at her. "I'm just, uh, going for a drive."

"Going for a drive," Violet repeated. "By yourself? At eight in the morning?"

George tilted her chin, but her cheeks were turning pink. "Mr. Pye will accompany me. He wishes to show me some things around the estate. Tenants and walls and crops and such, I suppose. Terribly boring, but necessary."

"Mr. Pye! But, George, you can't go out alone with him."

"Why not? He is my land steward, after all. It's his job to keep me informed about estate matters."

"But—"

"I really must go, dear. The man is apt to take off without me if I'm late." And with that, George all but ran down the stairs.

Violet followed more slowly, her brow knit in thought. What was George about? She couldn't still trust the land steward, could she? Not after the accusations she'd heard, not after Lord Granville had stormed the manor yesterday? Perhaps her sister was trying to find out more about Mr. Pye on her own. But in that case, why had she blushed?

Violet nodded to the footmen as she entered the morning room where breakfast was served. She had the gold and pale blue room to herself—Euphie never rose before nine in the morning, even in the country. She went to the sideboard and helped herself to a bun and a slice of gammon, and then sat down at the pretty gilt table. Only then did she notice the letter by her plate. The handwriting was distinctively slanted backward.

"When did this arrive?" She took a too-quick sip of tea and burned her mouth.

"This morning, my lady," one of the footmen murmured.

It was a silly question, and she wouldn't have asked it, but she'd been stalling before opening the letter. She picked it up and turned it over to pry up the seal with a butter knife. She took a deep breath before unfolding the paper and then had trouble releasing it. It was important she not show her emotions before the servants, but it was difficult. Her worst fears had been realized. She'd had two months of respite, but now that was over.

He'd found her.

ONE OF THE PROBLEMS WITH WOMEN—*and there are many—is they think nothing of messing about in a man's business.* Harry Pye remembered Da's words when he saw Lady Georgina's carriage the next morning at eight-thirty.

She wasn't taking any chances, his lady. She'd driven the old gig to the part of Woldsly drive that intersected the cutoff to his cottage. There was no way he could escape the estate without her seeing him. And she was a half hour earlier than their agreed-upon meeting time of nine o'clock. It was almost as if she'd feared he would try to leave without her. And since he'd planned exactly that, her appearance was all the more annoying.

"Good morning." Lady Georgina waved happily.

She was wearing some sort of red-and-white-patterned frock that should have jarred with her ginger hair but didn't. On her head was a wide-brimmed hat tilted rakishly down in front and up in back where her hair was massed. Red ribbons on the crown of the hat fluttered in the breeze. She looked dainty and aristocratic, like she was out for a picnic in the country.

"I've had Cook pack a luncheon," she called as he neared, confirming his worst fears.

Harry stopped himself in time from casting his eyes heavenward. *God help me.* "Good morning, my lady."

It was another dreary, gray day. No doubt they would be rained on before the morning was out.

"Would you like to drive?" She scooted across the seat to make room for him.

"If you don't mind, my lady." He climbed in, making the gig rock on its oversized wheels.

"Oh, no, I don't mind at all." He could feel her gaze as he gathered the reins. "I can drive, naturally; it's how I arrived here this morning, after all. But I find it's much nicer to watch the scenery without worrying about the horses and the road and all that."

"Indeed."

Lady Georgina sat forward, her cheeks flushed with the wind. Her lips were slightly parted like a child looking forward to a treat. He felt a smile form on his own lips.

"Where will we be going today?" she asked.

He brought his eyes back to the road. "I want to visit another of the farmers whose sheep were killed. I need to find out what exactly killed the animals."

"Wasn't it a poisonous weed?"

"Yes," he replied. "But no one I've talked to seems to know what kind, and it could be several. Wolfsbane is poisonous, though rare in these parts. Some folk grow belladonna and foxglove in their gardens—both can kill sheep and people as well. And there are common plants, such as tansy, that grow wild in pastures and will kill sheep if they eat enough."

"I had no idea there are so many poisons growing in the countryside. It quite makes one shiver. What did the Medicis use?"

"The Medicis?"

Lady Georgina wriggled her little rump on the carriage seat. "You know, those deliciously horrible Italians with the poison rings that went about killing anyone who looked at them askance. What d'you suppose they used?"

"I don't know, my lady." The way her mind worked.

"Oh." She sounded disappointed. "What about arsenic? That's very poisonous, isn't it?"

"It's poisonous, but arsenic isn't a plant."

"No? Then what is it?"

He had no idea. "A sort of seashell that is ground into a powder, my lady."

There was a short pause while she thought that one over.

Harry held his breath.

Out of the corner of his eye, he saw her squint at him. "You're making that up."

"My lady?"

"That bit about arsenic being a *sort of seashell*." She lowered her voice on the last words to mimic him.

"I assure you"—Harry kept his tone bland—"it's a pinkish seashell found only in the Adriatic Sea. The local villagers harvest the shells with long rakes and sieves. There is a yearly festival to celebrate the catch." He fought to prevent his lips from twitching. "The Annual Adriatic Arsenic Assail."

Silence—and, he was fairly certain—stunned silence at that. Harry felt a surge of pride. It wasn't just any man who could make Lady Georgina lose her power of speech.

Not that it lasted long.

"I shall have to watch you, Mr. Pye."

"My lady?"

"Because you are *evil*." But her words shook as if she barely held in the laughter.

He smiled. He hadn't felt so light in a very, very long time. He slowed the horse as they came to the stream that separated her estate from Granville's land. He scanned the horizon. Theirs was the only vehicle on the road.

"Surely Lord Granville wouldn't be so rash as to attack us here."

He glanced at her, brows raised.

She frowned impatiently. "You've been watching the hills since we neared the stream."

Ah. She'd been aware. He reminded himself not to underestimate her, even when she played the aristocratic ninny. "Granville would be insane to try an attack." Which didn't mean he wouldn't.

Reapers harvested barley to their right. Usually reapers sang as they worked, but these labored in silence.

"Lord Granville has his workers out on a misty day," Lady Georgina said.

He pressed his lips together to forestall a comment on Granville's agricultural practices.

A sudden thought occurred to her. "I haven't noticed anyone in my fields since I've arrived at Woldsly. Are you worried they might get the ague?"

Harry stared at her. *She didn't know.* "The grain is still too damp to store. Only a fool would order the reapers out on a morning like this."

"But"—she knitted her brows—"don't you need to harvest it before frost?"

"Yes. But if the grain is wet, it's worse than useless to harvest it. It would merely spoil in the storage bins." He shook his head. "Those workers are wasting their strength on grain that will rot, anyway."

"I see." She seemed to think about that for a minute. "What will you do with the Woldsly harvest, then?"

"There's nothing to do, my lady, except pray for a break in the rain."

"But if the harvest is ruined..."

He straightened a bit in the seat. "Your revenue will be considerably lessened from the estate this year, I'm afraid, my lady. If the weather clears, we might still get most of the crop in, maybe all of it. But every day that goes by lessens that chance. The tenants on your land need those crops to feed their families as well as pay you your share. The farmers won't have much left over—"

"I don't mean that!" Now she was frowning at him, looking insulted. "Do you think me such a... a *fribble* that I'd care for my income over a tenant's ability to feed his children?"

Harry couldn't think of anything to say. All the land-owners in his experience did indeed have more concern for their income than the well-being of the people who worked their land.

She continued, "We will, of course, waive the rent monies due me for this year if the harvest fails. And I will make available loans to any farmer who might need one to see him through the winter."

Harry blinked, startled by a sudden lightness in his heart. Her offer was more than generous. She'd removed a burden from his shoulders. "Thank you, my lady."

She looked down at her gloved hands. "Don't thank me," she said gruffly. "I should have realized. And I'm sorry for being cross with you. I was embarrassed to know so little about my own estate. You must think me an idiot."

"No," he replied softly, "only a lady who is city bred."

"Ah, Mr. Pye." She smiled, and his chest seemed to warm. "Ever the diplomat."

They crested a rise, and Harry slowed the gig to turn into a rutted lane. He hoped they wouldn't lose a wheel in the potholes. The lane led to a crofter's cottage, long and low, with a thatched roof. Harry pulled the horse to a halt and jumped from the gig.

"Who lives here?" Lady Georgina asked when he went to her side to help her down.

"Sam Oldson."

A shaggy terrier ran out from around the building and began barking at them.

"Sam!" Harry shouted. "You there, Sam! Are you home?"

He wasn't about to go nearer the cottage with that dog growling so seriously. It was a smallish dog, true, but the small ones were more apt to bite.

"Aye?" A burly man wearing a reaper's straw hat came from the shed. "Shuddup, dog!" He roared to the still-barking terrier. "Get on with you!"

The dog tucked its tail under its rear and sat.

"Good morning." Lady Georgina spoke brightly from beside Harry.

Sam Oldson snatched the hat from his head, baring a wild nest of black hair. "Ma'am. I didn't see you there at first." He ran a hand through his hair, making it stand up even more, and looked helplessly at the cottage. "My woman's not home. Visiting her mum she is, otherwise she'd be out here offering you a drink and a bite to eat."

"That's quite all right, Mr. Oldson. We did arrive unexpectedly, I know." She smiled at the man.

Harry cleared his throat. "This is Lady Georgina Maitland from Woldsly." He thought it best not to introduce himself, though Sam was no fool. Already he was beginning to scowl. "We've come to ask you about the sheep you lost. The ones that were poisoned. Did you find them yourself?"

"Aye." Sam spat into the dust at his feet, and the terrier cringed at his tone. "A little over a fortnight ago, it were. I'd sent my lad to bring them in and he come running back quick. Said I'd better come see myself. There they were, three of my best ewes, rolled on their sides with tongues sticking out and bits of green leaves still in their mouths."

"Do you know what they'd eaten?" Harry asked.

"False parsley." Sam's face turned purple. "Some son of a bitch had cut down false parsley and fed it to my sheep. And I says to my lad, I says, when I get my hands on the villain that's killed my sheep, he'll wish he'd never been born, he will."

Time to go. Harry grabbed Lady Georgina around the waist and threw her up onto the carriage seat. She squealed.

"Thank you." He walked swiftly around the front of the carriage, keeping an eye on Sam Oldson. The dog had begun to growl again.

"Here now, why're you asking questions?" Sam started toward them.

The dog lunged and Harry bound into the carriage and caught up the reins. "Good day, Sam."

He turned the horse's head and slapped it into a trot down the track. Behind them, Sam made a reply not fit for a lady's ears. Harry winced and glanced at Lady Georgina, but she was looking thoughtful rather than outraged. Maybe she hadn't understood the words?

"What is false parsley?" she asked.

"It's a weed that grows in wet places, my lady. About the height of a man with little white flowers at the top. It looks something like parsley or wild carrots."

"I've never heard of it before." Lady Georgina's brows were knit.

"You probably know it by its other name," Harry said. "Hemlock."

Chapter Five

"Do you know that when I first met you I didn't like you?" Lady Georgina asked idly as the old gig jolted over a hole in the road.

They were driving slowly down a track on the way to Tom Harding's cottage. Harding had lost two sheep last week. Harry only hoped he wasn't pushing their luck, staying on Granville land so long. He tore his mind away from thoughts of hemlock and dead sheep and stared at her. How was he supposed to answer a question like that?

"You were so stiff, so correct." She twirled her parasol. "And I had the distinct feeling you were looking down your nose at me as if you didn't particularly like me, either."

He remembered the interview many months before in her London town house. She'd kept him waiting in a pretty pink sitting room for over an hour. Then suddenly she'd blown in, chattering at him as if they'd already met. Had he glowered at her? He didn't know, but it was likely. Back then she'd conformed to all his expectations of an aristocratic lady.

Funny how his estimation of her had changed since.

"That's probably why Violet so dislikes you," she said now.

"What?" He'd lost the thread of her conversation. Again.

She waved a hand. "The sternness, the correctness that you display. I think that's why Violet doesn't care for you very much."

"I'm sorry, my lady."

"No, no, you needn't apologize. It's not your fault."

He raised an eyebrow.

"It's our father's." She glanced at him and must have read the puzzlement on his face. "Father was stern and terribly correct as well. You probably remind Violet of him."

"She said I reminded her of your father? An earl?"

"No, of course not. I doubt she consciously has noticed the superficial resemblance."

His mouth twisted. "I'm flattered to be compared to your father, my lady, superficially or not."

"Oh, Lord, and now you're using that terribly dry tone."

He shot a startled look at her.

Her eyes widened. "I never know if I should throw myself from a cliff when I hear it or simply slink into some corner and try and make myself invisible."

She could never make herself invisible. At least not to him. He'd smell her exotic fragrance if nothing else. He straightened. "I assure you—"

"Never mind." She cut him off with a wave. "If anyone should apologize, it should be me. My father was an awful man, and I had no business comparing the two of you."

How to reply to that? "Huh."

"Not that we saw Father all that much, of course. Only

once a week, sometimes less, when Nanny brought us down for inspection."

Inspection? He'd never understand the rich.

"It really was the most terrifying thing. I never could eat beforehand, or I'd be in danger of losing the meal on his boots, and wouldn't *that* be a horror." She shivered at the thought. "We'd line up, my brothers and I, all in a row. Scrubbed, polished, and silent, we'd wait for Father to give his approval. Quite, quite agonizing, I assure you."

He glanced at her. Despite her words, Lady Georgina's face was bland, almost careless, but she wasn't quite as good at disguising her voice. He wouldn't have noticed it a week ago, but today he detected the strain. Her old man must've been a right bastard.

She was looking down at her hands now, folded in her lap. "And, you see, at least we had each other, my brothers and I, when we went for inspection. But Violet is the youngest. She had to do it all alone after the rest of us grew up and left."

"When did the earl die?"

"Five years ago, now. He was on a foxhunt—he was very proud of his kennel of foxhounds—and his horse balked at a hedge. The horse stayed behind, but father went over and broke his neck. He was already dead when they brought him home. Mother had an hysterical fit and took to bed for the next year. She didn't even rise for the funeral."

"I'm sorry."

"So am I. Mostly for Violet's sake. Mother has always been delicate—her words. She spends a great deal of her time inventing illnesses and then calling for the latest ridiculous cure." She stopped suddenly and inhaled.

He waited, handling the reins as the horse trotted around a bend.

Then she said softly, "I'm sorry. You must think me terrible."

"No, my lady. I think that your sister is lucky to have you."

She smiled then, that bright, open smile that made his balls tighten and his breath catch. "Thank you. Although I don't know if she would agree with you at the moment."

"Why is that, my lady?"

"I don't know why, exactly," she said slowly. "But something seems to be wrong. She's angry at me... no, it's not that plain. She's distant, as if she's keeping part of herself back from me."

He was out of his depth here, but he tried. "Perhaps it is simply that she's growing out of the schoolroom."

"Maybe. But Violet has always been such a cheerful, open girl, and we've been very close. With Mother the way she is, well, I've had to step in. We're closer than most sisters." She smiled mischievously at him. "It's why I'm so sure of the reason she distrusts you."

"No doubt you're right about that." They'd come to a gate, and he pulled the horse to a stop. "But you're wrong on one other thing."

"What is that?"

He tied the reins and stood in preparation to swing down from the gig. "I never disliked you, my lady."

THE KEY TO A SUCCESSFUL alfresco picnic was in the packing. George peered into the wicker basket and hummed in approval. Squishy foods, like cream cakes, for instance, were bound to come to grief no matter how carefully the hamper was handled. She lifted out some smoked ham and placed it on a cutting board next to the cheese and crusty bread. If one forgot important utensils, one was likely to end up having to tear things apart with one's bare hands. She handed the corkscrew to Mr. Pye. It was also most imperative that the foods not spoil during the day. A pear tart followed. And the little details should not be forgotten in order to have a really splendid picnic. She took out a small jar of pickled gherkins and sighed in satisfaction.

"I just adore picnics."

Mr. Pye, wrestling with the cork in a bottle of white wine, looked up and smiled at her. "So I see, my lady."

For a moment, George felt lost in that smile, the first full one she'd ever seen on his face.

The cork let go with a soft *pop*. Mr. Pye poured a glass of the translucent liquid and handed it to her. She took a sip, savoring the tart bite on her tongue, and then set the glass down on the throw where they sat. A white butterfly that had been resting on the throw took off.

"Look." George gestured to the insect. "I wonder what kind it is?"

"It's a cabbage butterfly, my lady."

"Oh." She wrinkled her nose. "What an awful name for such a pretty thing."

"Yes, my lady." His tone was grave. Was he laughing at her?

The last farmer they'd visited hadn't been home, and as they'd driven away from the lonely cottage, she'd insisted that they stop for luncheon. Mr. Pye had found a grassy hill beside the road. The view from the top of the hill was glorious. Even on a cloudy day like this one they could see for miles, maybe all the way into the next county.

"How did you know of this place?" she asked as she fished for pickles with a fork.

"I used to come here as a boy."

"All alone?"

"Sometimes. I had a little pony as a lad, and I used to go wandering. Packed a picnic, not as grand as this one, of course, but enough to satisfy a boy for the day."

George listened with her pickle, speared on a fork, held in midair. "That sounds lovely."

"It was." He looked away.

She frowned at her pickle, and then popped it into her mouth. "Did you go alone, or were there other boys in the area to accompany you?" She squinted over his shoulder. Was that a horseman coming up the road?

"I usually had a mate."

Definitely a horseman. "I wonder who that is."

He twisted to look behind him. His back stiffened. "Damn."

"Do you know who it is?"

The rider was nearing, and by the narrowness of his shoulders, it wasn't Lord Granville.

"Maybe." Mr. Pye still stared.

The rider was now below the hill. He glanced up at them.

"Goddamn," Mr. Pye said.

George knew she should be shocked, but he didn't seem to realize that he'd sworn—twice—in front of her. Slowly she put down the pickle jar.

"Hullo," the man called. "Do you mind if I join you?"

She had a feeling Mr. Pye was about to reply in the negative to this friendly greeting, so she answered, "Not at all."

The man dismounted, tethered his horse, and began to climb the slope. George couldn't help but notice that, unlike when Mr. Pye had climbed the hill, the man was puffing by the time he reached them.

"Whew! A bit of a climb, what?" He brought out a handkerchief and wiped his sweating face.

George stared at him curiously. He dressed and spoke like a gentleman. Tall and long-boned, he had an ingratiating smile on thin lips, and his brown eyes were familiar.

"I'm sorry to bother you, but I noticed the carriage and thought I'd introduce myself." He bowed. "Thomas Granville at your service. And you are...?"

"Georgina Maitland. This is—"

But Mr. Granville interrupted, "Ah, I thought so... or rather, I *hoped* so. May I?" He gestured at the throw.

"Please."

"Thank you." He lowered himself carefully. "Actually, I wanted to apologize for my father's behavior yesterday. He told me that he'd visited you and that you'd disagreed. And knowing my father—"

"That's nice of you."

"Neighbors and all." Mr. Granville waved his hand vaguely. "I thought there must be a way we can settle this peacefully."

"How?" Mr. Pye's one word dropped onto the conversation, flattening it.

George glanced sharply at him.

Mr. Granville turned to speak, looked Mr. Pye in the face, and coughed.

Mr. Pye handed him a glass of wine.

"Harry," Mr. Granville gasped when he could draw breath. "I didn't realize that was you until I saw—"

"How," Harry Pye inquired, "do you plan to settle the problem without bloodshed?"

"It'll have to stop, of course—the sheep poisoning, I mean. And the other mischief."

"Plainly. But how?"

"You'll have to leave, I'm afraid, Harry." Mr. Granville shrugged one shoulder jerkily. "Even if you repaid the cost of the livestock and the damage to Father's stable, he's not going to let it go. You know what he's like."

Mr. Granville's gaze dropped to Harry Pye's mutilated right hand resting on his knee. George followed his eyes and felt a cold wave wash over her body when she saw Harry flex the remaining fingers.

"And if I don't leave?" Mr. Pye replied in a deadly calm voice, as if he were inquiring the time.

"You don't have a choice." Mr. Granville looked to George, apparently for support.

She raised her eyebrows.

He turned back to Mr. Pye. "It's for the best, Harry. I can't answer for what will happen if you don't."

Harry Pye didn't reply. His green eyes had grown stony.

Nobody spoke for an uncomfortable period of time.

Mr. Granville suddenly slapped his hand on the throw. "Disgusting things." He lifted his hand, and George saw that he'd squashed the cabbage butterfly.

She must've made a sound.

Both men looked at her, but it was Mr. Granville who spoke. "The butterfly. They come from worms that devour leafy crops. Nasty things. All farmers hate them."

She and Mr. Pye were silent.

Mr. Granville's face reddened. "Well. I must be going.

Thank you for the repast." He stood and clambered back down the hill to his horse.

Harry Pye watched him go, eyes narrowed.

George looked down at the pickle jar beside her hand. She hadn't the appetite for them anymore. She sighed mournfully. A perfect picnic ruined.

"YOU DON'T LIKE HIM." Lady Georgina frowned, looking down at the picnic blanket. She was trying to fold it, but it was turning into a tangled mess.

"Who?" Harry took it from her and shook out the fabric, then handed her the corners on one end.

"Thomas Granville, of course." She held her end of the blanket limply as if she didn't know what to do. Hadn't she ever folded a sheet before? "You swore when you saw him, you weren't going to invite him to join us, and when he did, you were barely civil to him."

"No, I don't like Thomas Granville." He backed up to draw the fabric taut, then brought his corners together so that a rectangle hung between them. She caught on. They folded the blanket once more, and then he walked toward her to take her corners from her. He met her eyes.

They were narrowed. "Why? What's wrong with Mr. Granville?"

He's his father's son. "I don't trust him."

"He knew you." Her head was cocked to the side, as if she were a curious thrush. "You knew each other."

"Aye."

She opened her mouth, and he expected more questions, but she simply pressed her lips together again. Silently they packed away the rest of the picnic. He took the basket from her, and they climbed down to the waiting gig. He stowed the basket under the seat, and then turned to her, steeling his features. It was harder to keep his emotions in check around her these days.

She watched him with thoughtful blue eyes. "Who do you think is poisoning the sheep?"

He put his hands around her waist. "I don't know." He felt the stiffness of her stays, and beneath that, warmth. He lifted her into the gig and let go before she could see the longing in his eyes. He jumped into the seat beside her and untied the reins.

"Maybe it's Thomas Granville," she said.

"Why?"

"To make it seem as if you were doing the crime? To enrage his father? Because he hates the smell of wet wool? I don't know."

He could feel her gaze on him, but he kept his eyes straight ahead as he guided the horse back to the road. The gelding liked to play games if the driver wasn't paying attention. He thought about her words. Thomas? Why would Thomas—

A sound like steam escaping from a lidded pot came from her lips. "You needn't blame me for his condescension, you know. I've already told you I don't believe you killed the sheep."

She was scowling at him. What had he done now? "I'm sorry, my lady. I was thinking."

"Well, try to think out loud. I don't handle charged silences well. They make me nervous."

His lips twitched. "I'll remember that."

"Do."

They rode another quarter mile in silence before she spoke again. "What else did you do when you were a boy?"

He glanced at her.

She caught the look. "Surely you can tell me that? All of your childhood can't be a secret."

"No, but it isn't very interesting. I mostly helped my da."

She leaned toward him. "And...?"

"We walked the land, checked traps, watched for poachers. That's what a gamekeeper does." A memory of his father's strong, leathery hands delicately setting a trap came to him. Strange how he could remember the hands but not the face.

"And did you find any poachers?"

"Aye, of course." He was pleased that his voice was steady. "There are always poachers, and Granville had more'n his fair share because he was so mean to his tenants. Many poached for food."

"What did your father do?" Her hand, which had been lying on her lap, slipped, resting now alongside his thigh.

Harry kept his gaze ahead and shrugged. "Mostly he'd turn a blind eye. If they took too much, he'd tell them to do their hunting elsewhere."

"But that would've put him in conflict with his employer, wouldn't it? If Lord Granville found out he wasn't arresting every poacher."

"It might've. If Granville found out. Turned out he didn't." He'd been more interested in other things, hadn't he?

"I would've liked to have known your father," she mused. He could've sworn he felt her fingers press against his leg.

He looked at her curiously. "Would you? A gamekeeper?"

"Yes. What else did you do when you were a boy?"

What did she want from him? Why all these questions, and why the hand against his leg? Her fingers felt as if they burned straight through his breeches to his skin beneath. "That's about it, my lady. Roaming the land, checking traps, looking for birds' eggs—"

"Birds' eggs?"

"Aye." He glanced at her, then down at her hand. "Used to collect them as a boy."

She was frowning and didn't seem to notice his gaze. "But where would you find them?"

"In the nest." She still looked puzzled, so he explained. "You watch the birds in spring. See where they go. Sooner or later, they all go back to their nests. Jackdaws in chimneys, plovers on the heath, pigeons in the crook of trees, and thrushes in a nest like a cup in the branches of hedges. You wait and you watch, and if you're patient, you see where the eggs are. Then you can take one."

"Just one?"

He nodded. "Never more than one, for my da said 'twas a sin to steal all the eggs from a nest. I'd watch the bird and slowly, slowly creep close until I could take an egg. Most of the time I'd have to wait until the bird left the nest. But sometimes if I was careful, I could reach right under the bird—"

"No!" She laughed up at him, her blue eyes crinkled at the corners, and suddenly his heart seemed to contract. Maybe he didn't really care why she asked her questions—just so long as she asked them. "You're teasing me now."

"It's true." He felt his lips curve. "I'd reach right under

the bird, feel its little downy body beating and warm on my fingers, and steal an egg straight from the nest it was sitting on."

"Really?"

"A fact."

"You're probably bamming me again, Mr. Pye, but for some reason I believe you." She shook her head. "But what did you do with the eggs after that? Eat them?"

"Eat them? Never!" He widened his eyes in an exaggeratedly horrified look that seemed to amuse her. That pleased him and he was puzzled. This silly conversation was like no other he could remember. Men took him dead seriously. Women were a little in awe of him. No one giggled at his words or attempted—

"Then what do you do with the eggs?" Her eyes were laughing up at him again.

He almost swore, he was so startled. Was Lady Georgina—an *earl's* daughter for Christ's sake—flirting with him?

He'd gone insane. "I'd take a pin and poke a tiny hole in each end of the egg and let it dry. I had a shelf next to my bed with a whole row of eggs, brown and white and clear blue. Blue as..." He trailed away. *Blue as your eyes,* he'd meant to say, but he remembered suddenly that this woman was his employer and he her servant. How could he forget that fact? Irritated with himself, he faced forward again.

She didn't seem to notice his pause. "Do you have the eggs still? I'd like to see them."

They'd rounded a bend in the road, and Harry saw that a tangle of branches blocked the way. A tree had fallen across the lane.

"Whoa!" He frowned. The lane was hardly wide enough for the gig as it was. It would be a devil's job to turn the carriage around. What—?

Four men suddenly appeared from behind the tangled branches. They were big, they looked mean, and they each held a knife in their hand.

Shit.

Chapter Six

George screamed as Harry Pye made a heroic attempt to pull the horse around. The lane was too narrow, and the men were upon him in seconds. Mr. Pye kicked the first in the chest with a booted foot. The second and third overwhelmed and dragged him from the carriage. The fourth dealt him a horrendous blow to the jaw.

Oh, my sweet Lord! They were going to kill him. George felt a second scream clog her throat. The gig jolted as the horse half-reared. It was frightened and trying to run, stupid animal, even though it had nowhere to go. George frantically scrabbled for the reins on the floor of the gig, cursing under her breath and banging her head against the seat.

"Watch it! He's got a knife!"

That wasn't Mr. Pye's voice. George chanced raising her head and saw to her relief that Harry Pye did indeed have a knife. He held a thin, gleaming blade in his left hand. Even from this distance it looked rather nasty. He was in a strangely graceful fighter's crouch in the road, both hands in front of him. He appeared to know what he was doing, too. One of the villains was bleeding from his cheek. But the other three were circling, trying to flank him, and the odds didn't look good.

The gig lurched again. She lost sight of the action as she fell and cracked her shoulder against the seat.

"Will you hold still, you silly beast?" she muttered.

The reins were sliding toward the front, and if she lost them, she'd never get control of the gig. Shouts and grunts came from the fighters, interspersed with the awful sound of fists hitting flesh. She daren't risk looking up again. She held on to the seat with one hand to steady herself and strained with the other toward the slithering reins. *Almost.* Her fingertips grazed the leather, but the horse jolted, sending her back against the seat. She just kept her footing. If the horse would only hold still.

One.

More.

Second.

She dived and triumphantly came up with the reins. Quickly she sawed them, little minding the horse's mouth, and tied them to the seat. She chanced a glance. Harry Pye was bleeding from his forehead. As she watched, an attacker lunged at him from his right. Mr. Pye whirled in a powerful move and kicked at the other man's legs. A second thug clawed at his left arm. Mr. Pye twisted and performed some sort of maneuver, too fast for her to see. The man screamed and staggered back with a bloody hand. But the first man took advantage of the distraction. He hit Mr. Pye again and again in the middle. Harry Pye grunted with each blow, doubling over, valiantly trying to swing his knife.

George set the carriage brake.

The third and fourth men advanced. The first man

punched Mr. Pye once more, and he fell to his knees, retching.

Mr. Pye was going to die.

Ohmygodohmygodohmygod! George scrambled under the seat and brought up a sackcloth-wrapped bundle. Shaking the cloth free, she clutched one of the dueling pistols in her right hand, raised it with a straight arm, aimed at the man standing over Mr. Pye, and fired.

Bang!

The explosion nearly deafened her. She squinted through the smoke and saw the man reel away, clutching his side. Got the bastard! She felt a thrill of bloodthirsty glee. The remaining men, including Harry Pye, had turned in her direction with varying degrees of shock and horror. She raised the second pistol and took aim at another man.

The man flinched and ducked. "Gorblimey! She's got a pistol!"

Apparently the thought that she might be dangerous had never crossed their minds.

Harry Pye rose, pivoted silently, and slashed at the man nearest him.

"Jaysus!" the man screamed, holding a hand to his bloody face. "Let's go, lads!" The thugs turned and dashed back the way they'd come.

The lane was suddenly quiet.

George heard the blood rushing in her veins. She carefully set the pistols down on the seat.

Mr. Pye still looked in the direction the men had disappeared. He seemed to decide that they were gone, for he lowered the hand holding the knife. Bending, he slipped it inside his boot. Then he turned to her. The blood from the wound on his forehead had mixed with sweat and smeared down the side of his face. Stray hairs from his queue stuck to the gore. He breathed deeply, his nostrils flaring as he tried to catch his breath.

George felt strange, almost angry.

He walked toward her, his boots scraping against the rocks in the road. "Why didn't you tell me you'd brought pistols?" His voice was raspy and deep. It demanded apology, concession, even submission.

George didn't feel like giving any.

"I—" she began firmly, strongly, even haughtily.

She didn't have a chance to finish because he was in front of her. He grabbed her about the waist and yanked her from the carriage. She half-fell against him. She put her hands on his shoulders to keep from toppling over. He pulled her against him until her breasts were quite squashed into his chest, which, strangely, felt very nice. She lifted her head to ask him what, exactly, he thought he was about—

And he kissed her!

Luscious, firm lips that tasted of the wine they'd drunk at luncheon. They moved over hers in an insistent rhythm. She could feel the prickle of his stubble and his tongue, running over the crease of her lips until she opened them and then... *Ohm.* Someone was moaning, and it might very well be her because she had never, never, *never* been kissed like this before in her whole life. His tongue was actually inside her mouth, stroking and teasing hers. She was about to melt—maybe she already was melting, she felt absolutely drenched. And then he lured her tongue into his mouth and suckled it, and she lost all control and wrapped her arms about his neck and suckled him back.

The horse—stupid, *stupid* animal—chose that moment to whicker.

Mr. Pye jerked his head away. He glanced around. "I can't believe I did that."

"Nor I," George said. She tried to pull his head back down so he would do it again.

But suddenly he picked her up and deposited her on the carriage seat. While she was still blinking, he crossed to the other side and jumped in.

Mr. Pye placed the still-loaded pistol in her lap. "It's dangerous here. They may decide to come back."

"Oh."

All her life she'd been warned that men were slaves to their desires, that they held their impulses in barely controlled check. A woman—a lady—must be very, very careful of her actions so she did not put spark to the gunpowder that was a man's libido. The consequences of a lady's carelessness were never fully explained, but the hints were dire indeed. George sighed. How deflating now to find Harry Pye was the exception to the rule of male instability.

He maneuvered the gig around, alternately cursing and cajoling the horse. Finally he got it turned back the way they'd come and urged the gelding into a brisk trot. George watched him. His face was grimly set. There was no evidence of the passion with which he'd kissed her only moments ago.

Well, if he could be sophisticated, then so could she. "Do you think Lord Granville had those men attack us, Mr. Pye?"

"They attacked only me. So, yes, it could be Lord Granville. He's the most likely." He looked thoughtful. "But Thomas Granville rode up the lane only minutes before we did. He could've warned the toughs if they were in his pay."

"You think he is in league with his father, despite his apology?"

Mr. Pye pulled a handkerchief out of an inside pocket and gently wiped her cheek with one hand. The handkerchief came away with blood on it. He must have rubbed his blood on her when they'd kissed. "I don't know. But there's one thing I'm sure of."

George cleared her throat. "What is that, Mr. Pye?"

He tucked away his handkerchief. "You can call me Harry now."

HARRY PUSHED OPEN THE DOOR to the Cock and Worm and was immediately smothered in smoke. West Dikey, the village closest to Woldsly Manor, was just large enough to boast two taverns. The first, the White Mare, was a half-timbered building with a few rooms and could be called an *inn*. Because of this, it offered meals and drew the more respectable business: passing travelers, local merchants, and even gentry.

The Cock and Worm was where everyone else went.

A series of dingy rooms with exposed beams that had caught more than one customer a nasty knock on the head, the Cock and Worm had windows permanently blackened from pipe smoke. A man could sit in peace here and not be recognized by his own brother.

Harry made his way through the crowd to the bar, passing a table of workmen and farmers. One of the men—a farmer named Mallow—looked up and nodded in greeting as he passed. Harry nodded back, surprised but pleased. Mallow had asked Harry for help back in June about an argument he was having over his neighbor's cow. The cow kept escaping its enclosure and had twice trampled the lettuce in the Mallow's kitchen garden. Harry had settled the difficulty by helping the elderly neighbor build a new wall for his cow. But Mallow was a taciturn man and had never thanked Harry for his trouble. Harry had assumed Mallow was ungrateful. Obviously, he'd been wrong.

The thought warmed him as he reached the bar. Janie was working tonight. She was sister to Dick Crumb, the owner of the Cock and Worm, and sometimes helped at the counter.

"Yeah?" she mumbled. Janie spoke to the air over his right shoulder. Her fingernails drummed an uneven beat on the counter.

"Pint of bitter."

She set the ale down in front of him, and he slid a few coppers across the scarred counter.

"Dick in tonight?" Harry asked quietly.

Janie was close enough to hear, but her face was blank. She'd gone back to the drumming.

"Janie?"

"Aye." She stared now at his left elbow.

"Is Dick in?"

She turned and walked into the back.

Harry sighed and found an empty table near a wall. With Janie it was hard to tell if she'd gone to tell Dick he was here, went to fetch more ale, or simply tired of his question. In any case, he could wait.

He'd gone stark, raving mad. Harry took a sip of his beer and wiped the foam from his mouth. It was the only explanation for kissing Lady Georgina this afternoon. He'd walked toward her, his head bleeding and his gut aching from the beating. He hadn't been thinking of kissing her at all. Then somehow she was in his arms, and there was nothing in the world that was going to stop him from tasting her. Not the possibility of being attacked again. Not the pain in his limbs. Not even the fact that she was aristocracy, for pity's sake, and all that meant to him and his ghosts.

Lunacy. Plain and simple. Next he'd be running through the high street, naked and waving his John Thomas. He took another glum sip. And what a fine sight that would be, the state his cock had been in lately.

He was a normal man. He'd felt lust for a woman before. But at those times he'd either bedded the woman, if she was free, or made do with his hand. Over and done with. He'd never had this aching, restless feeling, a longing for something he knew damn well he couldn't have. Harry scowled into his mug. Maybe it was time for another ale.

"Hope that look isn't for me, lad." Two mugs were slammed down in front of him, foam sloshing over their tops. "Have one on the house."

Dick Crumb slid his belly, covered in a stained apron, under the table and took a swig from his mug. Small, piggy eyes closed in ecstasy as the beer slid down his throat. He took out a flannel cloth and mopped his mouth, his face, and his bald pate. Dick was a large man, and he sweated all the time, the bare dome of his head shining greasy red. He sported a tiny gray pigtail, scraped together from the oily strands of hair still clinging to the sides and back of his head.

"Janie told me you were out here," Dick said. "Been a while since you stopped by."

"I was set on by four men today. On Granville land. Do you know anything about it?" Harry raised his mug and watched Dick over the rim. Something flickered in the piggy eyes. Relief?

"Four men, you say?" Dick traced a wet spot on the table. "Lucky you're alive."

"Lady Georgina had a pair of pistols."

Dick's eyebrows flew up to where his hairline should have been. "That so? You were with the lady, then."

"Aye."

"Well." Dick sat back and tipped his face to the ceiling. He took out the flannel and began wiping his head.

Harry was silent. Dick was thinking, and there was no point in hurrying him. He sipped his ale.

"See here." Dick sat forward. "The Timmons brothers usually stop in at night, Ben and Hubert. But tonight only Ben's been by, and he was limping a bit. Said he was kicked by a horse, but that don't seem likely, do it, seeing as how the Timmons haven't got a horse." He nodded triumphantly and upended his mug again.

"Who do the Timmons work for, d'you know?"

"We-ell." Dick stretched the word out as he scratched his head. "They're jacks-of-all-trades, see. But they mostly help out Hitchcock, who tenants for Granville."

Harry nodded, unsurprised. "Granville was behind it."

"Now I didn't say that."

"No, but you didn't have to."

Dick shrugged and raised his mug.

"So," Harry said softly, "who do you think killed Granville's sheep?"

Dick, caught as he swallowed, choked. Out came the flannel again. "As to that," he gasped when he could speak again, "I figured like everyone else in these parts that it was you."

Harry narrowed his eyes. "Did you?"

"Made sense, what Granville did to you, did to your father."

Harry was silent.

Which must've made Dick uneasy. He patted the air. "But after I'd mulled on it a bit, it didn't seem right. I knew your da, and John Pye wouldn't never hurt another man's bread and butter."

"Even after Granville?"

"Your da was the salt of the earth, lad. He wouldn't have harmed a fly." Dick raised his mug as if in toast. "The salt of the earth."

Harry was silent as he watched the other man make his tribute. Then he stirred. "If you've ruled me out, who do you think is poisoning the sheep?"

Dick frowned into the bottom of his empty mug. "Granville's a hard man, as well you know. Some say he's got the devil riding his back. It's as if he takes his joy in life from causing misery to others. There's more than your father that've been blasted by him over the years."

"Who?"

"Plenty of men were thrown off land their families had farmed for decades. Granville don't make allowances for bad years when he collects his money," Dick said slowly. "Then there was Sally Forthright."

"What about her?"

"She was Martha Burns's sister, as is the Woldsly gate-keeper's wife. Granville messed with her, it's said, and the lass ended her life in a well." Dick shook his head. "Wasn't more than fifteen."

"There are probably many like her in these parts"—Harry studied the depths of his own mug—"knowing Granville."

"Aye." Dick turned his face to the side and wiped it with the flannel. He sighed heavily. "Bad business. I don't like talking about it."

"Nor do I, but someone's killing those sheep."

Dick suddenly leaned across the table. His ale-soaked breath washed over Harry as he whispered, "Then maybe you should be looking a little closer to the Granville estate. They say Granville treats his firstborn son like a turd in his tea. The man must be your age, Harry. Can you imagine what that would do to your soul after thirty years?"

"Aye." Harry nodded. "I'll keep Thomas in mind." He drained his mug and set it down. "Is that everyone you can think of?"

Dick grabbed all three mugs in one fist and stood up. He hesitated. "You might try Annie Pollard's family. I don't know what went on there, but it was bad, and Granville was in the middle of it. And, Harry?"

Harry had risen and put on his hat. "Yes?"

"Stay away from aristo ladies." The piggy eyes were sad and old. "They won't do you any good, lad."

IT WAS WELL PAST MIDNIGHT, the moon hanging high and full like a swollen pale pumpkin, when Harry crossed through the Woldsly gates later that night. The first thing he saw was Lady Georgina's carriage standing in the drive. The horses hung their heads, asleep, and the coachman gave him a dirty look as Harry turned into the track leading to his cottage. The man had obviously been waiting a while.

Harry shook his head. What was she doing at his cottage, the second night in a row? Was she bent on plaguing him into an early grave? Or did she see him as something to amuse herself with here in the country? The last thought made him scowl as he stabled his mare. He was scowling still when he walked into his cottage. But the sight that met his eyes made him stop and sigh.

Lady Georgina was asleep in his high-backed chair.

The fire had died to glowing coals beside her. Had the coachman lit it for her, or had she managed on her own this time? Her head was tilted back, her long slim throat exposed trustingly. She'd covered herself with a cloak, but it had slid down, pooling at her feet.

Harry sighed again and picked up her cloak, laying it gently over her. She never stirred. He took off his own cloak, hung it on a knob by the door, and advanced to stir the coals. On the mantelpiece above the hearth, the carved animals had been placed into pairs, facing each other as if they were dancing a reel. He stared at them a moment, wondering how long she'd been waiting. He laid more wood on the fire and straightened. He wasn't sleepy, despite the hour and drinking two pints.

He went to the shelves, took down a box, and brought it to the table. Inside was a short, pearl-handled knife and a piece of cherrywood about half the size of his palm. He sat at the table and turned the wood over in his hands, rubbing the grain with a thumb. He'd thought at first of making a fox from it—the wood was the reddish-orange color of a fox's fur—but now he wasn't sure. He picked up the knife and made the first cut.

The fire crackled and a log fell.

After a while he looked up. Lady Georgina was watching him, her cheek cradled in one palm. Their eyes met, and he looked back down at the carving.

"Is that how you make all of them?" Her voice was low, throaty from sleep.

Did she sound like that in the morning, lying in her silk sheets, her body warm and moist? He pushed the thought aside and nodded.

"That's a pretty knife." She shifted to face him, curling her feet on the chair. "Much nicer than the other one."

"What other one?"

"The nasty-looking one in your boot. I like this one better."

He made a shallow cut, and a curling strip of wood fell to the table.

"Did your father give it to you?" She spoke slowly, sleepily, and it made him hard.

He opened his fist and stared at the pearl handle, remembering. "No, my lady."

She raised her head a little at that. "I thought I was to call you Harry and you could call me George?"

"I never said that."

"That isn't fair." She was frowning.

"Life seldom is, my lady." He shrugged his shoulders, trying to relieve the tightness. 'Course, the tightness was mostly in his balls, not his shoulders. And shrugging sure as hell wouldn't help that.

She stared at him a minute longer, and then turned to look into the fire.

He felt the moment her eyes left him.

She took a breath. "Do you recall the fairy tale I told you, the one about the enchanted leopard that was really a man?"

"Aye."

"Did I mention that he wore a golden chain around his neck?"

"Yes, my lady."

"And on the chain there was a tiny emerald crown? Did I say that?" She'd turned back to him again.

He frowned at the cherrywood. "I don't remember."

"Sometimes I forget the details." She yawned. "Well, he was really a prince, and on his chain there was a tiny crown with an emerald in it, the exact green color of the Leopard Prince's eyes—"

"That wasn't in your story before, my lady," he cut in. "The color of his eyes."

"I did just tell you that sometimes I forget the details." She blinked at him innocently.

"Huh." Harry started carving again.

"Anyway, the young king had sent the Leopard Prince to get the Golden Horse from the evil ogre. You do remember that part, don't you?" She didn't wait for an answer. "So the Leopard Prince changed into a man, and he held the emerald crown on his golden chain..."

Harry looked up as she trailed off.

Lady Georgina was staring into the fire and tapping a finger against her lips. "Do you suppose that was the *only* thing he was wearing?"

Oh, God, she was going to kill him. His cock, which had started subsiding, leaped up again.

"I mean, if he was a leopard before, he couldn't very well have been wearing clothes, could he? And then when he changed into a man, well, I think he'd have to be nude, don't you?"

"No doubt." Harry shifted on his chair, glad the table hid his lap.

"Mmm." Lady Georgina pondered a moment more, and then shook her head. "So he was standing there, evidently in the nude, grasping the crown, and he said, 'I wish for an impenetrable suit of armor and the strongest sword in the world.' And what do you suppose happened?"

"He got the armor and sword."

"Well, yes." Lady Georgina seemed put out that he'd guessed what any three-year-old could've. "But they weren't ordinary weapons. The armor was pure gold, and the sword was made of glass. What do you think of that?"

"I think it doesn't sound very practical."

"What?"

"Bet a woman made this story up."

Her eyebrows arched at him. "Why?"

He shrugged. "The sword would break the first time he swung it, and the armor would give to even a weak blow. Gold's a soft metal, my lady."

"I hadn't thought of that." She tapped her lips again.

Harry returned to his whittling. *Women.*

"They must've been enchanted, too." Lady Georgina waved away the problem of faulty equipment. "So he went and got the Golden Horse—"

"What? Just like that?" He stared at her, an odd sense of frustration filling his chest.

"What do you mean?"

"Wasn't there a grand fight, then?" He gestured with the wood. "A struggle to the death between this Leopard Prince and the evil ogre? The ogre must've been a tough bird, others would've tried to take his prize before. What made our fellow so special that he could defeat him?"

"The armor and—"

"And the silly glass sword. Yes, all right, but others would've had magical weapons—"

"He's an enchanted leopard prince!" Lady Georgina was angry now. "He's better, stronger, than all the others.

He could've defeated the evil ogre with a single blow, I'm sure."

Harry felt his face heat, and his words came too fast. "If he's as powerful as all that, my lady, then why doesn't he free himself?"

"I—"

"Why doesn't he just walk away from spoiled kings and ridiculous chores? Why is he enslaved at all?" He threw down his whittling. The knife skittered across the table and slid to the floor.

Lady Georgina bent to pick it up. "I don't know, Harry." She offered the knife to him on the palm of her outstretched hand. "I don't know."

He ignored her hand. "It's late. I think you'd better go back to your manor now, my lady."

She placed the knife on the table. "If your father didn't give you this, then who did?"

She asked all the wrong questions. All the questions he wouldn't—*couldn't*—answer, either for himself or for her, and she never stopped. Why was she playing this game with him?

Silently he picked up her cloak and held it out for her. She looked into his face, and then turned so he could drape it about her shoulders. The perfume in her hair reached his nostrils. He closed his eyes in something very like agony.

"Will you kiss me again?" she whispered. Her back was still toward him.

He snatched his hands away. "No."

He strode past her and opened the door. He had to occupy his hands so that he wouldn't grab her and pull her body into his and kiss her until there was no tomorrow.

Her gaze met his, and her eyes were deep pools of

blue. A man could dive in there and never care when he drowned. "Not even if I want you to kiss me?"

"Not even then."

"Very well." She moved past him and out into the night. "Good night, Harry Pye."

"Good night, my lady." He shut the door and leaned against it, breathing in the lingering traces of her perfume.

Then he straightened and walked away. Long ago he had railed against the order of things that deemed him inferior to men who had neither brains nor morals. It hadn't mattered.

He railed against fate no more.

Chapter Seven

"Tiggle, why do you think gentlemen kiss ladies?" George adjusted the gauze fichu tucked into the neckline of her dress.

Today she wore a lemon-colored gown patterned with turquoise and scarlet birds. Miniscule scarlet ruffles lined the square neck, and cascades of lace fell from the elbows. The whole thing was simply delicious, if she did say so herself.

"There's only one reason a man kisses a woman, my lady." Tiggle had several hairpins stuck between her lips as she arranged George's hair, and her words were a bit indistinct. "He wants to bed her."

"Always?" George wrinkled her nose at herself in the mirror. "I mean, might he kiss a woman just to show, I don't know, friendship or something?"

The lady's maid snorted and placed a hairpin in George's coiffure. "Not likely. Not unless he thinks bed-sport a part of friendship. No, mark my words, my lady, the better half of a man's mind is taken up with how to get a woman into bed. And the rest"—Tiggle stepped back to look critically at her creation—"is probably spent on gambling and horses and such."

"Really?" George was diverted by the thought of all the men she knew, butlers and coachmen and her brothers and vicars and tinkers and all manner of men, going about thinking primarily of bedsport. "But what about philosophers and men of letters? Obviously they're spending quite a lot of time thinking of something else?"

Tiggle shook her head sagely. "Any man not thinking about bedsport has something the matter with him, my lady, philosopher or no."

"Oh." She began arranging the hairpins on the vanity top into a zigzag pattern. "But what if a man kisses a woman and then refuses to do so again? Even when encouraged?"

There was silence behind her. She glanced up to meet Tiggle's gaze in the mirror.

The lady's maid had two lines between her brows that hadn't been there before. "Then he must have a very good reason not to kiss her, my lady."

George's shoulders slumped.

"'Course, in my experience," Tiggle spoke carefully, "men can be persuaded into kissing and the like awful easy."

George's eyes widened. "Truly? Even if he's... reluctant?"

The maid nodded once. "Even against their own will. Well, they can't help it, can they, poor dears? It's just the way they're made."

"I see." George rose and impulsively hugged the other woman. "You have the most interesting knowledge, Tiggle. I can't tell you how helpful this conversation has been."

Tiggle looked alarmed. "Just so you're careful, my lady."

"Oh, I will be." George sailed out of her bedroom.

She hurried down the mahogany staircase and entered the sunny morning room where breakfast was served. Violet was already drinking tea at the gilt table.

"Good morning, sweetheart." George crossed to the sideboard and was pleased to see that Cook had made buttered kippers.

"George?"

"Yes, dear?" Kippers started the morning so nicely. A day could never be all bad if it had kippers in it.

"Where were you last night?"

"Last night? I was here, wasn't I?" She sat down across from Violet and reached for her fork.

"I meant before you came in. At one o'clock in the morning, I might add." Violet's voice was a wee bit strident. "Where were you then?"

George sighed and lowered her fork. Poor kippers. "I was out on an errand."

Violet eyed her sister in a way that reminded George of a long-ago governess. That lady had been well past her fiftieth decade. How did a girl hardly out of the schoolroom manage so severe an expression?

"An errand at midnight?" Violet asked. "What could you possibly have been doing?"

"I was consulting Mr. Pye, if you must know, dear. About the sheep poisoning."

"Mr. Pye?" Violet squawked. "Mr. Pye is the one poisoning the sheep! What do you need to consult him about?"

George stared, taken aback at her sister's vehemence. "Well, we interviewed one of the farmers yesterday, and he told us that hemlock was the poison being used. And we were going to inquire of another farmer, but there was an incident on the road."

"An incident."

George winced. "We had a bit of trouble with some men attacking Mr. Pye."

"Attacking Mr. Pye?" Violet pounced on the words. "While you were with him? You might have been hurt."

"Mr. Pye acquitted himself very well, and I'd brought the pistols Aunt Clara left me."

"Oh, George," Violet sighed. "Can't you see the trouble he's causing you? You must turn him over to Lord Granville so he can be properly punished. I heard how you sent Lord Granville away the other day when he came for Mr. Pye. You're just being contrary; you know you are."

"But I don't believe he is the poisoner. I thought you understood that."

It was Violet's turn to stare. "What do you mean?"

George got up to pour herself some more tea. "I don't think a man of Mr. Pye's character would commit a crime like this."

She turned back to the table to find her sister gawking, horrified. "You're not infatuated with Mr. Pye, are you? It's so awful when a lady of your age starts mooning over a man."

Mooning? George stiffened. "Contrary to your opinion, eight and twenty is not actually in one's dotage."

"No, but it's an age when a lady should know better."

"What do you mean by that?"

"You should have some sense of propriety by now. You should be more dignified."

"Dignified!"

Violet slapped the table, making the silverware rattle. "You don't care what others think about you. You don't—"

"What are you talking about?" George asked, genuinely confused.

"Why are you doing this to me?" Violet wailed. "It's not fair. Just because Aunt Clara left you piles of money and land you think you can do anything you want. You *never* stop to consider those around you and how your actions might affect them."

"What is the matter with you?" George set down her cup. "I simply don't believe a *tendre* I may or may not have is any of your concern."

"It's my business when what you do reflects on the family. On *me*." Violet stood up so abruptly her teacup overturned. An ugly brown stain started migrating across the tablecloth. "You know very well it isn't proper to be alone with a man like Mr. Pye, and yet you're having sordid assignations with him at night."

"Violet! That's quite enough." George was startled at her own anger. She hardly ever raised her voice to her younger sister. Quickly she held out a hand in appeasement, but it was too late.

Violet was beet red and had tears in her eyes. "Fine!" she shouted. "Make a fool of yourself over some baseborn yokel! He's probably only interested in your money, anyway!" The last words hung horribly in the air.

Violet looked stricken for a moment; then she spun violently and ran out the door.

George pushed her plate aside and laid her head in her arms. It wasn't a day for kippers after all.

VIOLET POUNDED UP THE STAIRS, her vision blurred. Why, oh why must things change? Why couldn't everything stay the same? At the top, she turned right, striding as fast as possible in her voluminous skirts. A door ahead of her opened. She tried to duck away but wasn't quick enough.

"You're quite flushed, dear. Is something amiss?" Euphie looked at her worriedly, blocking Violet from her own room farther down the corridor.

"I... I have a slight headache. I was just going to lie down." Violet tried a smile.

"How horrible headaches are," Euphie exclaimed. "I shall send up a maid with a basin of cool water for your brow. Make sure to lay a damp cloth on your forehead and change it every ten minutes. Now, where did I put my powder? It's very useful for headaches."

Violet felt like screaming as Euphie went into a dither that looked like it might last for hours.

"Thank you, but I think I'll be all right if I just lie down." Violet leaned forward and whispered, "My woman's flow, you know."

If anything was likely to stop Euphie, it was mention of *women's matters*. She turned bright red and averted her eyes as if Violet was wearing a sign proclaiming her condition.

"Oh, I *comprehend,* dear. Well, then, you just go lie down. And I'll see if I can find my powder." She half-covered her mouth with her hand and hissed, "It's good for *that* as well."

Violet sighed, realizing there was no way she could get away without accepting Euphie's help. "That's sweet of you. Perhaps you can give it to my maid when you find it?"

Euphie nodded, and after further detailed instructions on how to deal with *that,* Violet was mercifully able to escape. In her room, she closed and locked the door, and then crossed to sit on the window seat. Her room was one of the prettiest in Woldsly, although it was by no means the biggest. Faded yellow and blue striped silk hung on the walls, and the carpet was an ancient Persian in blues and reds. Normally, Violet adored the room. But now it had begun to rain again outside, the wind spitting drops against the window and rattling the panes. Had the sun shone at all since she'd come to Yorkshire? She leaned her forehead against the glass and watched as her breath fogged the window. The fire had died on the grate, and her room was dim and cold, perfectly suiting her mood.

Her life was in utter shambles, and it was all her fault. Her eyes burned again, and she swiped at them angrily. She'd cried enough in the last two months to float a fleet of ships, and it hadn't done a lick of good. Oh, if only one could go back and have a second chance to do things over. She'd never do it again, not if she had a second chance. She'd know that the feelings—so desperate and urgent at the time—would fade soon enough.

She hugged a blue silk cushion to her chest as the window blurred before her eyes. It hadn't helped to run away. She'd thought that, surely, if she left Leicestershire, she'd soon forget. But she hadn't, and now all her problems had followed her to Yorkshire. And George—staid George, funny older sister so firmly on the shelf with her flyaway hair and love of fairy tales—*George* was acting strange, hardly noticing Violet at all and spending all her time with that dreadful man. George was so naïve, it probably never occurred to her that nasty Mr. Pye was after her fortune.

Or worse.

Well, that at least she could do something about. Violet tumbled off the window seat and ran to her escritoire. She pulled out drawers and rummaged through them until she found a sheet of writing paper. Uncapping her ink bottle, she sat down. George would never listen to her, but there was one person she had to obey.

She dipped her quill in the ink and began to write.

"WHY HAVE YOU NEVER MARRIED, Mr. *Pye?*" Lady Georgina stressed his surname just to irritate him, Harry was sure.

Today, she wore a yellow dress printed with birds like none he'd ever seen—some of them had three wings. She did look fetching in it, he had to admit. She had one of those scarf things that women wore tucked into her bodice. It was almost transparent, giving him a teasing hint of her titties. That irritated him as well. And the fact that she was beside him in the gig again, despite his strong objections, pretty much put a cap on things. At least the relentless rain had let up for a bit today, although the sky was an ominous gray. He hoped they could reach the first cottage before they were soaked.

"I don't know." Harry spoke curtly, a tone he would never have taken with her a week ago. The horse seemed to sense his mood and jogged sideways, jolting the gig. Harry tightened the reins to bring the nag back on the track. "I haven't met the right woman yet, likely."

"Who would be the right woman?"

"I don't know."

"You must have some idea," she stated with aristocratic certainty. "Do you fancy a golden-haired girl?"

"I—"

"Or do you prefer black-haired maidens? I once knew a man who would only dance with short, black-haired ladies, not that any of them wanted to dance with *him*, mind you, but that never seemed to occur to him."

"I'm not particular as to hair," he muttered when she paused to take a breath. Lady Georgina opened her mouth again, but he'd had enough. "Why haven't you married, my lady?"

There. Let her stew on that a bit.

She didn't miss a beat. "It is rather hard to find a promising gentleman. I sometimes think it would be easier to find a goose that really did lay golden eggs. So many of the gentlemen in society haven't a thought to their head, truly. They consider being knowledgeable about hunting or hounds sufficient and don't worry with anything else. And one must make conversation about *something* at the breakfast table. Wouldn't it be awful to be in a marriage with a lot of awkward pauses?"

He'd never thought about it. "If you say so."

"I do. Nothing but the clicking of the silverware against the china and the slurping of tea. Horrible. Then there are the ones who wear corsets and use rouge and patches." She scrunched up her nose. "Have you any idea how unappetizing it is to kiss a man wearing rouge on his lips?"

"No." Harry frowned. "Have you?"

"Well, no," she admitted, "but I have it on good authority that it's not an experience one would want to repeat."

"Ah." That was about the only thing he could think to say, but it seemed to do.

"I was engaged once." She gazed idly at a herd of cows they were passing.

Harry straightened. "Really? What happened?" Had some lordling jilted her?

"I was only nineteen, which, in my opinion, is a rather dangerous age. One is old enough to know quite a bit but not wise enough to realize there are many things that one *doesn't* know." Lady Georgina paused and looked around. "Where, exactly, are we going today?"

They had crossed into Granville land.

"To the Pollard cottage," he said. What had happened with her engagement? "You were talking about when you were nineteen."

"I found myself engaged to Paul Fitzsimmons; that was his name, you know."

"I understand that part," he nearly growled. "But how did you get engaged, and how did it end?"

"I'm a trifle fuzzy about how I got engaged."

He looked at her, brows raised.

"Well, it's true." She sounded defensive now. "One moment I was strolling on the terrace with Paul at a dance, discussing Mr. Huelly's wig—it was *pink,* can you imagine?—and then suddenly, *boom!* I was engaged." She looked at him as if this made perfect sense.

He sighed. That was probably the best he would get out of her. "And it fell through how?"

"Not long afterward, I discovered that my bosom beau, Nora Smyth-Fielding, was in love with Paul. And when I saw that, it was a short step to realizing that he was in love with her. Although"—Lady Georgina frowned— "I still don't understand why he asked me to marry him when he so obviously doted on Nora. Perhaps he was confused, poor man."

Poor man, my arse. This Fitzsimmons sounded like a half-wit. "What did you do?"

She shrugged. "I broke the engagement off, of course."

Of course. Too bad he hadn't been around to show the bastard proper manners. The fellow sounded like he could do with a bloody nose. Harry grunted. "Makes sense that you'd have trouble trusting a man after him."

"I hadn't thought of it like that. But you know, I think it's Aunt Clara's inheritance that is the bigger barrier to finding a husband."

"How could an inheritance be a barrier?" he asked. "I would have thought it would bring the men flocking like crows to a carcass."

"What a delightful simile, *Mr. Pye.*" Lady Georgina had narrowed her eyes at him.

He winced. "What I meant—"

"What *I* meant was that due to Aunt Clara's inheritance, I don't ever have to marry because of financial reasons. Thus, it becomes much less pressing to think about gentlemen in terms of marriage."

"Oh."

"Which doesn't stop me from thinking of gentlemen in other terms."

Other terms? He looked at her.

She was blushing. "Than marriage, that is."

He tried to work out that convoluted statement, but he had already turned the gig into a rutted lane. Now he pulled the horse to a stop beside a wretched cottage. Had he not been told otherwise, he would never have guessed anyone lived here. Built in the same shape as the Oldson cottage, this one was much different. The thatched roof was black and rotten, and one part had fallen in. Weeds grew along the walk, and the door hung at an angle.

"Perhaps you should stay here, my lady," he tried. But she was already climbing down from the gig without his help.

He gritted his teeth and held out his arm pointedly. She took it without protest, wrapping her fingers around him.

He could feel her warmth through his coat, and it soothed him somehow. They walked to the door. Harry knocked on it, hoping he wouldn't bring the whole place down.

Sounds of movement came from within, and then stopped. No one answered the door. Harry banged on the door again and waited. He was raising his arm to try a third time, when the old wood creaked open. A boy of about eight stood mutely in the doorway. His hair, greasy and overlong, hung in his brown eyes. He was barefoot and wore clothes gray with age.

"Is your mother at home?" Harry asked.

"Who is it, lad?" The voice was harsh, but it held no malice.

"Gentry, Gran."

"What?" A woman appeared behind the boy. She was nearly as tall as a man, rawboned and strong-looking despite her age, but her eyes were bewildered and fearful, as though angels had come calling at her doorstep.

"We've some questions to ask you. About Annie Pollard," Harry said. The woman simply continued to stare. He might've been speaking French. "This is the Pollard cottage, isn't it?"

"Don't like to talk about Annie." The woman looked down at the boy, who hadn't taken his gaze away from Harry's face. Abruptly, she cuffed him across the back of the head. "Go on! Go find something to do."

The boy didn't even blink, just walked past them and around the corner of the cottage. Maybe that was how his grandmother always spoke to him.

"What about Annie?" she asked.

"I've heard that she was involved with Lord Granville," he started cautiously.

"Involved? Aye, that's a pretty word for what it was." The woman curled her lip to reveal dark gaps where her front teeth had been. Her pink tongue poked through. "Why do you want to know about that?"

"Someone's killing sheep," Harry said. "I've heard that Annie or perhaps someone close to her might have a reason for doing it."

"I don't know nothing about those sheep." She started to close the door.

Harry stuck his boot in the crack. "Does Annie?"

She shook.

Harry thought at first that he might have driven her to tears, then she raised her head, and he saw her face was split by a grotesque smile.

"Maybe she does, does Annie," she wheezed. "If they know about the doings of the living in the fires of hell."

"Then she's dead?" Lady Georgina spoke for the first time.

Her crisp accent seemed to sober the woman. "Either that or might as well be." She leaned tiredly against the door. "Her name was Annie Baker, you know. She was married. At least she was until *he* came sniffing after her."

"Lord Granville?" Lady Georgina murmured.

"Aye. The devil hisself." The woman sucked in her upper lip. "Annie threw over Baker. She was Granville's whore for as long as he wanted her, which wasn't long. Came back here with her belly big and stayed just long enough to whelp. Then she took off again. Last I heard she was spreading her legs for a cup of gin." She looked suddenly wistful. "A lass don't last long as a gin slut, do she?"

"No," Harry said quietly.

Lady Georgina looked stunned, and he was sorry he

hadn't been able to talk her into staying behind at Woldsly Manor. He'd dragged her into a cesspit.

"Thank you for telling us about Annie, Mrs. Pollard," Harry spoke gently to the old woman. Despite her hardened manner, it must have pained her to talk about ancient hurts. "I've only one more question, and then we'll bother you no more. Do you know what happened to Mr. Baker?"

"Oh, him." Mrs. Pollard waved a hand as if flicking away a fly. "Baker took up with another lass. I've heard he even married her, though it can't be right in the church, him already married to Annie. Not that Annie cares. Not anymore." She closed the door.

Harry frowned, then decided he'd questioned the old woman enough. "Come, my lady." He took Lady Georgina's elbow and escorted her back up the path. As he was helping her into the gig, he glanced back.

The boy leaned on the corner of the cottage, head down, one bare foot on top of the other. He'd probably heard every word his grandmother had said about his mother. There weren't enough hours in the day to solve all the problems of this world. Da had said that often enough when Harry had been growing up.

"Wait a moment, my lady." Harry strode the short distance to the boy.

He looked up warily as Harry approached but didn't move otherwise.

Harry looked down at him. "If she dies, or you find yourself without, come to me. My name is Harry Pye. Repeat it."

"Harry Pye," the boy whispered.

"Good. Here, see if she'll get you some clothes."

He placed a shilling in the boy's hand and returned

to the gig without waiting for thanks. It had been a sentimental gesture and one that was probably useless. The old woman was as likely to use the shilling for gin as to buy the boy new clothes. He climbed in the gig, ignoring Lady Georgina's smile, and took up the reins. When he glanced again at the boy, he was staring at the coin in his hand. They pulled away.

"What an awful story." Her smile had died.

"Yes." Harry looked sideways at her. "I'm sorry you heard it." He urged the horse into a trot. Best to be off Granville land as soon as possible.

"I don't think anyone in that family could be poisoning the sheep. The woman is too old and afraid, the boy too young, and it sounds like Annie's husband has got on with his life. Unless Annie came back?"

He shook his head. "If she's been at the gin stalls all this time, she's no threat to anyone."

Sheep grazed on either side of the road, a peaceful scene, in spite of the lowering clouds and rising wind. Harry watched the surrounding area narrowly. After yesterday, he was wary of an attack.

"Have you another farmer to visit today?" Lady Georgina held her hat to her head with one hand.

"No, my lady. I—" They topped a rise, and Harry caught sight of what lay on the other side. Abruptly he pulled on the reins. "Goddamn."

The gig rolled to a stop. Harry stared at three lumps of wool lying just inside the dry stone wall bordering the road.

"Are they dead?" Lady Georgina whispered.

"Yes." Harry tied off the reins, set the brake, and leaped from the gig.

They weren't the first to make the discovery. A sleek chestnut was tethered to the wall, shaking its head nervously. The owner, a man, had his back toward them, bent over one of the prone sheep. The man straightened, revealing his height. His hair was brown. The cut of his coat, flapping in the wind, was that of a gentleman. Just his luck Thomas would find the poisoned sheep first.

The man turned, and Harry's thoughts scattered. For a moment he couldn't think at all.

The man's shoulders were broader than Thomas's, his hair a shade lighter, curling around his ears. His face was broad and handsome, laugh lines framed his sensual lips, and his eyes had heavy lids. It couldn't be.

The man approached and vaulted the stone wall easily. As he got nearer, his green eyes glowed like phosphorus. Harry felt Lady Georgina come alongside him. He realized absently that he'd forgotten to help her from the gig.

"Harry," he heard her say, "you never told me you had a brother."

Chapter Eight

It had always been her downfall: failing to think suffi-ciently before speaking. This was brought home to George rather emphatically when both men swung to look at her in shock. How was she to know it was some sort of dark secret? She'd never seen eyes as green as Harry's, and yet here they were, the same green eyes, staring at her from another man's face. True, the other man was taller, and his features were of a different cast. But who, looking at their eyes, could draw any other conclusion than that they were brothers? She really couldn't be blamed.

"Harry?" The stranger started forward. *"Harry?"*

"This is Bennet Granville, my lady." Harry had recov-ered quicker than the other man and was now expression-less. "Granville, Lady Georgina Maitland."

"My lady." Mr. Granville bowed correctly. "It's an honor to meet you."

She curtsied and muttered the proper words by rote.

"And Harry." For a moment, emotion flashed behind Mr. Granville's emerald eyes; then he controlled himself. "It's ... been a while."

George nearly snorted. In another year or so, he'd

be as adept as Harry at hiding his thoughts. "How long, exactly?"

"What?" Mr. Granville seemed startled.

"Eighteen years." Harry turned and glanced at the sheep, obviously avoiding the subject. "Poisoned?"

Mr. Granville blinked, but caught on quickly enough. "I'm afraid so. Would you like to take a look?" He turned and scrambled back over the wall.

Oh, for goodness sake! George rolled her eyes heavenward. Apparently both men were going to ignore her faux pas and the fact that they hadn't seen each other for eighteen years.

"My lady?" Harry was holding out his hand, presumably to help her over the wall.

"Yes, all right. I'm coming."

He looked at her oddly. When she placed her hand in his, instead of merely grasping it, he pulled her closer and then lifted her to sit on the wall. George suppressed a squeal. His thumbs were just under her breasts, and her nipples were suddenly sensitive. He gave her a warning look.

What was he about? She felt herself flush.

He vaulted the wall and walked to Mr. Granville. George, left to her own devices, swung her legs over and jumped down on the pasture side of the wall. The men were looking at a pile of wilted weeds.

"These aren't very old." Harry toed a sodden stem. "Probably placed here during the night. Hemlock again."

"Again?" Mr. Granville, squatting next to the plants, looked up at him.

"Yes. It's been going on for weeks now. Weren't you told?"

"I've just arrived from London. I haven't even been to Granville House yet. Who is doing this?"

"Your father thinks it's me."

"You? Why would he—?" Mr. Granville cut himself off, then laughed softly. "He's finally paying for his sins."

"Do you think?"

What was going on? George looked from one man to the other, trying to decipher the undercurrents.

Mr. Granville nodded. "I'll talk to him. See if I can get his mind off you and onto whoever's really doing this."

"Will he listen to you?" Harry's lips twisted cynically.

"Maybe." The two men exchanged a look. Despite their differing heights and features, their expressions were strikingly similar. They radiated grimness.

"Do try to get your father to listen, Mr. Granville," George said. "He's already threatened to arrest Harry."

Harry scowled at George, but Mr. Granville grinned charmingly. "I shall do my best, my lady, for *Harry*."

George realized she had been calling Mr. Pye, quite improperly, by his given name. *Oh, pish.* She tilted her nose into the air and felt a raindrop hit it.

Mr. Granville bowed again. "It's a pleasure to have met you, Lady Georgina. I hope that we can meet again under more amenable circumstances."

Harry moved closer to George's side, placing a hand at the small of her back. She had the feeling he was scowling at Mr. Granville now.

She smiled all the brighter at her neighbor. "Indeed."

"It's good to see you, Harry," Mr. Granville said.

Harry merely nodded.

The young man hesitated, then turned swiftly and leapt

the wall. He mounted and wheeled his horse in a half circle to wave good-bye before cantering away.

"Show-off," Harry muttered.

George blew out a breath and turned on him. "Is that all you've got to say after seeing your brother for the first time in eighteen years?"

He arched his eyebrows at her, silent.

She threw up her arms in disgust and stomped over to the stone wall, then stood dithering when she couldn't find a toehold for her shoe. Strong hands grabbed her from behind, again just under her breasts. This time she did shriek.

Harry lifted her up and held her against his chest. "He's not my brother," he growled in her ear, sending all sorts of interesting thrills down her neck and elsewhere. Who knew the nerves in one's neck were connected to—

He set her rather firmly on the wall.

She scrambled over it and marched to the gig. "Then what is his relationship to you?"

Instead of handing her into the carriage, Harry grasped her about the middle again. She might become accustomed to this.

"He was a boyhood playmate, my lady." He placed her on the seat.

George mourned the loss of his hands.

"You played with Thomas and Bennet Granville when you were little?" She craned her neck to follow him as he circled the gig.

More drops of rain began to fall.

"Yes." He climbed in and took up the reins. "I grew up on the estate, remember. Thomas is about my age and Bennet a few years younger." He guided the horse onto the lane and set him to a trot.

"Yet you had not seen them since you left the Granville estate?"

"I was—*am*—the gamekeeper's son." A muscle bunched in his jaw. "There was no reason we should see each other."

"Oh." She mulled over that. "Were you great friends? I mean, did you like Bennet and Thomas?"

The rain increased. George hugged her cloak about her and hoped her frock wouldn't be ruined.

Harry looked at her as if she'd asked something extremely silly. "We were boys growing up together. It didn't much matter if we liked each other." He watched the horse for a bit, then said almost grudgingly, "I daresay I got on better with Bennet even though Thomas was closer to my age. Thomas always seemed such a milksop. He didn't like fishing or exploring or other things boys like to do for fear of getting his clothes dirty."

"Is that why you don't trust Thomas now?"

"Because he was a milksop when he was a boy? No, my lady. Give me more credit than that. He was always trying to get his father's favor as a lad. I doubt he's changed much, just because he's a man now. And since Granville hates me..." He let his sentence trail away and shrugged.

His father's favor. A firstborn son usually had that without question. How strange that Thomas Granville did not. But she was more curious about something else. "So you spent a lot of time in Bennet's company when you two were boys?"

Rain was dripping off the brim of Harry's tricorn. "We played and I sat in on his lessons if the tutor was in a good mood that day—and if Granville wasn't around."

She frowned. "If Lord Granville wasn't around?"

He nodded grimly. "The man hated me, even then. Said

I had too much pride for a gamekeeper's son. But the tutor disliked his employer as well. I think he got some small revenge in teaching me."

"That's where you learned to read and write."

Harry nodded. "Bennet was better at letters than I, even though he was younger, but I best him at numbers. So, yes, I spent quite a bit of time with him."

"What happened?"

He looked at her. "His father whipped my father when I was twelve and he ten."

George thought about what it would be like if she'd lost someone close to her when she was twelve. Someone she saw every day. Someone she fought and played with. Someone she took it for granted would always be there. It would be like having a limb cut off.

How far would one go to correct such a wrong?

She shivered and looked up. They were at the river that divided the Granville land from her own. Harry slowed the horse to a walk as it splashed into the ford. The rain was coming down hard now, making the muddy water jump. George looked downstream where the water deepened and swirled in a whirlpool. A shape floated there.

"Harry." She touched his arm and pointed.

He swore.

The horse waded from the stream, and he pulled the gig over, tying the reins off quickly. He helped her down from the gig before walking to the bank ahead of her. George's shoes sank into the mud as she followed. When she reached him, Harry was very still. Then she saw why. The body of a sheep twisted slowly in the water; the rain pelting the fleece gave it a strange, lifelike movement.

She shuddered. "Why doesn't it float away?"

"It's tethered." Harry nodded grimly to a branch hanging over the water.

She saw that a rope was tied around the branch and disappeared into the water. Presumably, the other end attached to some part of the sheep. "But why would anyone do such a thing?" She felt a frisson run down her spine. "It's mad."

"Maybe to foul the stream." He sat and began to pull off his boots.

"What are you doing?"

"I'm going to cut it loose." He unbuttoned his coat. "It'll fetch up on a bank farther downstream and a farmer will pull it out. At least it won't spoil the whole stream."

By now he was in shirtsleeves, soaked through by the rain. He pulled his knife out of his boot and slid down the bank into the stream. The water came to midthigh, but as he waded slowly out, the water quickly rose to chest level. The rain had made the normally placid stream boil.

"Do be careful," George called. If he lost his footing, he might be swept downstream. Did he know how to swim?

He didn't acknowledge her call and kept wading. When he reached the rope, he grabbed it where it stretched above the water and started to saw. The strands unraveled rapidly, and suddenly the sheep spun away downstream. Harry turned and began to wade back, the water whirling angrily about him. He slipped and his head disappeared beneath the water without a sound.

Oh, God. George's heart leaped painfully in her chest. She started for the bank without knowing what she could do. But then he was upright again, his soaked hair plastered to his cheeks. He emerged and wrung out the front of his shirt, transparent now from the water. George could see his nipples and the swirl of dark hair where the shirt stuck against his chest.

"Someday I'd like to see a man nude," she said.

Harry froze.

Slowly he straightened from pulling on his boots. His green eyes met hers, and she could have sworn a fire burned there. "Is that an order, my lady?" he asked, his voice so deep it was almost a dark purr.

"I—" *Oh, goodness gracious, yes!* A part of George desperately wanted to see Harry Pye take off that shirt. To see what his shoulders and belly looked like naked. To find out if there really were curls of hair on his chest. And after that, if he removed his breeches... She really couldn't help it. Her eyes dropped to that part of a man's anatomy that a lady never, *ever,* under any circumstances let her gaze wander to. The water had done an exquisite job of molding Harry's breeches to his lower limbs.

George drew a breath. Opened her mouth.

And Harry cursed and turned away. A cart and pony were coming up the lane.

Well, damn.

"You can't really think Harry Pye is poisoning your sheep." Bennet's words were phrased as a question but said as a statement.

Not two minutes back and the lad was already setting himself against him. But then the boy had always taken Pye's part. Silas snorted. "I don't think. I *know* Pye is doing the killing."

Bennet frowned and poured himself a tumbler of whiskey. He held the decanter up in question.

Silas shook his head and leaned back in the leather-covered chair behind his study desk. The room was his favorite, all male in its feel. Mounted antlers circled the study, just below the ceiling. A deep, black fireplace took up the entire wall at the room's far end. Over it was a classical painting: *The Rape of the Sabine Women.* Swarthy men tearing the clothes from fair-skinned, screaming wenches. He sometimes got prick-proud just looking at the thing.

"But poison?" Bennet threw himself into a chair and started tapping his fingers on the arm.

His younger son aggravated him; but even now, Silas could not help feeling proud of him. This one should have been his heir. Thomas would never have the balls to confront his father. Silas had known it the moment he'd first seen Bennet, bawling and red-faced, in his mother's arms. He'd looked into the infant's face and a voice inside him had whispered, *this* one—this one out of all his other get—would be the son he, Silas, would be proud of. So he'd taken the babe from that whore's arms and brought him home. His wife had pouted and wept, but Silas had soon let her know he wouldn't change his mind and she'd had to relent. Some might still remember that Bennet wasn't legally born, that he'd come from the loins of the gatekeeper's wife, but they wouldn't dare speak that knowledge aloud.

Not while Silas Granville ruled this land.

Bennet shook his head. "Poison isn't the method Harry would use if he wanted revenge on you. He loves the land and the people who farm it."

"Loves the land?" Silas scoffed. "How can he? He doesn't own any land. He's naught but a paid custodian. The land he tends and works on belongs to someone else."

"But the farmers still come to him, don't they?" Bennet asked softly, his eyes narrowed. "They ask him his opinion; they follow his guidance. Even many of your own tenants go to Harry when they have a problem—or at least they did before all this started. They wouldn't dare come to you."

A line of pain shot along Silas's left temple. "Why should they? I'm not the tavern keep, someone for the farmers to bawl their troubles to."

"No, you're not interested in other people's troubles, are you?" Bennet drawled. "But their respect, their allegiance—that's a different matter."

He had the allegiance of the local people. Didn't they fear him? Stupid, dirty peasants, to seek the council of one of their own just because he'd risen a little from their ranks. Silas felt sweat drip down his neck. "Pye's envious of his betters. He wishes he was an aristocrat."

"Even if he was envious, he wouldn't use this method to get back at *his betters,* as you term it."

"Method?" Silas slammed the flat of his hand on his desk. "You talk as if he were a Machiavellian prince instead of a common land steward. He's the son of a whore and a thief. What type of method do you think he'd use other than sneaking around poisoning animals?"

"A whore." Bennet's lips thinned as he poured himself another finger of whiskey. Probably how he spent all his time in London—on drink and women. "If Harry's mother—*my* mother—was a whore, who do you think made her so?"

Silas scowled. "What do you mean, talking to me in that tone? I'm your father, boy. Don't you ever forget that."

"As if I'm likely to forget that you sired me." Bennet gave a bark of laughter.

"You should be proud—" Silas began.

His son sneered and emptied his glass.

Silas surged to his feet. "I saved you, boy! If it weren't for me—"

Bennet flung his tumbler into the grate. The glass exploded, flinging sparkling shards onto the carpet. "If it weren't for you, I would've had a mother, not your frozen bitch of a wife who was too proud to show affection for me!"

Silas swept the papers from his desk with his arm. "Is that what you want, boy? A mother's tit to suckle?"

Bennet turned white. "You've never understood."

"Understood? What's there to understand between a life lived in the muck and one in a manor? Between a starving bastard and an aristocrat who can afford all that's good in life? I gave you that. I gave you everything."

Bennet shook his head and stalked to the door. "Leave Harry alone."

He shut the door behind him.

Silas raised his arm to swipe at the only thing still on his desk, the inkstand, but he paused when he saw his hand. It was shaking. Bennet. He sank into his chair.

Bennet.

He'd brought him up strong, made sure he could ride like a demon and fight like a man. He'd always favored the boy and made no bones about it. Why should he? Couldn't anyone see that this was the son a man could be proud of? In return he'd expected... what? Not like or love, but respect, certainly. Yet, his second son treated him like a pile of dung. Came to Granville House only for money. And now took the side of a baseborn servant against his own sire. Silas pushed away from his desk. He needed to deal with Harry Pye before he became any more of a threat. He couldn't let Pye drive a wedge between himself and Bennet.

The door opened a crack, and Thomas peeked around it like a timid girl.

"What do you want?" Silas was too tired to yell.

"I saw Bennet rush by. He's back, eh?" Thomas eased into the room.

"Oh, yes, he's back. And that's why you invited yourself into my study? To exchange the news that your brother has returned?"

"I heard some of the words you had with him." Thomas crept another few steps forward as if approaching a wild boar. "And I wanted to offer my support. About seeing Harry Pye punished, I mean. He's quite obviously the one doing this, anyone can understand that."

"Lovely." Silas eyed his eldest with a curled lip. "And what, exactly, can you help me with?"

"I talked to Lady Georgina the other day. I tried to tell you." The muscle under Thomas's right eye had started to twitch.

"And she told you she would hand over Pye, tied with a pretty bow, at our convenience?"

"N-no, she seemed charmed by him." Thomas shrugged. "She is a woman, after all. But perhaps if there was further evidence, if we had men guarding the sheep..."

Silas chuckled hoarsely. "As if there are enough men in the county to watch all the sheep on my land every night. Don't be more of a fool than you can help." He crossed to the whiskey decanter.

"But if there was evidence linking him—"

"She wouldn't accept anything but a signed confession

from Pye. We *have* evidence—Pye's carving, found right by the dead sheep—and she still thinks him innocent. It'd be different if instead of a sheep, a man, or—" Silas stopped midsentence, staring sightlessly at his newly filled whiskey glass. Then he threw back his head and began to laugh, great, bellowing guffaws that shook his frame and spilled the whiskey in his glass.

Thomas looked at him as if he'd lost his mind.

Silas slapped the boy on the back, nearly bowling him over. "Aye, we'll give her evidence, boy. Evidence that not even she can ignore."

Thomas smiled tremulously, the pretty boy. "But we haven't any evidence, Father."

"Oh, Tommy, my lad." Silas took a gulp of the whiskey and winked. "Who says evidence can't be made?"

"That will be all. You may have the rest of the night off." George smiled in what she hoped was a casual manner. As if she always dismissed Tiggle before supper.

Apparently it didn't work.

"All, my lady?" The maid straightened from putting away a stack of linens. "What do you mean? You'll be undressing later, surely?"

"Yes, of course." She felt her face heat. "But I thought I'd manage it myself tonight."

Tiggle stared.

George nodded confidently. "I'm sure I'll be able. So you may go."

"What are you up to, my lady?" Tiggle placed her hands on her hips.

This was the problem with having the same servants for years on end. One didn't inspire the proper awe.

"I'm having a guest to dinner." She waved a hand airily. "I just thought you wouldn't want to wait for me."

"It's my job to wait for you," Tiggle said suspiciously. "Has Lady Violet's maid had the night off as well?"

"Actually"—George ran a fingertip along her dresser—"it's a very private dinner. Violet won't be attending."

"Won't be—"

The maid's exclamation was interrupted by a knock on the door. Darn! She'd hoped to have Tiggle out of the way by now.

George opened the door. "In my sitting room, please," she told the footmen outside.

"My lady," Tiggle hissed as George passed her on the way to the connecting door.

George ignored her and opened the door. In the sitting room, the footmen were busy rearranging the furniture and setting up the table they'd had to bring in. A fire was flickering in the grate.

"What...?" Tiggle dogged George into the sitting room but immediately quieted in the presence of the other servants.

"Is this how you want it, my lady?" one of the footmen asked.

"Yes, that will do nicely. Now, be sure and alert Cook when Mr. Pye arrives. We'll want supper promptly."

The footmen bowed out, which, unfortunately, freed the lady's maid from her self-imposed silence.

"You're having Mr. Pye to dinner?" Tiggle sounded scandalized. "All alone?"

George tilted her chin in the air. "Yes, I am."

"Oh, my Lord, why didn't you tell me, my lady?" Tiggle abruptly turned and ran back into the bedroom.

George stared after her.

The maid's head popped around the door frame, and she beckoned urgently. "Hurry, my lady! There's not much time."

Feeling like she'd been goosed, George followed her into the bedroom.

Tiggle was already at the vanity table, rummaging through bottles. She held up a small glass vial as George neared. "This'll do. Exotic, but not overwhelming." She snatched the fichu from around her mistress's neck.

"What are you—" George raised her hands to her suddenly bare décolletage.

The maid batted her hands away. She removed the bottle's glass stopper and stroked it down George's neck and between her breasts. The scent of sandalwood and jasmine hovered in the air.

Tiggle recapped the bottle and stepped back to look at her assessingly. "I think the garnet drops instead."

George obediently searched through her jewelry box.

From behind her Tiggle sighed. "It's a pity I haven't time to redo your hair, my lady."

"It was fine a moment ago." George squinted into the mirror as she replaced her earrings.

"A moment ago I didn't know you were meeting a gentleman."

George straightened and turned.

Tiggle knit her brows as she inspected her.

George ran a hand self-consciously across her green velvet gown. A row of black bows marched down the bodice, echoed at the elbows. "Will I do?"

"Yes." Tiggle nodded firmly. "Yes, my lady, I think you'll do." She walked swiftly to the door.

"Tiggle," George called.

"My lady?"

"Thank you."

Tiggle actually blushed. "Good luck, my lady." She grinned and disappeared.

George strolled back into the sitting room and shut the door to her bedroom. She sat down in one of the armchairs by the fire and immediately jumped up; then she crossed to the mantel and inspected the clock sitting upon it. Five minutes after seven o'clock. Perhaps he didn't have a timepiece? Or maybe he was just a habitually late man? Or perhaps he didn't intend to come—

Someone knocked at the door.

George froze and stared at it. "Come in."

Harry Pye opened the door. He hesitated, watching her with the door still ajar behind him.

"Won't you come in?"

He walked in but left the door open. "Good evening, my lady." He was at his most indecipherable.

George started babbling. "I thought we might have a quiet dinner to discuss the poisoning and the attack and what we might want to do—"

Footmen appeared at the door—*thank goodness!*— and started laying the table. Behind came more servants, bearing covered dishes and wine. There was a flurry of activity. She and Harry watched silently as the servants arranged the meal. Finally, most of the servants departed, leaving only one footman to serve dinner. That correct gentleman held the chairs, first for George and then for Harry. They sat and he began ladling the soup.

The room was deathly silent.

George looked from the footman to Harry. "I think we'll manage, thank you."

The footman bowed and left.

And they were alone. George peeked at Harry, who was frowning down at his soup. He didn't care for consommé?

She broke her roll, a thunderclap in the quiet. "I hope you didn't catch a chill from the stream this afternoon?"

Harry lifted his spoon. "No, my lady."

"Because the stream looked extremely cold."

"I am fine, my lady. Thank you."

"Good. Well… that's good." George chewed and furiously tried to think of something to say. Her mind was a complete blank.

Harry suddenly set his spoon down. "Why did you call me here tonight?"

"I just said—"

"You wanted to talk about the poisoning and the attack, yes, I know." Harry rose from the table. "But your breasts are all but naked, and you've sent the servants away. The *other* servants. Why do you really want me here?" He stood almost menacingly, his jaw bunched, his hands fisted.

"I…" George's heart quickened. Her nipples had tightened the moment he said *breasts*.

His eyes flickered down, and she wondered if he knew.

"Because I'm not what you think I am," Harry said evenly as he advanced around the table toward her. "I'm not a servant to jump to your bidding and then lie down when you've done with me." His voice was deepening. "I'm not someone you can dismiss like those footmen, like everyone else in this manor. I'm a man with blood in

his veins. If you start something with me, don't expect me
to turn into a lapdog, panting at your call." Harry seized
her upper arms and drew her against his hard body. "Don't
expect me to be your servant."

George blinked. The idea of confusing this man, who
fairly crackled with danger, with a lapdog was absurd.

He drew a finger slowly across the edge of her bodice,
watching her reaction. "What do you want with me, my
lady?"

Her breasts seemed to swell. "I..." She couldn't think
while he touched her; she didn't know what to say. What
did he need to hear? George looked around the room for
help but saw only the piles of food and dishes. "I'm not
sure, really. I don't have any experience in this."

He dipped two fingers below her bodice and brushed
her nipple. She shuddered. *Oh, my.* Harry pinched the
nipple, sending sparks all the way to her most private
places. George closed her eyes.

She felt his breath caress her cheek. "When you figure
it out, my lady, let me know."

He closed the door quietly behind him.

Chapter Nine

Bennet walked into the Cock and Worm at just after midnight that evening. The tavern was crowded and loud at that hour, the smoke from innumerable pipes hovering in a cloud near the ceiling. Harry sat in a dark corner and watched young Mr. Granville move with the overly cautious gait of a man who was already the worse for drink. Walking into a disreputable place like the Cock and Worm with one's senses impaired wasn't a particularly bright thing to do, but that wasn't Harry's worry. An aristocrat gambling with his own safety wasn't his business—now or ever.

Harry took a pull from his mug and switched his gaze to the two local harlots drumming up trade. The younger of the wenches, a blonde, sat on a ruddy-faced man's lap. Her titties were right under his chin—as if she was worried he was near-sighted. The man's eyes were glazed, and the harlot made stealthy movements at the front of his trousers. It wouldn't be long before the two came to an understanding.

The second harlot, a red-haired wench, caught his gaze and tossed her head. She'd already tried her charms with him, and he'd sent her away. Of course, if he flashed a purse now, she'd be smiling soon enough. The more ale he drank, the more he began to rethink turning the redhead down. He'd been randy for days now, and the object of his bone-on, despite her offer, wasn't likely to help him now, was she?

Harry scowled into his ale. What had she been after, his Lady Georgina, when she invited him to her private rooms? Not what he'd wanted to think, that's for sure. The lady was a virgin, and the first rule of aristocratic maidens was *Guard well thy virginity. Don't, whatever you do, go handing it out to the hired help.* The lady had been looking for the thrill of a stolen kiss or two. He was forbidden fruit to her. Good thing he'd resisted her blandishments. Few men he knew could've done so. He nodded and drank to his own wisdom.

But then he remembered how she'd looked earlier that night. Her eyes had been so blue and so unwary, belying the temptation of her low neckline. Her breasts had seemed to glow in the firelight. The thought of her even now made his too-alert prick come to attention. He frowned, disgusted at his own weakness. Actually, none of the men he knew—

Crash!

Harry jerked around.

Young Mr. Granville slid across a table, headfirst, knocking ale-filled glasses to the floor. Each glass detonated with a small, wet explosion upon impact with the floor.

Harry took another swig from his mug. This wasn't his worry.

The men at the table weren't pleased. One fellow with

hands the size of hams hauled Bennet upright by his shirtfront. Bennet flailed at the other man, catching him a blow to the side of the head.

Not his worry.

Two other men grabbed Bennet's wrists, jerking them behind him. The man in front buried his fist in Bennet's belly. Bennet doubled over. He tried to kick, but he was heaving bile from the blow to the stomach. His feet missed his attacker by miles. Behind them, a tall woman threw back her head and laughed drunkenly. She looked familiar, wasn't she...? The big man drew back his fist again in preparation.

Not his worry. Not his... oh, the hell with it.

Harry stood and drew the knife from his boot in one movement. No one was paying any attention to him and he was on the man about to hit Bennet before anyone noticed him. From this angle, a quick stab to the side followed by a twist of the wrist would kill the man before he even fell. But death wasn't what Harry was after. He sliced the man's face open instead. Blood gushed, blinding the man. He bellowed and dropped Bennet. Harry slashed one of the men holding Bennet's wrists, then waved his blade in front of the second man's eyes.

That one raised his hands. "Hold on! Hold on! We was only teaching him his manners!"

"Not anymore," Harry whispered.

The man's eyes flickered.

Harry ducked—in time to protect his head but not his shoulder—as a chair smashed across his side. He turned and stabbed. The man behind him howled, clutching a bleeding thigh. Another crash and the *thwack* of flesh hitting flesh. Harry realized that Bennet was standing back-to-back with him. The aristo wasn't as pie-eyed as he'd thought. He was able to fight, at least.

Three men charged at once.

Harry leaned to the side, helping a man pass him with a punch and a shove. A yellow-haired man with a knife came at him. This man had some experience with knife fighting. He gripped a cloak in his free hand and tried to foil Harry's dagger with it. But the yellow-haired man hadn't fought in the places Harry had.

Or ever fought for his life.

Harry grabbed the cloak and yanked the man hard. The man stumbled, tried to recover his balance, and found that Harry had him by the hair. Harry pulled the man back, arching his neck, and pointed his knife tip at the man's eye. Balls and eyes. Those were the two things men feared losing most. Threaten either, and you had a man's full attention.

"Drop it," Harry hissed.

Sweat and piss assaulted his nostrils. The yellow-haired man had lost control of his bladder. He'd also dropped his knife, and Harry kicked it. It skittered across the floor, sliding under a table. The tavern was quiet. The only sound was Bennet's labored breathing and the sobbing of one of the sluts.

"Let him go." Dick Crumb came out from the back.

"Tell them to back off." Harry pointed with his chin at the three men still standing.

"Go on. You don't want to be messing with Harry when he's in a mood."

No one moved.

Dick raised his voice. "Go on! There'll be more ale for them that wants it."

The mention of ale was magic. The men grumbled but

turned away. Harry let his hand drop. The yellow-haired man fell to his knees, whimpering.

"Better get Granville out of here," Dick muttered as he passed with mugs.

Harry took Bennet's arm and shoved him toward the door. The younger man wobbled, but at least he kept upright. Outside, the air was chill and Bennet gasped. He put out a hand to steady himself against the tavern wall, and for a moment Harry thought the man would be sick. But then he straightened.

Harry's bay mare stood beside a larger chestnut gelding. "Come on," he said. "Best to be away before they finish their drinks."

They mounted and started off. It had begun to drizzle again.

"Guess I should thank you," Bennet spoke suddenly. "Didn't think you'd come to the aid of a Granville."

"Do you always start brawls without anyone at your back?"

"Nah." Bennet hiccupped. "This was a spur-of-the-moment thing."

They rode in silence. Harry wondered if Bennet had fallen asleep. The horses splashed through puddles in the road.

"Didn't know you could fight like that." Bennet's slurred voice cut across the patter of the rain.

Harry grunted. "There's a lot you don't know about me."

"Where'd you learn?"

"The poorhouse."

Harry thought he'd shut the other man up with his stark statement, but then Bennet chuckled. "My father's a right sod, isn't he?"

There was no need to reply to that. They crested a rise and came to the river.

"Better not come any farther. You aren't safe on Granville land." Bennet peered at him in the dark. "He wants to kill you, did you know?"

"Yes." Harry turned the mare's head.

"Will you never call me by my name again?" Bennet sounded wistful. Perhaps he'd entered the maudlin stage of drink.

Harry nudged his horse down the track.

"I've missed you, Harry." Bennet's voice floated on the night air behind him and melted away like a ghost.

Harry didn't answer.

OUTSIDE THE COCK AND WORM, Silas peeled himself away from the shadows and watched bitterly as his beloved son rode away with the man he hated most in the world.

"Your boy be dead but for the Woldsly s-steward," a drunken voice slurred nearby.

Silas whirled and peered into the dark alley between the Cock and Worm and the neighboring building. "Who are you? How dare you speak to me thus?"

"I'm juss a little bird." A harsh feminine giggle.

Silas felt pressure building in his temple. "Come out of there or I'll—"

"You'll what?" the voice sneered. A face appeared, ghostly in the shadows. It was lined and worn and belonged to an old woman Silas couldn't remember ever seeing before. "You'll what?" she repeated, cackling like a demon. "He's been killing your sheep for weeks and you've done naught. You're juss an old man. Ol' man Granville, lord of nothing! How's it feel to be under the spur of the new cock?"

She turned and started staggering down the road, one hand held out to balance herself against the wall.

Silas was on her in two steps.

"My, THE SOFT-BOILED EGGS are good this morning." George mentally rolled her eyes at her own inanity.

She, Violet, and Euphie sat at the breakfast table. As per usual for the last several days, her sister refused to make any but the most desultory conversation, reducing George to commenting on the eggs.

"Mmm." Violet shrugged one shoulder.

At least she was still alive. What had happened to her vivacious younger sister? The one who was constitutionally unable to refrain from exclaiming about every little thing?

"I do like soft-boiled eggs," Euphie fluted from the other end of the table. "Of course, it is very important that they still be *moist* and not at all dried out."

George frowned as she took a sip of tea. Hadn't Euphie noticed the almost deathly quiet of her charge?

"Kidneys are nice as well," Euphie continued. "If they've been prepared in butter. But I can't abide gammon in the morning. I don't know how anyone can, really."

Perhaps it was time to find a younger companion for Violet. Euphie was a dear but a tad absentminded at times.

"Would you like to go riding today?" George asked. Maybe Violet just needed fresh air. "I saw a lovely vista the other day, and I thought if you brought your pencils, you could sketch it. Tony says—"

"I'm sorry." Violet leaped from her seat. "I... I can't go today."

She ran from the room.

"Young people are so abrupt, aren't they?" Euphie looked puzzled. "When I was a girl, I'm sure my mother told me a hundred times, 'Euphemia, do not rush about. The true mark of a lady is her ability to be sedate.'"

"Very enlightening, I'm sure," George said. "Do you know what is bothering Violet?"

"Bothering her, my lady?" Euphie cocked her head like a bird. "I don't know that she is actually *bothered*. I think any little change from her normal behavior might be blamed on her youth and certain *monthly* happenings." She blushed and hurriedly took a drink of tea.

"I see." George studied the older woman thoughtfully. Perhaps she would be better employed as M'man's companion. Her absentmindedness would certainly do no harm there. "Well, I thank you for your insight. And now if you will excuse me?" George stood and walked out of the breakfast room as Euphie was still murmuring her consent.

She hurried up the stairs to Violet's room.

"Violet, dear?" George knocked at her door.

"What is it?" Her sister's voice sounded suspiciously stuffy.

"I wanted to talk with you, if I may?"

"Go away. I don't want to see anyone. You never understand." The key turned in the lock.

Violet had locked her out.

George stared at the door. Fine, then. She was certainly not going to engage in an argument through solid wood. She stomped down the hallway. Euphie was in her own little world, Violet was sulking, and Harry... George opened the door to her bedroom so forcefully it banged against the wall. Harry wasn't anywhere to be found. She'd had her gig at his cottage at seven this morning, and he'd already left. *Coward!* And men thought women faint of heart. He was probably out doing male things in the delusion that work needed being done, when in reality, he was simply avoiding her. Ha! Well, two could play at that game. She struggled out of her day dress and yanked on a riding costume. She turned in a complete circle, trying to fasten the hooks in the back before she conceded defeat and rang for Tiggle.

The maid arrived wearing the same half-mournful, half-consoling expression she'd worn since the previous disastrous night.

George nearly lost control at the sight. "Help me do this up, please." She presented her back.

"You're going riding, my lady?"

"Yes."

"In this weather?" Tiggle looked doubtfully at the window. A wet tree branch lashed against it.

"Yes." George frowned at the tree branch. At least there was no lightning.

"I see." Tiggle bent behind her to reach the hooks at her waist. "It's a pity about last night—that Mr. Pye turned down your invitation."

George stiffened. Did all the servants feel sorry for her now? "He didn't turn me down. Well, not precisely."

"Oh?"

George could feel the heat stealing up her face. Drat pale complexions. "He asked me what I wanted from him."

Tiggle, who was picking up the discarded day dress, stopped and stared at her. "And what did you answer, my lady? If you don't mind me asking."

George threw up her hands. "I didn't know what to say. I mumbled something about never having done this before and he left."

"Oh." Tiggle frowned.

"What does he want me to say?" George paced to the window. " 'I want you naked, Harry Pye?' Surely it's usually done with more finesse than that? And why demand my intentions? I can't imagine most *affairs de coeur* begin on such a lawyerly note. I'm surprised he didn't ask for them in writing: 'I, Lady Georgina Maitland, do request Mr. Harry Pye to make very fine love to me.' Really!"

There was silence behind her. George winced. Now she'd shocked Tiggle. Could this day get any—

The maid started laughing.

George turned.

Her maid was doubled over, trying to catch her breath. "Oh, my lady!"

George's mouth twitched. "It isn't that funny."

"No, of course not." Tiggle bit her lip, plainly struggling. "It's just, 'I want you naked, Ha-Ha-Harry Pye.'" She went off again.

George plopped on the side of the bed. "What am I going to do?"

"I'm sorry, my lady." Tiggle sat beside her, the dress still in her arms. "Is that what you want from Mr. Pye? An affair?"

"Yes." George wrinkled her nose. "I don't know. If I'd met him at a ball, I wouldn't have asked him for an affair."

She would've danced with him, then flirted and exchanged witty banter. He would've sent flowers the next morning and maybe asked her to drive in the park. He would've courted her.

"But a land steward wouldn't be invited to the balls you attend, my lady," Tiggle said soberly.

"Exactly." For some reason this simple fact had George blinking back tears.

"Well, then"—Tiggle sighed and rose—"since there isn't any other choice, maybe you should just tell him what you've told me." She smiled without meeting George's eyes and left the room.

George flopped back on her bed. *I wish . . .* She sighed. If wishes were horses, then beggars would ride.

HARRY CLOSED THE DOOR TO his cottage and leaned his head against it. He could still hear the rain beating on the wood. The grain was rotting in the fields, and there wasn't a damn thing he could do about it. Despite Lady Georgina's kind offer of loans for the tenants, they would lose a great deal of money, a great deal of *food,* if the harvest failed. Not only that, but more dead sheep had been found on Granville land today. The poisoner was growing bold. In the last week, he'd struck three times, killing more than a dozen sheep. Even the most loyal of the Woldsly cottagers looked at him with suspicion now. And why not? To many he was a stranger here.

He pushed away from the door and set the lantern on the table beside a letter he'd opened this morning. Mrs. Burns had left his supper, but he didn't touch it. Instead, he lit the fire and put a kettle of water on to heat.

He'd ridden out before dawn and had worked ever since, inspecting crops. He couldn't stand the stink of his own body anymore. He swiftly stripped to the waist and poured the heated water into a basin. It was barely tepid, but he used it to wash under his arms, his chest, and his back. Finally, he poured clean water into the basin and dunked his head and face in. The cool water ran down his face, dripping off his chin. It seemed to wash away not only the filth of the day, but all the mental ills as well—the frustration and anger and helplessness. Harry caught up a cloth and toweled his face.

There was a knock at the door.

He froze, the cloth still in his hand. Had Granville's men finally come for him? He put out the lantern, drew his knife, and stole to the door. Standing to one side, he flung it wide.

Lady Georgina stood outside, the rain dripping from her hood. "May I come in?" Her gaze lowered and caught at his bare chest. Her blue eyes widened.

Harry felt his cock harden at her reaction. "I didn't think you waited on my permission to enter, my lady." He turned back to the table to put on his shirt.

"Sarcasm doesn't become you." She walked in and shut the door.

He uncovered his supper—bean soup—and sat to eat it.

Lady Georgina dropped her cloak untidily on a chair. He felt her glance at him before she wandered to the fireplace. She touched each of the animal carvings with a fingertip and then came back toward him.

He spooned up some of the soup. It was cold now but still tasty.

She trailed her fingers across the table, stopping at the letter. She picked it up. "You know the Earl of Swartingham?"

"We frequent the same coffeehouse in London." He poured himself a mug of ale. "Sometimes he writes me about agricultural matters."

"Really." She started reading the letter. "But he sounds like he considers you a friend. His language is certainly casual."

Harry choked and snatched the letter from her hand, startling her. Lord Swartingham's writing could be colorful at times—not fit for a lady. "How can I help you, my lady?"

Lady Georgina drifted away from the table. Her manner seemed off, and it took him a minute to place it.

She was nervous.

Harry narrowed his eyes. He'd never seen her flustered before.

"You wouldn't let me finish my tale last time," she said. "About the Leopard Prince." She halted by the fire and turned a curiously vulnerable face to him.

With one cold word, he could send her flying, this woman whose station so far outranked his. Had he ever had that much power over an aristocrat? He doubted it. The problem was that sometime in the last week she'd stopped being merely a member of the aristocracy and had become... a woman. Lady Georgina.

His lady.

"Please tell me your story, my lady." Harry ate some more of Mrs. Burns's soup, chewing on a piece of mutton.

She seemed to relax and turned back to the mantel, playing with the whittled animals as she spoke. "The Leopard Prince defeated the ogre and brought back the Golden Horse. Did I tell you that part?" She glanced at him.

Harry nodded.

"Yes, now..." She scrunched her nose in thought. "The young king, do you remember him?"

"Mmm."

"Well, the young king took the Golden Horse from the Leopard Prince, probably without even a 'thank you very much,' and carted it off to the princess"—she waved a hand—"or rather to her *father*, the *other* king. Because the princess doesn't have any say-so, does she?"

He shrugged. It was her fairy tale; he'd no idea.

"They very rarely do. Princesses, I mean. They get sold off to old dragons and giants and such all the time." Lady Georgina was frowning at a badger. "Where's the stag?"

"I beg your pardon?"

"The stag." She pointed at the mantel. "It's not here. You didn't knock it into the fire, did you?"

"I don't think so, but I might've."

"You'll have to find another place for them. It's too dangerous here." She began lining the carved animals at the back of the mantel.

"As you wish, my lady."

"Anyway," Lady Georgina continued, "the young king brought the Golden Horse to the father king and said, 'Here you are, and how about your beautiful daughter, then?' But what the young king didn't know was that the Golden Horse could speak."

"It's a talking metal horse?"

She appeared not to hear him. "The minute the young king left the room, the Golden Horse turned to the other king, the father king—are you following me?"

"Mmm." His mouth was full.

"Good. All these kings are very confusing." She heaved a sigh. "And the Golden Horse said, 'That's not the man who freed me. You've been tricked, Your Majesty.' And didn't that make the father king mad."

"Why?" Harry drank some ale. "The father king had

possession of the Golden Horse. Why would he care one way or the other who actually stole it?"

She set her hands on her hips. "Because stealing the Golden Horse is a test. He wants only the man who can do that to marry his daughter."

"I see." The whole thing sounded silly. Wouldn't a noble father be more interested in the richer man rather than the stronger? "So, then, he didn't really want the Golden Horse."

"He probably wanted the Golden Horse as well, but that's neither here nor there."

"But—"

"What *is* important"—Lady Georgina glared at him—"is that the father king marched straight back to the young king and said, 'See here, the Golden Horse is all very well, but what I really want is the Golden Swan that belongs to a very nasty witch. So if you want the princess, off you go to get it.' What do you think of that?"

It took a moment for Harry to realize that the last was said to him. He swallowed. "There seem to be a lot of golden animals in this fairy tale, my lady."

"Ye-es," Lady Georgina said. "That did occur to me, too. But they can't very well be anything else, can they? I mean, it wouldn't do to have a copper horse or a lead swan." She frowned and switched a mole with a sparrow.

He watched her thoughtfully. "Is that all, my lady?"

"What?" She didn't look up from the little animals. "No, there's lots more." But she didn't elaborate.

He pushed the remains of his supper away. "Are you going to tell me the rest?"

"No. Not right now, anyway."

He got up from the table and took a step closer. He

didn't want to frighten her. He felt as if he had his own golden swan within reach. "Then, will you tell me why you've really come, my lady?" he asked. He could smell the perfume in her hair, an exotic scent like spices from distant lands.

She set a thrush next to a cat. The bird toppled over, and he waited while she carefully righted it. "I need to tell you something. Besides the fairy tale." Her face was half turned away, and he could see the glistening trail of a tear on her cheek.

A kind man—an *honorable* man—would leave her alone. He would pretend he didn't see the tears and would turn away. He would not trespass upon her fears and desires. But long ago Harry had lost what little honor he'd ever had.

And he had never been kind.

He touched her hair with a fingertip, feeling the soft strands. "What do you need to tell me?"

She turned to face him, and her eyes were bright in the firelight, uncertain and hopeful and as alluring as Eve herself. "I know now what I want from you."

Chapter Ten

Harry stood so near, his breath caressed her face. "And what is it you want from me, my lady?"

George's heart beat in her throat. This was so much harder than she'd imagined back in her room at Woldsly. She felt like she was laying her soul before him. "I want you."

He bent closer, and she thought she felt his tongue touch her ear. "Me?"

She gasped. This was what drove her on, despite her embarrassment, despite her fear: desire for this man.

"Yes. I... I want you to kiss me like you did before. I want to see you naked. I want to be naked for you. I want..."

But her thoughts scattered because this time she was sure of it—he was tracing the rim of her ear with his tongue. And while the *idea* of such a caress might seem rather odd, in reality it was *divine*. She shivered.

Harry's chuckle puffed against her wet ear. "You want many things, my lady."

"Mmm." George swallowed as another thought occurred to her. "And I want you to stop calling me *my lady*."

"But you order me about so masterfully." His teeth closed on her earlobe.

George had to press her knees together to contain her own excitement. "E-even so—"

"Maybe I should call you George, as your sister does." He trailed a line of kisses up to her temple.

She frowned as she tried to concentrate on his words. It wasn't very easy. "Well—"

"Although I'm afraid I don't see you in the same way as your sister. George is such a mannish name." His hand wandered to her breast. "And I don't find you mannish at all." One thumb brushed her nipple.

She almost stopped breathing.

He circled the tip through the fabric of her dress. *Oh, dear Lord.* She didn't know it was possible to feel so much from such a little touch.

"I could call you Georgina, but it's long." He watched his hand, his eyes dark.

What?

"And then there is Gina, a pet name, but it's too common for you." He squeezed her nipple, and she felt the jolt all the way to the center of her being.

She moaned helplessly.

Harry's gaze flicked up to hers. He no longer smiled. "So, you see, I think I'll have to continue calling you *my* lady."

His head dipped. His mouth was on hers before she could even think. Biting, licking, sucking. His kiss—if such a ravenous devouring could be called a kiss—overwhelmed her senses. She tunneled her fingers through his hair and hung on for dear life. *Oh, thank the Lord!* She'd begun to think she would never taste him again. She suckled his tongue, murmuring her enjoyment.

He made a sound—a growl?—and placed a hand frankly on her bottom and pulled her roughly against himself. She would've bet her life that the hard rod she felt poking into her lower belly was his manhood. Just to be sure, she rubbed against it, and his rod now had almost all of her attention. He rewarded her daring by shoving a knee between her legs. The effect was so exciting that she almost forgot about the rod. He'd somehow found *that* spot, that little place that could bring her so much pleasure. He rubbed that spot with his leg while thrusting his tongue repeatedly into her mouth.

She nearly whimpered at the sensation. Did he know? Did all men have a secret understanding of that part of a woman's anatomy? George pulled at his hair until Harry's lips broke away from hers. His knee continued its maddening motion. She looked into his eyes, heavy-lidded and burning green, and saw devastating knowledge. Harry knew exactly what he was doing to her. It wasn't fair! He would have her lying in a puddle of want before she could even discover him.

"Stop."

The word came out more a gasp than a command, but Harry stilled at once. "My lady?"

"I said I wanted to see *you*." George dismounted his knee. That really was the only word for it.

Harry spread his arms wide. "Here I am."

"Naked."

For the first time, there was a trace of unease in his face. "As my lady wishes." But he made no move.

She saw it in his eyes; she'd have to undress him herself. She bit her lip, excited and uncertain at the same time. "Sit there." She pointed to the armchair by the fire.

He obeyed, lounging back, his legs sprawled.

She hesitated.

"I'm yours to do with as you wish, my lady," he said. The words came out a purr, as if a great cat had granted her leave to pet it.

If she balked now, she'd never find out. She knelt and carefully undid the buttons on his shirt. His hands were draped casually over the chair's arms, and he made no move to help. She reached the last button and spread the halves of his shirt wide, examining him. The lines of his neck tendons ran down into the hills of his shoulders, smooth and taut. Below, he had small brown nipples, puckered like her own. She touched one with a fingertip and then traced the bumpy ridge of the surrounding dark circle.

He made a sound.

Her gaze flicked to his. His eyes glowed under lowered lids, and his nostrils were flared; otherwise he was still. She looked back to his bare chest. In the center grew dark hairs, and she brushed over them to feel their texture. They were smooth, damp underneath with his sweat. She followed the trail of hair down to his belly where it encircled his navel. How strange. And the hair skimmed lower. It must meet up with... She searched the placket of his trousers for the buttons that closed it. His manhood stood up stiffly within the fabric. From the corner of her eye, she saw his hands grip the chair arms, but he let her have her way. She found the buttons. Her hands trembled and one button popped off. She undid the placket and slowly peeled it back while struggling to draw breath.

It stood up all by itself, larger than she'd ever imagined, poking through his smallclothes. The statues lied. There was no way this could fit beneath those puny fig leaves.

It was ruddier than the flesh of his belly, and she could see veins throbbing along the length. The head was bigger than the rest, shining and red. The hair at the base was damp, and when she leaned forward—oh, dear Lord— she could smell him. Male musk, heavy and intoxicating.

George didn't know the etiquette of the situation, whether it was done or not, but she reached out. If she died tomorrow and had to make accounting for her eternal soul before the gates of heaven and St. Peter himself, she would not regret it: She touched Harry Pye's cock.

He groaned and lifted his hips.

But she was distracted by her discovery. The skin was soft, like the finest kid glove, and it moved separately from the muscle beneath. She skimmed her palm over the shaft up to the head and found liquid leaking from a slit. Was this the seed of life?

He groaned again. This time he grabbed her and lifted her to his lap, obscuring that most interesting part of his body.

"You're going to kill me, my lady." He worked at the hooks at the back of her gown. "I promise on my father's grave that you may look at my naked body for hours, or as long as I can stand it, *later.* But right now"—her gown gaped forward, and he pulled it and her shift down— "I need to see *your* naked body."

She frowned, about to protest, but he had the entire bodice off now, and he bent his head and sucked on her nipple. She gazed down at his head, shocked; then the sensation caught up with the act and she inhaled. She knew men were fascinated with breasts, but she'd no idea.

Oh, my, was this usual? Perhaps it didn't matter—he tongued his way to her other breast and sucked on that one as well—because it felt so erotic. So evocative. Now her hips moved, swiveling of their own accord. He chuckled and she felt the vibration through her nipple.

And then he bit gently.

"Oh, please." She was startled at the huskiness of her own voice. She didn't know for what she begged.

But Harry knew. He shifted and dragged her gown from off her body. He pulled off her slippers one at a time and let them drop to the floor. She lay across his lap like some odalisque, naked except for her stockings and garters, his cock pressed into her hip. She should have been embarrassed, she knew. If she were proper at all, she would've run away, screaming. Which only proved what she'd suspected for some time: She'd lost all sense of propriety. For when Harry lifted his head and slowly, *very* slowly, perused her naked body, she actually arched her back as if to display herself.

"You're so beautiful." His voice was guttural, deep and rasping. "Here"—he touched her swollen nipples—"they look like red berries in snow. Here"—he smoothed his hand on the curve of her belly—"so soft, like down. And here." His fingers combed into the auburn curls surrounding her womanhood. His hand tightened on her mound for a moment. His face was carnal in the firelight, the lines in sharp relief, his lips drawn back. He slid his long middle finger between her folds.

She shut her eyes as he touched her there.

"Do you like it softly?" His finger brushed over her. "Or firmly?" He stroked.

"L-like that," she sighed. She spread her thighs a little more.

"Kiss me," he whispered, and turned his head to brush feather kisses across her lips.

.

She moaned into his mouth. Her hands tangled in his hair and roamed over the warm skin of his shoulders. And all the while his finger stroked until the tension built to unbearable levels, and he thrust his tongue into her mouth. George arched, feeling her heart beat out of her chest and the warmth seeping, spreading, from her middle. She felt shaken, as if she'd taken a journey from which there was no return.

He petted her, gentle and consoling.

When she began to drift, he lifted her, stood, and walked to his bedroom. He lay her down on his narrow bed and stepped back deliberately. Harry watched her—for resistance?—as he stripped out of his remaining clothes. She lay there limply, anticipating whatever he would do next. Then he climbed over her and poised for a moment on all fours, a hungry beast about to devour his prey.

His very willing prey.

"It may hurt." He searched her eyes.

"I don't care." She pulled his head down to hers.

He met her lips and nudged her legs apart with his own. She felt him at her entrance. He lifted his head and braced himself on one hand, then thrust himself into her. Or at least she thought he did. He drew back a little and thrust again, and more flesh entered her. Good Lord, would all of him . . . ? Another thrust and she gasped. It hurt. It pinched. It burned. He glanced at her face, grit his teeth, and thrust powerfully. His pelvis met hers.

She whimpered. She felt full—too full.

Above her, he was still. A bead of sweat dripped off the side of his face and fell on her collarbone. "All right?" It was a grunt.

No. She nodded and hazarded a smile.

"Brave girl," he whispered.

He leaned down to kiss her and slowly moved his hips. He seemed to grind against her without actually shifting his manhood. That was quite nice. She explored his back, the bunched shoulder muscles, the valley of his spine, damp with sweat. She moved lower and felt his buttocks flex as he finally moved inside her. It wasn't painful, but it wasn't as nice as his finger had been before. She concentrated on teasing his tongue with her own. And pressing her fingers into the muscles of his bottom because they were oddly fascinating to her. She wished she could see his backside right now. She felt tender. He pumped. The feel of his manhood sliding in and out of her was rather interesting.

George idly wondered what they must look like.

Then all thought fled, for he had pressed his hand against her *there*. And somehow, the combination of his fingers and his thrusting cock was really altogether perfect. She gripped his hips and began to move her own. Utterly without rhythm, but it didn't seem to matter. Almost... *Oh, heavens!* She actually saw stars. She broke their kiss to arch her head into the pillow in a bliss like none she'd ever felt before.

He was suddenly gone from her body, and she felt warmth splattering onto her belly. She opened her eyes in time to see Harry throw his head back and shout. The tendons in his neck stood out, and his upper body glistened with sweat.

He was the most magnificent thing she'd ever seen.

AMAZING, REALLY, HOW SIMPLE it was to kill.

Silas looked down at the woman lying in the gorse. He'd had to drag her here after keeping her locked up for over a day. It'd been important, after all, that she die in the proper way, and he'd had to find and prepare the poisonous herbs. A rather tedious job. The woman had convulsed at the end, and the body was twisted. Before she died, she had vomited and lost control of her bowels, shitting quite disgustingly all over the place. He curled his lip. The whole process had taken too much of his time and had been foul to boot.

But it had been simple.

He'd chosen a sheep pasture on his own land. Isolated at night but close enough to the road so she'd be found before she rotted entirely away. It was important to associate this with the sheep poisonings. These farmers were a dull lot, and if the connections weren't made for them, they might not see the obvious.

He could have tried to get the woman to drink the brew he'd made, but it'd been quicker to simply force it down her throat. Then he'd sat back and waited. The woman had sworn and cried at his treatment—she had already been drunk when he'd found her. Then, after a while, she'd clutched her stomach. Vomited. Shat.

And finally died.

Silas sighed and stretched, his muscles cramped from sitting so long on a damp boulder. He stood up and pulled a handkerchief out of his pocket. He walked over to the stinking corpse and unwrapped the carved stag. Carefully he placed it a few steps from the woman. Close enough to be found but far enough away to have been dropped. He looked critically at the scene he'd created and found it good.

He smiled to himself and walked away.

A WEIGHT LAY ON HIS CHEST. Harry opened his eyes but didn't move. He saw a cloud of ginger hair floating over his chest and right arm.

She'd stayed the night.

He glanced at the window and cursed silently. It was dawn already. He should've been up an hour past, and Lady Georgina should have left well before that. But lying here in a too-small bed with his lady was nice. He could feel the cushion of her breast against his side. Her breath puffed on his shoulder, and her arm was flung across his chest as if she had taken possession of him. And maybe she had. Perhaps he was like some enchanted prince in one of her tales and now she held the key to his heart.

The key to his very soul.

He closed his eyes again. He could smell her scent mingled with his. She stirred, her hand moving down over his belly, almost to his morning cockstand. He held his breath, but she stopped.

He needed to piss, and besides, she would be too sore this morning. He eased her arm off him. Harry sat up. Lady Georgina's hair was a tangle around her face. He gently pushed it back, and she scrunched her nose in her sleep. He smiled. She looked like a wild gypsy lass. He bent, kissed her bare tit, and rose. He stoked the fire, then pulled on his trousers to take a piss outside. When he returned, he put water on to boil and glanced into the little bedroom again. His lady still slept.

He was taking down the teapot when someone started pounding on the cottage door. Quickly he shut the bedroom door. He palmed his knife and opened the cottage door a crack.

A gentleman stood outside. Tall, with reddish-brown hair. The stranger flicked a riding crop in one bony hand. A horse was tethered behind him.

"Aye?" Harry braced his right hand above his head. The other hand held the knife, hidden on his side of the doorjamb.

"I'm looking for Lady Georgina Maitland." The stranger's voice, clipped and upper crust, would have frozen most men.

Harry raised one eyebrow. "And who might you be?"

"The Earl of Maitland."

"Ah." He started to close the door.

Maitland wedged his crop in the doorway to prevent him. "Do you know where she is?" There was warning in his voice now.

"Yes." Harry stared flatly at Maitland. "She'll be at the manor soon."

Anger sparked in the other man's eyes. "Within the hour or I'll kick this bloody hovel down around your ears."

Harry closed the door.

When he turned, he saw Lady Georgina peeking from the bedroom. Her hair was loose around her shoulders, and she had used a bedsheet as a wrap.

"Who was it?" Her voice was husky with sleep.

Harry wished he could pick her up and carry her back to his bed and make her forget about this day, but the world and everything in it waited.

He replaced the teapot on the shelf. "Your brother."

HER BROTHER HAD TO BE the one person in all the world a woman didn't want to meet directly after a night of ecstasy. George fiddled with the ribbon at her neck.

Tiggle batted her hand away and set a last pin in her hair. "There you are, my lady. As ready as you'll ever be." At least the maid was no longer sending her mournful looks.

Instead, she was now commiserating. Did everyone know what had happened last night? She really should've been more discreet than to spend the night. George sighed and contemplated feigning a headache. But Tony was nothing if not stubborn. He might not drag her from her room to interview her, but he'd be right outside the minute she tried to emerge. Best to get it over with.

She threw back her shoulders and marched downstairs like a Christian going to meet a particularly irate lion. Greaves sent her a sympathetic look as he held the breakfast room door for her.

Inside, Tony was standing by the mantelpiece, staring down his bony nose into the fire. He evidently hadn't touched the food on the sideboard. Tony was the spitting image of their late father, tall and angular with a face dominated by prominent cheekbones and heavy eyebrows. The only difference was the auburn hair he'd inherited from their mother. That, and the fact that he was a much nicer man than Father had been.

Usually, anyway.

George noticed that Violet was conspicuously absent. She had a very good idea why, too. She'd corner the minx later.

"Good morning, Tony." George strolled to the sideboard. Buttered kippers. Even Cook knew. She helped herself to a large serving. She was going to need her strength.

"George," Tony greeted her coolly. He advanced swiftly to the door and flung it open. Two footmen looked at him, startled. "We won't be needing you. Make sure we're not disturbed."

The footmen bowed. "Yes, my lord."

Tony closed the door and yanked down on his waistcoat

to straighten it. George rolled her eyes. When had her brother become this stuffy? He must have been practicing in his room at nights.

"Are you having breakfast?" she asked as she sat down. "Cook has made some lovely kippers."

Tony ignored her pleasantry. "What could you have been thinking?" His tone was unbelievably dour.

"Well, really, if you want to know the truth, I wasn't thinking at all." She took a sip of tea. "I mean, not after the first kiss. He does kiss very well."

"George!"

"If you didn't want to know, why ask?"

"You know very well what I mean. Don't play the flib-bertigibbet with me."

George sighed and put down her fork. The kippers tasted like ashes in her mouth, anyway. "It's no concern of yours."

"Of course it's my concern. You're my sister and you're unmarried."

"Do I poke into your affairs? Do I ask about what ladies you see in London?"

Tony crossed his arms and stared down his large nose at her. "It's not the same and you know it."

"Yes"—George poked a kipper—"but it should be."

He sighed and took a chair opposite her. "Maybe so. But that isn't how the world works. We don't deal with how society ought to be but rather how it is. And society will judge you rather harshly, my dear."

She felt her lips tremble.

"Come back to London with me," Tony said. "We can forget about this. There are some fellows I can introduce you to—"

"It's not like choosing a horse. I don't want to exchange a bay for a chestnut."

"Why not? Why not find a man from your own class? One who could marry you and give you children."

"Because," George said slowly, "I don't want just any man. I want *this* one."

Tony slammed the flat of his hand down on the table, making her jump. He leaned over her. "And the rest of the family can just go to hell? You're not like this. Think about the example you're setting for Violet. Would you want her doing what you're doing?"

"No. But I can't live my life as an example for my sister."

Tony pursed his lips.

"You don't," George accused. "Can you honestly say that with every action you take, you stop to think, 'Is this a good example for my brothers?'"

"For God's sake—"

The door swung open.

They both looked up in surprise. Tony frowned. "I thought I said to admit no—"

"My lord. My lady." Harry closed the door on the two harassed footmen outside and advanced into the room.

Tony straightened away from the table. He was easily half a head taller than Harry, but the shorter man did not break stride.

"Are you well, my lady?" Harry spoke to George, but his eyes never left Tony.

"Yes, thank you, Harry." She'd assured him back at the cottage that Tony would never hurt her, but he must have decided to see for himself. "Would you like a kipper?"

A corner of Harry's mouth twitched upward, but Tony

forestalled his answer. "We have no need of you. You may go."

"*Tony,*" George gasped.

"My lord." Harry inclined his head. His expression was once again carefully blank.

George's heart felt like it was breaking into tiny pieces. *This isn't right.* She started to rise, but Harry had already turned back to the door.

Her lover left the room, dismissed like a common servant by her brother.

NOTHING LEVELED A MAN QUITE like being unable to protect his woman. Harry jerked on his tricorn and cloak and strode to the stables, the heels of his boots kicking up gravel. But Lady Georgina wasn't really his, was she? She wasn't bound to him by law or society. She was a woman who'd allowed him to make love to her. Once.

And maybe only that once.

It had been her first time, and inevitably, he'd hurt her. He'd given her pleasure before, but was it enough to make up for the pain afterward? Did she understand that only the first time was painful? Maybe she wouldn't let him prove that he could give her pleasure with his flesh inside hers.

Harry swore. The stable hand holding his mare's head eyed him warily. He scowled at the boy and took the reins. The fact that he wanted Lady Georgina didn't help his mood. Now. Under him or above him, it didn't matter; he just wanted to sink his flesh into hers and feel the world fall away again.

"Mr. Pye!"

Harry looked over his shoulder. The Earl of Maitland was hailing him from Woldsly's steps. Jesus Christ, now what?

"Mr. Pye, if you'll wait while my horse is brought around, I'd like to accompany you."

He didn't have much of a choice, now, did he? "Very well, my lord."

He watched the earl stroll up while stable hands ran to do his bidding. Even if the other man hadn't introduced himself at the cottage this morning, Harry would have known him. His eyes were his sister's—clear, piercing blue.

A saddled horse was brought, and both men mounted. They rode out from the stable yard without saying a word. At least the earl was discreet.

Dark clouds glowered overhead, threatening yet more rain where none was wanted.

They were nearly to the gates when the earl spoke. "If it's money you're after, I can give you a pretty purse to speed you on your way."

Harry looked at the earl—Tony, Lady Georgina had called him. His face was stony, but his lips curled ever so slightly at the corners, giving away his distaste. Harry almost felt sorry for him. "I'm not after money, my lord."

"Don't take me for a fool." Tony's nostrils flared. "I've seen the hut you're living in, and your attire doesn't bespeak even modest wealth. You're after my sister's money."

"You see no other reason for me to seek the company of Lady Georgina?"

"I—"

"I wonder if you realize how close you are to insulting my lady," Harry said.

A flush spread over the other man's cheekbones. Harry remembered that the earl was Lady Georgina's younger brother. He couldn't be more than, what, five or six and twenty? His air of authority made him seem older.

"If you do not take my money and leave her alone, I'll see that you're dismissed without reference," Tony said.

"I'm employed by your sister, not you, my lord."

"Have you no pride, man?" Tony pulled his horse up short. "What kind of a cur preys on a lonely woman?"

Harry halted his horse as well. "Do you really think your sister wouldn't see straight through a man trying to take advantage of her?"

Tony frowned. "You've put her in danger. Violet says our sister was attacked while in your company."

Harry sighed. "Did Lady Violet also tell you that Lady Georgina fired a pistol at the attackers?" The other man's eyes widened. "Or that if I'd had my way, she wouldn't have been in the gig with me in the first place?"

Tony winced. "Rode roughshod over you, did she? She does have a persistent streak."

Harry raised one eyebrow.

Tony coughed and started his horse. "Be that as it may, a gentleman doesn't continue to press his attentions on a lady who can't return them."

"Then, as I see it, you have two problems, my lord," Harry said.

Tony's eyes narrowed.

"One, that the lady does, in fact, return my attentions, and two"—Harry turned to meet the earl's gaze—"I am no gentleman."

Chapter Eleven

"Violet, open this door!" George held her breath and applied her ear to the wood. Nothing. "I know you're in there. I can hear you breathing."

"You can't." Her sister's voice came petulantly from inside.

Ha! "Violet Elizabeth Sarah Maitland. Open this door at once or I shall have Greaves take the hinges off."

"No, you won't. The hinges are inside." Violet sounded triumphant.

So they were, the little minx. George inhaled and gritted her teeth. "Then I shall have him bash the door in."

"You wouldn't." Violet's voice was closer.

"I don't believe you should count on that." She crossed her arms and tapped one foot.

There came a scraping from the other side; then the door cracked open. One tear-stained eye peeped out.

"Oh, my dear." George pushed the door the rest of the way open and walked in, closing it behind her. "Time to cut line. Whatever possessed you to write to Tony?"

Violet's lower lip began to tremble. "That man has you

in his clutches. He's beguiled you with his caresses and his carnal wiles."

Caresses and carnal wiles? George knit her brows. "What do you know about carnal wiles?"

Violet's eyes widened. "Nothing," she said much too fast. "Well, only what everybody hears."

George stared as her younger sister blushed. It always was a problem, trying to lie with fair skin. "Violet," she said slowly, "is there something you want to tell me?"

Violet let out a squeaking wail and flung herself into George's arms. *Oh, dear.*

"There, there, sweet." She stumbled back—Violet was an inch or two taller—and sat in the cushioned window seat. "It can't be as bad as all that."

Violet tried to speak, choked, and cried some more. George rocked her, murmuring the inanities one whispers to a distressed child, and brushed the hair back from her sister's damp brow.

Violet inhaled, shuddering. "Y-you don't understand. I've done something really awful." She scrubbed her eyes with a hand. "I... I've *sinned,* George!"

George couldn't help the twitch of her lips—Violet was always so dramatic—but she firmed her mouth at once. "Tell me."

"I... I've lain with a man." The words were indistinct because Violet had buried her head, but George couldn't mistake them.

She immediately sobered, dread clutching at her throat. "What?" She pried Violet away from her breast. "Look at me. What do you mean?" Perhaps her sister had mistaken the matter somehow; confused an embrace for something more.

Violet raised a ravaged face. "I gave my virginity away to a man. There was blood."

"Oh, my Lord." No, not Violet, not her baby sister. George felt tears prick at her own eyes, but she willed them away and framed her sister's face with her hands. "Did he force you? Did he hurt you?"

"N-no." Violet choked on a sob. "It's almost worse. I did it of my own free will. I'm a wanton. A ... a *harlot*." She broke down again and hid her face in George's skirts.

George stroked her sister's back and waited and thought. She had to handle this well the first time. When Violet had calmed again, George said, "I don't think we can go as far as saying that you're a harlot. I mean, you didn't take any money, did you?"

Violet shook her head. "Of course—"

George held up her hand. "And as for being a wanton, well ... it was only the one man. Am I correct?"

"Y-yes." Violet's lower lip trembled.

"Then, I think you will have to forgive my bias in saying that it is at least as much the gentleman's fault as yours. How old is he?"

Violet looked a bit mutinous at having been demoted from wanton. "Five and twenty."

Five and twenty! The seducing, lecherous ... George inhaled. "And do I know him?" she asked calmly.

Violet pushed away from her sister. "I won't tell you! I'll not be made to marry him."

George stared, her heart stopping in her chest. "Are you increasing?"

"No!" Violet's horror was unfeigned, thank goodness.

George blew out a relieved breath. "Then why do you think I would make you marry him?"

"Well, maybe not you, but Tony . . ." Violet got up and paced around the room. "He's been writing me letters."

"Tony has?"

"No!" Violet turned to glare at her. *"Him."*

"Oh, *him.*" George frowned. "What about?"

"He wants me to marry him. He says he loves me. But, George"—Violet picked up a candlestick from the bedside table and gestured with it—"I don't love him anymore. I did. I mean, I thought I did. That's why I, well, *you* know."

"Quite." George felt herself blushing.

"But then afterward I started noticing how far apart his eyes were and that he says *ain't* in such an affected way." Violet shrugged and set the candlestick down on the dresser. "And then it was gone, the love or whatever. I don't hate him; I just don't love him."

"I see."

"Is that how you feel about Mr. Pye?" Violet asked. "Are you over him now?"

George had a vision of Harry Pye, his head arched back, the tendons in his neck straining as he convulsed over her. A slow heat invaded her loins. She caught herself dropping her eyelids.

She snapped them open, sitting up straight at the same time. "Uh, not exactly."

"Oh." Violet looked forlorn. "Maybe it's me, then."

"I don't think so, sweetheart. Maybe it's that you're only fifteen. Or," she added hastily when Violet stuck out her lip, "maybe it's that he's just not the right man for you."

"Oh, George!" Violet flopped backward onto her bed. "I'll never have another suitor. How would I explain that I've lost my maidenhead? Perhaps I should marry *him.* No other man will ever have me." Violet stared at the canopy over her bed. "I'm just not sure I can bear the way he takes snuff for the rest of my life."

"Yes, that would be torturous," George murmured, "but I'm afraid I'll have to put my foot down and forbid you to marry him. So you're saved."

"You're a peach." Violet smiled tremulously from the bed. "But he's said he will have to reveal all if I don't become his bride."

"Ah." If she ever got her hands on the blackmailing bastard... "Then I think you will really have to tell me his name, sweetheart. I know"—she held up her hand as Violet started to protest—"but it's the only way."

"What will you do?" her sister asked in a small voice.

George met her eyes. "We'll have to tell Tony who he is so Tony can convince him that you aren't interested in marriage."

"But Tony, George?" Violet flung her arms wide across the bed, unconsciously taking the position of a martyr. "You know the way he inspects one so coldly down his nose. It makes me feel like a worm. A *squashed* worm."

"Yes, dear, I am aware of his look," George said. "I was the recipient of it just this morning, thanks to you."

"I'm sorry about that." Violet looked contrite before reverting to her own dilemma. "Tony will make me marry him!"

"No, you're maligning Tony, now," George said. "He may have lost all sense of humor since he assumed the title, but that doesn't mean he'll force a marriage on a sister, especially his fifteen-year-old sister."

"Even though I've—"

"Even though." George smiled. "Think how useful

Tony will be when he convinces this gentleman. Really, it is the only advantage I can think of to having an earl for a brother."

THAT NIGHT GEORGE SHIVERED and pulled the hood of her cloak tighter around her face. It was late, almost midnight, and Harry's cottage was dark. Perhaps he had already retired for the evening? At any other time, for any other reason, she would've turned around. But this compulsion drove her on. She had to see him again. Except it wasn't to *see* him that she'd come here so late in the evening, was it? She felt a blush start high on her cheekbones. She wanted to do more, much more, than see Harry Pye. And she didn't want to examine too closely the reasons behind that urge.

She knocked at his door.

It swung open almost immediately, as if he'd been waiting for her. "My lady." His green eyes were heavy.

Harry's chest was bare, and her gaze was drawn to it. "I hope you don't mind," she began vapidly, addressing his left nipple.

He reached out a long arm and drew her in. Slammed the door and pushed her up against it. Shoved back her hood and seized her lips. He tilted her head back and slanted his mouth over hers, thrusting his tongue between her lips. Oh, heavens, she needed this. Had she become so wanton after only one taste? His hands gripped the back of her head, and she felt the pins falling out. Her hair came undone down her back. Her hands roamed, kneading, stroking his back. She could taste ale on his tongue and smell his musk. Her nipples were already peaked and aching as if they recognized him and what he was.

He drew his lips down her neck, open-mouthed. "I don't mind," he rasped.

And while she was trying to remember to what he replied, he hooked his hand in her bodice. He pulled down savagely, tearing the fine fabric and exposing her naked breasts. George gasped and felt moisture between her legs. Then he had his mouth on her breast, nipping at it. She actually worried that he would bite her. He seemed animal, fundamental, male to her female. He reached her nipple and did bite, a sharp pinching.

She couldn't help but arch her head back and moan.

He had his hand under her skirts now, pushing and shoving them up as if he were impatient to find her center. She clutched at his shoulders when he reached his goal. He brushed his fingers over her, touching, feeling.

He lifted his head from her breast and chuckled. "You're wet for me." His voice was dark. Sexual.

He brought both hands under her legs and lifted her, bracing her back against the door; all her weight was on him. She was helplessly spread as he moved between her thighs. She felt the brush of his trousers. And then the brush of *him*. Her eyes opened wide and met his, gleaming and green like a predator's.

Oh, my.

He rocked his hips, just a little. She felt the intrusion. She imagined that wide head, splitting her lips down there, and she panted, eyes half closed. He rocked again, and his cock pushed in a little farther.

"My lady." His breath puffed over her lips.

With an effort, she opened her eyes. "What?" she gasped. She felt drunken, dazed, as if she floated in a marvelous daydream.

"I hope you do not mind"—he rocked—"my boldness."

What? "No. I, *uh,* don't mind." She could hardly get the words out.

"You're sure?" He licked her nipple, the devil, and she jumped.

She was so sensitive, the feeling was almost painful. *I'm going to get him for this.*

He rocked.

Some other time. "Very sure," she whimpered.

He grinned, but a bead of sweat ran down his temple. "Then with your permission."

He didn't wait for her nod but slammed his entire length into her, shoving her up the door and hitting with exquisite accuracy *that* place. George wrapped her legs, her arms, and her heart around Harry. He withdrew with agonizing slowness and repeated the process, this time swiveling a bit when he crashed into her. The impact sent shards of ecstasy skittering through her.

She was going to die from pleasure.

He withdrew again, and she could feel every inch dragging against her sensitive flesh. She waited, suspended in time and air, for him to mate her once more. And he did, his cock thrusting into her and his pelvis rubbing her exposed center. Then he seemed to lose control. He began a rapid pistoning, his movements short and jerky. But just as effective, damn him. And it began for her, spreading in waves that seemed to have no end. She couldn't catch her breath, couldn't see or hear, could only moan in primitive abandon and open her mouth and fill it with his shoulder, salty and warm.

She *bit* Harry.

He came, withdrawing from her suddenly but keeping his arms around her as he shook and spasmed his release between them. He leaned into her, his weight keeping her pinned to the wall as they both drew deep, shuddering breaths. George felt heavy. Listless. Like she'd never be able to move her limbs again. She stroked his shoulder, rubbing at the bite mark she'd made.

Harry sighed against her hair. He let her legs fall to the floor as he steadied her. "I wish I could carry you to my bed, but I fear you've just drained me, my lady. That is"—he pulled away enough to look her in the eye—"if you mean to stay the night?"

"Yes." George tested her legs. Wobbly but adequate. She made her way to the small bedroom. "I'll stay the night."

"And your brother?" he asked from behind her.

"My brother does not control my life," George said loftily. "Besides, I snuck out the servants' entrance."

"Ah." He had followed her into the bedroom, and she saw now that he carried a basin of water.

She raised her eyebrows.

"I should have done this last night." Was he embarrassed?

Harry set down the basin beside the bed and helped her remove her gown and chemise, then knelt to take off her shoes and stockings. "Lie down, my lady."

George lay back on the bed. For some reason she was shy now when she hadn't been before during their wild lovemaking. He took a cloth and dipped it in the basin, wringing it out; then he stroked it down her neck. She closed her eyes. The wet cloth left coolness and goose bumps in its wake. She heard him dip and wring out the cloth again, the trickle of the water somehow erotic in the room's stillness. He washed down her chest, over her breasts, and across her belly, leaving a trail of cold heat.

Her breath was coming faster now, anticipating what would come next.

But he started again at her feet, trailing the cloth up her calves. Gently, he spread her thighs and washed the inner curves. He wet the cloth, and she felt the coolness against her mons. He stroked the cloth deliberately between her folds and her breath caught. Then his weight left the bed.

George opened her eyes and watched Harry strip his breeches down. Nude, his eyes on hers, he took the cloth and rubbed it across his chest. Dip. Wring. He washed under his arms. Across his belly.

Her eyes dropped and she licked her lips.

His penis jumped. George looked up, and her gaze met his. Harry dipped the cloth in the water. He lifted his manhood to wash the heavy sac underneath. Another dip in the basin and he drew the wet cloth up his cock, pulling the cloth around, leaving the skin glistening. He scrubbed the rag in his pubic hair and then threw it to the floor. Harry advanced on the bed, his penis stiff. George couldn't take her eyes off him.

He placed one knee beside her, making the bed dip. The ropes holding the mattress creaked. "Are you going to finish your fairy tale, my lady?"

She blinked. "Fairy tale?"

"The Leopard Prince, the young king." He brushed his lips over her collarbone. "The beautiful princess, the Golden Swan."

"Oh. Well." She scrambled to think. Harry's mouth was wandering to the underside of her left breast. "I think we'd got to when the father king told the young king to get—" She squeaked.

He'd reached the nipple. Her breast was already tender from their play before.

Harry lifted his head. "The Golden Swan held by the nasty witch." He blew cool air on the wet nipple.

George gasped. "Yes. Of course, the young king sent the Leopard Prince after it."

"Of course," Harry murmured to the other nipple.

"And the Leopard Prince turned into ... ahhh ..."

He had sucked that nipple into his mouth.

He let it pop out. "A man," he prompted, and blew.

"Mmm." George went under for a few seconds. "Yes. And the Leopard Prince held his emerald crown in his hand..."

He was trailing kisses down her abdomen.

"... and wished for ..."

"Yes?"

Was he licking her belly button? "A cloak to make him invisible."

"Really?" Harry propped his chin on her lower belly, his arms resting across her pelvic bones.

George craned her neck to see him. He was lying between her spread legs, his face only inches from her ... And he was looking gravely interested in her story.

"Yes, really." She let her head drop back on the pillow. "And he put on the cloak and went and stole the Golden Swan without the nasty witch even knowing. And when he got back"—what was Harry doing down there?—"he gave the Golden Swan to ... *Oh, my Lord!*"

Harry finished leisurely licking up through the flanges of her woman's place, then kissed *that* spot. He raised his head. "Is that part of the fairy tale, my lady?" he inquired politely.

George tunneled her fingers in his silky hair. "No. I'm through telling the story for now." She pulled his head back down. "Do. Not. Stop."

She thought he may have laughed, as she seemed to feel a vibration, but then Harry lowered his mouth, placed it over her nubbin, and *sucked* on it.

And, frankly, after that she no longer cared.

"WHAT DO YOU DREAM ABOUT at night?" Lady Georgina asked him a long time later.

"Mmph?" Harry tried to focus his mind. His body was a dead loss. His limbs were leaden, almost liquid with fatigue, and he was struggling to stay awake.

"I'm sorry. Are you asleep?" His lady obviously wasn't. He could feel her fingers stroking through the hair on his chest.

He made a heroic effort. "No." He opened his eyes. Wide. "What did you say?"

"What do you dream about at night?"

Rats. He suppressed a shudder. "Nothing." He winced. That wasn't what a gently born lady wanted to hear. "Besides you," he added hastily.

"No." She tapped him on the shoulder. "I'm not fishing for a compliment. I want to know what you think about. What you want. What you care for."

What he cared for? At this time of night? After he'd loved her, not once, but twice? "Ah." He felt his eyelids drifting shut and struggled to open them again. He was just too tired for this. "I'm afraid I'm a simple man, my lady. I think mostly about the harvest."

"What do you think?" Her voice was intent.

What did she want from him? He stroked her hair as her head lay on his chest and tried to think, but it was too great an exertion. He let his eyes close and said whatever came to mind. "Well, I worry about the rain, as you know. That it won't stop in time this year. That the crop will be ruined." He sighed, but she was quiet beneath his hand. "I think about next year's planting, whether we should try hops this far north."

"Hops?"

"Mmm." He yawned gigantically. "For ale. But then we'd have to find a market for the harvest. It would be a good cash crop, but would the farmers have enough of their own to keep them through the winter?" She traced a circle on his breastbone, her touch almost tickling. He was waking up now as he thought about the problem. "It's hard to introduce a new crop to the farmers. They're set in their ways, don't like innovations."

"How would you convince them, then?"

He was silent a minute, considering, but she didn't interrupt. He had never told anyone of this idea. "Sometimes I think that a grammar school in West Dikey would be a good idea."

"Really?"

"Mmm. If the farmers or their children could read, were educated even a little, innovation might be easier. And then each generation would be more learned, and they in turn would be more open to new thoughts and ways of doing things. It would be an improvement measured in decades, not years, and it would affect not only the landowner's income, but also the lives of the farmers themselves." Harry was wide awake now, but his lady was silent. Perhaps she thought educating farmers a foolish idea.

Then she spoke. "We'd have to find a teacher. A gentleman who was patient with children."

Her *we* warmed him. "Yes. Someone who likes the country and understands the seasons."

"The seasons?" The hand on his chest had stilled.

He covered it with his own and rubbed the back of her hand with his thumb as he talked. "Spring, cold and wet, when the farmers must get the seed into the ground, but not too soon or it'll frost, and the ewes are all lambing at once, or so it seems. Summer, long and hot, tending the sheep under the wide, blue skies and watching the grain grow. Fall, hoping for the sun to shine so the harvest will be good. If the sun shines, the people celebrate and there are festivals; if it doesn't, they go about with thin, fearful faces. And winter, long and dreary, the farmers and their families sitting by a little fire in the cottages, telling tales and waiting for spring." He stopped and squeezed her shoulder self-consciously. "The seasons."

"You know so much," she whispered.

"Only what goes on in this part of Yorkshire. I'm sure you could find many who would think that little enough."

She shook her head, her springy hair brushing against his shoulder. "But you're aware. You know how the people around you think. What they're feeling. I don't."

"What do you mean?" He tried to see her face, but her head was tilted down against his chest.

"I get caught up in silly things like the cut of a gown or a new pair of earrings, and I lose track of the people around me. I don't think about whether Tiggle is being courted by the new footman or how Tony is doing all by himself in London. You wouldn't know it to look at Tony, he seems so big and strong and in control, but he can get lonely. And Violet..." She sighed. "Violet was seduced this summer at our family home in Leicestershire and I didn't know. I never even suspected."

He frowned. "Then how did you find out?"

"She confessed just this morning."

Her face was still hidden, and he tried to brush the hair away from her eyes. "If it was a secret, if she didn't want to tell you before now, it would be hard to know. Children of that age are very mysterious sometimes."

She bit her lip. "But I'm her sister. I'm the closest one to her. I should have known." She sighed again, a small, sad sound that made him want to shield her from all the world's worries. "He's pressing her to marry."

"Who?"

"Leonard Wentworth. He's a penniless nobody. He seduced her simply to get her to wed him."

He smoothed his mouth over her forehead, unsure of what to say. Did she see how similar her sister's situation was to her own? Was she afraid that he, too, would demand marriage as a forfeit for their lovemaking?

"Our mother..." She hesitated, then began again. "Our mother is not always well. M'man has many illnesses and complaints, most imagined, I'm afraid. She spends so much of her time looking inward for the next disease that she doesn't often notice those around her. I've tried to be a mother to Violet in her stead."

"That's quite a burden."

"Not really. That's not the point. Loving Violet isn't the problem."

He frowned. "Then what is?"

"I've always despised M'man." She spoke so low, he stopped breathing so he could hear her. "For being so withdrawn, so uncaring, so very selfish. I never thought I was like her, but maybe I am." She finally looked at him, and he saw crystal tears in her eyes. "Maybe I am."

Something in his chest twisted. Harry bent his head and licked the salt from her cheeks. He kissed her gently, softly, feeling the tremble beneath his mouth, wishing he knew the words to comfort her.

"I'm sorry," she sighed. "I don't mean to lay all my woes on your shoulders."

"You love your sister," he said. "And I would bear your woes, my lady, whatever they might be."

He felt the brush of her lips against his collarbone. "Thank you."

He listened, but she said no more, and, after a while, her breath evened out into sleep. But Harry stayed awake long into the night, staring at the dark and holding his lady.

Chapter Twelve

Lady Georgina's rump, smooth and soft, nestled against his morning bone-on. Harry opened his eyes. She'd spent the night again. Her shoulder was a dim outline in front of him. His arm was draped over her hip, and he curved his hand, cupping her belly.

She didn't move, her soft breathing slow in sleep.

He tilted his head forward so that her hair tickled his nose. He could smell that exotic scent she wore, and his cock throbbed, like a trained dog sitting up at his master's signal. He searched through her hair until he found the back of her neck, warm and damp with sleep. He opened his mouth to taste her.

She mumbled and hunched her shoulder.

He smiled and inched his hand down, slowly, slyly, until he felt her bush tangling about his fingers. He touched her pearl. That bit of female flesh had been his greatest discovery as a young man. The revelation that women held such secrets in their bodies had been heady. He didn't even recall the face of his first lover, but he could remember his awe at the way women were made.

He flicked his lady's pearl now. Not hard, barely a

feather touch, really. She didn't move, so he grew bolder and pressed down gently. Sort of petted. Her hips twitched. Harry licked the back of her neck and could almost taste what he'd licked last night—the place where his fingers played. She had liked that, his lady, when he'd kissed and licked and sucked her there. She'd arched her back and moaned so loudly he'd wanted to laugh out loud. Now he slowly stroked, playing with her sleek, soft folds, and felt her wetness build. His cock was almost aching, as hard as he could ever remember it. He lifted her upper leg and draped it over his hip. Her breathing hitched, and he felt a smile break his face.

Harry took his prick in hand and guided it to that warm, wet place. He flexed his arse and slid in, so tight, so smooth, he wanted to groan in pain and in pleasure. He shoved again, gently but steadily, and slid farther in. One more time, and the hair around his cock met her bum. She was panting. He lowered her leg and finally had to groan aloud. *So perfect.* Harry reached around and found her pearl again. He pressed. Christ, he could feel her squeezing around him. Instead of thrusting, he ground against her, pressing that part of her until she squeezed again.

"Harry," she moaned.

"Shh," he whispered, kissing the back of her neck.

She was pushing back against him. So impatient. He grinned and ground some more.

"Harry."

"Dearling."

"Tup me, Harry."

And he thrust hard, in surprise and in pure lust. Good God, he never thought she'd know that word, let alone say it.

"Ohhh, yes," she breathed.

He was humping now, nearly out of control, and her moans were so erotic. Each time was better than before, and he thought uneasily that it was possible he could never get enough of her. That he'd always want her this much. But then he felt her spasm around him as he gripped her hips and that thought fled. It was so agonizingly good that he nearly forgot; he was almost too late. But in the end, he pulled his cock out of her in time and spent, shuddering, in the sheets next to her.

He stroked her hip and tried to calm his breathing. "Good morning, my lady."

"Mmm." She turned to face him. Her face was flushed and sleepy and satisfied. "Good morning, Harry." Lady Georgina pulled his face to hers and kissed him.

It was a light, gentle touch, but it made something in his chest contract. Harry knew suddenly that he would do anything for her, his lady. Lie. Steal. Kill.

Relinquish his pride.

Was this how Da had felt? He sat up and grabbed his trousers.

"Are you always this active in the morning?" she asked behind him. "Because I must tell you that some do not consider it a virtue."

He stood up and pulled on his shirt. "I'm sorry, my lady." He finally turned to face her.

She was propped on one elbow, the bed linens about her waist. Her orange hair cascaded around her white shoulders, tangled and wanton. Her nipples were pale rose-brown, darker pink at the tips. He'd never seen a more beautiful woman in his life.

He turned away.

"I'm not exactly disappointed. More like tired," Lady Georgina said. "I don't suppose you ever just lay around in bed in the morning?"

"No." He finished buttoning his shirt.

He started into the other room and heard a faint scrape. He stopped.

It came again.

He looked back at her. "I thought your brother didn't mind."

Lady Georgina looked as indignant as a naked woman could. "He wouldn't dare."

Harry merely raised an eyebrow and closed the door to the bedroom. He crossed to the cottage door and opened it. On the step huddled a small bundle of rags. What...? The mop of hair raised its head, and Harry stared into the face of the boy he'd seen at the Pollard cottage.

"She went drinking and didn't come back." The boy said it flatly, as if he'd been expecting to be abandoned someday.

"You'd best come in," Harry replied.

The boy hesitated, then stood and ducked inside.

Lady Georgina poked her head around the corner of the bedroom door. "Who is it, Harry?" She caught sight of the small shape. "Oh."

Boy and lady stared at each other.

Harry put the kettle on for tea.

She recovered first. "I'm Lady Georgina Maitland from the manor. What's your name?"

The boy merely stared.

"Best to nod when a lady talks to you, lad," Harry said.

She frowned. "I hardly think that's necessary."

But the boy tugged his forelock and dipped his head.

Lady Georgina sidled into the room. She'd thrown a bed linen over her gown from the night before. Harry remembered he'd torn the bodice. "Do you know his name?" she whispered in his ear.

He shook his head. "Would you like tea? I don't have much else. Some bread and butter."

Lady Georgina brightened, whether at the offer of food or something to do he wasn't sure. "We can make toast," she said.

Harry cocked an eyebrow, but she'd already found the bread and butter, the knife, and a bent fork. She hacked at the bread and sawed off a shapeless lump.

All three of them stared at it.

She cleared her throat. "I think cutting may be more of a man's job." She handed the knife to Harry. "Now, don't make the slices too thick or they won't toast and they'll have that awful spongy bit in the center. And it's important they're not too thin or they'll burn, and I detest burnt toast, don't you?" She turned to the boy, who nodded his head.

"I'll do my best," Harry said.

"Good. I'll butter. And I suppose"—she looked critically at the boy—"you can toast. You *do* know how to toast bread properly, don't you?"

The lad nodded and took the fork as if it were the sword of King Arthur.

Soon there was a pile of crusty bread, dripping with butter, in the center of the table. Lady Georgina poured tea, and the three of them sat down to break their fast.

"I wish I could just stay here," she said, licking butter from her fingers, "but I suppose I shall have to return to the manor at least to dress properly."

"Did you leave word to have the carriage come for you?" Harry asked. If she hadn't, he would lend her his horse.

"I saw a carriage this morning," the boy piped up.

"You mean waiting on the drive?" Lady Georgina asked.

"No." The boy swallowed a huge mouthful. "It was going up the drive at a gallop, fair flew by, it did."

Lady Georgina and Harry looked at each other.

"Black with red trim?" she asked. The color of Tony's carriage.

The boy reached for his fifth piece of toast and shook his head. "Blue. All over blue."

Lady Georgina gave an exclamation and choked on her tea.

Harry and the boy stared at her.

"Oscar," she gasped.

He raised an eyebrow.

"My middle brother."

Harry set his teacup down. "Just how many brothers do you have, my lady?"

"Three."

"Hell."

"YOUR LAND STEWARD, GEORGIE?" Oscar picked up an iced bun from the tray Cook had prepared. "It's just not the thing, darling. I mean"—he waved the bun—"either one should choose someone from one's own class or go all the way and seduce a brawny young stable hand."

Oscar grinned at George, his treacle-brown eyes crinkling devilishly at the corners. His hair was darker than Tony's, almost black. Only when he stood in sunlight could you sometimes make out the red highlights.

"You aren't helping." Tony pinched the bridge of his nose between forefinger and thumb.

"Yes, Oscar," Ralph, the youngest Maitland brother, put in his two pence. Gangly and large-boned, his frame was just beginning to show the bulk of manhood. "Georgina couldn't seduce anyone. She's not married. He must have seduced *her,* the bounder."

Oscar and Tony stared at Ralph for a moment, apparently stunned into silence by his recitation of the obvious.

George sighed, and not for the first time since entering her library. *Stupid. Stupid. Stupid.* At first sight of Oscar's carriage she should've tucked her tail between her legs and made a run for the hills. They might not have found her for days; weeks, if she'd been lucky. She could've slept under the stars and lived on wild strawberries and dew—never mind that strawberries didn't fruit in September. Instead, she'd meekly dressed in her most demure gown and presented herself to her three younger brothers.

Who were all now glaring at her. "Actually, I believe it was a mutual seduction, if that's important."

Ralph looked puzzled, Tony groaned, and Oscar laughed, nearly choking on a mouthful of his bun.

"No, that's not important," Tony said. "What is important—"

"Is that you break it off at once." Oscar finished for him. He started to shake a finger at George and realized he still held the bun. He looked around for a plate and set his bun down. "Now, after you have married a suitable gentleman, *then* you may take up with whoever—"

"I think not!" Ralph jumped to his feet, an effective move, since he was the tallest. "Georgina isn't like the macaronis and libertines and whores you hang about with. She's—"

"I have never, *ever,* in my entire life, consorted with macaronis." Oscar arched an awful eyebrow at his younger brother.

"Gentlemen, please," Tony said. "Save your teasing for later. George, what do you plan to do with your land steward? Do you want to marry him?"

"I say!"

"But, Tony!" Both Oscar and Ralph started.

Tony held up a hand, silencing them. "George?"

George blinked. What did she want from Harry? To be close to him, she knew, but beyond that, matters became complicated. Why, oh why, couldn't she muddle along as she always had?

"Because," Tony said, "much as I hate to admit it, Oscar and Ralph are right. You must either break it off or marry the fellow. You aren't the type of lady to engage in this kind of behavior."

Oh, Lord. George's chest felt suddenly tight, as if someone had crept up behind her and yanked her corset strings taut. She always felt this sensation at the thought of marriage. What could she say? "Well..."

"He kills sheep. Violet says so in her letter." Ralph crossed his arms. "Georgina cannot marry a madman."

No wonder Violet was hiding. She must've sent letters to all three of their brothers. George narrowed her eyes. Her sister was probably in the hills at this very moment, trying to figure out exactly how one went about drinking dew.

"You've been reading my mail again." Oscar selected a tart from the tray, apparently having forgotten the bun, and shook it at Ralph. "That letter was to me. Yours said nothing about sheep."

Ralph opened his mouth and closed it a few times, like

a mule unsure of the bit between its teeth. "How would you know that if you hadn't been reading my letters?"

Oscar smirked in a loathsome way. One day someone was going to hit him. "I'm older than you. It's my duty to keep tabs on my impressionable young brother."

Crash!

Everyone jerked around to the fireplace, where shards of glass lay on the hearth.

Tony leaned on the mantel and frowned sternly back. "I hope you didn't care for that crystal vase, George?"

"Uh, no, not at—"

"Good," Tony clipped, "Now, then, Edifying as this display of brotherly love is, I think we've wandered from the main point." He held up a hand and ticked off his large-knuckled fingers. "One, do you think Harry Pye is a madman going about the countryside killing Granville's sheep?"

"No." That might be the only thing she was sure of.

"Fine. Ah. Ah." Tony shook his head at Ralph, who'd begun to protest. "Do you both trust George's judgment?"

"Of course," Ralph said.

"Implicitly," Oscar replied.

Tony nodded, then turned back to her. "Two, do you want to marry Harry Pye?"

"But, Tony, a land steward!" Oscar burst out. "You know he's only in it for..." He stopped and looked flustered. "Sorry, Georgie."

George tilted her chin away. She felt as if something fluttered in her throat, impeding the air.

Only Tony met the objection head-on. "Do you think he wants your money, George?"

"No." *Beastly, beastly brothers.*

He raised his eyebrows and stared pointedly at Oscar.

Oscar threw up his arms and pushed his open palms at Tony. "Fine!" Oscar went to brood by the window, taking his plate of food with him.

"Do you want to marry him?" Tony persisted.

"I don't know!" She couldn't breathe. When had it come to marriage? Marriage was like a fluffy coverlet that enveloped its occupants closer and closer, the air growing thin and stale, until they stifled to death and didn't even realize they were already dead.

Tony closed his eyes for a moment, then opened them. "I know you've avoided marriage thus far, and I can understand. We all can."

At the window, Oscar shrugged one shoulder.

Ralph looked at his feet.

Tony just stared at her. "If you've given yourself to this man, don't you think the choice has already been made?"

"Maybe." George got to her feet. "Maybe not. But in either case, I won't be pushed. Give me some time to think."

Oscar looked up from the window and exchanged glances with Tony.

"We'll give you time," Tony said, and the sympathy in his eyes made her want to cry.

George bit her lip and turned to a nearby wall of books. She trailed a fingertip over the spines. Behind her she heard Ralph say, "Up for a bit of a ride, Oscar?"

"What?" Oscar sounded irritable—and like his mouth was full again. "Are you mad? It's begun to rain."

A sigh. "Come with me, anyway."

"Why? Oh. *Ooh.* Yes, of course." Her two younger brothers quietly exited the room.

George almost smiled. Oscar had always been the least perceptive of her siblings. She turned to look behind her. Tony was frowning into the fire. She winced. Oh, damn, she'd forgotten to tell him yesterday.

Tony must have uncanny peripheral vision. He glanced up sharply. "What?"

"Lord, you're not going to like this. I meant to tell you right away and then..." She turned over a palm. "I'm afraid there's another sisterly problem you must deal with."

"Violet?"

George sighed. "Violet has gotten herself into a bit of a fix."

He raised his eyebrows.

"She was seduced this summer."

"Bloody hell, George," Tony said, his voice more sharp than if he'd yelled. "Why didn't you tell me at once? Is she all right?"

"Yes, she's fine. And I'm sorry, but I only got the story out of her yesterday." George blew out a breath. She was so weary, but it was best to get it over with. "She didn't want to tell you; she thought you'd make her marry him."

"That is the usual response to a lady of good family being compromised." Tony frowned at her, his eyebrows ferocious. "Is the fellow suitable?"

"No." George pressed her lips together. "He has been threatening her. He says he'll expose her if she doesn't marry him."

He stood still for a moment before the fireplace, a big hand propped against the mantel. One forefinger tapped slowly on the marble. She held her breath. Tony could be unbelievably stuffy and conventional at times. It probably came from growing up the heir.

"I don't like the sound of that," he said abruptly, and George let out her breath. "Who is this man?"

"Leonard Wentworth. It took me forever to get it out of her. She'd only tell me when I promised that I wouldn't let you force her into marriage."

"Glad to know I've been cast as the choleric father in this drama," Tony muttered. "I've never heard of Wentworth. What is he?"

George shrugged. "I had to think about it, but he must be one of the young men who came up with Ralph this summer. Remember when you had that hunting party in June?"

Tony nodded. "There were three or four friends with Ralph. Two of them I know, the Alexander brothers; they're from an old Leicestershire family."

"And Freddy Barclay was there; he didn't bag any grouse, and the others teased him about it unmercifully."

"But one of the others shot ten birds," Tony said thoughtfully. "He was older than the rest of Ralph's party, nearer my own age."

"Violet says he's five and twenty." George grimaced. "Can you imagine a man of that age seducing a girl not even out of the schoolroom? And he's pressing her for marriage."

"A fortune hunter," Tony said. "Damn it. I'll have to question Ralph about him and find out where to look for this scoundrel."

"I'm sorry," George said. Nothing she did recently seemed to work out well.

Tony's wide mouth softened. "No, I'm sorry. I shouldn't get cross at you for this man's sins. Oscar, Ralph, and I will sort this out, never fear."

"What will you do?" George asked.

Tony frowned, his heavy brows drawn together. He looked just like Father. For a moment he didn't answer, and she thought perhaps he hadn't heard. Then he looked up, and she drew in her breath at the steel she saw in his blue eyes.

"What will I do? Make him understand how very foolish it is to threaten a Maitland," he said. "He won't be bothering Violet again."

George opened her mouth to ask for details, then thought better of it. This was one time when it might be better to mind her own business. "Thank you."

He quirked an eyebrow. "It's one of my duties, after all, to look after the family."

"Father didn't."

"No," Tony said. "He didn't. And between him and M'man it's a wonder that we survived at all. But then that's part of the reason I vowed to do better."

"And you have." If only she had done as well with her own responsibilities.

"I've tried." He smiled at her, his wide mouth curved boyishly, and she realized how rarely he smiled anymore. But then his smile died. "I'll take care of Violet's problem, but I can't do the same for you until you tell me which way I should start. You need to make a decision about Harry Pye, George, and you need to make it soon."

"DOES SHE HAVE A GOLDEN cunt, Pye?"

Harry stiffened and slowly turned to the speaker, his left hand flexed and loose by his side. He'd taken the boy on his rounds this morning after Lady Georgina had left his cottage; then they'd ridden to West Dikey. He'd hoped to find a pair of shoes for the lad.

The oaf who'd spoken was the big-fisted man from the brawl at the Cock and Worm. The knife wound that Harry had given him stood out a livid red on his face. It started at one side of his forehead, slashed across the bridge of his nose, and ended on the far cheek. He was flanked on either side by two big men. They'd chosen a good place to confront him. A deserted lane, not much more than an alley. The stink of the open sewer running through the middle of the lane was powerful in the sun.

"You ought to put a poultice on that," Harry said, nodding at the crusted scar on the man's face. It was oozing pus.

The other man grinned, stretching the end of the scar on his cheek until it broke open and leaked blood. "Does she give you pretty things for your stud work?"

"Maybe she dresses his pud with gold rings." One of the man's cronies giggled.

Beside him, Harry felt the boy tense. He laid his right hand on his shoulder. "I can open that wound for you, if you like," Harry said gently. "Drain the poison away."

"Poison. Aye, you'd know about *poison*, wouldn't you, Pye?" The scarred man sneered in amusement at his own wit. "Hear you've turned your poisoning from animals to women now."

Harry frowned. What?

His opponent correctly interpreted his frown. "Didn't you know, then?" The man cocked his head. "They found her body on th' moor this morning."

"Who?"

"That's a hanging offense, that is. Murder. There're those who say your neck should be stretched right away. But you've been busy with your mistress, haven't you?"

The big man leaned forward, and Harry's left hand dropped to his boot.

"Does she tell you when to spend, Pye? Or maybe she doesn't let you spend at all. Would soil her fine, white body, wouldn't it? Having common spunk on her. Don't bother with that." He gestured to where Harry's hand hovered near his knife. "I wouldn't want to hurt a man-whore."

The three men walked off, laughing.

Harry froze. *Whore*. The name they'd called his mother so long ago.

Whore.

The boy moved beneath his hand. Harry looked down and realized he was clutching his shoulder too tightly. The boy didn't complain, just shrugged a bit.

"What's your name?" Harry asked.

"Will." The boy looked up at him and wiped a hand across his nose. "My ma's a whore."

"Aye." Harry released Will's shoulder. "So was mine."

GEORGE PACED THE LIBRARY THAT EVENING. The windows were black mirrors, reflecting the darkness outside. For a second she paused and studied her ghostly reflection. Her hair was perfect, a rarity, but Tiggle had redressed it after supper. She wore a lavender gown, one of her favorites, and her pearl drops. Perhaps she flattered herself, but she felt she looked well, almost handsome, in the frock.

If only she felt as confident inside.

She was beginning to think that the library was the wrong place for this meeting. But what other choice was there, really? With her brothers in residence at Woldsly, she couldn't ask Harry to her rooms, and the last two times she'd gone to his cottage… George felt her face warm. They hadn't done much talking, had they? So there wasn't an alternative. But still. The library felt somehow wrong.

The sound of booted footsteps rang in the hall. George squared her shoulders and faced the door, a lonely offering waiting for the dragon. Or maybe the leopard.

"Good evening, my lady." Harry prowled into the library.

Definitely the leopard. She felt the hairs stand on the back of her neck. Harry gave off a sort of volatile energy tonight.

"Good evening. Won't you have a seat?" She gestured to the settee.

He flicked his eyes in the direction she indicated and back to her. "I think not."

Oh, dear. "Well…" George inhaled and tried to remember what she'd planned to say to him. Her speech had made sense in her rooms. But now, with Harry staring at her, *now* it fell apart like wet paper tissue.

"Yes?" He cocked his head as though to better hear her thoughts. "Do you want it on the settee or the floor?"

Her eyes widened in confusion. "I don't—"

"The chair?" Harry asked. "Where do you want to make love?"

"Oh." She felt a flush start on her cheeks. "I haven't called you here for that."

"No?" His eyebrows raised. "Are you sure? You must've ordered me here for something."

"I didn't order you…" She closed her eyes and shook her head and began again. "We need to talk."

"Talk." The word was flat. "Do you want my resignation?"

"No. What makes you think that?"

"My lady." Harry laughed, a nasty, hoarse sound. "I may be merely your servant, but credit me with some intelligence. You were closeted with your three aristocratic brothers all day, and then you summoned me to your library. What is this if not a dismissal?"

She was losing control of the conversation. She spread her hands helplessly. "I just need to talk to you."

"What do you wish to talk about, my lady?"

"I...I don't know." George squeezed her eyes shut, trying to think. He wasn't making this any easier for her. "Tony is pressing me to make a decision about us. And I don't know what to do."

"Are you asking me what to do?"

"I..." She drew a breath. "Yes."

"It seems simple enough to me, poor commoner that I am," Harry said. "Let us continue as we have."

George looked down at her hands. "But that's just it. I can't."

When she looked up again, Harry's expression was so blank she might've been staring in the eyes of a dead man. Lord, how she'd begun to hate that wooden face. "Then you'll have my resignation by tomorrow."

"No." She wrung her hands. "That isn't what I want at all."

"But you can't have it both ways." Harry seemed suddenly weary. His beautiful green eyes were dulled by something close to despair. "You can either be my lover or I will leave. I'll not stay as some convenience for you, like that gelding in your stable here. You ride him when at Woldsly and forget him the rest of the year. Do you even know his name?"

Her mind went blank. The fact was, she didn't know the horse's name. "It isn't like that."

"No? Pardon, but what is it like, my lady?" Anger was breaking through Harry's wooden mask, painting scarlet flames across his cheekbones. "Am I a stud for hire? Nice for a romp in bed, but after the tupping, not good enough to show your family?"

George could feel a blush heat her own cheeks. "Why are you being so crude?"

"Am I?" Harry was suddenly in front of her, standing too close. "You must forgive me, my lady. That's what you get when you take a common lover: a crude man." His fingers framed her face, his thumbs hot against her temples. She felt her heart skitter in her chest at his touch. "Isn't that what you wanted when you chose me to take your maidenhead?"

She could smell spirits on his breath. Was that the reason for this hostility? Was he drunk? If so, he showed no other signs. She inhaled deeply to steady her own emotions, to try to counter his terrible sorrow. "I—"

But he would not let her speak. He whispered in a cruel, hard voice instead, "A man so crude he takes you against a door? A man so crude he makes you scream when you come? A man so crude he doesn't have the grace to melt away when he's no longer wanted?"

George shuddered at the awful words and scrambled to frame a reply. But it was too late. Harry claimed her mouth and sucked on her bottom lip. He pulled her to him roughly and ground his hips against hers. There it was again, that wild, desperate desire. He bunched her skirts in one hand, pulling them up. George heard a tear but couldn't bring herself to care.

He reached underneath and found her mound with ruthless accuracy. "*This* is what you get with a common lover." He speared two fingers into her sheath.

She gasped at the sudden intrusion, feeling him stretch her as he stroked with his fingers. She shouldn't feel anything, shouldn't respond when he—

His thumb pushed down on her most sensitive spot. "No finesse, no pretty words. Just hard cock and hot cunny." His tongue trailed across her cheek. "And your cunny is hot, my lady," he whispered into her ear. "It's fairly dripping on my hand."

She moaned then. It was impossible for her not to respond to him, even when he touched her in anger. He covered her mouth with his own, swallowing her wail, ravishing her at will. Until she broke all at once and waves of pleasure rushed over her so fast she felt dizzy. George shook in the after-tremors, clinging to Harry as he bent her backward over his arm and fed on her mouth. His fingers left her to stroke over her hip soothingly.

His mouth gentled.

Then Harry broke away to hiss in her ear, "I told you, decide what you want before coming to me. I'm not a goddamned lapdog you can pick up and pet and then send away again. You can't get rid of me that easily."

George stumbled, both from his words and from the fact that he'd let her go. She clutched at the back of a chair. "Harry, I—"

But he'd already left the room.

Chapter Thirteen

Harry woke with the taste of stale ale in his mouth. He waited a moment before opening his eyes. Although it had been a very long time, he never quite forgot the painful torture of sunlight and a hangover. When he finally cracked open his dry eyes, he saw the room was too bright for early morning. He'd overslept. Groaning, he lurched up and sat for a moment on the edge of his bed, head in hands, feeling uncommonly old.

God, what an idiot he'd been to drink too much yesterday eve. He'd been trying to track down the rumors about the woman poisoned on the moor, had gone first to the White Mare and then to the Cock and Worm, but Dick wasn't at his tavern, and no one else would speak to him. In every face he'd seen suspicion and, in some, loathing. Meanwhile, what the scarred man had said to him in West Dikey had sounded in his skull like a chant. *Man-whore. Man-whore. Man-whore.* Perhaps he'd been trying to drown the words when he'd drunk multiple tankards of ale last night.

A clatter came from the cottage's main room.

Harry swiveled his head carefully in that direction and

sighed. Will was probably hungry. He staggered to the door and stared.

The fire blazed and a steaming teapot sat on the table.

Will crouched on the floor, strangely still. "I dropped the spoons. I'm sorry," he whispered. He hunched his body as if he was trying to make himself smaller, maybe disappear altogether.

Harry knew that posture. The boy expected to be hit.

He shook his head. "Doesn't matter." His voice sounded like the scrape of a shovel on stony ground. He cleared his throat and sat down. "Made tea, have you?"

"Aye." Will stood up, poured a cup, and carefully handed it to him.

"Ta." Harry sipped and scalded his throat. He winced and waited, but his stomach felt better, so he took another mouthful.

"I cut some bread for toast, too." Will brought a plate for his inspection. "They're not so nice as yours, though."

Harry looked at the uneven slices with a jaundiced eye. He wasn't sure his belly could take solids at the moment, but the boy needed praise. "Better than Lady Georgina's try."

His painful smile died as he thought about what he'd said and done to his lady last night. He gazed at the fire. He'd have to go apologize sometime today. Assuming she would still talk to him, that is.

"I'll toast them." Will must be used to sudden, awkward silences. He went about skewering the bread on the crooked fork and finding a spot to hold it over the fire.

Harry watched him. Will had no father, thanks to Granville, nor mother, either. Just that old woman, his grandmother, and a less loving woman he'd rarely seen.

Yet here he was, competently tending to an adult sick from too much drink. Perhaps he'd had to care for his grandmother after a night of swilling. The thought was bitter in Harry's mouth.

He took another sip of tea.

"Here we are, then," Will said, sounding like an elderly woman. He set a pile of buttered toast on the table and bustled around to another chair.

Harry bit into a piece of toast and licked melting butter off his thumb. He noticed that Will was looking at him. He nodded. "Good."

The boy smiled, revealing a gap in his upper teeth.

They ate companionably for a while.

"Did you have a fight with her?" Will swiped up a drip of butter and licked it off his finger. "Your lady, I mean."

"You could say that." Harry poured himself more tea, stirring in a large spoonful of sugar this time.

"My gran said gentry was evil. Didn't care if regular folk lived or died, so long as they'd gold plates to eat off of." Will traced a circle on the table with a greasy finger. "But your lady was nice."

"Aye. Lady Georgina's not like most."

"And she's pretty." Will nodded to himself and took another piece of toast.

Aye, pretty as well. Harry looked out the cottage window, a feeling of uneasiness beginning to build in him. Would she let him apologize?

"'Course, she's not much of a cook. Couldn't cut the bread straight. You'll have to help her with that." Will wrinkled his forehead in thought. "Does she eat off of gold plates?"

"I don't know."

Will eyed him suspiciously, as if Harry might be with-holding important information. Then his look turned to pity. "Haven't you been invited to supper, then?"

"No." Well, there'd been that dinner in her rooms, but he wasn't telling Will about that. "I've had tea with her, though."

"She didn't have gold plates for that?"

"No." Why was he explaining himself?

Will nodded sagely. "You'll have to go to supper before you know." He finished his toast. "Have you brought her presents?"

"Presents?"

Will's pitying look was back. "All girls like presents; that's what my gran said. And I think she must be right. I like presents."

Harry propped his chin in his hands and felt wire-stiff stubble. His head was feeling bad again, but Will seemed to think presents were important. And this was the most the boy had talked since he'd shown up the day before.

"What kind of presents?" Harry asked.

"Pearls, gold boxes, sweetmeats." Will waved a piece of toast. "Things like that. A horse would be good. Have you got any horses?"

"Just the one."

"Oh." Will sounded disappointed in him. "Then I suppose you can't give her that."

Harry shook his head. "And she has many more horses than my one."

"Then what can you give her?"

"I don't know."

He didn't know what she wanted from him. Harry frowned into the dregs of his tea. What could a man like him give a lady like her? Not money or a house. She already had that. And the physical love he gave her—any halfway competent man could do as well. What could he give her that she didn't already have? Maybe nothing. Maybe she would realize that soon enough, and especially after last night, choose never to see him again.

Harry stood. "More important than a present, I need to speak to Lady Georgina today." He moved to the cupboard, took down his shaving things, and began stropping his razor.

Will looked at the dirty plates on the table. "I can wash these."

"Good boy."

Will must have refilled the kettle after making tea. It was already full and boiling. Harry divided the hot water between his basin and a big bowl the boy could wash the dishes in. The little mirror he used for shaving showed a ragged face. Harry frowned, then carefully started scraping the stubble from his cheeks. His razor was old but very sharp, and a nick on his chin wouldn't help his appearance. Behind him, he could hear Will swishing in the water.

By the time Will finished the dishes, Harry was as ready as he was ever going to be. He'd washed, brushed his hair, and changed into a clean shirt. His head still pounded steadily, but the circles under his eyes had begun to fade.

Will looked him over. "You'll do, I guess."

"Ta."

"Am I to stay here?" The lad's face was too stoic for his young age.

Harry hesitated. "Would you like to see the Woldsly stables while I speak to my lady?"

Will was immediately on his feet. "Yes, please."

"Then come on." Harry led the way out the door. The boy could ride behind him on the back of his horse.

Outside, clouds gathered in the sky. But it hadn't yet rained today, and saddling the mare would take time. It was unreasonable, but he was anxious to see Lady Georgina.

"Let's walk."

The boy followed at his heels, silent, but with suppressed excitement. They were almost to the Woldsly drive when Harry heard the rumbling of carriage wheels. He quickened his pace. The sound grew rapidly closer.

He broke into a run.

Just as he burst from the cover of the copse, a carriage passed, shaking the ground beneath his feet and sending up globs of mud. He glimpsed her ginger hair, then the carriage turned the corner and was gone, only the diminishing sound of wheels marking its passage.

"Don't think you'll be able to talk to her today."

Harry had forgotten Will. He stared blindly down at the boy panting at his side. "No, not today."

A fat raindrop splattered on his shoulder, and then the clouds let go.

TONY'S CARRIAGE JOLTED AROUND the corner, and George swayed as she peered out the window. It had begun to rain again, soaking the already sodden pastures, dragging tree branches earthward, and turning everything into the same gray-brown color. Monotonous veils of dingy water fell, blurring the landscape and trickling down the window like tears. From inside the carriage it appeared that the whole world wept, overcome by a grief that would not fade.

"Perhaps it won't stop."

"What?" Tony asked.

"The rain," George said. "Perhaps it won't stop. Perhaps it will continue forever until the mud in the highway turns to a stream and rises up and becomes a sea and we float away." She traced a finger through the condensation on the inside of the window, making squiggly lines. "Do you think your carriage is buoyant?"

"No," Tony said. "But I shouldn't worry. The rain will stop sometime, even if it doesn't seem so at the moment."

"Mmm." She stared out the window. "And if I don't care if it goes on? Perhaps I wouldn't mind floating away. Or sinking."

She was doing the right thing, everyone assured her so. Leaving Harry was the only proper choice left to her. He was of a lower class, and he resented the difference in their ranks. Last night, he'd been ugly in his resentment; and yet, she couldn't fault him. Harry Pye wasn't meant to be anyone's lapdog. She hadn't thought she was confining him, but he obviously felt demeaned. There was no future for them, an earl's daughter and a land steward. They knew that; *everyone* knew that. This was a natural conclusion to an affair that should never have been begun in the first place.

But, still, George couldn't shake the feeling that she was running away.

As if reading her thoughts, Tony said, "It's the correct decision."

"Is it?"

"There was no other."

"I feel like a coward," she mused, still looking out the window.

"You're not a coward," he said softly. "This course

wasn't easy for you, I know. Cowards are people who take the least difficult path, not the hardest."

"Yet I've abandoned Violet when she needs me most," George objected.

"No, you haven't," Tony said firmly. "You've turned her problem over to me. I've sent Oscar and Ralph ahead of us to London. By the time we arrive, they should have learned where this cad lives. In the meantime, rusticating for another few weeks in the country won't hurt her, and she has Miss Hope to keep her company. That is what we pay her for, after all," he finished dryly.

But Euphie had failed Violet once already. George closed her eyes. And what about the poisoned sheep— the reason she'd traveled to Yorkshire in the first place? The attacks were growing more frequent. As she'd left, George had overheard two footmen talking about a poisoned woman. She should've stopped and found out if the dead woman was connected to the sheep, but instead she'd let Tony hustle her out the door. Once she'd made the decision to leave Woldsly, it was as if a strange lethargy had taken over her body. It was so hard to concentrate. So hard to know what to do. She felt wrong in her bones, but she couldn't seem to make things right.

"You must stop thinking about him," Tony said.

His tone made George glance at her brother, sitting in the blood-red leather seat across from hers. Tony looked sympathetic and worried. And sad, his shaggy eyebrows drawn down. Sudden tears clouded her eyes, and she turned to the window again, although she couldn't see a thing now.

"It's just that he was so . . . good. He seemed to understand me in a way nobody has before, not even you or

Aunt Clara. And I couldn't figure him out." She laughed under her breath. "Maybe that's what attracted me to him. He was like a puzzle that I could have spent the rest of my life studying and never grow tired of." They rumbled over a bridge. "I don't think I'll ever find that again."

"I'm so sorry," Tony said.

George laid her head back on the seat. "You're awfully kind for a brother. Did you know that?"

"I've been most lucky in my allotment of sisters." Tony smiled.

George tried to smile back but found she couldn't. She went back to looking out the carriage window instead. They passed a field of drenched sheep, poor miserable creatures. Could sheep swim? Maybe they'd float if their pasture flooded, like tufts of down in a puddle.

They were already out of her lands, and in another day Yorkshire would be behind them altogether. By the end of the week she'd be in London, resuming her life as if this trip had never happened. Three or four months from now, Harry, acting as her land steward, might write to ask if she wanted him to present his report on her lands in person. And she, having just returned from a soiree, might turn the letter over in her hand and muse, *Harry Pye. Why, I once lay in his arms. I looked up into his illuminated face as he joined his flesh with mine, and I was alive.* She might toss the letter on her desk and think, *But that was so long ago now and in a different place. Perhaps it was only a dream.*

She might think that.

George closed her eyes. Somehow she knew that there would never come a day when Harry Pye was not her first memory when she woke and her last thought as she drifted into sleep. She would remember him all the days of her life.

Remember and regret.

"TOLD YOU NOT TO HAVE no truck with aristo ladies." Dick Crumb sat down across from Harry without invitation late that afternoon.

Wonderful. Now he was getting romantic advice from Dick. Harry studied the Cock and Worm's proprietor. Dick looked like he'd been sampling too much of his own brew. His face was creased with sleeplessness, and his hair was thinner, if that was possible.

"Aristos ain't nothing but trouble. And here's you, sticking your meat where it don't belong." Dick wiped his face.

Harry glanced at Will sitting beside him. He'd finally bought him new shoes this morning. The boy's eyes had been fixed on his feet, swinging under the table, the entire time they'd been in the tavern. But now he was staring at Dick.

"Here." Harry dug a few coppers out of his pocket. "Go see if the baker has any sweet buns left."

Will's attention was immediately caught by the coins. He grinned up at Harry, grabbed the money, and was out the door in a flash.

"That's Will Pollard, ain't it?" Dick asked.

"Aye," Harry said. "His gran abandoned him."

"So he's living with you now?" Dick's long forehead wrinkled in confusion, and he swiped his cloth over it. "How's that?"

"I have room. I'll have to find him a better home soon, but for now, why not?"

"I dunno. Don't he get under foot when she comes calling?" The older man leaned forward and lowered his voice, but his whisper was loud enough to be heard clear across the room.

Harry sighed. "She's gone back to London. It won't come up."

"Good." Dick took a giant gulp from the mug he'd set down in front of him when he'd joined Harry. "I know you don't want to hear this, but it's for the best. Common folk and gentry ain't meant to mix. That's the way God intended it. They stay in their marble halls with their servants to wipe their arses—"

"Dick—"

"And we do an honest day's work and go home to a hot meal. If we're lucky." Dick slammed down his mug to make his point. "And that's the way it's meant to be."

"Right." Harry hoped to stem this sermon.

No such luck.

"And what would you do with the lady if she'd have you?" the older man plowed on. "She'd have your dangly bits hanging by her bed for a bellpull afore a week was out. You'd probably have to wear a pink wig and yellow hose, learn to do that tippy-toe dancing the gentry do and beg like a dog to have your own pin money. No"—he took another swallow of ale—"that ain't no life for a man."

"I agree." Harry cast about for a change of subject. "Where's your sister? I haven't seen Janie lately."

Out came the cloth. Dick polished the dome of his head. "Oh, you know Janie. She were born a bit off, and ever since Granville got done with her, she's been even worse."

Harry slowly set down his mug. "You didn't tell me that Granville had abused Janie."

"Didn't I?"

"No. When did this happen?"

"Fifteen years ago. It wasn't long after your mother caught that fever and died." Dick wiped his face and neck almost frantically now. "Janie was five and twenty or thereabouts, a grown woman, except maybe in her head. Anyone but Granville would've respected that. Would've let her alone. But him." Dick spat onto the flagstones at his feet. "He just saw her as easy pickings."

"He raped her?"

"Maybe, at the beginning. I dunno." Dick stared off. His hand was stopped on top of his head, still holding the cloth. "I didn't know about it, see, not for a long time. She was living with me, like she does now, but Janie's ten years the younger of me. Our da had passed years before, and Janie's mum died when she were born." The big man swallowed from his mug.

Harry didn't say anything for fear of stopping the flow of the story.

"Janie's more like a niece or a daughter to me than a sister," Dick said. He took his hand away from his head and looked at the cloth blankly. "And by the time I noticed that she was sneaking out at night, it'd been going on a while." He gave a bark of laughter. "When I found out and told her to stop, she said he was going to marry her." He was silent a moment.

Harry took another drink to wash away the bile gathering in his throat. *Poor, poor Janie.*

"Can you see it?" Dick looked up, and Harry saw tears glittering in his eyes. "He was widowed, so she thought Lord Granville would marry her. Nothing I said could keep her from creeping out and meeting him at night. Went on for weeks and I thought I'd go mad. Then, of course, he dropped her. Like a dirty rag he'd wiped his spunk on."

"What did you do?"

Dick gave another bark of laughter and finally put away his cloth. "Nothing. Wasn't aught I could do. She came back and stayed to herself like a good girl. I spent a couple months worried I'd have to house another of Granville's bastards, but she was lucky." He lifted his mug to drink, noticed it was empty, and set it down again. "Probably the only time she ever lucked out in her whole life, Janie. And not much luck at that, was it?"

Harry nodded. "Dick, do you think—"

A tug at his elbow interrupted him. Will had returned so silently that the two men hadn't noticed.

"Just a moment, Will."

The boy tugged again. "She's dead."

"What?" Both men looked at the boy.

"She's dead. Me gran. She's dead." He spoke in a dull tone that worried Harry more than the news.

"How do you know?" he asked.

"They found her on the heath. A farmer and his boys out looking for a stray. In a sheep pasture." Will suddenly focused on Harry's face. "They said the sheep poisoner killed her."

Harry closed his eyes. Christ, why did the dead woman have to be Will's gran, of all people?

"No." Dick was shaking his head. "Can't be. The sheep poisoner couldn't have killed her."

"They found false parsley by her, and she was all twisted..." Will's face screwed up.

Harry put his arms around Will's shoulders and drew the boy close. "I'm sorry." The boy must still love the old witch, even after she'd thrown him out like the slops. "There, there, lad." He patted the boy's back and felt stupidly angry at Will's gran for letting herself get killed.

"You best be going," Dick's voice broke in.

Harry glanced up, puzzled. The big man was looking thoughtful—and worried.

He met Harry's eyes. "If folks think you're the poisoner, they're going to believe you did this, too."

"For God's sake, Dick." All Will needed was to believe Harry had killed his grandmother.

Will lifted his wet face from Harry's shirt.

"I didn't kill your gran, Will."

"I know, Mr. Pye."

"Good." He took out a handkerchief and gave it to the boy. "And call me Harry."

"Yes, sir." Will's lower lip began to tremble again.

"Dick's right, we best be going. It's getting late anyway." Harry studied the boy. "Are you ready?"

Will nodded.

They made their way to the tavern entrance. Already men were gathering in knots and talking. Some seemed to look up and glare at him as they passed, but he might have imagined it after Dick's comment. If Will's gran had truly been murdered by the same man who'd been killing the sheep, it did not bode well. The people hereabouts were worried about their livestock. How much more fearful would they be if they now had to worry about their children, their wives, maybe themselves?

As they neared the entrance, someone shoved him. He stumbled but had his knife in his hand almost instantly. When he turned, a wall of hostile faces stared back.

Someone whispered, "Murderer." But no one moved.

"Come on, Will." Harry slowly backed out of the Cock and Worm.

Quickly, he found his mare and boosted Will onto her back. Mounting, Harry looked around. A drunk was pissing against the tavern wall, but otherwise the darkening street was deserted. News of a murder would travel fast, but maybe night falling would delay it a bit. He should have until morning to figure out how to deal with this.

Harry chirruped to the mare and set out into the gathering dusk, Will clinging to his back. They turned onto the road home. The road passed through Granville land before going over the river to Woldsly. The lights of the town faded, leaving the dark to shroud them. No moon was out to light the road. Or to give them away.

Harry urged the mare into a trot.

"Are they going to hang you?" Will's voice sounded scared in the dark.

"No. They need more evidence than a bunch of gossip to hang a man."

Hoofbeats came from behind them.

Harry cocked his head. More than one horse. And coming up on them fast. "Wrap your arms around me, Will."

He nudged the mare into a gallop as soon as he felt the clench around his waist. The mare thundered down the road. But she was carrying two, and he knew the riders behind would soon overtake them. They were in open pasture land. Nowhere to hide. He could take the mare off the road, but in the dark she'd have a fair chance of putting her hoof in a hole and killing them all. And he had Will to think of. The boy's small hands clung to his waist. Foam flew from the mare's mouth, and Harry leaned low over her sweating neck, muttering words of encouragement. If they could make it to the ford, there were places along the bank to hide. Or they could even go into the stream if necessary and follow the water downstream.

"We're almost to the ford. We'll be all right there," Harry shouted to the boy.

Will must have been afraid, but he never made a sound. Another turn. The mare's lungs heaved like bellows. The riders behind them were growing closer, their hoofbeats louder. *There!* The mare raced down the track to the stream. Harry almost sighed in relief. Almost. Then he saw and realized there had never been any hope at all. On the stream's far side, shadows shifted in the gloom. More men on horseback were waiting for him there.

They were herding him into a trap.

Harry glanced over his shoulder. He had maybe half a minute before the riders were upon them. He hauled on the reins, cutting the poor mare's mouth. There was no help for it. The mare half reared, skidding to a stop. Harry pried Will's hands from his waist. He grabbed the boy's wrist and flung the crying child to the ground.

"Hide. Now!" Harry shook his head as the boy sobbed a protest. "There isn't time for that. You have to stay hidden—no matter what they do. Go back to Dick, tell him to get Bennet Granville. Now run!"

Harry kicked the mare and drew his knife. He didn't look back to see whether Will had done as instructed. If he could draw the attackers far enough away from Will, maybe they wouldn't bother going back for one small boy. He charged full gallop into the stream. Harry felt a grin stretch his lips just before the mare slammed into the first horse.

He was surrounded by plunging horses and foaming

water. The man nearest raised his arm, and Harry drove his knife into the exposed armpit. The man didn't even groan when he fell into the stream. Around him, the horses whinnied and the men shouted. Hands grabbed for him and Harry swung his knife viciously. Desperately. Another man fell into the stream, screaming. Then they pulled him from his horse. Someone caught his knife hand. Harry closed his right hand, the one with the missing finger—into a fist and hammered at any flesh near enough to hit. But there were many of them and only one of him, and they were raining down a storm of kicks and blows.

In the end, it was only a matter of time before he went under.

Chapter Fourteen

"Men do have their uses," Lady Beatrice Renault said as if conceding a dubious point of debate, "but giving advice on *affaires de coeur* is not one of them." She raised the dish of tea to her lips and took a small sip.

George repressed a sigh. She'd been in London over a week and up until this morning had successfully managed to avoid Aunt Beatrice. This was all Oscar's fault. If he hadn't been so careless as to leave a letter from Violet laying around, their Aunt Beatrice would never have found out about Harry and would never have felt compelled to come and lecture George on the proper way to conduct an affair. True, Oscar had placed the damning letter in the drawer of his desk, but any fool knew that would be the first place Aunt Beatrice would start browsing when the butler left her alone in the study when she'd come to call.

Definitely Oscar's fault.

"They are much too sentimental, poor dears," Aunt Beatrice continued. She bit into a piece of cake and then frowned down at it. "Is this a prune filling, Georgina? I've specifically told you that prunes do not agree with me."

George glanced at the offending slice of cake. "I believe it is chocolate cream, but I can ring for a different pastry."

Aunt Beatrice had invaded George's London town house, settled into a gilt chair in her pretty blue and white sitting room, and all but demanded tea. George thought Cook had done an outstanding job, considering she'd had no notice of potential guests.

"Humph." Lady Beatrice poked at the cake on her plate, disemboweling it. "It looks like prunes, but if you are quite sure." She took another bite, masticating thoughtfully. "As a result, they are competent—barely—at running the government but a complete wash at domestic doings."

George was at a loss for a second before remembering that her aunt had been discussing men before prunes. "Quite."

Perhaps if she feigned an attack of the vapors... But knowing Aunt Beatrice, she'd probably throw cold water in her face until George admitted consciousness and then continue with her lecture. Best to sit it out.

"Now, contrary to what men will tell you," her aunt continued, "an affair or two or more is good for a lady. Brings a certain mental alertness and, naturally, roses to the cheeks."

Lady Beatrice touched her own cheek with one manicured fingernail. It was indeed rosy, but more from rouge than nature. It was also decorated by three black velvet patches: two stars and a crescent moon.

"The most important thing for a lady to remember is to be discreet." Aunt Beatrice sipped her tea. "For instance, I have found that if one is engaged with two or more gentlemen over the same period of time, it is imperative they not find out about each other."

Aunt Beatrice was the youngest of the Littleton sisters. Aunt Clara, who'd left George her fortune, had been the eldest, and George's own mother, Sarah, the middle sister. The Littleton sisters had been considered beauties in their day, cutting a devastating swath through London society. All three sisters had married unhappily. Aunt Clara had wed an insanely religious man who had died young, leaving her childless but wealthy. Aunt Beatrice had married a much older man who had kept his wife constantly pregnant while he lived. Tragically, all her babies had died in miscarriages or stillbirth.

As for Sarah, her own mother... George took a sip of her tea. Who knew what exactly was wrong with her parents' marriage? Maybe only that her mother and father had not cared for each other. In any case, Lady Maitland was bedridden with imagined ills and had been for years.

"Even the most sophisticated man becomes like a little boy unable to share his toys," Lady Beatrice continued now. "No more than three is my motto, and really with three one has to do a fine balancing act."

George choked.

"Whatever is the matter with you, Georgina?" Lady Beatrice looked at her with annoyance.

"Nothing," George gasped. "A bit of crumb."

"Really, I do worry about the English as a race with—"

"What luck to find not one, but two examples of womanly pulchritude." George's sitting room door was flung open to reveal Oscar and a fair young man who bowed to the ladies.

Lady Beatrice frowned and lifted her cheek for Oscar's

buss. "We are busy, dear. Go away. Not you, Cecil." The other man had started to back out the door. "You may stay. You are the only man I know with any sense, and that should be encouraged."

Cecil Barclay smiled and bowed again. "Your ladyship is kind indeed."

He quirked an eyebrow at George, who patted the settee cushion next to her. She'd known Cecil and his younger brother, Freddy, since they'd all been in leading strings.

"But if Cecil stays, then I beg leave to do so also." Oscar sat down and helped himself to a slice of cake.

George glared at her brother.

Oscar mouthed *What?* at her.

She rolled her eyes in exasperation. "Will you take tea, Cecil?"

"Yes, please," Cecil said. "Oscar dragged me all over Tattersall's this morning to look at horses. He wants a matched set for his new carriage and claims none in London will do."

"Gentlemen spend entirely too much money on horseflesh," Lady Beatrice pronounced.

"What other type of flesh would you have us spend our blunt upon?" Oscar opened his wicked brown eyes wide.

Lady Beatrice tapped him overhard on the knee with her fan.

"Ow!" Oscar rubbed the spot. "I say, is this a prune filling in the cake?"

George repressed another sigh and looked out her town house windows. It wasn't raining here in London, but there was a kind of gray mist that covered everything and left behind a sticky grime. She'd made a mistake. She knew that now after more than a week away from Harry and Yorkshire. She should've stuck it out and made him talk. Or talked herself until he broke down and told her... what? His fears? Her faults? Why he didn't care for her? If it was the last, at least she would know. She wouldn't be stuck here in this limbo, not able to return to her old life and yet unable to go on with what might be a new one.

"Can you come, George?" Cecil was speaking to her.

"What?" She blinked. "I'm sorry, I'm afraid I didn't catch that last bit."

Her aunt and the gentlemen exchanged a look that said they had to make allowances for her mental state.

George grit her teeth.

"Cecil said he was going to the theater tomorrow night and wanted to know if he could escort you," Oscar explained.

"Actually, I—" George was saved from making an excuse by the entrance of her butler. She knit her brows. "Yes, Holmes?"

"I beg your pardon, my lady, but a messenger has just arrived from Lady Violet." Holmes proffered a silver plate on which lay a rather muddy letter.

George took it. "Thank you."

The butler bowed and exited.

Had Wentworth pursued Violet north? They'd thought it best to leave Violet at Woldsly in the assumption that she was safest there away from society, but perhaps they'd been wrong.

"If you don't mind?" George didn't wait for her guests' permission but used a butter knife to break the seal on the letter. Violet's handwriting sprawled frantically across the page, obliterated here and there by inkblots.

*My Dear Sister... Harry Pye beaten and arrested...
in Granville's custody... denied access... please
come at once.*

Beaten.

George's hand shook. *Oh, dear Lord, Harry.* A sob
caught in her throat. She tried to remember Violet's fondness for melodrama. Perhaps she'd overstated or otherwise
exaggerated. But, no, Violet didn't lie. If Lord Granville
had Harry in his hands, he might already be dead.

"Georgie." She looked up to find Oscar kneeling
directly in front of her. "What is it?"

Mutely, she turned the letter so he could read it.

He frowned. "But there was no concrete evidence of
his culpability, was there?"

George shook her head and drew a ragged breath.
"Lord Granville has a grudge against Harry. He doesn't
need evidence." She closed her eyes. "I should have never
left Yorkshire."

"There's no way you could have foreseen this."

She rose and started for the door.

"Where are you going?" Oscar caught her elbow.

George shook him off. "Where do you think? To him."

"Wait, I—"

She turned on her brother savagely. "I cannot wait. He
may already be dead."

Oscar held up his hands as if surrendering. "I know,
I know, Georgie. I meant I'll go with you. See what I can
do." He turned to Cecil. "Can you ride and tell Tony what's
happened?"

Cecil nodded.

"Here." Oscar pried the letter from George's hand. "Give him this. He'll need to come when he can."

"Of course, old chap." Cecil looked curious but took the letter.

"Thank you." Tears began to run down George's face.

"It's all right." Cecil started to say more, then shook his head and left.

"Well, I can't say that I approve of all this, whatever it is." Lady Beatrice had been quiet through the scene, but she rose now. "I do not like being kept in the dark. Not at all. But I will wait just this once to find out what you are all rushing about for."

"Of course, Aunt." George was already half out the door, not really listening.

"Georgina." Lady Beatrice laid a palm on her niece's tear-stained face, halting her. "Remember, dear, we cannot stay the hand of God, but we can be strong." She looked suddenly old. "Sometimes it is the only thing we can do."

"OLD MISTRESS POLLARD WAS MURDERED, plain and simple." Silas sat back in his leather armchair and looked at his younger son with satisfaction.

Bennet paced the library like a young lion. In contrast, his brother cowered in a too-small corner chair, his knees drawn nearly to his chin. Why Thomas was in the library at all, Silas couldn't fathom, but he didn't really care either way. All his attention was on his younger son.

In the week since his men had brought in Harry Pye, Bennet had railed and raged against his father. But however much he tried, he couldn't get away from that one fact: A woman had been murdered. An old woman, true, and a poor one at that. One that nobody had much cared about when alive. Nevertheless, she was human and so, no matter how decrepit, several steps up from a dead sheep.

At least in the popular estimation.

In fact, Silas had begun to wonder if he'd made a mistake in his haste to catch Pye. Local sentiment was running very high. No one liked a murderer on the loose. Had he simply left Pye to his own devices, someone might have taken matters into their own hands and lynched the bastard. He might already be dead by now. But in the long run it made very little difference. Dead now or dead in a week, either way, Pye would soon be very, very dead. And then his son would no longer be arguing with him.

"She may have been murdered, but it wasn't Harry Pye who did it." Bennet stood in front of his father's desk, arms crossed, eyes blazing.

Silas felt impatience rise in him. Everyone else believed the land steward guilty. Why couldn't his own son?

He sat forward and tapped on his desktop with a forefinger as if he could drill through the mahogany. "Hemlock killed her, same as the sheep. His carving was found by her corpse. The second carving, remember, discovered with these crimes." Silas thrust his hands forward, palms upward. "What more do you want?"

"I know you hate Harry Pye, Father, but why would he leave his own carvings by the bodies? Why incriminate himself?"

"Mayhap the man is mad," Thomas said quietly from the corner. Silas frowned at him, but Thomas was too intent on his brother to notice. "Pye's mother was a slut, after all; perhaps he inherited her bad blood."

Bennet looked pained. "Tom—"

"Don't call me that!" Thomas said shrilly. "I'm your

elder. I'm the heir. Give me the respect I deserve. You're only a—"

"Shut up!" Silas roared.

Thomas shrank at the bellow. "But, Father—"

"No more!" Silas glared until his elder son flushed blotchily; then he sat back in the chair and turned his attention back to Bennet. "What would you have me do?"

Bennet shot an apologetic glance at Thomas, which the other ignored, before answering. "I don't know."

Ah, the first outward show of uncertainty. It was like balm to his soul. "I am the magistrate for this county. I must uphold the law as I see fit."

"At least let me see him."

"No." Silas shook his head. "He's a dangerous criminal. It would not be responsible of me to let you near him."

Not until his men got a confession. The way Pye took a beating—absorbing blow after blow until he could no longer stand, until he staggered and fell, but still refused to talk—it might be several more days before he was broken. But break he would. And then Silas would hang him by the neck until dead, and no one, not the king nor God, would be able to gainsay him.

Aye, he could wait.

"Oh, for pity's sake." Bennet was pacing agitatedly now. "I've known him since we were lads. He's my—" He broke off and dismissed the sentence with a wave. "Just let me talk to him. Please."

It had been a long, long while since the boy had begged. He should know by now that begging only gave the opponent ammunition.

"No." Silas shook his head regretfully.

"He is still alive?"

Silas smiled. "Yes. Alive, but not particularly well."

Bennet's face paled. He stared at his father as if he would hit him, and Silas actually braced himself for a blow.

"Goddamn you," Bennet whispered.

"He might indeed."

Bennet swung to the study door and pulled it open. A small, scrawny boy tumbled in.

"What's this?" Silas frowned.

"He's with me. Come on, Will."

"You ought to teach your servants not to listen at doors," Silas drawled after his son.

For some reason his words caused Bennet to stop and swing around. His son looked between Silas and the boy. "You really don't know who he is, do you?"

"Should I?" Silas studied the lad. Something about his brown eyes did look familiar. He waved away the question. It didn't matter. "The boy is nobody."

"Jesus, I don't believe you." Bennet stared at him. "We're all just pawns to you, aren't we?"

Silas shook his head. "You know I'm not fond of puzzles."

But Bennet had taken the boy's shoulder and was guiding him from the room. The door shut behind them.

"He's ungrateful," Thomas whispered from the corner. "After all you did for him, after all I suffered, he's ungrateful."

"What's your point, boy?" Silas growled.

Thomas blinked, then he stood, looking oddly dignified. "I've always loved you, Father, always. I would do anything for you." Then he, too, left the room.

Silas stared after his son for a moment, then shook his

head again. He swiveled to a small door set in the wood paneling behind his desk and rapped on it. For unknown reasons, an earlier Granville had made a passage from the library to the cellars. After a small wait, the door opened. A burly man emerged, ducking his head. He was bare-chested. Heavy, muscled arms hung by his sides. The brown body hair covering his upper torso was gruesomely flecked with blood.

"Well?" Silas demanded.

"He still won't talk." The big man held out swollen hands. "My knuckles are fair bloodied, and Bud has had a go as well today."

Silas scowled. "Do I have to bring in someone else? He's only one man and not nearly your size. He should've been whistling any tune you asked by now."

"Aye, well, he's a tough bugger, that one. I've seen blokes crying like a baby after what we've been giving him."

"So you say," Silas taunted. "Wrap your hands and keep at it. He's bound to break soon, and when he does, there'll be a bonus in it for you. And if you can't do it in the next day, I'll find someone who can and replace you and your mate."

"Aye, my lord." The big man stared at Silas, suppressed anger firing behind his eyes before he turned away. Good, he'd take it out on Pye.

The door closed behind him and Silas smiled. Soon, very soon now.

SOMEWHERE WATER WAS dripping.

Slowly.

Steadily.

Endlessly.

It had dripped when he had first woken in this room, it had dripped every day since then, and it dripped now. The dripping might very well break him before the beatings did.

Harry hunched a shoulder and dragged himself painfully upright against the wall. They held him in a tiny room. He thought it must have been at least a week since they'd taken him, but time was hard to judge here. And there were hours, maybe days, that he'd lost to insensibility. There was a window the size of a child's head high on one wall, covered by a rusted iron grill. Outside, a few weeds poked through, so he knew the window was at ground level. It gave enough light to illuminate his cell when the sun was at a certain height. The walls were of damp stone, the floor of dirt. There was nothing else in the room save himself.

Well, usually, that is.

At night he could hear the scratching of tiny feet, scurrying here and there. Squeaks and rustlings would suddenly still and then begin again. Mice. Or perhaps rats.

Harry hated rats.

When he'd gone to the poorhouse in the city, he'd quickly figured out that he and Da would starve if he couldn't fight off the others to keep their ration of food. So he'd learned to fight back, fast and ruthless. The other boys and men stayed away after that.

But the rats didn't.

When dusk fell, they would come out. The wild creatures of the countryside feared people. Rats did not. They would creep right into a man's pocket to steal his last bite of bread. They would nose through a boy's hair, looking for crumbs. And if they couldn't find any leavings, they'd make their own. If a man slept too deeply, whether from drink or sickness, the rats would take a nibble. From toes or fingers or ears. There were men in the poorhouse whose ears were ragged flowers. You knew those wouldn't last much longer. And if a man died in his sleep, well, by morning sometimes you didn't know his face.

You could kill the rats, of course, if you were quick enough. Some boys even roasted them over a fire and ate them. But however hungry Harry got—and there'd been days when his insides twisted with need—he could never imagine putting that meat in his mouth. There was an evil in rats that would surely transfer to your belly and infect the soul if you ate them. And no matter how many rats you killed, there were always more.

So now at night, Harry didn't really sleep. Because there were rats out there and he knew what they could do to an injured man.

Granville's thugs had been beating him daily, sometimes twice a day, for a week now. His right eye was swollen shut, the left not much better, his lip split and resplit. At least two ribs were cracked. Several of his teeth were loose. There wasn't more than a handspan on his entire body that wasn't covered with bruises. It was only a matter of time until they hit him too hard or in the wrong place or until his body just gave out.

And then the rats...

Harry shook his head. What he couldn't understand was why Granville hadn't killed him at once. When he'd woken the day after he'd been caught at the stream, there'd been a moment when he had been stunned just to find himself alive. Why? Why capture him alive when Granville surely meant to kill him anyway? They kept telling him to confess to killing Will's gran, but surely that didn't really matter to Granville. The baron didn't need a confession to hang him. Nobody would care much about Harry's death or would protest it, except maybe Will.

Harry sighed and leaned his aching head against the mildewed stone wall. That wasn't true. His lady would care. Wherever she was, either in her fancy London town house or her Yorkshire mansion, she'd weep when she heard of her lowborn lover's death. The light would go out of her beautiful blue eyes, and her face would crumple.

In this cell he'd had many hours to ponder. Of all the things in his life that he regretted, he regretted that one thing the most: that he would cause Lady Georgina pain.

A mutter of voices and the scuff of boots on stone came from without. Harry cocked his head to listen. They were coming to beat him again. He flinched. His mind might be strong, but his body remembered and dreaded the pain. He closed his eyes in that moment before they opened the door and it all began again. He thought about Lady Georgina. In another time and place, if she'd not been so highborn and he not so common, it might have worked. They might have married and had a little cottage. She might have learned to cook, and he might have come home to her sweet kiss. At night he might have lain beside her and felt the rise and fall of her body and drifted into dreamless sleep, his arm draped over her.

He might have loved her, his lady.

Chapter Fifteen

"Is he alive?" George's face looked like a piece of paper scrunched up and smoothed out again. Her gray dress was so rumpled, she must have been sleeping in it all the way from London.

"Yes." Violet hugged her sister, trying not to show shock at the change in her appearance. She'd only been gone from Woldsly less than a fortnight. "Yes, he's alive as far as I know. Lord Granville isn't letting anyone see him."

George's expression didn't lighten. Her eyes still stared too intently as if she'd miss something important if she blinked. "Then he might be dead."

"Oh, no." Violet widened her own eyes frantically at Oscar. *Help!* "I don't think so—"

"We'd know if Harry Pye was dead, Georgie," Oscar cut in, rescuing Violet. "Granville would be crowing. The fact that he isn't means Pye is still alive." He took George's arm as if he were guiding an invalid. "Come into Woldsly. Let's sit down and have a cup of tea."

"No, I have to see him." George flung Oscar's hand off as if he were a too-eager vender importuning her with wilted flowers.

Oscar didn't turn a hair. "I know, dear one, but we need to show strength when we confront Granville, if we hope to get in. Better to be fresh and rested."

"Do you think Tony got the message?"

"Yes," Oscar said as if repeating something for the hundredth time. "He'll be on the road right behind us. Let's be ready for him when he comes." He put his hand on George's elbow again, and this time she let him lead her up Woldsly's front steps.

Violet followed behind, absolutely amazed. What was wrong with George? She'd expected her sister to be upset, to cry even. But this—this was a kind of harrowing, tearless grief. If she heard today that Leonard, her summer lover, had died, she would feel a certain melancholy. Maybe shed a tear and mope about the house for a day or two. But she wouldn't be as devastated as George seemed to be now. And Mr. Pye wasn't even dead, as far as they knew.

It was almost as if George loved him.

Violet stopped in her tracks and watched the retreating back of her sister leaning on her brother. Surely not. George was too old for love. Of course she'd been too old for a love affair as well. But, love—real love—was different. If George loved Mr. Pye, she might want to marry him. And if she married him, why... he'd be part of the family. Oh, no! He probably had no idea which fork to use for fish, or how to address a retired general who was also a hereditary baron, or the proper way to help a lady mount a horse sidesaddle or... Good Lord! What if he started dropping his *H*s!

George and Oscar had reached the drawing room, and Oscar looked around as he guided her in. He saw Violet and frowned at her. She hurried to catch up.

Inside the drawing room, he was helping George to a seat. "You've ordered tea and refreshments?" he asked Violet.

She felt her face heat guiltily. Quickly she leaned out the door and told a footman what was wanted.

"Violet, what do you know?" George was looking at her fixedly. "Your letter said Harry was arrested but not why or how."

"Well, they found a dead woman." She sat and tried to order her thoughts. "On the heath. Mistress Piller or Poller or—"

"Pollard?"

"Yes." Violet stared at her, startled. "How did you know?"

"I know her grandson." George waved the interruption away. "Go on."

"She was poisoned in the same manner as the sheep. They found those weeds by her, the ones that were by the dead sheep."

Oscar frowned. "But a woman wouldn't be so stupid as to eat poison weeds like a sheep."

"There was a cup by her." Violet shuddered. "With some kind of dregs in it. They think he—the poisoner— forced her to drink it." She looked uneasily at her sister.

"When was this?" George asked. "Surely someone would have told us had they found her before we left."

"Well, it appears they didn't," Violet replied. "The local people found her the day before you left, but I only heard the day after you'd gone. And there was a carving, an animal of some sort. They say that Mr. Pye made it, so he must have done it. Murdered her, that is."

Oscar darted a glance at George. Violet hesitated,

anticipating a reaction from her sister, but George merely raised her eyebrows.

So Violet soldiered on. "And the night you left they arrested Mr. Pye. Only no one will tell me much about his arrest, except that it took seven men to do it and two were very badly wounded. So," she inhaled and said carefully, "he must have put up quite a fight." She gazed expectantly at George.

Her sister stared off into space, worrying her lower lip with her teeth. "Mistress Pollard was killed the day before I left?"

"Well, no," Violet said. "Actually, they're saying it might've been three nights before."

George suddenly focused on her.

Violet hurried on. "She was seen alive in West Dikey four nights before you left—some people at a tavern saw her—but the farmer swears she wasn't there the morning after she'd been seen in West Dikey. He distinctly remembers moving his sheep to that pasture the next morning. It was several days before he went back again to the pasture where she was found. And they think, by the condition of the body, because of the . . . uh"—she wrinkled her nose in disgust—"the *deterioration,* that it had been on the heath more than three nights. Ugh!" She shuddered.

The tea was brought in, and Violet looked at it queasily. Cook had seen fit to include some cream cakes oozing a pink filling, which under the circumstances were quite disgusting.

George ignored the tea. "Violet, this is very important. You are sure it was three nights before the morning I left that she is thought to have been killed?"

"Mmm." Violet swallowed and dragged her eyes from the ghastly cream cakes. "Yes, I'm sure."

"Thank the Lord." George closed her eyes.

"Georgie, I know you care for him, but you can't." Oscar's voice held a warning. "You simply can't."

"His life is at stake." George leaned toward her brother as if she could infuse him with her passion. "What sort of a woman would I be if I ignored that?"

"What?" Violet looked from one to the other. "I don't understand."

"It's quite simple." George finally seemed to notice the steaming teapot and reached to pour. "Harry couldn't have killed Mistress Pollard on that night." She handed a cup to Violet and met her eyes. "He spent it with me."

HARRY WAS DREAMING.

In the dream there was an argument going on between an ugly ogre, a young king, and a beautiful princess. The ugly ogre and the young king looked more or less as they should, considering it was a dream. But the princess didn't have ruby lips or raven black hair. She had ginger hair and Lady Georgina's lips. Which was just as well. It was his dream after all, and he had a right to make his princess look like anyone he wanted. In his opinion, springy ginger hair was far more beautiful than smooth raven locks any day of the week.

The young king was nattering on about the law and evidence and such in an upper-crust accent so refined it made your teeth ache. Harry could quite understand why the ogre was bellowing in reply, trying to drown out the young king's monologue. He'd bellow at the blighter if he could. The young king seemed to want the ogre's tin stag. Harry suppressed a laugh. He wished he could tell the young king that the tin stag wasn't worth anything.

The stag had long ago lost the better part of its rack and stood on only three legs. And besides, the animal wasn't magic. It couldn't talk and never had.

But the young king was stubborn. He wanted the stag, and he was going to have the stag, by God. To that end, he was badgering the ogre in that overbearing way the aristocracy had, as if everyone else was put on this earth merely for the joy of licking his lordship's boots clean. *Thank you, m'lord. It's been a pleasure, it really has.*

Harry would have sided with the ogre, just on principle, but something was wrong. Princess Georgina seemed to be weeping. Great drops of liquid rolled down her translucent cheeks and slowly turned to gold as they fell. They tinkled as they hit the stone floor and rolled away.

Harry was mesmerized; he couldn't take his eyes away from her sorrow. He wanted to yell at the young king, *Here is your magic! Look to the lady beside you.* But, of course, he couldn't speak. And it turned out he was wrong: It was actually the princess, not the young king, who wanted the tin stag. The young king was merely acting as the princess's agent. Well, here was an entirely different matter. If Princess Georgina desired the stag, she should have it, even if it was a ratty old thing.

But the ugly ogre loved the tin stag; it was his most precious possession. To prove it, he threw the stag down and stamped on it until the stag groaned and broke into pieces. The ogre stared at it, lying there at his feet, bleeding lead, and smiled. He looked into the princess's eyes and pointed. *There, take it. I've killed it, anyway.*

Then a wondrous thing happened.

Princess Georgina knelt beside the shattered stag and wept, and as she did, her golden tears fell upon the beast.

Where they lay, they formed a bond, soldering together the tin until the stag was whole again, made of both tin and gold. The princess smiled and held the strange animal to her breast, and there the stag nuzzled his head. She lifted him up, and she and the young king turned with their dubious prize.

But Harry could see over her shoulder that the ogre did not like this outcome. All the love he'd borne the tin stag had now turned to hatred of the princess who had stolen it away. He wanted to shout to the young king, *Be careful! Watch the princess's back! The ogre means her harm and will not rest until he has his revenge!* But however much he tried, he could not speak.

You never can in dreams.

GEORGE CRADLED HARRY'S HEAD in her lap and tried not to sob at the terrible marks on his face. His lips and eyes were swollen black. Fresh blood was smeared from a cut across an eyebrow and another beneath an ear. His hair was stringy and dirty, and she very much feared that part of the dirt was actually dried blood.

"The sooner we're out of here, the better," Oscar muttered. He slammed the carriage door behind him.

"Indeed." Tony rapped sharply on the ceiling, signaling the driver.

The carriage pulled away from Granville House. George didn't need to look back to know that its owner stared malevolently after them. She braced her body to cushion the bumps from Harry as he lay on the seat beside her.

Oscar studied him. "I've never seen a man beaten so badly," he whispered. The words *and live* hung in the air unspoken.

"Animals." Tony looked away.

"He'll live," George said.

"Lord Granville didn't think so; otherwise he'd never have let us take him. As it was, I rather had to throw my title around." Tony's lips pressed together. "You need to prepare yourself."

"How?" George almost smiled. "How do I prepare myself for his death? I can't, so I won't. I'll believe in his recovery instead."

"Oh, my dear," Tony said, and sighed, but he made no further remark.

It seemed like forever before they eventually drew up in front of Woldsly. Oscar tumbled out, and Tony followed more sedately. George could hear them organizing footmen and finding a door to lay Harry on. She looked down. Harry hadn't moved an inch since he'd been laid on her lap. His eyes were so swollen, she wasn't sure he'd be able to open them even if he was awake. She placed her palm against his neck and felt his pulse, slow but strong.

The men came back and took over. They wrestled Harry out of the carriage and onto the door they'd found. Four men carried him up the steps and into Woldsly. Then they had to take him up more steps, sweating and cursing despite George's presence. Finally, they placed Harry on a bed in a little room in between Tony's and her own, a compromise. The room was hardly big enough to hold a bed, chest of drawers, bedside table, and chair. It was really meant to be a dressing room. But it was near her own, and that was all that mattered. All the men, even her brothers, trooped out, leaving the room suddenly quiet. Harry hadn't so much as twitched during the entire process.

George sat down wearily next to him on the bed. She

laid her hand at his neck again, feeling for that heartbeat and closed her eyes.

Behind her, the door opened.

"Dear Lord, what they've done to that bonny man." Tiggle stood beside her with a basin of hot water. The lady's maid met George's eyes, then squared her shoulders. "Let's make him comfortable, anyway, shall we, my lady?"

SIX DAYS LATER, HARRY OPENED his eyes.

George was sitting by his bed in the dim little room as she had every day and almost every night since he'd been laid there. She didn't let her hopes get away from her when she saw his eyelids flicker. He'd opened his eyes briefly before and hadn't seemed to recognize her or even to be fully awake.

But this time his emerald eyes settled on her and stayed. "My lady." His voice was a whispered croak.

Oh, sweet Lord, thank you. She could have sung hallelujahs. She could have danced a reel around the room all by herself. She could have fallen upon her knees and offered up a prayer of thanksgiving.

But she merely lifted a cup to his lips. "Are you thirsty?"

He nodded without ever taking his eyes from hers. When he had swallowed, he whispered, "Don't cry."

"I'm sorry." George replaced the cup on the bedside table. "They're tears of joy."

He watched her a few minutes longer; then his eyes closed again, and he fell asleep.

She put her hand to his neck as she had innumerable times over the last terrible week. She'd done it so often that it had become habit. The blood beneath his skin beat strong and steady. Harry murmured at her touch and shifted.

George sighed and rose. She spent an hour in a luxurious, slow bath and took a nap that somehow lasted until nightfall. When she woke, she dressed in a yellow dimity gown with lace at the elbows and requested that her supper be brought to Harry's room.

He was awake when she entered his room, and she felt her heart skip. Such a small thing, seeing his eyes alert, but it made all the difference in her world.

Someone had helped him to sit up. "How's Will?"

"He's fine. Will is staying with Bennet Granville." George went to open the curtains.

The sun was dying, but even that little light made the room seem less gloomy. She made a mental note to have the maids open the one window in the morning to get rid of the stuffy sickroom odor.

She came back beside the bed. "Apparently, Will hid when they took you and then ran all the way back to West Dikey to tell the Cock and Worm's landlord what had happened. Not that the landlord could do much."

"Ah."

George frowned at the thought of Harry in that cell being beaten every day with no one to help him. She shook her head. "Will was most anxious about you."

"He's a good lad."

"He told us what happened that night." George sat down. "You saved his life, you know."

Harry shrugged. Obviously he didn't want to talk about it.

"Would you like some beef tea?" She removed the cover to the tray of food the maids had already brought.

On her side was a plate of roast beef, steaming in juice and gravy. There were potatoes and carrots and a savory pudding. On his side of the tray stood a single cup of beef tea.

Harry eyed the food and sighed. "Beef tea would be very nice, my lady."

George brought the cup to his face, intending to hold it as she had before while he drank from it, but he took the cup from her fingers. "Thank you."

She busied herself arranging her tray and pouring a glass of wine, but she watched him from the corner of her eye. He drank from the cup and rested it on his lap without spilling. His hands seemed steady. She relaxed a bit inside. She hadn't wanted to embarrass him by hovering, but only a day ago he'd been quite insensible.

"Will you tell me your fairy tale, my lady?" His voice had strengthened since this afternoon.

George smiled. "You've probably been on tenterhooks, wondering about the ending."

Harry's bruised lips twitched, but he replied gravely, "Yes, my lady."

"Well, let's see." She popped a piece of beef into her mouth and thought as she chewed. The last time she had told him the story . . . Suddenly she remembered that she'd been quite naked and Harry had . . . George swallowed too suddenly and had to grab for her wine. She just *knew* she was blushing. She snuck a look at Harry, but he was looking resignedly down at his beef tea.

She cleared her throat. "The Leopard Prince turned into a man. He grasped his crown pendant and wished for a cloak of invisibility. Which would have been quite handy since, as we discussed before, he was most probably nude when he turned into a man."

He raised his eyebrows at her over the rim of his cup.

She nodded primly. "He put the cloak on and set out to defeat the nasty witch and win the Golden Swan. And while there was a small setback when she turned him into a toad—"

Harry smiled at her. How she gloried in his smiles!

"Eventually he was able to resume his natural form and steal the Golden Swan and bring it to the young king. Who, of course, immediately carted it off to the beautiful princess's father."

She cut a piece of beef and held it out to Harry. He eyed the fork, but instead of taking it, he merely opened his lips. His eyes met hers and held them as George placed the food in his mouth. For some reason this transaction made her breath quicken.

George looked down at her plate. "But the young king was out of luck again, for the Golden Swan could talk just as well as the Golden Horse. The father king took the Golden Swan aside and quizzed it and soon discovered the young king wasn't the one who'd stolen the Golden Swan from the nasty witch. Potato?"

"Thank you." Harry closed his eyes as his lips took a piece from her fork.

George's mouth watered in sympathy. She cleared her throat. "So the father king went storming out to confront the young king. And the father king said, 'Right. The Golden Swan is very nice, but not exactly useful. You must bring me the Golden Eel guarded by the seven-headed dragon that lives on the Mountains of the Moon.'"

"An eel?"

She held out a spoonful of pudding, but Harry was looking at her dubiously.

She waved it under his nose. "Yes, an eel."

He captured her hand and guided the spoon to his lips.

"It does seem rather odd, doesn't it?" George continued breathlessly. "I did question Cook's aunt about it, but she was quite certain." She speared another piece of beef and held it out. "I myself would have thought, oh, a wolf or a unicorn."

Harry swallowed. "Not a unicorn. Too close to the horse."

"I suppose. But, anyway, something more exotic." She wrinkled her nose at the pudding. "Eels—even golden eels—don't sound exotic to you, do they?"

"No."

"Nor I." She poked at the pudding. "Of course, Cook's aunt is getting on in years. She must be at least eighty." George looked up to find him staring at the pudding she'd just destroyed. "Oh, I'm sorry. Would you like some more?"

"Please."

She fed him some pudding, watching as his lips enveloped the spoon. Goodness, he had lovely lips, even when they were bruised. "Anyway, the young king trotted off back home, and I'm sure he was quite nasty when he told the Leopard Prince that he had to retrieve the Golden Eel. But the Leopard Prince had no choice, did he? He turned into a man and took his emerald crown pendant in his hand, and guess what he asked for this time?"

"I don't know, my lady."

"One-hundred-league boots." George sat back in satisfaction. "Can you imagine? You put them on and the wearer can cross one hundred leagues in a single step."

Harry's mouth quirked. "I shouldn't ask, my lady,

but how would that help the Leopard Prince get to the Mountains of the Moon?"

George stared. She'd never thought of that. "I haven't any idea. They would be wonderful on land, but would they work in the air?"

Harry nodded solemnly. "It is a problem, I fear."

George absently fed him the rest of her beef while pondering this question. She was offering the last bite when she realized that he'd been watching her the entire time.

"Harry . . ." She hesitated. He was weak, barely recovered enough to sit upright. She shouldn't take advantage of him, but she needed to know.

"Yes?"

She asked before she could rethink the idea. "Why did your father attack Lord Granville?"

He stiffened.

She immediately regretted asking. It was more than clear he didn't want to talk about that time. How mean of her.

"My mother was Granville's whore." His words were flat.

George stopped breathing. She'd never heard Harry mention his mother before.

"She was a beautiful woman, my mother." He looked down at his right hand and flexed it. "Too beautiful for a gamekeeper's wife. She was all black hair and blazing green eyes. When we went to town, men used to watch her pass. Even as a lad it made me uneasy."

"Was she a good mother?"

Harry shrugged. "She was the only mother I had. I've none other to compare her with. She kept me fed and clothed. My da did most everything else."

George looked down at her own hands, fighting back tears, but she still heard his words, rasping and slow.

"When I was small, she used to sing to me sometimes, late at night if I couldn't sleep. Sad love songs. Her voice was high, and not very strong, and she wouldn't sing if I looked at her face. But it was lovely when she sang." He sighed. "At least I thought so at the time."

She nodded, barely moving, too afraid to interrupt the flow of his words.

"They moved here, my da and my mother, when they were first married. I don't know exactly—I've had to piece the story together from conversations I've overheard—but I think she took up with Granville soon after they came here."

"Before you were born?" George asked carefully.

He looked at her with steady emerald eyes and nodded once.

George let out a slow breath. "Did your father know?"

Harry grimaced. "He must've. Granville took away Bennet."

She blinked. She couldn't have heard correctly. "Bennet Granville is . . .?"

"My brother," Harry said quietly. "My mother's son."

"But how could he do such a thing? Didn't anyone notice when he brought a baby into his house?"

Harry made a sound that was almost a laugh. "Oh, everyone knew—quite a few hereabouts probably still remember—but Granville has always been a tyrant. When he said the baby was his legitimate son, none dared disagree. Not even his lawful wife."

"And your father?"

Harry looked down at his hands, frowning. "I don't

remember, I was only two or so, but I think Da must've forgiven her. And she must've promised to stay away from Granville. But she lied."

"What happened?" George asked.

"My father caught her. I don't know if Da always knew that she'd gone back to Granville and looked away or if he fooled himself that she had turned over a new leaf or..." He shook his head impatiently. "But it doesn't matter. When I was twelve, he found her in bed with Granville."

"And?"

Harry grimaced. "And he went for Granville's throat. Granville was a much larger man, and he beat my father off. Da was humiliated. But Granville still had him horsewhipped."

"And you? You said he horsewhipped you as well."

"I was young. When they started on Da with that big whip..." Harry swallowed. "I darted in. It was a stupid thing to do."

"You were trying to save your father."

"Aye, I was. And all I got for the effort was this." Harry held up his mutilated right hand.

"I don't understand."

"I tried to shield my face, and the whip caught me across this hand. See?" Harry pointed at a long scar that cut across the inside of his fingers. "The whip nearly severed them all, but the third finger was the worst. Lord Granville had one of his men cut it off. Said he was doing me a favor."

Oh, God. George felt bile rise in her throat. She covered Harry's right hand with her own. He turned it over so they were palm to palm. George carefully linked her fingers with his.

"Da was out of work and so badly crippled by the whipping that after a while we went into the poorhouse." Harry looked away from her, but he still clasped his hand with hers.

"And your mother? Did she go into the poorhouse as well?" George asked in a low voice.

Harry's hand squeezed hers almost painfully. "No. She stayed with Granville. As his whore. I heard many years later that she'd died of the plague. But I never spoke to her again after that day. The day Da and I were horsewhipped."

She breathed deeply. "Did you love her, Harry?"

He smiled then, crookedly. "All boys love their mothers, my lady."

George closed her eyes. What kind of woman would abandon her child to be a rich man's mistress? So many things about Harry were explained, but the knowledge was almost too painful to bear. She laid her head down in his lap and felt him stroke her hair. It was strange. She should be comforting him after his revelations. Instead, he consoled her.

He drew a breath like a sigh. "Now you understand why I must leave."

Chapter Sixteen

"But why must you leave?" George asked.

She paced the small bedroom. She wanted to pound on the bed. Pound on the chest of drawers. Pound on Harry. It had been almost a fortnight since he'd first said it. A fortnight in which he'd regained his feet, his bruises had faded to the greenish-yellow color of recovery, and he hardly limped. But in that fortnight he'd remained adamant. He would leave her as soon as he was well.

Every day she came to visit him in his tiny room, and every day they had the same argument. George couldn't stand this cramped room anymore—Lord knew what Harry thought of it—and she was about ready to scream. He was going to leave her soon, just walk out the door, and she still didn't know *why*.

Harry sighed now. He must be weary of her badgering him. "It's not going to work, my lady. You and me. You must know that, and you'll agree with me soon." His voice was low and calm. Reasonable.

Hers was not.

"I won't!" George cried like a small child told she must go to bed. All she lacked was the stomp of one foot.

Oh, Lord, she knew she was making herself ugly. But she couldn't stop. Couldn't help pleading and whining and pestering. The thought of never seeing Harry again brought blind panic flooding into her chest.

She took a deep breath and tried to speak more sedately. "We could get married. I love—"

"No!" He slammed his hand against the wall, the sound like a cannon shot in the room.

She stared at him. She knew damn well Harry loved her. She knew by the way he said *my lady* so low it was almost a purr. The way his eyes lingered when he looked at her. The way he had made love to her so intently before he'd been injured. Why couldn't he—?

He shook his head. "No, I'm sorry, my lady."

Tears started in her eyes. She rubbed them away. "You can at least do me the favor of explaining why you don't think we should marry. Because I just can't see why not."

"Why? *Why?*" Harry laughed sharply. "How about this reason: If I married you, my lady, the whole of England would think I did it for your money. And how exactly would we work out the money part? Eh? Would you give me a quarterly allowance?" He stood with his hands on his hips and stared at her.

"It wouldn't have to be that way."

"No? Perhaps you'd like to sign all your money over to me?"

She hesitated for a fatal second.

"No, of course not." He flung up his arms. "So I'd be your pet monkey. Your male whore. Do you even think any of your friends would invite me to dine with them? That your family would accept me?"

"*Yes*. Yes, they would." She stuck out her jaw. "And you're *not*—"

"Aren't I?" There was pain in his green eyes.

"No, never," she whispered. She held out her hands in supplication. "You know you're not that to me. You're much more. I love—"

"*No*."

But she spoke over him this time. "*You*. I love you, Harry. I love you. Doesn't that mean anything to you?"

"Of course it does." He closed his eyes. "It's all the more reason not to let you be pilloried by society."

"It won't be as bad as all that. And even if it was, I don't care."

"You'd care after they figured out why you married me. You'd care then." Harry was advancing on her, and George didn't like the look in his eyes.

"I don't—"

He grasped her upper arms almost too gently, as if he held himself back by an unraveling willpower. "They'd know soon enough," he said. "Why else would you marry me? A commoner with no money or power? You, the daughter of an earl?" He leaned close and whispered, "Can't you guess?" His breath on her ear sent shivers down her neck. It had been so very long since he'd last touched her.

"I don't care what they think of me," she repeated stubbornly.

"No?" The word was whispered in her hair. "But, you see, my lady, it still won't work between us. We have one remaining problem."

"What?"

"*I* care what they think of you." His lips came down on hers in a kiss that tasted of anger and despair.

George grabbed his head. She yanked the ribbon from his hair and ran her fingers into it. And she kissed him back, countering fury with fury. If he would just stop thinking. She nipped his bottom lip, felt the groan go through him, and opened her mouth in seductive invitation. And he took it, thrusting his tongue into her mouth and angling his face over hers. Framing her face with his hands, caressing and punishing her mouth with his. He kissed her as if it were the last embrace they would ever share.

As if he would leave her tomorrow.

George tightened her grasp in his hair at that thought. It must have hurt him, but she wasn't letting go. She pressed her body to his until she felt his arousal even through the bulk of both their clothing. She rubbed herself against him.

Harry broke their kiss and tried to pull his head up. "My lady, we can't—"

"Shhh," George murmured. She trailed kisses along his jaw. "I don't want to hear *can't*. I want you. I need you."

She licked the pulse at his throat, tasting salt and man. He shuddered. She bared her teeth against his neck. She released his hair with one hand and ripped at his shirt, tearing it open and off one shoulder.

"My lady, I, uhh…" He lapsed into a moan when she licked his exposed nipple.

From the way he took her bottom and pulled her hard into his groin, he was no longer interested in protesting. Just as well. She'd never realized a man's nipples were sensitive. Someone should make this information known to the general female population. She took the tiny nubbin between her teeth and delicately bit down. He squeezed her bottom in his big hands. She lifted her head and pulled

the shirt entirely off. Definitely better. Of all the things
God had made on this earth, surely a man's chest must be
one of the most beautiful. Or perhaps it was just Harry's
chest. George ran her hands across his shoulders, skim-
ming gently over the scars from his beating.

She'd come so close to losing him.

Her fingers drifted down to circle his nipples, making
him close his eyes, then lower, into the slim line of hair
below his navel. Her fingernails must have tickled. Harry
sucked in his stomach. Then she reached his breeches. She
explored the flap and found the hidden buttons. George
flicked them open, conscious all the while that his penis
was underneath, already hard and tenting the fabric. She
glanced up once to find him watching her under lowered
lids. The emerald fire in his eyes made her squirm. A slow
seep of wetness began at her core.

She opened the breeches and found her prize, poking
up through the top of his smallclothes.

"Take them off." She forced her gaze to his face.
"Please."

Harry crooked an eyebrow but obediently stripped off
his breeches, smallclothes, stockings, and shoes. Then he
reached for the front of her dress.

"No. Not yet." George danced out of his way. "I can't
think when you touch me."

Harry stalked her. "That's the point, my lady."

Her rear bumped against the bed. She held up her hands
to ward him off. "Not *my* point."

He leaned close without actually touching her, the heat
from his bare chest almost menacing. "The last time you
played with me I nearly died."

"But you didn't."

He watched her, his eyes unconvinced.

"Trust me."

He sighed. "You know I can deny you nothing, my lady."

"Good. Now get on the bed."

Harry grimaced but he did as she ordered, stretching on his side. His cock arced up, nearly touching his navel.

"Unhook me."

She presented her back and felt his fingers as he undid her gown. When he reached the end, she walked out of his reach and turned. She let the bodice fall. She wasn't wearing stays, and his eyes immediately dropped to her nipples, peaking the fabric of her shift. She placed her hands at her waist and wriggled the dress down.

He narrowed his eyes.

She sat on a chair and pulled off her garters and rolled down her stockings. Wearing only her shift, she walked to the bed. When she crawled on the bed beside him, Harry reached for her at once.

"No, this won't do." George frowned. "You can't touch me." She looked at the row of carved spindles on the bed's headboard. "Hold those."

He twisted to look and then lay down and grasped one spindle in each hand. With his arms over his head, the muscles in his upper arms and chest bunched.

George licked her bottom lip. "You can't let go until I tell you."

"As you wish," he growled, sounding not at all submissive. He should've appeared weak in such a compromising position. Instead, he reminded her of a wild leopard captured and tethered. He lay there, eyeing her speculatively, a trace of a sneer on his lips.

Best not to get too close.

She ran a fingernail down his chest. "Perhaps I ought to tie your wrists to the bed."

Harry's eyebrows shot up.

"Just to be safe," she reassured him sweetly.

"My lady," he warned.

"Oh, never mind. But you must promise not to move."

"On my honor, I will not let go of the bedposts until you permit me."

"That's not what I said."

But it was close enough. She leaned over him and licked the tip of his penis.

"Jesus Christ."

George lifted her head and frowned.

"You never said anything about talking," Harry panted. "For God's sake, do that again."

"Maybe. If I feel inclined." She inched nearer, ignoring his grumbled curse.

This time she lifted his cock aside and planted a series of tiny, wet kisses on his belly. She ended when she came to the dark, wiry hair above his erection. She opened her mouth and scraped her teeth against his skin.

"Shit." Harry sucked in a breath.

His scent was pungent here. George nudged his legs apart and ran her fingers over his sac. She could feel the things that men called *stones* rolling about inside. Very, very carefully she squeezed.

"God*damn.*"

She smiled at his profanity. George grasped his cock between forefinger and thumb. She glanced up at Harry's face.

He looked worried.

Good. Now, what if she ...? George bent her head and licked the underside of his manhood. She tasted salt and skin and inhaled his aroma. She shifted her fingers and ran her tongue around the head, just where it began to swell out. Harry groaned. So she repeated the process and then thought to kiss the very tip where drops of seed welled.

"Put it in your mouth." His voice was a deep rasp, dark and prayerful.

It excited her unbearably. She didn't want to take his order. On the other hand... She opened her mouth over him. He was very big. Surely he didn't mean the whole thing? She fit the head into her mouth, like a small peach. Except peaches were sweet and he was musky. Tasting of man.

"Suck me."

She was startled. Really? She pursed her mouth and his hips came off the bed, startling her again.

"Ahhh. *God*."

His reaction, his obvious enjoyment of what she was doing, aroused her. She could feel that part of herself throbbing. She pressed her thighs together tightly and sucked on Harry's cock. She tasted his semen and wondered if he would reach completion in her mouth. But she wanted him in her when that happened. George licked one last time and rose to straddle his hips. She guided his erection to where it should be, but it seemed so big now. She pressed and felt him begin to part her. To tunnel and push. She glanced down. The smooth red skin of his cock disappeared into her feminine hair. She moaned and almost came apart right there.

"Let me move," he whispered.

She couldn't speak. She nodded.

He placed one hand on his penis to steady it and the other on her bottom. "Lean toward me."

She did and he slid in suddenly, almost all the way. She caught her breath and felt unexpected tears. *Harry.* Harry was making love to her. She closed her eyes and ground her hips into his. Felt at the same time his thumb touch that spot. She moaned and drew up until only the head remained inside her, concentrating on her pleasure and his. Down, grinding herself into him. Up, balancing precariously on a peak. Down, his thumb pressing against that most sensitive part of her. Up...

But suddenly he broke. He gripped her bottom tightly and rolled her underneath him. Then he braced himself on his hands and ploughed into her, fast and furious. She tried to move, to respond, but he pinned her to the mattress with his weight, dominated and mastered her with his flesh. She arched her head and widened her legs helplessly. Allowed him full access. Gave herself to him as he continued his relentless pounding. He grunted with each thrust into her body, and it almost sounded like sobbing. Did he feel it as much as she?

Then she fell apart and saw stars, a glorious stream of light filling her being. Dimly she heard his cry and felt his withdrawal, like a little death.

Then he lay next to her, panting.

"I wish you wouldn't do that." George stroked his neck. Her tongue was thick with satiation. "I wish you would stay with me until the end."

"You know I can't do that, my lady." His voice sounded no better.

She rolled over and snuggled against him. Her hand stroked down his sweaty belly until she found his penis again. She held it. The argument could wait for tomorrow.

But when she woke in the morning, Harry was gone.

BENNET LAY WITH ONE ARM flung over his head and a foot hanging off the bed. In the moonlight, something metallic shone dully around his neck. He snored.

Harry stole across the darkened bedroom, placing his feet carefully. He should've quit the area the night he'd left his lady's bed, a week ago now. And he had meant to. It had been harder than it should've been to watch his lady sleep, see her relaxed body after he'd given her pleasure, and know he must leave her. There was simply no other choice. They had kept secret his recovery from Granville, but it was only a matter of time before Silas found out. And when he did, Lady Georgina's life would be in danger. Granville was insane. Harry had seen that firsthand during his stay in the lord's dungeon. Whatever was driving Granville to seek Harry's death had been let off its leash. Lord Granville would stop at nothing—not even an innocent woman—to see Harry dead. It would be irresponsible to put his lady's life in danger for an affair that had no future.

He knew all this, and yet something still held him here in Yorkshire. As a result, Harry had become a master at sneaking. He hid from Granville's watchful eyes and the men who had begun roaming the hills in the last few days, seeking him. Tonight he made almost no noise, just a faint creak from his leather boots. The man on the bed stirred not at all.

Still, the boy on the pallet beside the bed opened his eyes.

Harry stopped and watched Will. The boy nodded slightly. Harry returned the nod. He walked to the bed. For a moment, he stood looking down at Bennet. Then he leaned over and covered the other man's mouth with his hand. Bennet jackknifed convulsively. He threw out his arms and managed to knock Harry's hand aside.

"Wha——?"

Harry slapped his hand back down again, grunting as Bennet elbowed him. "Hist, you beef-wit. It's me."

Bennet fought for a second more, and then Harry's words seemed to reach his brain. He froze.

Cautiously, Harry lifted his hand.

"Harry?"

"You'd better hope." He spoke barely above a whisper. "The way you sleep, it could be marauders. Even the boy woke before you."

Bennet leaned over the bed. "Will? Are you there?"

"Yes, sir." Will had sat up sometime during the struggle.

"Jesus." Bennet flopped back on the bed, covering his eyes with an arm. "You nearly gave me apoplexy."

"You've gotten soft living in London." The corner of Harry's mouth twitched. "Hasn't he, Will?"

"We-ell." The boy clearly didn't want to say anything against his new mentor. "Wouldn't hurt to be more alert."

"Thank you, young Will." Bennet removed his arm to glare at Harry. "What're you doing, creeping into my bedroom in the wee hours?"

Harry sat on the bed, his back against one of the posts at the end. He nudged Bennet's legs with a boot. The other man stared at the boot indignantly before moving.

Harry stretched out his legs. "I'm leaving."

"So you've come to say good-bye?"

"Not exactly." He looked down at the fingernails on his right hand. To the place where one should be but wasn't. "Your father is hell-bent on having me killed. And he's none too happy with Lady Georgina for saving me."

Bennet nodded. "He's been rampaging around Granville House the last week, roaring that he'd have you arrested. He's insane."

"Aye. He's also the magistrate."

"What can you do? What can anybody do?"

"I can find whoever is really killing the sheep." Harry glanced at Will. "And Mrs. Pollard's murderer as well. It might dampen his temper." And turn it away from his lady.

Bennet sat up. "Very well. But how are you going to find the killer?"

Harry stared. A pendant on a thin chain around Bennet's neck had swung forward: a small, crudely carved falcon.

Harry blinked, remembering.

Long, long ago. A morning so bright and sunny it hurt to open your eyes wide to the full, blue sky. He and Benny had stretched on their backs on top of the hill, chewing grass.

"Lookee here." Harry took the carving out of his pocket and handed it to Benny.

Benny turned it over in his dirty fingers. "A bird."

"It's a falcon. Can't you see?"

"'Course I can see." Benny glanced up. "Who made it?"

"Me."

"Really? You carved it?" Benny stared at him with awe.

"Aye." Harry shrugged. "My da taught me. It's only my first, so it's not so good."

"I like it."

Harry shrugged again and squinted into the blinding blue sky. "You can keep it if you want."

"Thanks."

They had lain for a while, almost falling asleep in the warm sun.

Then Benny sat up. "I've got something for you."

He'd turned out both pockets and then dug down again, finally bringing up a small, dirty penknife. Benny rubbed it on his breeches and handed it to Harry.

Harry looked at the pearl handle and tested the edge with his thumb. "Ta, Benny. It'll be good for whittling."

Harry couldn't remember what he and Bennet had done the rest of that day. Probably rode their ponies about. Maybe fished in the stream. Come home hungry. That was how they'd spent most days back then. And it didn't really matter. The next afternoon Da had found his mother humping old Granville.

Harry looked up and met eyes as green as his own.

"I've always worn it." Bennet touched the little falcon.

Harry nodded and glanced away from Bennet for a moment. "I had started asking around, before I was arrested, and I've tried again this last week, discreetly, lest your father track me." He looked back at Bennet, his face under control now. "Nobody seems to know much, but there's plenty besides me who have a reason to hate your father."

"Probably most of the county."

Harry ignored the sarcasm. "I thought maybe I should search a bit further back."

Bennet raised his eyebrows.

"Your nurse is still alive, isn't she?"

"Old Alice Humboldt?" Bennet yawned. "Yes, she's alive. Her cottage was the first place I stopped when I got back into the district. And you're right, she might know something. Nanny is very quiet, but she always noticed everything."

"Good." Harry stood up. "Then she's the person to question. Want to come?"

"What, now?"

Harry's mouth twitched. He'd forgotten how fun it was to bait Bennet. "I had thought to wait for sunrise," he said gravely, "but if you're eager to go now..."

"No. No, sunrise is fine." Bennet winced. "I don't suppose you could wait until nine o'clock?"

Harry looked at him.

"No, of course not." Bennet yawned again, nearly unhinging the back of his head. "I'll meet you at Nanny's cottage, shall I?"

"I'll go, too," Will spoke up from the pallet.

Harry and Bennet glanced at the boy. He'd nearly forgotten Will. Bennet raised his eyebrows at Harry, leaving the decision to him.

"Aye, you'll go, too," Harry said.

"Ta," Will said. "I've got something for you."

He burrowed under his pillow and came out with a long, thin object wrapped in a rag. He held it out. Harry took the bundle and unrolled it. His knife, cleaned and oiled, lay on his palm.

"Found it in the stream," Will said, "after they took you. I been taking care of it for you. Until you was ready for it again."

It was the most Harry had ever heard from the boy's mouth.

Harry smiled. "Ta, Will."

* * *

GEORGE TOUCHED THE LITTLE SWAN swimming on her pillow. It was the second carving Harry had given her. The first had been a rearing horse. He'd been gone from her seven days, but he hadn't left the neighborhood. That much was obvious from the tiny carvings he'd somehow placed on her bed.

"Gave you another one, has he, my lady?" Tiggle bustled about the room, putting away her dress and gathering soiled things for the laundry.

George picked up the swan. "Yes."

She'd questioned the servants after the first carving. Nobody had seen Harry enter or leave Woldsly, not even Oscar, who kept the irregular hours of a bachelor. Her middle brother had remained behind after Tony had left for London. Oscar said it was to keep her and Violet company, but she suspected the real reason had more to do with his creditors in London.

"Romantic of Mr. Pye, isn't it?" Tiggle sighed.

"Or irritating." George wrinkled her nose at the swan and placed it carefully on her dressing table beside the horse.

"Or irritating, I guess, my lady," Tiggle agreed.

The maid came over and laid a hand on George's shoulder, gently pressing her into the chair before the dressing table. She took up the silver-backed brush and began to stroke it through George's hair. Tiggle started at the ends and worked to the roots, teasing out the tangles. George closed her eyes.

"Men don't always see things the same way we do, if you don't mind me saying so, my lady."

"I can't help but think that Mr. Pye was dropped on his head as a baby." George squeezed her eyes shut. "Why won't he come back to me?"

"Can't say, my lady." The tangles worked out, Tiggle began stroking from her crown down to the ends of her hair.

George sighed in pleasure.

"But he hasn't gone too far away, now, has he?" the maid pointed out.

"Mmm." George tilted her head so Tiggle could do that side.

"He wants to go—you've said so yourself, my lady— but he hasn't." Tiggle started on the other side, brushing gently from the temple. "Stands to reason, then, that maybe he can't."

"You're speaking in riddles and I'm too tired to understand."

"I'm just saying maybe he can't leave you, my lady." Tiggle set down the brush with a thump and began braiding her hair.

"A lot of good that does me if he can't bring himself to face me, either." George frowned in the mirror.

"I think he'll be back." The maid tied a ribbon at the end of George's braid and leaned over her shoulder to meet her eyes in the mirror. "And when he comes, you'll be needing to tell him, if you don't mind my saying so, my lady."

George blushed. She had hoped Tiggle wouldn't notice, but she should have realized the maid kept track of everything. "There's no way of knowing yet."

"Aye, there is. And you being so regular like…"

Tiggle gave her an old-fashioned look. "Good night, my lady."

She left the room.

George sighed and dropped her head into her hands. Tiggle had better be right about Harry. Because if he waited too long to return, there would be no need to tell him she was expecting.

He'd see it.

Chapter Seventeen

"Aye?" The wizened face peeped out the door crack.

Harry looked down. The old woman's head didn't come to his breastbone. The hump on her back bent her until she had to peer sideways and up to see her caller.

"Good morning, Mistress Humboldt. My name is Harry Pye. I'd like to talk with you."

"Best come in, then, hadn't you, young man?" The tiny figure smiled at Harry's left ear and opened the door wider. Only then, in the light let in by the open door, did he see the cataracts that clouded the old woman's blue eyes.

"Thank you, ma'am."

Bennet and Will were there before him. They sat by a smoldering fire, the only light in the dim room. Will was munching on a scone and eyeing another on a tray.

"Late, aren't you?" Bennet was more alert than he'd been five hours before. He looked quite pleased to have got the first dig in.

"Some of us have to travel by back lanes."

Harry helped Mistress Humboldt lower herself into a fan-backed chair piled with knitted pillows. A calico cat padded over, meowing. It leaped into the old lady's lap and purred loudly even before she started stroking its back.

"Have a scone, Mr. Pye. And if you don't mind, you can help yourself to tea." Mistress Humboldt's voice was thin and whistling. "Now. What have you lads come to talk to me about that you must do it in secret?"

Harry's mouth twitched. The old woman's eyes might be fading, but her mind surely wasn't. "Lord Granville and his enemies."

Mistress Humboldt smiled sweetly. "Have you got all day, then, young man? For if I was to list everyone who ever had a grudge against that lord, I'd still be talking tomorrow morning."

Bennet laughed.

"You're quite right, ma'am," Harry said. "But what I'm after is the person poisoning the sheep. Who has such hatred of Granville that they'd want to do these crimes?"

The old woman cocked her head and stared at the fire for a moment, the only sound in the room the purring of the cat and Will eating his scone.

"As it happens," she said slowly, "I've been thinking on these sheep killings myself." She pursed her lips. "Bad things they are and evil because while it hurts the farmer, it merely bothers Lord Granville. Seems to me that what you really should be asking, young man, is who has the heart to do this." Mistress Humboldt took a sip of tea.

Bennet started to speak. Harry shook his head.

"It takes a hard heart to not care that others are hurt along the way to getting at the lord." Mistress Humboldt tapped a shaking finger on her knee to punctuate her point.

"A hard heart and a brave one as well. Lord Granville is the law and the fist in this county, and whoever goes against him is gambling their very life."

"Who fits your description, Nanny?" Bennet leaned forward impatiently.

"I can think of two men that answer, at least in parts." She wrinkled her brow. "But neither are quite right." She raised her teacup to her lips with a wavering hand.

Bennet shifted in his chair, jiggled one leg up and down, and sighed.

Harry leaned forward in his own chair and selected a scone.

Bennet shot him an incredulous glare.

Harry raised his eyebrows as he bit into the scone.

"Dick Crumb," the old woman said, and Harry lowered the scone. "A while back, his sister, Janie, the one who's weak in the head, was seduced by the lord. A terrible thing, preying on that child-woman." The corners of Mistress Humboldt's mouth crumpled in a frown. "And Dick, when he found out, why, he nearly lost his head. Said he'd have killed him had it been any man but the lord. Would have, too."

Harry frowned. Dick hadn't said he'd threatened Granville's life, but then what man would? Surely that by itself . . .

Mistress Humboldt held out her cup, and Bennet silently poured tea for her and placed the cup back in her hand.

"But," she continued, "Dick isn't a mean man. Hard, yes, but not hard-hearted. As for the other man—Mistress Humboldt looked in Bennet's direction—"perhaps it's best to let sleeping dogs lie."

Bennet seemed bewildered. "What sleeping dogs?"

Will stopped eating. He looked between Bennet and the old woman. *Damn.* Harry had a feeling he knew what Mistress Humboldt was getting at. Perhaps it would be better to leave it alone.

Bennet caught some of Harry's unease. He leaned forward tensely, his elbows on his knees, both heels tapping now. "Tell us."

"Thomas."

Shit. Harry looked away.

"Thomas who?" It seemed to hit Bennet all at once. He stopped moving for a second, then exploded out of the chair, pacing in the tiny space before the fire. "Thomas, my *brother?*" He laughed. "You can't be serious. He's a... a *milksop.* He wouldn't say nay to Father if he told him the sun rose in the west and he shat pearls."

The old woman compressed her lips at the profanity.

"I'm sorry, Nanny," Bennet said. "But Thomas! He's lived under my father's thumb so long he has calluses on his buttocks."

"Yes, I know." In contrast to the young man, Mistress Humboldt was calm. She must have expected his reaction. Or maybe she was simply used to his constant movement. "That's exactly why I name him."

Bennet stared.

"A man so long under his father's power isn't natural. Your father took a dislike to Thomas when he was very young. I've never understood it." She shook her head. "Lord Granville hating his own son so thoroughly."

"But even so, he'd never..." Bennet's words trailed off, and he abruptly turned away.

Mistress Humboldt looked sad. "He might. You know it

yourself, Master Bennet. The way your father has treated him shows. He's like a tree trying to grow through a crack in a rock. Twisted. Not quite right."

"But—"

"Do you remember the mice he'd catch sometimes when he was a boy? I found him once with one he'd caught. He'd cut off it's feet. He was watching it try to crawl."

"Oh, Jesus," Bennet muttered.

"I had to kill it. But then I couldn't punish him, poor lad. His father beat him enough already. I never saw him again with a mouse, but I don't think he stopped. He just got better at hiding it from me."

"We don't have to pursue this," Harry said.

Bennet swung around, his eyes desperate. "And what if he is the sheep poisoner? What if he kills someone else?"

His question hung in the air. No one could answer it but Bennet.

He seemed to realize it was up to him. He squared his broad shoulders. "If it is Thomas, he's murdered a woman. I need to stop him."

Harry nodded. "I'll talk to Dick Crumb."

"Fine," Bennet said. "You've helped us, Nanny. You see things nobody else does."

"Maybe not with my eyes anymore, but I always could read a person." Mistress Humboldt held out a wavering hand to her former charge.

Bennet grasped it.

"God save and protect you, Master Bennet," she said. "It's not an easy task you have."

Bennet leaned down to kiss the withered cheek. "Thank you, Nanny." He straightened and clapped Will on the shoulder. "We best be going, Will, before you finish those last two scones."

The old woman smiled. "Let the lad take the rest. It's been so long since I had a boy to feed."

"Thank you, ma'am." Will stuffed the scones into his pockets.

She saw them to the door and stood and waved as they rode away.

"I'd forgotten how sharp Nanny is. Thomas and I could never get anything past her." Bennet's face darkened when he spoke his brother's name.

Harry glanced at him. "If you want, you can put off talking to Thomas until tomorrow, after I've sounded out Dick Crumb. I'll have to wait until nightfall to find him, anyway. Best time to catch Dick is at the Cock and Worm after ten o'clock."

"No, I don't want to wait another day to talk to Thomas. Better to do it right away."

They rode for a half mile or more in silence, Will clinging behind Bennet.

"So once we find whoever's doing this," Bennet said, "you'll be leaving?"

"That's right." Harry watched the road ahead but could feel the other man's gaze on him.

"I was under the impression that you and Lady Georgina had an... uh... understanding."

Harry gave Bennet a look that usually shut a man up. Not him.

"Because, I mean, it's a bit thick, what? A fellow just up and leaving a lady."

"I'm not from her class."

"Yes, but that obviously doesn't matter to her, does

it? Or she'd never have taken up with you in the first place."

"I—"

"And if you don't mind me being blunt, she must be pretty gone on you." Bennet looked him up and down as if he were a side of spoiled beef. "I mean, you don't exactly have the sort of face that women swoon over. More in my line, that."

"Bennet—"

"Not to blow my own horn, but I could tell you quite a tale of a delectable bird in London—"

"Bennet."

"What?"

Harry nodded at Will, who was wide-eyed and listening to every word.

"Oh." Bennet coughed. "Quite. Shall I see you tomorrow, then? We'll meet and exchange information."

They had neared a copse of trees that marked where the main road crossed the lane they traveled on.

"Fine." Harry pulled his mare to a halt. "This is where I must turn off, anyway. And Bennet?"

"Yes?" He turned his face and the sun fell full upon it, tracing the laugh lines around his eyes.

"Be careful," Harry said. "If it is Thomas, he'll be dangerous."

"You be careful as well, Harry."

Harry nodded. "Godspeed."

Bennet waved and rode off.

Harry spent the rest of the daylight hours laying low. When dusk fell, he made his way to West Dikey and the Cock and Worm. He ducked his head as he entered and scanned the crowd from under his low hat brim. A table of farmers, smoking clay pipes in the corner, burst into boisterous laughter. A weathered-looking barmaid dodged with practiced ease a heavy hand aimed at her rump and made her way to the counter.

"Dick in tonight?" Harry bawled in her ear.

"Sorry, luv." She pivoted and shouldered a tray of drinks. "Maybe later."

Harry frowned and ordered a pint from the counterman, a lad he remembered seeing once or twice before. Was Dick hiding in back or was he really not in the building? He leaned on the wood counter while he thought and watched a gentleman, obviously a traveler, judging from the mud on his boots, enter and stare bemusedly around. The man's face was handsome but long and bland, rather like a goat's. Harry shook his head. The traveler must've missed the sign for the White Mare. He wasn't the Cock and Worm's usual type of customer.

The boy slid Harry his mug of ale, and Harry rolled a few coins back. He moved over and took a sip as the traveler came to the counter.

"Pardon me, but do you know the way to Woldsly Manor?"

Harry froze for a second, his mug at his lips. The stranger hadn't paid him any attention; he was leaning over the counter to the boy.

"Say again?" the boy shouted.

"Woldsly Manor," the stranger raised his voice. "Lady Georgina Maitland's estate. I'm an intimate of her younger sister, Lady Violet. I can't seem to find the road—"

The boy's gaze darted to Harry.

Harry clapped his hand on the other's shoulder, making the stranger start. "I can show you the way, friend, soon as I finish my ale."

The man turned, his face brightening. "Would you?"

"No problem at all." Harry nodded at the boy. "Another pint for my friend here. I'm sorry, didn't catch your name?"

"Wentworth. Leonard Wentworth."

"Ah." Harry suppressed a feral smile. "Let's find a table, shall we?" As the other man turned, Harry leaned over the counter and murmured urgent instructions to the boy, then passed him a coin.

An hour later, when the middle Maitland brother strolled into the Cock and Worm, Wentworth was on his fourth pint. Harry had been nursing his second for some time now and felt as if he needed a bath. Wentworth had been quite forthcoming about bedding a fifteen-year-old, his marriage hopes, and what he would do with Lady Violet's money once he got his hands on it.

So it was with some relief that Harry spotted the red Maitland hair. "Over here," he shouted at the newcomer.

He'd only spoken to Lady Georgina's middle brother once or twice, and the man hadn't been all that friendly. But all of Maitland's animosity was reserved for Harry's companion at the moment. He made his way to them with a look that would've sent Wentworth running, had he been sober.

"Harry." The redheaded man nodded at him; only then did Harry remember his name: Oscar.

"Maitland." Harry nodded. "Like you to meet an acquaintance of mine, Leonard Wentworth. Says he seduced your younger sister this last summer."

Wentworth paled. "Now w-w-wait a—"

"Really?" Oscar drawled.

"Indeed," Harry said. "He's been telling me about his debts and how her dowry will help settle them, once he's blackmailed her into marriage."

"Interesting." Oscar grinned. "Perhaps we should discuss this outside." He took one of Wentworth's arms.

"May I assist you?" Harry asked.

"Please."

Harry took the other.

"Uhh!" was all Wentworth got out before they frogmarched him through the doors.

"I've got a carriage over here." Oscar was no longer smiling.

Wentworth whimpered.

Oscar casually cuffed him over the head and Wentworth subsided. "I'll take him to London and my brothers."

"Do you need my help on the road?" Harry asked.

Oscar shook his head. "You've got him pretty far gone with drink. He'll sleep most of the way."

They heaved Wentworth's now-inert body into the carriage.

Oscar dusted his hands. "Thanks, Harry. We owe you."

"No, you don't."

Maitland hesitated. "Well, thanks, anyway."

Harry raised his hand in a salute, and the carriage pulled away.

Oscar poked his head through the retreating carriage window. "Hey, Harry!"

"What?"

"You fit in." Oscar waved and ducked back.

Harry stared as the carriage barreled around the corner.

GEORGE DIDN'T SLEEP WELL ANYMORE. Maybe it was the life growing inside of her, making its presence known by disturbing her sleep. Maybe it was the thought of the decisions she must make soon. Or maybe it was wondering where Harry was spending the night. Was he sleeping under the stars, shivering in a bundled up cloak? Had he found sanctuary with friends somewhere? Was he keeping another woman warm tonight?

No, best not to think of that.

She rolled over and stared out her black bedroom window. Maybe it was just the chill of the autumn air. A tree branch rattled in the wind. George drew the covers up to her chin. She'd found Harry's latest gift earlier when she'd prepared for bed. A small, rather funny eel. She'd thought it a snake at first, before remembering the fairy tale. Then she could see the tiny fin running along the creature's back. Did that complete her collection? He'd made all the animals the Leopard Prince had obtained for the princess. Perhaps it was his way of saying good-bye.

A shadow shifted outside her window, and the frame slid smoothly up. Harry Pye swung a leg over the sill and climbed into her room.

Thank goodness. "Is that how you've been getting in and out?"

"Mostly I've been sneaking in the kitchen door." Harry gently shut the window.

"That's not nearly as romantic as the window." George sat up and hugged her knees to her chest.

"No, but it's a lot easier."

"I had noticed that it's a three-story drop to the ground."

"With prickly rose bushes at the base, my lady. I hope you saw those, too." He strolled to the bed.

"Mmm. I did see the roses. Of course, now that I know you were merely using the kitchen entrance..."

"Not tonight."

"No, not tonight," George agreed. Oh, how she loved him. His green, ever-watchful eyes. His words, so carefully chosen. "But, even so, I'm afraid it has shattered some of my dreams."

Harry's lips twitched. His mouth sometimes gave him away.

"I found the eel tonight." She nodded at her dressing table.

He didn't follow her gaze. Instead, he continued to watch her. "I have one more." He held out his fist and opened his fingers.

A leopard lay on his palm. "Why is it caged?"

George took it from him and looked closely. The workmanship was incredibly cunning. The cage was all of one piece but separate from the leopard within. He would've had to whittle the animal inside the cage. The leopard in turn wore a miniscule chain about its neck, each link carefully delineated. A tiny, tiny crown hung from the chain.

"It's marvelous," she said, "but why did you carve the leopard in a cage?"

He shrugged. "It's enchanted, isn't it?"

"I suppose, but—"

"I thought you'd ask me why I'm here." He paced to the dresser.

She'd have to tell him soon, just not yet. Not while he seemed on the verge of flight. George set the caged leopard on her knees. "No. I'm just glad you're with me." She poked a finger through the bars and gently moved the leopard's necklace. "I'll always be happy when you come to me."

"Will you?" Harry was looking down at the carved animals.

"Yes."

"Hmm," he murmured noncommittally. "Sometimes I've asked that question of myself: Why I keep coming back when I've already said good-bye."

"And do you have an answer for yourself?" George held her breath, hoping.

"No. Except that I can't seem to stay away."

"Maybe that's your answer, then."

"No. It's too simple." He turned to look at her. "A man should be able to lead his life, make his decisions, in a more reasoned way. I said I would leave you, and so I should have."

"Really?" She set the leopard on the little table beside her bed and propped her chin on her knees. "But then what are emotions for? The good Lord gave them to men just as much as he gave intellectual thought. Surely He meant us to use our feelings as well?"

He frowned. "Emotions shouldn't hold sway over reasoned thought."

"Why not?" George asked softly. "If the Lord gave us both, then surely your emotion—your love of me—is just as important as what you think about our match. Perhaps it's more important."

"Is it for you?" Harry began to walk back to the bed.

"Yes." George lifted her head. "My love for you is more important than the fears I might have of marriage or of letting a man have dominion over me."

"What fears are those, my lady?" He had reached her bedside again. He stroked a finger down her cheek.

"That you might betray me with another woman." She

leaned her cheek on his hand. "That we might eventually grow apart and even come to hate each other." She waited, but he didn't try to allay her worries. She sighed. "My own parents didn't have a happy marriage."

"Nor did mine." Harry sat on the bed to take off his boots. "My mother betrayed Da for years; perhaps for the whole of their marriage. Yet he forgave her again and again. Until he could forgive her no more." He removed his coat.

"He loved her," George said softly.

"Yes, and it made him weak and eventually led to his death."

She could no more reassure him than he'd been able to reassure her. She wouldn't ever betray him with another man; she knew that. But who was to say she wouldn't lead to his destruction in another way? Did loving her make Harry weak?

George studied the caged leopard. "He gets free, you know."

He paused in unbuttoning his waistcoat and raised his eyebrows.

She held up the carving. "The Leopard Prince. He's freed in the end."

"Tell me." He shrugged off the waistcoat.

She took a deep breath, and said slowly, "The young king brought the Golden Eel to the father king, just as he had the other gifts. But the Golden Eel was different."

"It was ugly." Harry started on his shirt.

"Well, yes," George admitted. "But besides that, it could speak, and it was wise. When the father king got it alone, it said, 'Tush! That weakling no more stole me than the wind did. Listen now, tell the young king that the beautiful princess will only marry the man who wears the golden chain with the emerald crown on it. Then you will have the man who has done all these wonderful things. That man and no other shall be her bridegroom.' "

"I'm beginning to suspect you are making parts of this fairy tale up, my lady." Harry tossed his shirt to a chair.

George held up her hand. "On my honor as a Maitland. This is exactly how Cook's aunt told it to me in the kitchen of my town house over tea and crumpets."

"Huh."

She leaned back against the headboard. "So the father king marched back to the young king and told him the Golden Eel's words. The young king smiled and said, 'Oh, that's easy enough!' And he didn't even have to return home, for he'd brought the Leopard Prince with him. He went to the Leopard Prince and said, 'Give me that chain that hangs about your neck.' " She paused a moment to watch as Harry started to unbutton his breeches. "And what do you think the Leopard Prince said?"

He snorted. "Shove it up your"—he glanced at her—"nose?"

"No, of course not." She frowned severely. "No one talks like that in fairy tales."

"Perhaps they ought."

She ignored his mutter. "The Leopard Prince said, 'Impossible, my liege, for if I remove this chain, I will soon sicken and die.' The young king replied, 'Well, that's a pity, for I've found you quite useful, but I need the chain now, so you must give it to me at once.' And so the Leopard Prince did." George looked at Harry, expecting a protest, a comment, something.

But he simply returned her gaze and removed his

breeches. This made her temporarily forget where she was in the fairy tale. She watched as he sat on the bed beside her, quite nude.

"And?" he murmured. "Is that it? The Leopard Prince dies and the young king marries the beautiful princess?"

George reached up and untied the black ribbon holding his queue. She ran her fingers through his brown hair, spreading it on his shoulders. "No."

"Then?"

"Turn around."

Harry arched his eyebrows, but turned so his back was to her.

"The young king presented himself to the father king," George said quietly as she stroked her hands down his back, feeling the bumps of his spine. "And the father king had to admit that he wore the chain described by the Golden Eel. Reluctantly, he sent for his daughter, the beautiful princess." She paused to dig her thumbs into the muscles that sloped up from his shoulders to his neck.

Harry let his head fall forward. "Ahhh."

"But the beautiful princess took one look at the young king and started laughing. Naturally, all the courtiers and ladies and lords and the people who hang about a royal court just stared at the beautiful princess. They could not understand why she laughed." She worked her fingers into the muscles at the back of his head.

Harry groaned.

George leaned forward and whispered in his ear as she bore down on his shoulder muscles. "Finally her father, the king, said, 'What causes such mirth, my daughter?' And the beautiful princess said, 'Why, the chain doesn't fit him!' "

"How can a chain not fit?" Harry mumbled over his shoulder.

"Shhh." George pushed his head back down. "I don't know. It probably hung to his knees or something." She dug her thumbs into the hills along his spine. "Anyway, the beautiful princess looked around the court and said, 'There. That is the man the chain belongs to.' And, of course, it was the Leopard Prince—"

"What, she just picked him out of the crowd?" He twisted out of her hands this time.

"Yes!" George placed her hands on her hips. "Yes, she just picked him out of the crowd. He was an enchanted Leopard Prince, remember. I'm sure he looked quite distinguished."

"He was dying, you said." Harry was almost surly now. "He probably looked a right mess."

"Well, he didn't after the beautiful princess put the chain back on him." George crossed her arms. Really. Men were quite unreasonable sometimes. "He got better right away, and the beautiful princess kissed him, and they were married."

"Probably it was the kiss that revived him." Harry's mouth quirked. He leaned toward her. "And was the spell broken? He never turned into a leopard again?"

She blinked. "Cook's aunt didn't say. I would think so, wouldn't you? I mean, that is the usual thing in fairy tales, the spell is broken and they marry."

She was frowning thoughtfully and was consequently caught off guard when Harry lunged and captured her wrists. He pulled her hands above her head and loomed over her menacingly. "But perhaps the princess would have preferred that he remain a Leopard Prince."

"Whatever do you mean?" George asked, batting her eyelashes.

"I mean"—he nibbled at her neck—"it might have been more interesting on their wedding night."

She squirmed under the sensations he was arousing and stifled a giggle. "Wouldn't that be bestiality?"

"No." Harry took her wrists in one hand and used the other to whip off her covers. "I'm afraid you are mistaken in that, my lady." He flung up her shift, exposing her nude legs. She spread them invitingly, and he settled his hips there, making her gasp at the contact. "Bestiality," Harry murmured in her ear, "is congress between a human and a common animal, such as a horse or bull or rooster. Sexual activity with a leopard, on the other hand, is merely exotic." He nudged his hips, burrowing the length of his penis between her folds and touching her just *there*.

George's eyes closed. "A rooster?"

"In theory." He licked along her neck.

"But how could a rooster—?"

He used his free hand to pinch her nipple.

She moaned and arched beneath him, spreading her knees wider.

"You seem very interested in roosters," he purred. Harry rubbed his thumb over her nipple.

He hadn't moved his hips since that first time. George tried to bump hers up to encourage him, but his full weight lay heavily on her, and she realized he wasn't going to move until he wanted to. "Actually, you could say I'm more interested in one *cock* in particular."

"My lady." He raised his head, and she could see the censorious frown on his lips. "I'm afraid I do not approve of such language."

She felt a gush of erotic desire. "I'm sorry." She lowered her eyelashes demurely. "Whatever can I do to win your approval?"

There was silence.

George began to wonder if she had overstepped some boundary. But then she glanced up and saw Harry trying to repress a smile.

He bent his head until they were nose-to-nose. "It won't be easy to get in my good graces again." He flicked her nipple with a fingernail.

"No?"

"No." Almost casually he tugged the ribbon on her chemise and pulled it down. He cupped her breast in his hand. His palm felt incredibly hot. "You will have to work very hard." He flexed his hips, sliding between her folds.

"Mmm."

Harry stopped moving. "My lady?"

"What?" George muttered irritably. She nudged up, but he wouldn't move.

"Pay attention." He pinched her nipple again.

"I *am*." She opened her eyes wide to prove it.

He moved again. Agonizingly slow. She could feel the head of his erection slipping down, almost to her entrance and then back up to kiss her clitoris.

"You want to win my approval," he reminded her.

"Yes." She would have agreed to just about anything he said.

"And how are you going to do that?"

She had an inspiration. "By pleasing you, sir?"

He appeared to give that serious thought. All the while, his cock rubbed against her and his hand fondled her breast. "Well, yes, that might be one way to do it. Are you sure that's the way you want to choose?"

"Oh, yes." George nodded fervently.

"And how will you please me?" His voice had lowered to that deep tone that meant he was very aroused.

"By tupping you, sir?"

Harry froze. She was afraid for a moment that she might have shocked him.

Then he lifted his hips. "That'll do." And he thrust himself into her, hard and fast.

She felt a scream building in her throat as he pounded her into the mattress, all trace of playfulness wiped from his face. She wrapped her legs high over his hips, digging her heels into his buttocks. He'd let go of her wrists, and she dragged his head down by his hair to kiss him. Deeply. Ravenously. Desperately.

Please, please, dear Lord, don't let this be the last time.

He was relentless, and she could feel the explosion building within her, but she held it off, forcing open her eyes. It was important that she see him, that they be together at the end. His face was shining with sweat, his nostrils flared. As she watched, his rhythm broke. She let go of his hair to clutch at his shoulders, her entire being focused on keeping him within her.

And she felt it, at the end.

He reared back, his hips still locked with hers. She could feel his cock jump within her. Feel the spurt and warmth of his seed filling her. She arched her head and gave herself over to the waves of her own release, creaming and flooding with his. It was magnificent, like no other thing she had ever felt, having Harry spend in her body. Tears ran down her temples into her tangled hair. How could she ever let him go after this?

Harry suddenly shifted and tried to withdraw. "I'm sorry. I didn't mean to—"

"Shhh." George placed her fingers against his mouth, silencing his apology. "I'm increasing."

Chapter Eighteen

The word *increasing* seemed to echo around Lady Georgina's room, bouncing off the china-blue walls and dainty lace bed curtains. For a moment, Harry thought she meant that he'd made her pregnant just now when he'd filled her with his seed. When he'd been seduced by the force of his orgasm and the accompanying surge of his feelings for her.

Love for his Lady Georgina.

Even knowing he had to withdraw, he'd simply been unable to resist the moment. Unable to resist the woman.

Then sense returned. He rolled off Lady Georgina and stared at her. She was pregnant. He felt a spurt of ridiculous anger, hurt, that all his self-debate and worry didn't in the end even matter.

She was pregnant.

He'd have to marry her. Whether or not he wanted to marry her. Whether he could bring himself to let go and trust in their love. Whether he was able to fit himself into her life, so far out of his experience. All of that was beside the point now. Put simply, it was no longer of any importance. He'd been trapped by his own seed and a woman's body. He almost felt like laughing. That least-smart part of himself had made the decision for him.

Harry realized that he'd been staring at his lady far too long. Her hopeful expression had closed into one more guarded. He opened his mouth to reassure her when he caught a flicker from the corner of his eye. He raised his head. Yellow and orange lights danced at the window.

He stood up and strode to the window.

"What is it?" Lady Georgina called from behind him.

In the distance, a pyramid of light lit the night, glowing like something out of hell itself.

"Harry." He felt Lady Georgina's fingers on his bare shoulder. "What—?"

"Granville House is burning." *Bennet.* Panic, pure and instinctual, flooded his veins.

Lady Georgina gasped. "Oh, my dear Lord."

Harry whirled and caught his shirt, flinging it on. "I need to go. See if I can help in any way." Was Bennet asleep in his father's house tonight?

"Of course." She bent to pick up his breeches. "I'll come with you."

"No." He snatched the breeches from her hand and tried to control his voice. "No. You must stay here."

Lady Georgina frowned in that stubborn way of hers.

He didn't have time for this. Bennet needed him now.

"But I—" she began.

"Listen to me." Harry finished tucking in his shirt and grabbed his lady's upper arms. "I want you to do as I tell you. Granville is dangerous. He doesn't like you. I saw the look he gave you when you took me from his tender care."

"But surely you'll need me."

She wasn't listening to his words. She thought herself invincible, his beautiful lady, and she was simply going to do as she pleased. Regardless of what he thought. Regardless of Granville. Regardless of the danger to herself and the babe.

Harry felt fear build to an unbearable level inside him.

"I don't need you there." He shook her. "You'll only get in the way. You might get yourself killed. Do you understand?"

"I understand you are worried, Harry, but—"

Would she never give up? "Goddamn it!" He frantically looked around for his boots. "I can't fight the fire and you at the same time. Stay here!"

There they were, half under the bedskirts. He pulled his boots out and stamped them on, then snatched up his coat and waistcoat. He ran to the door. No use going out the window again—all of England would know soon enough that he'd been in his lady's bed.

He twisted at the door to repeat, "Stay here!"

On his last glimpse of her, Lady Georgina seemed to be pouting.

He thundered down the stairs, pulling on his coat. He would have to do a lot of apologizing when he returned, but he didn't have time to think of that now. His brother needed him. He dashed to the front door, waking a sleeping footman as he passed, and then he was out in the night. Gravel crunched beneath his boots. He ran around the corner of Woldsly. He'd tied the mare not far from his lady's window.

Come on. *Come on.*

The mare was standing in the shadows, dozing. He

vaulted into the saddle, startling the horse. He kicked her into a gallop, rounding the manor. By the time they hit the drive, the mare was going flat out. Here in the open, the fire seemed to loom larger in the sky. Even from this distance, he could see the flames leaping into heaven. He thought he smelled the smoke. It looked huge. Was the whole of Granville House engulfed? The mare reached the road and he slowed just enough to make sure there were no obstacles ahead. If Bennet and Will had been inside asleep...

Harry shook the thought away. He would not think until he reached Granville House and saw the damage.

Past the stream, lights glowed in the cottages dotting the hills. The farmers who lived and worked on Granville land were awake and must know of the blaze. But strangely he met no one else hurrying to the fire. Had they gone on ahead or were they huddled inside their cottages, pretending they didn't see? He topped the rise before the Granville gates, and the wind blew smoke and dancing ashes in his face. The mare was flecked with foam, but he urged her on down the drive.

And then he saw. The blaze had enveloped the stables, but Granville House was yet untouched.

The mare reared at the sight of the fire. Harry fought her down and forced her closer. As they neared, he could hear the shouting of men and the dreadful roar of the flames consuming the stables. Granville prided himself on his horseflesh, and he probably had twenty or more horses stabled here.

Only two horses were outside the stables.

Harry clattered into the yard, unnoticed by the lord or his servants. Men milled, half-dressed, seemingly in a daze. Their blackened faces were weirdly lit by the flames, the whites of eyes and teeth reflecting the glow. A few had formed a line and threw puny buckets of water on the inferno, merely making the monster more angry. In the middle of it all, Silas Granville was a figure out of hell. In his nightshirt, his bare legs sticking out of buckle shoes, his gray hair standing wildly on end, he surged around the courtyard, shaking his fists.

"Get him! Get him!" Granville cuffed a man, sending him sprawling to the cobblestones. "Goddamn all of you! I'll see you run out of my lands! I'll see you hung, you filthy curs! *Someone get my son!*"

Only on the last word did Harry realize a man was trapped in the inferno. He stared at the burning stables. The flames licked hungrily at the walls. *Was it Thomas or Bennet?*

"Nooo!"

Somehow, over the roaring and shouting, he heard the thin wail. He swung in its direction and saw Will, held physically off the ground by a burly footman. The boy struggled and fought, his gaze fixed on the flames all the while. "Nooo!"

It was Bennet in there.

Harry jumped from his horse and ran to the line of men hauling water. He grabbed a full bucket and upended it over his own head, gasping as the cold water slapped him.

"Oy!" someone yelled.

Harry ignored the shout and plunged into the stable.

It was like diving into the sun. The heat embraced and overwhelmed him, pulling him greedily down. The water in his hair and clothes hissed as it turned to steam. A black wall of smoke blocked his way. Around him, horses screamed their fear. He smelled ashes and, horribly, burning flesh. And everywhere, over all the rest, the awful flames eating the stable and everything within.

"Bennet!" He had the breath for one bellow.

His second breath brought ashes and burning heat into his lungs. Harry choked, unable to speak. He pulled his damp shirt up and covered his nose and mouth, but it made little difference. He stumbled forward like a drunkard, desperately feeling with his hands. How long could a man live without air? His foot struck something. Unable to see, he fell forward. He landed on a body, felt hair.

"Harry." A ghastly rasp. *Bennet.*

Harry searched quickly with his hands. He'd found Bennet. And another man.

"Have to get him out." Bennet was on his knees, struggling to pull the man, moving the dead weight only an inch or two.

Nearer the floor, the air was a little better. Harry gasped, taking in a lungful, and grabbed one of the unconscious man's arms. He heaved. His chest burned and his back ached as if the muscles were tearing. Bennet had the man's other arm, but he'd obviously reached the end of his rope. He pulled only feebly. Harry hoped, *prayed,* that they moved in the direction of the stable door, that he'd not gotten turned around in the smoke and screaming and ashes and death. If they went in the wrong direction, they would die here. Their bodies would be so thoroughly burned that no one would know which man was which.

My lady needs me. He grit his teeth and pulled against the agony in his arms.

I will be a father soon. His foot caught and he staggered, but kept himself upright.

My child will need me. He could hear Bennet sobbing behind him, whether from the smoke or from fear, he didn't know.

Please, God, they both need me. Let me live.

And Harry saw it: the stable door. He gave an inarticulate shout and coughed convulsively. One last, terrible heave and they were through the stable doors. The cool night air embraced them like the kiss of a mother. Harry staggered, still clutching the unconscious man. Then other men were there, shouting and helping them away from the flames. He fell to the cobblestones, Bennet beside him. He felt small fingers on his face.

He opened his eyes to see Will in front of him. "Harry, you came back."

"Aye, I did." He laughed and then started coughing, hugging the wiggling boy to himself. Someone brought a cup of water, and he sipped at it gratefully. He turned to Bennet, a smile on his face.

Bennet still wept. He coughed convulsively and clutched the unconscious man in his arms.

Harry frowned. "Who—?"

"It's Mr. Thomas," Will said in his ear. "He went into the stables when he saw the fire. Because of the horses. But he didn't come out, and Bennet ran in after him." The boy patted Harry's face again. "He made me stay with that man. I thought he'd never come out again. And then you went in, too." Will wrapped his thin arms around Harry's neck, nearly throttling him.

Harry gently pried loose the boy's arms and looked at the man they'd pulled from the stable. Half his face was blistered and red, the hair singed black and short on that side. But the other half was recognizable as Bennet's older brother. Harry held the side of his hand beneath Thomas's nose. Then he moved his fingers to the man's neck.

Nothing.

He touched Bennet's shoulder. "He's dead."

"No," Bennet rasped in an awful voice. "No. He grasped my hand inside. He was alive then." He raised red-rimmed eyes. "We pulled him out, Harry. We saved him."

"I'm sorry." Harry felt helpless.

"You!" Granville's roar came from behind them.

Harry jumped to his feet, fists clenched.

"Harry Pye, you goddamn criminal, you started this fire! Arrest him! I'll see you—"

"He saved my life, Father," Bennet choked out. "Leave Harry alone. You know as well as I that he didn't set the fire."

"I know nothing of the sort." Granville advanced menacingly.

Harry took out his knife and sank into a fighting crouch.

"Oh, for God's sake. Thomas is dead," Bennet said.

"What?" Granville looked for the first time at his eldest son, lying by his feet. "Dead?"

"Yes," Bennet said bitterly. "He went in after your damn horses and died."

Granville scowled. "I never told him to go in there. Stupid thing to do, just like everything else he's ever done. Foolish and pointless."

"Jesus Christ," Bennet whispered. "He's still warm. He breathed his last only minutes ago, and you're already demeaning him." He glared up at his father. "They were your horses. He probably ran in there to win your approval, and you can't even give him that after death." Bennet laid Thomas's head down on the hard cobblestones and rose to his feet.

"You're a fool, too, for going in after him," Granville sputtered.

For a moment Harry thought Bennet would hit his father. "You're not even human, are you?" Bennet said.

Granville frowned as if he hadn't heard, and maybe he hadn't. His son's voice was nearly ruined.

Bennet turned away nevertheless. "Did you talk to Dick Crumb?" he asked Harry in a voice so low no one else could hear. "I don't think Thomas set this fire and then ran into it."

"No," Harry replied. "I went to the Cock and Worm earlier, but he never showed."

Bennet's face was grim. "Then let's go find him now."

Harry nodded. There was no longer any way to put it off. If Dick Crumb had set this fire, he would hang for it.

GEORGE WATCHED THE DAWN BREAK with resignation. Harry had said he didn't need her, and he had not returned last night.

The message was quite clear.

Oh, she knew he'd spoken in haste, that when Harry had said, *I don't need you,* he'd feared Lord Granville might harm her. But she couldn't help feeling that he had spoken a hidden truth in that moment of frantic hurry. Harry guarded his words so well, was always so careful not to offend her. Would he ever have told her that he just didn't want to be with her had he not been driven to it?

She turned the little carved leopard in her hands. He looked back at her, his eyes blank inside his cage. Did Harry see himself in the animal? She hadn't meant to cage Harry; she'd only wanted to love him. But no matter how she wished, she could not change the fact that she was an aristocrat and Harry a commoner. The very circumstance of their disparate ranks seemed to be the basis of Harry's anguish. And that would never change.

She rose carefully from her bed, hesitating when her stomach gave an unpleasant roll.

"My lady!" Tiggle burst into the bedroom.

George looked up, startled. "What is it?"

"Mr. Thomas Granville is dead."

"Good Lord." George sat back down on the edge of the bed. She had almost forgotten the fire in her misery.

"The Granville stables burned last night," Tiggle continued, oblivious to her mistress's consternation. "They say it was set afire on purpose. And Mr. Thomas Granville ran in to save the horses, but he didn't come out. Then Mr. Bennet Granville went in despite his father's pleas not to."

"Was Bennet killed as well?"

"No, my lady." Tiggle shook her head, dislodging a pin. "But he was inside so long that everyone thought them both dead. And then Mr. Pye rode up. He ran inside right away—"

"Harry!" George leaped to her feet in terror. The room spun about her sickeningly.

"No, no, my lady." Tiggle caught her before George

could run to the door. Or fall down. "He's all right. Mr. Pye is fine."

George slumped with a hand over her heart. Her stomach was backing up into her throat. "Tiggle, for shame!"

"I'm sorry, my lady. But Mr. Pye, he pulled them both out, Mr. Thomas and Mr. Bennet."

"He saved Bennet, then?" George closed her eyes and swallowed.

"Yes, my lady. After what Lord Granville did to Mr. Pye, no one could believe it. Mr. Pye, would have saved them both, but Mr. Thomas was already dead. Burned fearfully, he was."

George's stomach lurched at the thought. "Poor Bennet. To lose a brother in such a manner."

"Aye, it must have been bad for Mr. Bennet. They say he held his brother's body as if he'd never let go. But that Lord Granville didn't turn a hair. Hardly looked at his dead son."

"Lord Granville must be mad." George closed her eyes and shuddered.

"There's some who think so, indeed." Tiggle frowned down at her. "Gracious, my lady, you're that pale. What you need is a nice cup of hot tea." She bustled to the door.

George lay back down, closing her eyes. Maybe if she was very still for a bit...

Tiggle returned, her heels tapping across the wood floor. "I thought that pale green gown would look very good when Mr. Pye comes to call—"

"I'll wear the brown print."

"But my lady." Tiggle sounded scandalized. "It's

simply not the thing to see a gentleman in. At least not a special gentleman. Why, after last night—"

George swallowed and tried to summon the strength to battle her lady's maid. "I won't be seeing Mr. Pye again. We'll be leaving for London today."

Tiggle drew in a sharp breath.

George's stomach gurgled. She braced herself.

"My lady," Tiggle said, "just about every servant in this house knows who came to call last night in your private rooms. And then the brave thing he did at Granville House! The younger maids have been sighing over Mr. Pye all morning, and the only reason the older maids aren't sighing as well is the look in Mr. Greaves's eyes. You cannot leave Mr. Pye."

The whole world was against her. George felt a wave of self-pity and nausea well up in her. "I'm not leaving him. We've simply come to an agreement that we're better off apart."

"Nonsense. I'm sorry, my lady. I don't usually speak my mind," Tiggle said with apparent sincerity, "but that man loves you. He's a good man, Harry Pye is. He'll make a good husband. And you're carrying his babe."

"I'm well aware of that." George belched ominously. "Mr. Pye may love me, but he doesn't want to. Please, Tiggle. I can't remain, hoping and clinging to him." She opened her eyes wide in desperation. "Can't you see? He'll marry me out of honor or pity and he'll spend the rest of his life hating me. I must go."

"Oh, my lady—"

"Please."

"Very well," Tiggle said. "I think you're making a mistake, but I'll pack to leave if that's what you want."

"Yes, it's what I want," George said.

And promptly threw up into the chamber pot.

THE SUN HAD LIT THE morning sky for more than an hour by the time Harry and Bennet rode up to the small, dilapidated cottage. They'd spent most of the night waiting at the Cock and Worm, even though Harry had suspected it was useless within the first half hour.

They'd first made sure of Will's safety by taking the sleepy boy to Mistress Humboldt's cottage. Despite the unholy hour, that lady had been glad to have the boy and they'd left him contentedly stuffing his face with muffins. Then they'd ridden to the Cock and Worm.

Dick Crumb and his sister both lived above the tavern in low-ceilinged rooms that were surprisingly tidy. Searching the rooms, his head grazing the lintels, Harry had thought that Dick must have to continuously stoop in his own house. Of course, neither Dick nor Janie had been there; in fact, the tavern had never opened that night, much to the disgust of several yokels hanging about the door. Dick and Janie had so few possessions, it was hard to tell if anything had been removed from the rooms. But Harry didn't think they'd taken anything. That was odd. Surely if Dick had decided to run with his sister, he would have taken at least Janie's things? But her few clothes—an extra dress, some chemises, and a pathetic pair of stockings riddled with holes—still hung from the pegs in her room beneath the eaves. There was even a small leather pouch with several silver coins hidden under Dick's thin mattress.

So, thinking the tavern keeper would come back for the money if nothing else, Harry and Bennet had lurked in the dark tavern. They had coughed and spit up black phlegm once or twice, but they hadn't talked. Thomas's death had stunned Bennet. He stared into space, his eyes far, far away. And Harry had considered his future life with a wife and a child and a whole new way of living.

As the dawn gave light to the dim room and it became evident that Dick wasn't going to show up, Harry remembered the cottage. The Crumb cottage, the hovel where Dick and his sister had been raised, had long ago fallen into ruin. But maybe Dick might use it as temporary shelter? Far more likely he was in the next county by now, but they might as well check it.

Now as they neared, the cottage looked deserted. The thatched roof had mostly fallen in, and one wall was crumbled, leaving the chimney pointing nakedly to the sky. They dismounted and Harry's boots sank into mud, no doubt the reason for the cottage having been abandoned. The river behind the tiny house spread over her banks here, making a marshy area. Every spring the cottage probably flooded. It was an unhealthy place to live. Harry couldn't think why anyone would build here.

"Don't know if we should even try the door," he said.

They looked at the door, tilting inward under a leaning lintel.

"Let's check around back," Bennet said.

Harry walked as quietly as he could in the mud, but his boots made a squishing sound as the muck sucked at them with each step. If Dick was here, he was already warned.

He was in the lead when he rounded the corner and stopped short. Plants as tall as a man grew in the boggy ground behind the cottage. They had delicate, branching fronds, and some still bore flat seed heads.

Water hemlock.

"Jesus," Bennet breathed. He'd come around Harry, but it wasn't the plants he looked at.

Harry followed the direction of his gaze and saw that the entire back wall of the cottage was gone. From one of the remaining rafters a rope was tied and a pathetic bundle dangled at its end.

Janie Crumb had hung herself.

Chapter Nineteen

"She didn't know what she was doing." Dick Crumb sat with his back against the decayed stone of the cottage. He still wore his stained tavern apron, and one hand clutched a crumpled handkerchief.

Harry looked at Janie's body, swaying only feet away from where her brother sat. Her neck was grotesquely elongated, and her blackened tongue protruded from swollen lips.

Nothing could be done for Janie Crumb now.

"She was never right, poor lass, not after what he did to her," Dick continued.

How long had he been sitting there?

"She used to slip away at night. Wander the fields. Maybe do other things I didn't want to know about." Dick shook his head. "It took me a while to realize she might be up to something else. And then Mistress Pollard died." Dick looked up. His eyes were bloodshot, his eyelids reddened. "She came in after they took you, Harry. She was wild, her hair all flying away. Said she hadn't done it. Hadn't killed Mistress Pollard like she killed the sheep. Was calling Lord Granville the devil and cursing him."

The big man knit his brows like a puzzled little boy. "She said Lord Granville killed old woman Pollard. Janie was crazy. Just plum crazy."

"I know," Harry said.

Dick Crumb nodded, as if relieved by his agreement. "I didn't know what to do. She was my little sister, crazy or no." He wiped the dome of his head with a shaking hand. "The only family I had left. My baby sister. I loved her, Harry!"

The body on the rope seemed to twist in horrible reply.

"So I did nothing. And last night, when I heard that she'd fired the Granville stables, I came a running down here. The old place had always been her hidey-hole. Don't know what I would've done. Only I found her like this." He threw his hands out to the corpse as if in prayer. "Like this. I'm so sorry." The big man began to cry, great heaving sobs that shook his shoulders.

Harry looked away. What could one do in the face of such overwhelming grief?

"You have no reason to apologize, Mr. Crumb," Bennet spoke from beside Harry.

Dick raised his head. Snot shone beneath his nose.

"The blame lies with my father, not you." Bennet nodded curtly and walked back around the cottage.

Harry took out his knife. Dragging a chair over beneath the corpse, he climbed up and cut the rope. Janie slumped, suddenly freed from her self-imposed punishment. He caught the body and gently lowered her to the ground. As he did so, he felt something small and hard fall out of Janie's pocket. He bent to look and saw one of his own carvings: a duck. Quickly, he palmed the little bird. Had Janie been placing his carvings at the poisonings all

along? Why? Had she meant to set him against Granville?
Perhaps she'd seen Harry as her instrument of revenge.
Harry darted a glance at Dick, but the older man was
simply staring into the face of his dead sister. It would
only grieve Dick further to tell him Janie had meant for
Harry to take the blame for her crimes. Harry pocketed
the duck.

"Ta, Harry," Dick said. He took off his apron and covered his sister's distorted face.

"I'm sorry." Harry laid his hand on the other man's
shoulder.

Dick nodded, grief overtaking him again.

Harry turned to join Bennet. The last sight he had of
Dick Crumb was the big man bending, a mountain of sorrow, over the slight form of his sister's body.

Behind them, the water hemlocks danced gracefully.

"THERE CERTAINLY HAS BEEN a lot of traveling of late,"
Euphie murmured, smiling benignly around the carriage.
"Back and forth between Yorkshire and London. Why, it
seems that everyone barely draws breath before they rush
off again. I don't believe I remember so much coming and
going since, well, since ever."

Violet sighed, shook her head slightly, and gazed out
the window. Tiggle, sitting with Violet, looked puzzled.
And George, scrunched next to Euphie on the same seat,
closed her eyes and gripped the tin basin she'd brought
along just in case. *I will not cast up. I will not cast up.
I will not cast up.*

The carriage lurched around the corner, jostling her
against the rain-streaked window. She decided abruptly
that her stomach was better with her eyes open.

"This is ridiculous," Violet huffed, and folded her arms. "If you're going to marry, anyway, I simply do not see what is wrong with Mr. Pye. He likes you, after all. I'm sure we can help him if he has trouble with his *H*s."

His *H*s? "You were the one who thought he was a sheep murderer." She was getting tired of the almost universal disapproval aimed at her head.

One would think Harry a veritable saint from the shocked reaction of her servants at her decampment. Even Greaves had stood on the Woldsly steps, the rain trickling off his long nose, staring mournfully at her as she climbed into the carriage.

"That was before," Violet said with unarguable logic. "I haven't thought him the poisoner for at least three weeks."

"Oh, Lord."

"My lady," Euphie exclaimed. "We should, as gentlewomen, never take the good Lord's name in vain. I am sure it was a mistake on your part."

Violet stared at Euphie in exaggerated astonishment while beside her Tiggle rolled her eyes. George sighed and rested her head on the cushions.

"And besides, Mr. Pye is quite handsome." Violet wasn't going to let go of this argument. Ever. "For a land steward. You aren't likely to find a nicer one."

"Land steward or husband?" George asked nastily.

"Are you contemplating marriage, my lady?" Euphie inquired. Her eyes opened wide, like an interested pigeon.

"No!" George said.

Which was almost drowned out by Violet's "Yes!"

Euphie blinked rapidly. "Marriage is a hallowed state, becoming to even the most respectable of ladies. Of course, I myself have never experienced that heavenly communion with a gentleman, but that is not to say that I do not wholeheartedly endorse its rites."

"You're going to have to marry *someone*," Violet said. She gestured crassly toward George's abdomen. "Unless you intend to take a protracted tour of the continent."

"Broadening the mind by travel—" Euphie started

"I have no intention of touring the continent." George cut Euphie off before she could gather wind and babble about traveling until they reached London. "Perhaps I could marry Cecil Barclay."

"Cecil!" Violet gaped at her sister as if she'd announced her intention of wedding a codfish. One would think Violet would be a little more sympathetic, considering her own near predicament. "Have you gone raving mad? You'll trample Cecil as if he were a fluffy bunny rabbit."

"What do you mean?" George swallowed and pressed her hand to her belly. "You make me sound like a harpy."

"Well, now that you mention it . . ."

George narrowed her eyes.

"Mr. Pye is quiet, but at least he never backed down from you." Violet's eyes widened. "Have you considered what he'll do when he finds out you've run away from him? It's the silent ones who have the worst tempers, you know."

"I don't know where you get these melodramatic ideas. And besides, I haven't run away." George ignored her sister, pointedly glancing around the carriage, which was presently bumping out of Yorkshire. "And I don't think he will do anything." Her stomach rolled at the thought of Harry finding her gone.

Violet looked doubtful. "Mr. Pye didn't strike me as the kind of man to just sit back and let his woman find another man to marry."

"I am not Mr. Pye's woman."

"I'm not sure what else you would call it—"

"Violet!" George clutched the tin basin under her chin. *I will not cast up. I will not cast up. I will no—*

"Are you feeling quite the thing, my lady?" Euphie piped. "Why, you look almost green. Do you know, your mother bore that exact same face when she was"—the companion leaned forward and hissed as if a gentleman might somehow hear her inside the moving carriage—"*increasing* with Lady Violet." Euphie sat back and blushed a bright pink. "But of course that can't be your problem."

Violet stared at Euphie as if mesmerized.

Tiggle buried her face in her hands.

And George groaned. She was going to die before she made it to London.

"WHAT DO YOU MEAN SHE'S GONE?" Harry tried to keep his voice even. He stood in the front hall of Woldsly. He'd come here to see his lady, only to have the butler tell him that she'd left over an hour ago.

Greaves backed up a step. "Exactly that, Mr. Pye." The butler cleared his throat. "Lady Georgina accompanied by Lady Violet and Miss Hope left quite early this morning for London."

"The hell you say." Had she received urgent news about a relative, maybe one of her brothers?

"Mr. Pye." The butler drew himself up in offense.

"I've had a very hard night, Mr. Greaves." And a harder

morning. Harry passed a hand over his aching forehead. "Was a letter brought to my lady? Or a rider? Did a rider come bearing some kind of news?"

"No. Not that it is any concern of yours, Mr. Pye." Greaves stared down his thin nose. "Now, if I may show you the door?"

Harry took two quick steps and grabbed the butler by the shirtfront. One step more and he slammed the man against the wall, cracking the plaster. "As it happens, what my lady does *is* my concern." Harry leaned close enough to smell the powder on Greaves's wig. "She's carrying my child and will soon be my wife. Is that understood?"

The butler nodded, sending a fine dusting of powder onto his shoulders.

"Good." Harry released the other man.

What would make her leave so suddenly? Frowning, he took the curving main stairs two at a time and headed down the long hall to his lady's room. Had he missed something? Said the wrong thing? The problem with women was that it could be damn near anything.

Harry threw open the bedroom door, scaring a maid cleaning out the hearth. He strode to Lady Georgina's vanity table. The top had been cleared. He opened drawers and flung them shut just as fast. They were empty save for a few hairpins and a forgotten handkerchief. The maid scurried from the room. Harry straightened from the vanity and surveyed the room. The wardrobe doors stood ajar and empty. A lone candlestick sat on the table by her bed. The bed itself had already been stripped. There wasn't anything to indicate where she'd gone.

He quit the room and ran back down the stairs, knowing the servants were aware of his movements. He knew he must seem a madman, racing about the manor and claiming the daughter of an earl as his bride. Well, damn them all to hell. He wasn't backing down. She was the one who had brought it this far. She'd laid down the gauntlet and then run for it. This time around he wasn't going to wait for her to come to her senses. Who knew how long it would take her to get over whatever snit she'd gotten herself into? He might be a commoner, he might be poor, but by God, he was going to be Lady Georgina's husband, and his wife needed to learn that she couldn't just light out every time she got a bee in her bonnet.

Harry mounted the poor mare, already half asleep, and turned her in the direction of his own little cottage. He'd pack the barest essentials. If he was fast, he might catch her before Lincoln.

Five minutes later, he opened the door to his cottage, thinking about what to bring, but all thought stopped when he saw the table. The leopard stood on it. Harry picked up the carved animal. It was exactly the same as the last time he'd seen it in her palm. Except that it was no longer in a cage.

She'd set the leopard free.

He stared at the wooden creature in his hands for a minute, rubbing his thumb over the smooth back he'd so carefully whittled. Then he looked at the table again. There was a note. He picked it up with a shaking hand.

My Dear Harry,
I'm sorry. I never meant to cage you. I see now that it wouldn't be right for me to force myself on you.

I'll take care of matters myself. Enclosed is something I had drawn up when last in London.
—Georgina

The second paper was a legal document. Lady Georgina had given him the Woldsly estate.

No.

Harry reread the fine script. The document remained the same.

No. No. *No.* He crumpled the paper in his fist. Did she hate him that much? Hate him enough to give up part of her inheritance to get him out of her life? He sank into a chair and stared at the balled scrap in his hand. Perhaps she'd finally come to her senses. Finally realized how very far beneath her he lay. If so, there would be no redemption for him. He laughed, but it came out more a sob, even to his own ears. He'd spent the last weeks pushing Lady Georgina away, but even as he'd done so, he'd known.

She was the one.

The one and only lady for him in this lifetime. If she left him, there would be no other. And he'd thought that was fine. His life had been adequate up until now, hadn't it? He could continue without her. But somehow in the last weeks she had burrowed into his life. Into him. And the things she had offered him so casually, a wife and family, a home, those things had become like meat and wine put before a man who had eaten only bread and water his entire life.

Vital.

Harry looked down at the crushed piece of paper and realized that he was afraid. Afraid he couldn't make this right. Afraid he'd never be whole again.

Afraid he'd lost his lady and their child.

* * *

TWO HORSES.

Silas snorted and kicked a still-smoldering beam. Two horses out of a stable of nine and twenty. Even Thomas's last act had been a piss-poor one; he'd managed to save only the pair of nags before succumbing to the flames. The air was thick with the stench of burned meat. Some of the men pulling out the carcasses were gagging, despite the scarves they wore over their mouths. Like little girls they were, whining over the stink and filth.

Silas looked at the remains of the great Granville stables. A heap of smoking debris now. All because of a deranged woman, so Bennet said. A pity she'd taken her own life. It would've set a nice example for the local peasants had she been fodder for the hangman. But in the end, perhaps he would've thanked the crazy wench. She'd murdered his elder son, which made Bennet his heir now. No more jaunting off to London for that young man. As the heir, he would have to stay at Granville House and learn how to run the estates. Silas curled his upper lip back in a grin. He had Bennet now. The boy might buck and paw, but he knew his duty. The heir to Granville must oversee the estates.

A rider clattered into the yard. Silas nearly choked when he saw who it was. "Get out! Get out, you young cur!" How dare Harry Pye just dance onto Granville land? Silas started for the horse and rider.

Pye dismounted his horse without even looking in his direction. "Out of my way, old man." He started for the house.

"You!" Fury clogged Silas's throat. He turned to the

gawking workmen. "Seize him! Throw him off my land, damn you!"

"Try it," Pye spoke softly behind him.

Several of the men backed up, the cowards. Silas turned and saw that Pye had a long, thin knife in his left hand.

The bounder pivoted in his direction. "How about acting for yourself, Granville?"

Silas stood still, clenching and unclenching his fists. Had he been twenty years younger, he wouldn't have hesitated. His chest burned.

"No?" Pye sneered. "Then you won't mind if I have a word with your son." He ran up the steps to Granville House and disappeared inside.

Filthy, common lout. Silas backhanded the servant nearest him. The man was caught off guard and went down. The other workmen stared at their fellow wallowing in the stable yard muck. One offered his hand to the man on the ground.

"You're all sacked after this day's work," Silas said, and didn't wait to hear the grumbling behind him.

He mounted his own stairs, rubbing at the fire in his chest. He'd throw the bastard out himself if it killed him. He didn't have far to go. Entering the great hall, he could hear men's voices coming from the front room where Thomas's body had been laid out.

Silas swung the door open, banging it against the wall.

Pye and Bennet looked up from where they stood near the table bearing Thomas's charred corpse. Bennet deliberately turned away from his father. "I can go with you, but I'll have to see Thomas properly buried first." His voice was a whispered rasp from the fire.

"Of course. My horse will need to rest after last night, anyway," Pye replied.

"Now wait just a minute," Silas interrupted the cozy pair. "You're not going anywhere, Bennet. Especially not with this bastard."

"I'll go where I want."

"No, you'll not," Silas said. The burning pain was spreading to his arm. "You're the heir to Granville now. You'll stay right here if you want a penny more from me."

Bennet finally looked up. Silas had never seen such hatred in another man's eyes. "I don't want a penny or anything else from you. I'm traveling to London as soon as Thomas has been decently buried."

"With him?" Silas jerked his head in Pye's direction, but he didn't wait for an answer. "So your baseborn blood has begun to tell, has it?"

Both men turned.

Silas grinned in satisfaction. "Your mother was a whore, you know that, don't you? I wasn't even the first she'd cuckolded John Pye with. That woman had an itch that just couldn't be scratched by one man. If she hadn't died so soon, she'd be spreading her legs in the gutter right now, just to feel a cock."

"She may have been a faithless lying whore, but she was a saint compared to you," Pye said.

Silas laughed. He couldn't help it. What a joke! The boy must have no idea. He gasped for breath. "Can't you do sums, lad? Must not be something they teach in the poorhouse, eh?" Another chuckle shook him. "Well let me spell it out for you, nice and slow. Your mother came here before you were conceived. You're as likely my son as John Pye's. More like, the way she panted after me."

"No." Strangely, Pye showed no reaction. "You may well have planted the seed in my mother, but John Pye and only John Pye was my father."

"*Father,*" Silas spat. "I doubt John Pye was even capable of getting a woman with child."

For a moment Silas thought Pye would go for his throat, and his heart leapt painfully. But the bastard turned aside and walked to the window, as if Silas were not worth the effort.

Silas scowled and gestured scornfully. "Do you see what I saved you from, Bennet?"

"Saved me?" His son opened his mouth as if laughing, but no sound came out. "Saved me how? By bringing me to this mausoleum? By putting me in the tender care of your bitch of a wife? A woman who must have felt the sting of her humiliation every single time she looked at me? By favoring me over Thomas so there was no way we would ever have a normal relationship?" Bennet was shouting hoarsely now. "By banishing Harry, my *brother?* God! Tell me, Father, how exactly have you saved me?"

"You walk out that door, boy, and I'll never welcome you back, heir or no." The pain in his chest was back again. Silas rubbed his breastbone. "You'll get no more money, no more help from me. You'll starve in a ditch."

"Fine." Bennet turned away. "Harry, Will is in the kitchen. I can have my bags packed in a half hour."

"Bennet!" The word felt as if it were ripped from Silas's lungs.

His son walked away from him.

"I've killed for you, boy." Damn it, he would not go groveling after his own son.

Bennet turned, a look of mingled horror and loathing on his face. "You *what?*"

"Murdered for you." Silas thought he bellowed, but the words weren't as loud as before.

"Jesus Christ. Did he say he murdered someone?" Bennet's voice seemed to float around him.

The pain in his chest had spread and become a fire burning through to his back. Silas staggered. Tried to grab a chair and fell, toppling the chair next to him. He lay on his side and felt the flames licking hungrily down his arm and over his shoulder. He smelled ashes from his son's body and piss from his own.

"Help me." His voice was a thin trickle.

Someone stood over him. Boots filled his vision.

"Help me."

Then Pye's face was in front of his own. "You killed Mistress Pollard, didn't you, Granville? That's who you murdered. Janie Crumb never had the strength to feed another woman poison."

"Oh, my God," Bennet whispered in his ruined voice.

Bile suddenly filled Silas's throat, and he heaved, choking on the contents of his own stomach. The carpet wool chafed his cheek as he convulsed.

Dimly, Silas saw Pye step aside, avoiding the pool of vomit.

Help me.

Harry Pye's green eyes seemed to bore into him. "I never begged for mercy when you had me beaten. Do you know why?"

Silas shook his head.

"It wasn't pride or bravery," he heard Pye say.

The fire crawled up into his throat. The room was going dark.

"My da begged you for mercy when you had him horse-whipped. You ignored him. There is no mercy in you."

Silas choked, coughing on hot coals.

"He's dead," someone said.

But by that time, the fire had reached Silas's eyes and he no longer cared.

Chapter Twenty

"You've gone mad." Tony sat back in the settee as if his pronouncement settled the matter.

They were in his elegant town house sitting room. Across from him, George sat stiffly in an armchair, the now-ever-present basin at the ready by her feet. Oscar prowled the room, munching on a muffin. No doubt, Violet and Ralph were taking turns pressing their ears to the door.

George sighed. They'd arrived in London yesterday, and she seemed to have spent all the time since debating her condition with her brothers. *I should have just eloped with Cecil.* She could have informed her family in a note and not even have been around to hear the resulting commotion.

"No, I've gone sane," she replied. "Why is it that everyone was against my being with Harry before and now they keep pushing me at him?"

"You weren't increasing before, Georgie," Oscar pointed out kindly. He had a fading bruise high on one cheek, and she briefly stared at it, wondering where he'd got it.

"Thank you very much." She winced as her tummy gave a bubbling rumble. "I think I'm aware of my state. I don't see that it matters."

Tony sighed. "Don't be obtuse. You know very well that your state is the reason you need to marry. The problem is the man you've chosen—"

"It's a bit thick, you must admit." Oscar leaned forward from his place at the mantelpiece and waved a muffin at her, scattering crumbs. "I mean, you are carrying the fellow's child. Seems only right he should have a chance at marrying you."

Wonderful. Oscar, of all people, was lecturing her on propriety.

"He's a land steward. You told me only recently that a land steward just *wasn't done*." George lowered her voice in a fair imitation of Oscar's tone. "Cecil comes from a very respectable family. And you like him." She folded her arms, sure of her point.

"I'm terribly disappointed in your lack of morals, Georgie, old girl. Can't tell you how disillusioning this insight into the female mind is for me. Might very well make me cynical for years to come." Oscar frowned. "A man has a right to his own progeny. Doesn't matter what class he comes from, the principle is the same." He bit into his muffin for emphasis.

"Not to mention poor Cecil," Tony muttered, "foisted off with someone else's get. How are you going to explain that?"

"Actually, that probably won't be a problem," Oscar muttered sotto voce.

"No?"

"No. Cecil's not that interested in females."

"Not inter—*oh*." Tony cleared his throat and yanked down on his waistcoat. She noticed for the first time that his knuckles were raw. "Well. And that's another consideration for you, George. Surely you don't mean to have *that* kind of marriage?"

"It doesn't really matter what kind of marriage I'll have, does it?" Her lower lip trembled. *Not now.* The last few days she'd found herself almost constantly on the verge of tears.

"Of course it matters." Tony was obviously affronted.

"We want you to be happy, Georgie," Oscar said. "You seemed happy with Pye before."

George bit her lip. She would not cry. "But he wasn't happy with me."

Oscar exchanged a look with Tony.

Tony drew his heavy eyebrows together. "If Pye needs to be persuaded to marry you—"

"No!" George drew a shuddering breath. "No. Can't you understand that if he's forced to marry me, it would be far worse than marriage to Cecil? Or no marriage at all?"

"Don't see why." Oscar scowled. "He might balk at first, but I think he'd soon come around once married."

"Would you?" George stared at Oscar.

He looked taken aback.

She switched her gaze to Tony. "Either of you? If you were forced to marry by the brothers of your bride, would you soon forgive and forget?"

"Well, maybe—" Oscar began.

Tony spoke over him. "No."

She raised her eyebrows.

"Look—" Oscar started.

The door opened and Cecil Barclay stuck his head around it. "Oh, sorry. Didn't mean to interrupt. Come back later, shall I?"

"No!" George lowered her voice. "Come in, Cecil, do. We were just talking about you."

"Oh?" He looked warily at Tony and Oscar, but he closed the door behind him and advanced into the room. He shook out a sleeve, spraying drops of water. "Ghastly weather out. Can't remember when it's rained so much."

"Did you read my letter?" George asked.

Oscar muttered something and flopped into an armchair. Tony propped his chin in a hand, long bony fingers covering his mouth.

"Quite." Cecil glanced at Tony. "It seems an interesting proposition. I take it you have discussed this idea with your brothers and it meets with their approval?"

George swallowed down a wave of nausea. "Oh, yes."

Oscar muttered, more loudly this time.

Tony arched a hairy eyebrow.

"But does it meet with your approval, Cecil?" George forced herself to ask.

Cecil started. He'd been looking rather worriedly at Oscar, slumped in the armchair. "Yes. Yes, actually it does. Solves a rather tricky problem, in fact. Due to a childhood illness, I doubt I'm able to, uh, father a... a..." Cecil petered out, staring a bit fixedly at her tummy.

George pressed a hand to her belly, wishing desperately that it would calm down.

"Quite. Quite. Quite." Cecil had regained his power of speech. He brought out a handkerchief and blotted his upper lip. "There is only one hitch, as it were."

"Oh?" Tony dropped his hand.

"Yes." Cecil sat in an armchair next to George, and she realized guiltily that she'd forgotten to offer him a seat. "It's the title, I'm afraid. It isn't much of one, only a obscure baronetcy that Grandfather has, but the estate that goes with it is rather large." Cecil passed the handkerchief over his brow. "Huge, to be quite vulgar."

"And you wouldn't want the child inheriting it?" Tony spoke quietly.

"No. That is, *yes,*" Cecil gasped. "Whole point of the proposition, isn't it? Having an heir? No, the problem is in my aunt. Aunt Irene, that is. The bally woman has always blamed me for being next in line to inherit." Cecil shuddered. "Fact is, I'd be afraid to meet the old bat in a dark alley. Might take the opportunity to make the succession a little closer to her own son, Alphonse."

"Fascinating as this family history is, Cecil, old man, how does it pertain to Georgie?" Oscar asked. He'd sat up during Cecil's recitation.

"Well, don't you see? Aunt Irene might challenge any heir that arrived, er, a little early."

Tony stared. "What about your younger brother, Freddy?"

Cecil nodded. "Yes, I know. A sane woman would see that too many stood between her Alphonse and the inheritance, but that's just it. Aunt Irene ain't sane."

"Ah." Tony sat back, apparently in thought.

"So what are we to do?" George just wanted to retire to her rooms and go to sleep.

"If t'were done, t'were best done quickly," Oscar said softly.

"What?" Cecil knit his brow.

But Tony sat up and nodded. "Yes. You've mangled

the quote, of course, but you're quite right." He turned to Cecil. "How soon can you get a special license?"

"I . . ." Cecil blinked. "In a fortnight?"

Oscar shook his head. "Too long. Two, three days at the most. Knew a fellow got one within a day of applying."

"But the archbishop of—"

"Canterbury's a personal friend of Aunt Beatrice's," Oscar said. "He's in London right now. She was telling me only the other day." He clapped Cecil on the back. "Come on, I'll help you find him. And congratulations. I'm sure you'll make an excellent brother-in-law."

"Oh, er, thanks."

Oscar and Cecil slammed out of the room.

George looked at Tony.

He turned down one corner of his wide mouth. "You'd better start looking for a wedding dress, Georgie."

Which was when George realized she was engaged—to the wrong man.

She grabbed the basin just in time.

THE RAIN POUNDED DOWN. Harry stepped unwarily and sank ankle-deep in oozing muck. The entire road was more a moving stream than solid ground.

"Jesus Christ," Bennet panted from atop his horse. "I think I'm growing mildew between my toes. I can't believe this rain. Can you? Four days straight without any letup."

"Nasty," Will mumbled indistinctly from his place behind Bennet. His face was all but hidden in Bennet's cape.

It had started raining the day of Thomas's funeral and continued through Lord Granville's internment the day after, but Harry didn't say that. Bennet knew the facts well enough. "Aye, it's nasty all right." The mare nuzzled the back of his neck, blowing a warm, musty breath against his skin.

The horse had gone lame a mile back. He'd tried looking at the mud-clogged hoof but hadn't found anything obviously wrong. Now he was reduced to walking her to the next town. Slowly walking her.

"What do you intend to do once we catch up with Lady Georgina?" Bennet asked.

Harry turned to peer at him through the downpour. Bennet had an expression of studied nonchalance.

"I'm going to marry her," Harry said.

"Mmm. I'd got the idea that was your overall plan." Bennet scratched his chin. "But she did take off for London. You must admit it looks rather as if she might be, well, *unreceptive* to the idea."

"She's carrying my child." A gust of wind flung a spatter of icy raindrops playfully against Harry's face. His cheeks were so numb with cold he hardly felt it.

"That part puzzles me." Bennet cleared his throat. "Because a lady in such a state, you'd think she'd be running to you with open arms. Instead, she appears to be running away."

"We've already been over that."

"Yes," Bennet agreed. "But, I mean, did you say something to her before?"

"No."

"Because women can be awfully sensitive when they're in the family way."

Harry raised an eyebrow. "And you would you know this how?"

"Everyone…" Bennet tilted his chin down, causing a

trickle of water to pour off his tricorn into his lap. "Damn!" He straightened. "Everyone knows about women with child. It's just common knowledge. Perhaps you didn't pay enough attention to her."

"She got quite a bit of attention from me," Harry growled irritably. He noted Will's brown eyes peering curiously around Bennet's back and grimaced. "Especially on the night before she left."

"Oh. Ah." Bennet frowned thoughtfully.

Harry searched for a change of subject. "I'm grateful to you for coming with me," he said. "Sorry you had to rush Thomas's funeral. And your father's."

"Actually"—Bennet cleared his throat—"I was glad you were there, rushed or not. Thomas and I weren't close, but he was my brother. And it was hard dealing with the succession on top of his funeral. As for Father..." Bennet swiped a drip of water off his nose and shrugged.

Harry splashed through a puddle. Not that it mattered. He was already soaked to the skin.

"Of course, you're my brother, too," Bennet said.

Harry shot a glance at him. Bennet was squinting down the road.

"The only brother I have now." Bennet turned and gave him a surprisingly sweet smile.

Harry half grinned. "Aye."

"Excepting Will, here." Bennet nodded to the boy clinging to his back like a monkey.

Will's eyes widened. "What?"

Harry scowled. He hadn't wanted to tell Will, as he was afraid it would confuse the boy's already complicated life, but it appeared that Bennet wasn't waiting to discuss the matter.

"It seems that my father might very well be yours as well," Bennet said now to the child. "We have similar eyes, you know."

"But mine are brown." Will frowned.

"The shape, he means," Harry said.

"Oh." Will thought about that for a bit, then peeked at him. "What about Harry? Am I his brother, too?"

"We don't know," Harry said quietly. "But since we don't, we might as well say we are. If you don't mind. Do you?"

Will vigorously shook his head.

"Good," Bennet said. "Now that's settled, I'm sure Will is as concerned as I am about your impending nuptials."

"What?" Harry lost the smile that had begun to form on his lips.

"The thing is, Lady Georgina is the Earl of Maitland's sister." Bennet pursed his lips. "And if she decides to dig in her heels ... might be a problem, the two of us going up against an earl."

"Huh," Harry said. It hadn't occurred to him before that he might have to go through his lady's brothers in order to speak to her. But if she was well and truly mad at him ... "Damn."

"Exactly." Bennet nodded. "It'd help if we could send word ahead to someone in London when we reach the next town. Have them reconnoiter, so to speak. Especially if it takes a while to get you a fresh horse." Bennet looked at the mare, who was definitely lagging.

"Aye."

"Not to mention, it would be nice to have someone at our back when we confront Maitland," Bennet continued. "I know a couple of blokes in London, of course. Might

be up for it, if we can convince them it's a sort of lark."
His brow furrowed. "They aren't usually sober, but if
I impress upon them the seriousness—"

"I have some friends," Harry said.

"Who?"

"Edward de Raaf and Simon Iddesleigh."

"The Earl of Swartingham?" Bennet's eyes widened.
"And Iddesleigh's titled, too, isn't he?"

"He's Viscount Iddesleigh."

"How the hell do you know them?"

"Met through the Agrarian Society."

"The Agrarians?" Bennet wrinkled his nose as if at a
bad smell. "Don't they debate turnips?"

Harry's mouth quirked. "It's for gentlemen interested
in agriculture, yes."

"I suppose it takes all kinds." Bennet still looked dubious.
"Christ, Harry, I had no idea. If you have friends like that,
why the hell are you playing around with me and Will?"

"You two are my brothers, aren't you?"

"Aye!" Will shouted.

"So we are." Bennet's face broke into a broad smile.

And then he tipped back his head and laughed into the
rain.

"THIS BLUE IS VERY NICE, my lady." Tiggle held up the
gown in question, spreading the skirts over her arm.

George glanced at the frock so enticingly displayed
and tried to muster some enthusiasm. Or at the very
least care one way or the other. It was her wedding day.
She and Tiggle were in her bedroom in her London
town house, which was presently strewn with the bright
colors of rejected frocks. George was having a hard time

convincing herself the wedding was real. It was only a scant week since she and her brothers had talked to Cecil, and now she was readying herself to marry him. Her life had taken on the aspect of one of those horrid dreams where a ghastly doom was inevitable and nobody could hear the screams.

"My lady?" Tiggle prompted.

If she screamed now, would anyone hear? George shrugged. "I don't know. The neckline doesn't really suit me, does it?"

Tiggle pursed her lips and set aside the blue. "Then what about the yellow brocade? The neckline is square and quite low, but we could put in a lace fichu, if you like."

George wrinkled her nose without looking. "I don't fancy all the ruffles about the bottom of the skirt. Makes me look like a cake with too much marzipan decoration."

What she really ought to wear was black. Black with a black veil. She looked down at her vanity and touched with one finger the little carved horse standing on it. The swan and the eel sat to either side of the horse. They looked rather forlorn without the leopard to guard them, but she'd left him behind for Harry.

"You'll have to decide soon, my lady," Tiggle said from behind her. "You're to be wed in less than two hours."

George sighed. Tiggle was being awfully kind to her. Normally, a bit of vinegar would have shown through her lady's maid façade by now. And she was right. It was no use holding on to dreams. Soon she would have a baby. Its welfare was of far greater importance than the silly fantasies of a woman who liked to collect fairy tales.

"I think the green, the one embroidered with lilies," she

said. "It isn't as new as the others, but it's rather fine and I've always felt it became me."

Tiggle gave a sigh of what sounded like relief. "A good choice, my lady. I'll get it out."

George nodded. She pulled out one of the shallow drawers at the top of her vanity. Inside was a plain wooden box. She opened the box and carefully laid the horse, the swan, and the eel inside.

"My lady?" Tiggle was waiting with the gown.

George closed the box and the drawer and turned to prepare for her wedding.

"*THIS* IS WHERE THE AGRARIANS MEET?" Bennet looked incredulously at the low-slung entrance to the coffee-house. It was on the bottom floor—really the cellar—of a half-timbered building in a narrow back lane. "The place isn't going to fall, is it?" He eyed the second floor looming over the lane.

"It hasn't yet." Harry ducked and entered the smoky room, Will sticking close to his side. He'd asked de Raaf to meet him here.

Behind him, he heard Bennet swear as he caught his head on the lintel. "The coffee had better be good."

"It is."

"Harry!" A large, pockmarked man hailed him from a table.

"Lord Swartingham." Harry made his way to the table. "Thank you for coming, my lord. May I present my brothers, Bennet Granville and Will?"

Edward de Raaf, fifth Earl of Swartingham, frowned. "I've told you to call me Edward or de Raaf. This *my lord* stuff is ridiculous."

Harry merely smiled and turned to the second man at the table. "Lord Iddesleigh. I hadn't expected you. Bennet, Will, this is Simon Iddesleigh."

"How d'you do?" Bennet bowed.

Will merely ducked his head.

"Charmed." Iddesleigh, a lean aristocrat with ice-gray eyes, inclined his head. "I had no idea Harry had relations. I was under the impression that he'd sprung fully formed like Athena from a rock. Or maybe a mangel-wurzel. It goes to show one can't always go by impressions."

"Well, I'm glad you came." Harry held up two fingers to a passing boy and took a seat, making room for Bennet and Will.

Iddesleigh flipped a lace-trimmed wrist. "Wasn't much else going on today, anyway. Thought I'd tag along. It was either that or attend Lillipin's lecture on compost layering, and fascinating though the subject of decay may be, I can't think how one could take up three whole hours on it."

"Lillipin could," de Raaf muttered.

The boy banged down two steaming mugs of coffee and whirled away.

Harry took a scalding sip and sighed. "Do you have the special license?"

"Right here." De Raaf patted his pocket. "You think there will be objections from the family?"

Harry nodded. "Lady Georgina is the Earl of Maitland's sister—" But he cut himself off because Iddesleigh was choking on his coffee.

"What's wrong with you, Simon?" de Raaf barked.

"Sorry," Iddesleigh gasped. "Your intended is Maitland's sister?"

"Yes." Harry felt his shoulders tense.

"The *older* sister?"

Harry merely stared, dread filling him.

"For God's sake, just spit it out," de Raaf said.

"You could have told me the bride's name, de Raaf. I only heard the news this morning from Freddy Barclay. We happened to meet at my tailor's, wonderful chap on—"

"Simon," de Raaf growled.

"Oh, all right." Iddesleigh suddenly sobered. "She's getting married. Your Lady Georgina. To Cecil Barclay—"

No. Harry closed his eyes, but he couldn't shut out the other man's words.

"Today."

TONY WAS WAITING OUTSIDE, hands clasped behind his back, when George emerged from her town house. Raindrops speckled the shoulders of his greatcoat. His carriage, which had the Maitland crest in gilt on the doors, stood ready at the curb.

He turned as George descended the steps and frowned with concern. "I was beginning to think I would have to come in after you."

"Good morning, Tony." George held out her hand.

He enveloped it in his own big hand and helped her into the carriage.

Tony took his seat across from her, the leather squeaking as he settled. "I'm sure the rain will stop soon."

George looked at her brother's hands resting on his knees and noticed again the scabbed knuckles. "What happened to you?"

Tony flexed his right hand as if testing the scrapes. "It's nothing. We sorted out Wentworth last week."

"We?"

"Oscar, Ralph, and I," Tony said. "That's not important now. Listen, George." He leaned forward, his elbows on his knees. "You don't have to go through with this. Cecil will understand, and we can work something out. Retiring to the country or—"

"No." George cut him off. "No, I thank you, Tony, but this is the best way. For the baby, for Cecil, and even for me."

She took a deep breath. She hadn't wanted to admit it, even to herself, but now George faced it: Somewhere deep inside, she'd secretly hoped Harry would stop her. She grimaced ruefully. She'd expected him to come charging up on a white stallion and sweep her off her feet. Perhaps wheel his stallion around while fighting ten men and go galloping off into the sunset with her.

But that wasn't going to happen.

Harry Pye was a land steward with an old mare and a life of his own. She was a pregnant woman of eight and twenty years. Time to put the past behind her.

She managed a smile for Tony. It wasn't a very good one, judging by the doubt on his face, but it was the best she could do at the moment. "Don't worry about me. I'm a grown woman. I have to face my responsibilities."

"But—"

George shook her head.

Tony bit off whatever he was going to say. He stared out the window, tapping long fingers against his knee. "Damn, I hate this."

Half an hour later, the carriage pulled up before a dingy little church in an unfashionable part of London.

Tony descended the carriage steps, then helped George down. "Remember, you can still end this," he murmured in her ear as he tucked her hand in the crook of his arm.

George just thinned her lips.

Inside, the church was dark and somewhat chilly with the faint smell of mildew lingering in the air. Above the altar, a small rose window hung in the shadows, the light outside too dim to tell what color the glass might be. Tony and George walked down the uncarpeted nave, their footsteps echoing off the old stones. Several candles were lit at the front near the altar, supplementing the feeble light from the clerestory. A small group was gathered there. She saw Oscar, Ralph, and Violet as well as her imminent husband, Cecil, and his brother, Freddy. Ralph was sporting a yellowing black eye.

"Ah, the bride, I presume?" The vicar peered over half-moon glasses. "Quite. Quite. And your name is, umm"—he consulted a piece of notepaper stuck in his Bible—"George Regina Catherine Maitland? Yes? But what an odd name for a woman."

She cleared her throat, tamping down hysterical laughter and sudden nausea. *Oh, please, Lord, not now.* "Actually, my given name is Georgina."

"Georgiana?" the vicar asked.

"No, *Georgina.*" Did it really matter? If this silly man said the wrong name during the service, would she not be married to Cecil?

"Georgina. Quite. Now, then, if we are all here and ready?" The assembled nobility nodded meekly. "Then let us proceed. Young lady, please stand here."

He shuffled them around until George and Cecil were side by side with Tony at George's side and Freddy as best man at Cecil's.

"Good." The vicar blinked at them, then spent a prolonged minute ruffling his paper and Bible. He cleared his throat. "Dearly beloved," he began in a strange falsetto.

George winced. The poor man must think it more carrying.

"We are gathered here—"

Bang!

The sound of the church doors smacking against the wall reverberated throughout the church. The group turned as one to look.

Four men marched grimly up the aisle, trailed by one small boy.

The vicar frowned. "Rude. Quite rude. Astonishing what people think they can get away with these days."

But the men had reached the altar now.

"Excuse me, but I believe you have my lady," one of them said in a quiet, deep voice that sent veritable chills down George's spine.

Harry.

Chapter Twenty-one

The shriek of steel against steel echoed from the walls of the little church as every man in the wedding party drew his sword simultaneously. Followed immediately by Bennet, de Raaf, and Iddesleigh unsheathing their weapons. Bennet looked very serious. He'd shoved Will into a pew as soon as they'd neared the altar, and now he held his sword high and his body angled. De Raaf's pale, pock-marked face was alert, his arm steady. Iddesleigh had a bored expression and handled his sword carelessly, his long, lace-draped fingers nearly limp. Of course, Iddesleigh was probably more dangerous than any of them with a sword.

Harry sighed.

He hadn't slept in two days. He was muddy and no doubt smelled. He couldn't remember his last meal. And he'd spent the last terror-stricken, heart-stopping, god-awful hour riding hell for leather across London, thinking they would never make it in time to stop his lady from marrying another man.

Enough.

Harry strode through the mess of weapon-wielding

aristocrats to his lady's side. "If I might have a word, my lady?"

"But, I mean..." the skinny blond man by her side, presumably the groom, damn his hide, protested.

Harry turned his head and looked the man in the eye.

The groom backed up so fast he nearly stumbled. "Jolly good! Jolly good! No doubt it's important, what?" He sheathed his sword with a shaking hand.

"Who are you, young man?" The vicar peered over his spectacles at Harry.

Harry gritted his teeth and pulled back his lips in something like a smile. "I'm the father of the child Lady Georgina is carrying."

De Raaf cleared his throat.

One of his lady's brothers muttered, "Christ."

And Lady Violet giggled.

The cleric blinked his myopic light blue eyes rapidly. "Well, then, I suggest you indeed have a word with this lady. You may use the vestry." He closed his Bible.

"Thank you." Harry latched one hand around his lady's wrist and pulled her toward the little door off to the side. He needed to make the room before his pain exploded from him. Behind them there was absolute silence.

He dragged his lady into the room and kicked the door closed. "What the *hell* did you mean by this?" Harry took out the legal document deeding Woldsly to him. He held it up to her face and shook it, his anger—his anguish—barely contained. "Did you think I could be bought off?"

Lady Georgina retreated before the paper, her face confused. "I—"

"Think again, my lady." Harry tore the paper into shreds and threw them on the floor. He gripped her upper arms, flexing his trembling fingers against her flesh. "I'm not a lackey to be dismissed with a too-generous present."

"I only—"

"I won't be dismissed at all."

Lady Georgina opened her lips again, but he didn't wait for her to speak. He didn't want to hear her reject him. So Harry covered her lips with his own. He ground down on her soft, lush mouth, thrusting in his tongue. He placed his hand under her chin and felt the vibration of her moan in her throat. His cock was already hard and aching. He wanted to pound it against her, pound it into her. Put himself inside her and stay there until she told him why she had run away. Until she promised never to do it again.

He crowded her against a heavy trestle table and felt her body yield to his. That submission brought him a small measure of control.

"Why?" he groaned against her lips. "Why did you leave me?"

She made a small sound, and he nipped her bottom lip to silence her.

"I need you." He licked her bruised lip to soothe it. "I can't think straight without you. My world is all turned around, and I go through it in pain, wanting to hurt someone."

He kissed her again, open-mouthed, to reassure himself that she was really here in his arms. Her mouth was warm and wet and tasted of her morning's tea. He could spend the rest of his life just tasting her.

"I hurt. Here." He grabbed her hand and placed her palm against his chest. "And here." He pulled it lower and thrust his prick crudely into her fingers.

That felt good, to have her hand on him again, but it wasn't enough.

Harry picked his lady up and sat her on the table. "You need me as well. I know you do." He flung up her skirts and burrowed his hand under them, feeling along her thighs.

"Harry—"

"Shhh," he murmured against her mouth. "Don't talk. Don't think. Just feel." His fingers found her cunny, and she was wet. "Ahh, there. Do you feel it?"

"Harry, I don't—"

He touched her pea-shaped bit of flesh and she moaned, eyes closed. The sound inflamed him.

"Hush, my lady." He unbuttoned his breeches and parted her thighs wider, stepping between them.

She moaned again.

He didn't care much, but she might be embarrassed. Later. "Shhh. You have to be quiet. Very quiet." His flesh pressed against her weeping opening.

Her eyes suddenly flew open at the touch of his cock. "But, Harry . . ."

"My lady?" He gently pushed in. *Ah, God, so tight.*

She clutched him as if she would never let him go. And that was fine with him. He was more than glad to stay right here for eternity. Or maybe a little farther in.

He shoved again.

"Oh, Harry," his lady sighed.

Someone pounded on the door.

She started, squeezing him inside. He bit back a groan.

"George? Are you all right?" One of the brothers.

Harry withdrew a little and thrust carefully. Tenderly. "Answer him."

"Is it locked?" His lady arched her back as he thrust. "Is the door locked?"

He grit his teeth. "No." He wrapped his hands around her bare rump.

The pounding started again. "George? Should I come in?" His lady panted.

He somehow grinned through his terrible desire. "Should he?" He thrust deeply, burying himself in her heat. Whatever happened, he wasn't fleeing. He didn't think he could, anyway.

"No," she gasped.

"What?" From the door.

"No!" she yelled. "*Unh.* Go away, Tony! Harry and I need to converse a little longer."

Harry cocked an eyebrow. "Converse?"

She glared at him, her face flushed and damp.

"You're sure?" Tony apparently cared deeply for his sister.

Harry knew he would appreciate that fact later. He brought one hand to where he was joined with her. He touched her.

"Yes!" she screamed.

"Fine, then." Footsteps retreated.

His lady wrapped her legs high over his hips and leaned forward to bite his mouth. "Finish it."

His eyes half closed at the feel, the perfection, of her. This was his lady, and he was going to claim her. His chest filled with gratitude that he'd been given this second chance.

But she was still waiting. "As you wish." He pressed his thumb firmly on her and at the same time thrust hard and quick, shaking the table.

"Oh, my Lord!" she moaned.

"Bite my shoulder," he panted, picking up his pace even more.

He felt the pinch even through his coat's broadcloth. And then he burst within her, flinging his own head back and grinding his teeth to keep from shouting in ecstasy. "*God!*"

His entire body trembled in the aftermath, and he had to prop one arm on the table to brace both of them. He locked his knees to stay upright and gasped, "Will you marry me, my lady?"

"You're asking *now?*" Her voice was weak.

At least he wasn't the only one affected. "Yes. And I'm not leaving until you give me an answer."

"WHAT COULD THEY POSSIBLY be talking about this long?" Violet asked no one in particular. She shivered and wished she'd thought to bring a wrap. The church was chilly.

The vicar muttered and settled more deeply into a front pew. His eyes were closed. She suspected he'd fallen asleep.

She tapped her foot on the flagstones. When Harry and his friends had first shown up, it had been quite tense, exciting really, with all those swords waving about. She'd thought for sure that some type of fight would break out. She'd been all ready to start tearing up her underskirts in the proscribed manner should any blood be spilled. But as the minutes wore on, the gentlemen had begun to look, well, *bored.*

The big man with the scarred face started poking the tip of his sword into the cracks in the church flagstones. The elegant-looking man was glaring at the big man and lecturing him on the proper maintenance of blades. The third man in Harry's group had brown hair and was wearing a terribly dusty coat. That was all she knew about him because his back was to everyone else as he idly inspected the church's stained-glass windows. He had a small boy by his side and appeared to be pointing out to him the biblical scenes depicted in the glass.

Meanwhile, Oscar, Ralph, Cecil, and Freddy, the defenders of George's honor, were arguing about the correct way to hold a sword. Ralph's eye was swollen and turning greenish yellow, and Oscar was limping. She'd have to find out about that later.

Violet sighed. It was all rather disappointing.

"I say, aren't you de Raaf?" Tony had returned from knocking on the vestry with an odd, almost embarrassed expression. He addressed the scarred man. "The Earl of Swartingham, I mean?"

"Yes?" The big man frowned ferociously.

"Maitland here." Tony stuck out his hand.

Lord Swartingham stared at the proffered appendage for a moment, then sheathed his sword. "How d'you do?" He tilted his head toward the elegant man. "This is Iddesleigh, viscount."

"Ah, indeed." Tony shook hands with him as well. "Heard of you, de Raaf."

"Oh?" The big man looked wary.

"Yes." Tony was unperturbed. "Read a manuscript of yours a while back. About crop rotation?"

"Ah." The big man's face cleared. "Do you practice crop rotation on your lands?"

"We've begun to. We're a bit farther north than you, and peas are a major crop in the area."

"And barley and swedes," Oscar cut in. He and Ralph wandered over.

"Naturally," Lord Swartingham murmured.

Swedes? Violet stared. They were discussing farming

as if they were at an afternoon tea. Or rather, in this case, at the neighborhood tavern.

"Sorry." Tony indicated his brothers. "This is Oscar and Ralph, my younger brothers."

"How d'you do?"

Another round of masculine handshaking.

Violet shook her head dumbly. She would never, never, *never* understand the human male.

"Oh, and this is Cecil and Freddy Barclay." Tony cleared his throat. "Cecil was to marry my sister."

"Not anymore, I fear," Cecil said ruefully.

They all chuckled, the boobies.

"And you must be the little sister," a male voice said in her ear.

Violet whirled to find Harry's third friend standing behind her. He'd left the boy kicking his heels in a pew. Up close, the man's eyes were a beautiful green, and he was suspiciously handsome.

Violet narrowed her own eyes. "Who are you?"

"Granville, Bennet Granville." He bowed.

Violet didn't curtsy. This was too confusing. Why would a Granville be helping Harry?

"Lord Granville nearly killed Mr. Pye." She scowled up at Bennet Granville.

"Yes, I'm afraid he's my father." His smile slipped a bit. "Not my fault, I assure you. I had very little to do with my conception."

Violet felt her mouth start to relax into a smile and suppressed it ruthlessly. "What are you doing here?"

"Well, that is a story—" Mr. Granville cut himself off, and his gaze moved over her head. "Ah, I think they're emerging."

And the questions Violet had been about to ask slid from her mind. She turned to see if George had decided which man she would marry.

GEORGE SIGHED LUXURIOUSLY. She could fall asleep right here in Harry's arms. Even if she was perched on a vestry table.

"Well?" He nudged her with his chin.

Apparently he wanted an answer now. She tried to think, hoping her brain hadn't turned to mush like her legs. "I love you, Harry, you know I do. But what about your reservations? That others would think you my pet"—she gulped, hating to say the word—"monkey?"

He nuzzled the hair at her temple. "I can't deny that it will bother me. That and what they will say about you. But the thing is"—he raised his head and she saw that his emerald eyes had grown soft, almost vulnerable—"I don't think I can live without you, my lady."

"Oh, Harry." She cradled his face in her palms. "My brothers like you, as does Violet. And, really, they're all that matter in the end. The rest can go hang for all I care."

He smiled, and as always, her heart sang at the sight. "Then will you marry me and be my lady for all our lives?"

"Yes. Yes, of course I'll marry you." She felt tears start in her eyes. "I love you desperately, you know."

"And I love you," he said rather absently, in her opinion. He carefully removed himself from her sensitive flesh.

"Oh, must you?" George tried to hold on to him.

"I'm afraid so." Harry was swiftly rebuttoning his breeches. "They're waiting for us out there."

"Oh, let them wait." She wrinkled her nose. He'd just proposed to her in a most romantic manner. Couldn't she savor the moment?

Harry leaned forward to flip down her skirts and kiss her nose. "We'll have plenty of time to lounge about after."

"After?"

"After our marriage." Harry frowned at her. "You did just agree to marry me."

"But I didn't imagine right away." She checked her bodice. Why wasn't there a mirror in here?

"You were ready to marry that popinjay out there right away." Harry gestured with an outflung arm.

"That was different." Did she look like she'd been doing what she had been doing? "And Cecil isn't a popinjay; he's—" She noticed that his expression had darkened alarmingly. Perhaps it was time to change the subject. "We can't get married. We need a license."

"I already have one." Harry patted his coat pocket. It crinkled.

"How—?"

He cut her off with a kiss that could only be described as masterful. "Are you going to marry me or not?"

George clutched at his arms. Really, some of Harry's kisses left her quite weak. "I'm going to marry you."

"Good." Harry tucked her arm through his and marched her to the door.

"Stop!"

"What?"

Men could be so obtuse. "Do I look like I've just been tumbled?"

Harry's lips twitched. "You look like the most beautiful

woman in the world." He kissed her soundly again. He hadn't exactly answered her question, but it was too late now.

He opened the door.

The two camps had merged into one lump, crowded around the altar. Good Lord, they hadn't been fighting, had they? Everyone turned expectantly.

George cleared her throat, trying to put together the right words. Then she saw something and stopped dead. "Harry..."

"My lady?"

"Look." She pointed.

A Persian carpet of lights danced on the formerly dingy floor: cobalt blues, ruby reds, and amber yellows. She followed the beam of light back to its source, the rose window above the altar. It glowed, lit from without by sunshine.

"The sun has come out," George whispered in awe. "I'd almost forgotten what it looked like. Do you think it's shining in Yorkshire as well?"

Harry's green eyes sparkled down at her. "I have no doubt, my lady."

"Ahem." George looked up to see Violet staring at them in a rather exasperated manner. *"Well?"*

She smiled. "I shall be marrying Mr. Pye today."

Violet squealed.

"About time," someone, probably Oscar, muttered.

George ignored that and tried to look contrite as she turned to poor Cecil. "I am so sorry, Cecil. I—"

But Cecil interrupted, "Don't worry your head, old thing. I shall dine out on this tale for the next year. It isn't every day a fellow is left at the altar."

"Eh?" A cry from the front pew brought everyone around. The vicar straightened his wig. He returned his spectacles to his nose and searched the gathering until his eyes lit on George. "Now, then, young lady. Which of these gentlemen will you marry?"

"This one." She squeezed Harry's arm.

The vicar inspected Harry and sniffed. "Doesn't look that much different from the other one."

"Nevertheless"—she fought to remain sober-faced—"this is the man I want."

"Very well." The vicar frowned at Harry. "Have you a license?"

"Yes." He produced the piece of paper. "And my brothers will serve as groomsmen."

Bennet walked to Harry's side and stood with Will just a little behind him. The boy looked both terrified and excited.

"Brothers?" Violet hissed.

"I'll explain later," George said. She blinked back sudden tears.

"My dinner is waiting, so let us commence." The vicar cleared his throat noisily. He began again in the same falsetto voice he'd used before, "Dearly beloved..."

Everything else was different.

The sun shone through the rose window, lighting and warming the little church. Tony looked relieved, as if a terrible burden had been lifted from his shoulders. Ralph grinned next to him. Oscar winked at George as she caught his eye. Violet kept shooting puzzled glances at Bennet, but in between she grinned at George. Bennet stood a little awkwardly beside Harry, but he seemed proud as well. Will was bouncing on his toes in excitement.

And Harry . . .

George looked at him and felt a great bubble of joy well up inside her. Harry watched her as if she were the center of his soul. He wasn't smiling, but his beautiful emerald eyes were warm and serene.

When it came time to pledge herself to Harry, George leaned toward him and whispered, "I forgot one thing when I told you about the end of the fairy tale."

Her almost husband smiled down at her and asked gravely, "What was that, my lady?"

She savored the moment and the love in his eyes, then declared, "And they lived happily ever after!"

"So they did." Harry whispered back, and kissed her.

Vaguely she heard the vicar moan, "No, no, not yet!" and then, "Oh, never mind. I pronounce you man and wife."

And that was how it should be, George thought as she opened her mouth beneath her husband's. She was Harry's wife.

And Harry was her man.

About the Author

Elizabeth Hoyt lives in central Illinois with three untrained dogs, two angelic but bickering children, and one long-suffering husband. There is some debate on whether a golden hamster resides with her family as well. The hamster was a free-thinking rodent and decided to live *sans* cage sometime in the summer of '05. It has not been reliably spotted since, although Elizabeth's youngest child holds out hope of its return. The hermit crabs are best not mentioned at all.

Winters are long, cold, and monotonous in central Illinois. Elizabeth would be most appreciative of any mail you'd care to send her. You may e-mail her at elizabeth@elizabethhoyt.com or mail her at PO Box 17134, Urbana, Illinois 61803. Please visit her website at elizabethhoyt.com for giveaways, book excerpts, and author updates.

Chapter One

The dead man at Lucinda Craddock-Hayes's feet looked like a fallen god. Apollo, or more likely Mars, the bringer of war, taken human form and struck down from the heavens to be found by a maiden on her way home. Except that gods rarely bleed.

Or die, for that matter.

"Mr. Hedge," Lucy called over her shoulder. She glanced around the lonely lane leading from the town of Maiden Hill to the Craddock-Hayes house. It appeared the same as before she'd made her find: deserted, except for herself; her manservant, puffing a ways behind her; and the corpse lying in the ditch. The sky hung low and wintry gray. The light had already begun to leak away, though it was not yet five o'clock. Leafless trees lined the road, silent and chill.

Lucy shivered and drew her wrap more closely about her shoulders. The dead man lay sprawled facedown, naked and battered. The long lines of his back were marred by a mass of blood on his right shoulder. Below were lean hips, muscular, hairy legs, and curiously elegant, bony feet. She blinked and returned her gaze to his face. Even in death he was handsome. His head, turned to the side, revealed a patrician profile: long nose, high bony cheeks, and a wide mouth. An eyebrow, winging over his closed eye, was bisected by a scar. Closely cropped pale hair grew flat to his skull, except where it was matted by blood. His left hand was flung above his head and on the index finger was an impression where a ring had once been. His killers must've stolen it along with everything else. Around the body the mud was scuffed, the imprint of a boot heel stamped deep beside the dead man's hip. Other than that, there was no sign of whoever had dumped him here like so much offal.

Lucy felt silly tears prick at her eyes. Something about the way that he'd been left, naked and degraded by his murderers, seemed a terrible insult to the man. It was so unbearably sad. *Ninny,* she chided herself. She became conscious of a muttering drawing steadily closer. Hastily, she swiped at the moisture on her cheeks.

"First she visits the Joneses and all the little Joneses, snotty-nosed buggers. Then we march up the hill to old woman Hardy—nasty biddy; don't know why she hasn't been put to bed with a shovel yet. And is that all? No, that's not all by half. Then, *then* she must needs call round the vicarage. And me carting great jars of jelly all the while."

Lucy suppressed an urge to roll her eyes. Hedge, her manservant, wore a greasy tricorne smashed down over a shock of gray hair. His dusty coat and waistcoat were equally disreputable, and he'd chosen to highlight his bowlegs with scarlet-clocked stockings, no doubt Papa's castoffs.

He halted beside her. "Oh, gah, not a deader!"

In his surprise, the little man had forgotten to stoop, but when Lucy turned to him, she saw his wiry body decay before her eyes. His back suddenly curved, the shoulder bearing the awful weight of her now empty basket fell, and his head hung to the side listlessly. As the pièce de résistance, Hedge took out a checkered cloth and laboriously wiped his forehead.

Lucy ignored all this. She'd seen the act hundreds, if not thousands, of times in her life. "I don't know that I would have described him as a *deader*, but he is indeed a corpse."

"Well, best not stand here gawping. Let the dead rest in peace, I always say." Hedge made to sidle past her.

She placed herself in his path. "We can't just leave him here."

"Why not? He was here before you trotted past. Wouldn't never have seen him neither, if we'd've taken the shortcut through the common like I said."

"Nevertheless, we did find him. Can you help me carry him?"

Hedge staggered back in patent disbelief. "Carry him? A great big bloke like that? Not unless you want me crippled for sure. My back's bad as it is, has been for twenty years. I don't complain, but still."

"Very well," Lucy conceded. "We'll have to get a cart."

"Why don't we just leave him be?" the little man protested. "Someone'll find him in a bit."

"Mr. Hedge..."

"He's stabbed through the shoulder and all over bloody. It's not nice, that." Hedge screwed up his face until it resembled a rotten pumpkin.

"I'm sure he didn't mean to be stabbed, through the shoulder or not, so I don't think we can hold that against him," Lucy chided.

"But he's begun to go off!" Hedge waved the handkerchief in front of his nose.

Lucy didn't mention that there hadn't been any smell until he'd arrived. "I'll wait while you go fetch Bob Smith and his cart."

The manservant's bushy gray eyebrows drew together in imminent opposition.

"Unless you would prefer to stay here with the body?"

Hedge's brow cleared. "No, mum. You knows best, I'm sure. I'll just trot on over to the smithy—"

The corpse groaned.

Lucy looked down in surprise.

Beside her, Hedge jumped back and stated the obvious for both of them.

"Jaysus Almighty Christ! That man ain't dead!"

Dear Lord. And she'd been standing here all this while, bickering with Hedge. Lucy swept off her wrap and threw it across the man's back. "Hand me your coat."

"But—"

"Now!" Lucy didn't bother giving Hedge a look.

She rarely used a sharp tone of voice, making it all the more effective when she did employ it.

"Awww," the manservant moaned, but he tossed the coat to her.

"Go fetch Doctor Fremont. Tell him it's urgent and that he must come at once." Lucy gazed sternly into her manservant's beady eyes. "And Mr. Hedge?"

"Yes'm?"

"Please run."

Hedge dropped the basket and took off, moving surprisingly fast, his bad back forgotten.

Lucy bent and tucked Hedge's coat around the man's buttocks and legs. She held her hand under his nose and waited, barely breathing, until she felt the faint brush of air. He was indeed alive. She sat back on her heels and contemplated the situation. The man lay in the ditch on half-frozen mud and in the weeds, which were cold and hard. That couldn't be good for him, considering his wounds. But as Hedge had noted, he was a big man and she wasn't sure she could move him by herself. She peeled back a corner of the wrap covering his back. The slit in his shoulder was crusted with dried gore, the bleeding already stopped to her admittedly inexperienced eyes. Bruises bloomed across his back and side. Lord only knew what the front of him looked like.

And then there was the head wound.

She shook her head. He lay so still and white. No wonder she'd mistaken him for dead. But all the same, Hedge could've already been on his way to Doctor Fremont in the time they'd taken to argue over the poor man.

Lucy checked again that he was breathing, her palm hovering above his lips. His breath was light, but even. She smoothed the back of her hand over his cold cheek. Almost invisible stubble caught at her fingers. Who was he? Maiden Hill was not so big that a stranger could pass through it without notice. Yet she had heard no gossip about visitors on her rounds this afternoon. Somehow he'd appeared here in the lane without anyone noticing. And the man had obviously been beaten and robbed. Why? Was he merely a victim or had he somehow brought this fate upon himself?

Lucy hugged herself on the last thought and prayed Hedge would hurry. The light was fading fast and was taking with it what little warmth the day had held. A wounded man lying exposed to the elements for Lord knows how long... She bit her lip.

If Hedge didn't return soon, there would be no need of a doctor.

THE ANGEL WAS SITTING by his bed when Simon Iddesleigh, sixth Viscount Iddesleigh, opened his eyes.

He would've thought it a terrible dream—one of an endless succession that haunted him nightly—or worse, that he'd not survived the beating and had made that final infinite plunge out of this world and into the flaming next. But he was almost certain hell did not smell of lavender and starch, did not feel like worn linen and down pillows, did not sound with the chirping of sparrows and the rustle of gauze curtains.

And, of course, there were no angels in hell.

Simon watched her. His angel was all in gray, as befit

a religious. She wrote in a great book, eyes intent, level black brows knit. Her dark hair was pulled straight back from a high forehead and gathered in a knot at the nape of her neck. Her lips pursed slightly as her hand moved across the page. Probably noting his sins. The scratch of the pen on the page was what had woken him.

When men spoke of angels, especially those of the female sex, usually they were employing a flowery fillip of speech. They thought of fair-haired creatures with pink cheeks—both kinds—and red, wet lips. Insipid Italian putti with vacant blue eyes and billowy, soft flesh. That was not the type of angel Simon contemplated. No, his angel was the biblical kind—Old Testament, not New. The not-quite-human, stern-and-judgmental kind. The type that was more apt to hurl men into eternal damnation with a flick of a dispassionate finger than to float on feathery pigeon wings. She wasn't likely to overlook a few flaws here and there in a fellow's character. Simon sighed.

He had more than just a few flaws.

The angel must have heard his sigh. She turned her unearthly topaz eyes on him. "Are you awake?"

He felt her gaze as palpably as if she'd laid a hand on his shoulder, and frankly the feeling bothered him.

Not that he let his unease show. "That depends on one's definition of *awake*," he croaked. "I am not sleeping, but yet I have been more alert. I don't suppose you have such a thing as coffee to hasten the awakening process?" He shifted to sit up, finding it more difficult than it should have been. The coverlet slipped to his abdomen.

The angel's gaze followed the coverlet down and frowned at his bare torso. Already he was in her bad graces.

"I'm afraid we don't have any coffee," she murmured to his navel, "but there is tea."

"Naturally. There always is," Simon said. "Could I trouble you to help me sit up? One finds oneself at a distressing disadvantage flat on one's back, not to mention the position makes it very hard to drink tea without it spilling into the ears."

She looked at him doubtfully. "Perhaps I should get Hedge or my father."

"I promise not to bite, truly." Simon placed a hand over his heart. "And I hardly ever spit."

Her lips twitched.

Simon stilled. "You're not really an angel after all, are you?"

One ebony brow arched ever so slightly. Such a disdainful look for a country miss; her expression would've fit a duchess. "My name is Lucinda Craddock-Hayes. What is yours?"

"Simon Matthew Raphael Iddesleigh, viscount of, I'm afraid." He sketched a bow that came off rather well in his opinion, considering he was prostrate.

The lady was unimpressed. "You're the Viscount Iddesleigh?"

"Sadly."

"You're not from around here."

"Here would be . . . ?"

"The town of Maiden Hill in Kent."

"Ah." Kent? Why Kent? Simon craned his neck to

try and see out the window, but the gauzy white curtain obscured it.

She followed his gaze. "You're in my brother's bedroom."

"Kind of him," Simon muttered. "No, I can't say I've ever been to the lovely town of Maiden Hill, although I'm sure it's quite scenic and the church a famous touring highlight."

Her full, red lips twitched again bewitchingly. "How did you know?"

"They always are in the nicest towns." He looked down—ostensibly to adjust the coverlet, in reality to avoid the strange temptation of those lips. *Coward.* "I spend most of my wasted time in London. My own neglected estate lies in Northumberland. Ever been there?"

She shook her head. Her lovely topaz eyes watched him with a disconcertingly level stare—almost like a man. Except Simon had never felt stirred by a man's glance.

He tsked. "Very rural. Hence the appellative *neglected.* One wonders what one's ancestors were thinking, precisely, when they built the old pile of masonry so far out of the way of anything. Nothing but mist and sheep nearby. Still, been in the family for ages, might as well keep it."

"How good of you," the lady murmured. "But it does make me wonder," she continued, "why we found you only a half mile from here if you've never been in the area before?"

Quick, wasn't she? And not at all sidetracked by his blather. Intelligent women were such a bother.

"Haven't the foggiest." Simon opened his eyes wide. "Perhaps I had the good fortune to be attacked by industrious thieves. Not content to leave me lie where I fell, they spirited me off here so I might see more of the world."

"Humph. I doubt they meant for you to see anything ever again," she said quietly.

"Mmm. And wouldn't that've been a shame?" he asked, feigning innocence. "For then I wouldn't have met you." The lady raised a brow and opened her mouth again, no doubt to practice her inquisition skills on him, but Simon beat her to it. "You did say there was tea about? I know I spoke of it disparagingly before, but really, I wouldn't mind a drop or two."

His angel actually flushed—a pale rose wash coloring her white cheeks. Ah, a weakness. "I'm sorry. Here, let me help you sit up."

She placed cool little hands on his arms—an unsettlingly erotic touch—and between them they managed to get him upright; although, by the time they did so Simon was panting. His shoulder felt as if little devils—or maybe saints, in his case—were poking red-hot irons into it. He closed his eyes for a second, and when he opened them again there was a cup of tea under his nose. He reached for it, then stopped and stared at his own bare right hand. His signet ring was missing. They'd stolen his ring.

She mistook the reason for his hesitation. "The tea is fresh, I assure you."

"Most kind." His voice was embarrassingly weak. His hand shook as he grasped the cup, the familiar clink of his ring against the porcelain absent. He hadn't taken it off since Ethan's death. *"Damn."*

"Don't worry. I'll hold it for you." Her tone was soft, low and intimate, though she probably didn't know it. He could rest on that voice, float away on it and let his cares cease.

Dangerous woman.

Simon swallowed the lukewarm tea. "Would you mind terribly writing me a letter?"

"Of course not." She set the cup down and withdrew safely to her chair. "To whom would you like to write?"

"My valet, I think. Bound to be teased if I alert any of my acquaintances."

"And we certainly wouldn't want that." There was laughter in her voice.

He looked at her sharply, but her eyes were wide and innocent. "I'm glad you understand the problem," he said dryly. Actually, he was more worried that his enemies would learn that he was still alive. "My valet can bring down miscellaneous things like clean clothes, a horse, and money."

She laid aside her still-open book. "His name?"

Simon tilted his head, but he couldn't see the book's open page from this angle. "Henry. At 207 Cross Road, London. What were you writing before?"

"I beg your pardon?" She didn't look up.

Irritating. "In your book. What were you writing?"

She hesitated, the pencil immobile on the letter, her head still bent downward.

Simon kept his expression light; though, he grew infinitely more interested.

There was a silence as she finished scratching out the letter; then she laid it aside and looked up at him. "I was sketching, actually." She reached for the open book and placed it on his lap.

Drawings or cartoons covered the left page, some big, some small. A little bent man carrying a basket. A leafless tree. A gate with one broken hinge. On the right was a single sketch of a man asleep. Him. And not looking his best, what with the bandage and all. It was an odd feeling, knowing she had watched him sleep.

"I hope you don't mind," she said.

"Not at all. Glad to be of some use." Simon turned back a page. Here, some of the drawings had been embellished by a watercolor overwash. "These are quite good."

"Thank you."

Simon felt his lips curve at her sure reply. Most ladies feigned modesty when complimented on an accomplishment. Miss Craddock-Hayes was certain of her talent. He turned another page.

"What's this?" The sketches on this page were of a tree changing with the seasons: winter, spring, summer, and fall.

The rose tinted her cheeks again. "They're practice sketches. For a small book of prayers I want to give

Mrs. Hardy in the village. It's to be a present on her birthday."

"Do you do this often?" He turned another page, fascinated. These weren't the pallid drawings of a bored lady. Her sketches had a kind of robust life to them. "Illustrate books, that is?" His mind was furiously working.

She shrugged. "No, not often. I only do it for friends and such."

"Then maybe I can commission a work." He looked up in time to see her open her mouth. He continued before she could point out that he didn't fall in the category of *friends.* "A book for my niece."

She closed her mouth and raised her eyebrows, waiting silently for him to continue.

"If you don't mind humoring a wounded man, of course." Shameless. For some reason it was important that he engage her.

"What kind of a book?"

"Oh, a fairy tale I think, don't you?"

She took back her book and settled it on her lap, slowly turning to a blank page. "Yes?"

Oh, Christ, now he was on the spot, but at the same time he felt like laughing aloud. He hadn't felt this lighthearted in ages. Simon glanced hurriedly around the little room and caught sight of a small, framed map on the opposite wall. Sea serpents frolicked around the print's edges. He smiled into her eyes. "The tale of The Serpent Prince."

She arched a brow. "I've never heard it."

"I'm surprised," he lied easily. "It was quite a favorite

of my youth. Brings back fond memories of bouncing on my old nurse's knee by the fire while she thrilled us with the tale." *In for a penny, in for a pound.*

She gave him a patently skeptical look.

"Now let me see." Simon stifled a yawn. The pain in his shoulder had died to a dull throb, but his headache had increased as if to make up for it. "Once upon a time—that's the proscribed way to begin, isn't it?"

The lady didn't help. She merely sat back in her chair and waited for him to make a fool of himself.

"There lived a poor lass who made a meager living tending the king's goats. She was orphaned and quite alone in the world, except, of course, for the goats, who were rather smelly."

"Goats?"

"Goats. The king was fond of goat's cheese. Now hush, child, if you want to hear this." Simon tilted his head back. It was aching terribly. "I believe her name was Angelica, if that's of any interest—the goat girl, that is."

She merely nodded this time. She'd picked up a pencil and begun sketching in her book, although he couldn't see the page, so he didn't know if she was illustrating his story or not.

"Angelica toiled every day, from the first light of dawn until the sun had long set, and all she had for company were the goats. The king's castle was built on top of a cliff and the goat girl lived at the cliff's base in a little stick hut. If she looked far, far up, past the sheer rocks, past the shining, white stone of the castle walls, to the very turrets themselves, sometimes she could just catch a glimpse of the castle folk in their jewels and fine robes. And once in a very great while she would see the prince."

"The Serpent Prince?"

"No."

She cocked her head, her eyes still on her drawing. "Then why is the fairy tale called 'The Serpent Prince' if he isn't the Serpent Prince?"

"He comes later. Are you always this impatient?" he asked sternly.

She glanced up at him then as her lips slowly curved into a smile. Simon was struck dumb, all thought having fled from his mind. Her fine, jeweled eyes crinkled at the corners and a single dimple appeared on the smooth surface of her left cheek. She positively glowed. Miss Craddock-Hayes really was an angel. Simon felt a strong, almost violent, urge to thumb away that dimple. To lift her face and taste her smile.

He closed his eyes. He didn't want this.

"I'm sorry," he heard her say. "I won't interrupt again."

"No, that's all right. I'm afraid my head hurts. No doubt from having it bashed in the other day." Simon stopped babbling as something occurred to him. "When, exactly, was I found?"

"Two days ago." She rose and gathered her book and pens. "I'll leave you to rest. I can address the letter to your valet in the meantime and post it. Unless you would like to read it first?"

"No, I'm sure you'll do fine." Simon sank into the

pillows, his ringless hand lax on the coverlet. He kept his voice casual. "Where are my clothes?"

She paused halfway out of the room and shot him an enigmatic look over her shoulder. "You didn't have any when I found you." She closed the door quietly.

Simon blinked. Usually he didn't lose his clothes until at least the second meeting with a lady.

THE DISH

Where authors give you the inside scoop!

♥ ♥ ♥ ♥ ♥ ♥ ♥ ♥ ♥ ♥ ♥ ♥ ♥ ♥ ♥ ♥

From the desk of Samantha Graves

There are some characters who will haunt a writer until their story is told. Raven Callahan from SIGHT UNSEEN (on sale now) was one such character.

She was born from a One-Page Workshop exercise at my local writing chapter, where she fended off an attacker in an underwater cave. Call it intuition or inspiration, I decided that psychic touch was the edge Raven needed to be a world-class art thief and give her a humanity she didn't always welcome. Fearless, capable, and fiercely independent, I knew I had a character I would never forget. But when the workshop was over, I filed her scene into the "Someday" folder on my desk as other obligations called.

For three years, Raven waited impatiently for me to create a story worthy of her courage and skill, full of high-stakes adventure, danger, and a hero who would challenge her at every turn, yet accept her just the way she was—the one man she couldn't walk away from. Enter David Maddox, an ex-cop surviving on guilt and vengeance. With nothing left to lose, he needed redemption as much as Raven did, even if she would *never* admit it. They would learn the hard way that the only thing they could depend on was each other.

But I have to admit that half the fun of writing this book was the opportunity to research some remarkable locales I have always wanted to visit myself. From the excitement of Miami to the tropical paradise of Key West to the sultry heat of Havana, I made their adventure mine.

So now their story is told in SIGHT UNSEEN, and although my "Someday" file doesn't look much smaller, Raven Callahan can finally rest.

Happy reading!

Samantha Graves

www.samanthagraves.com

♥ ♥ ♥ ♥ ♥ ♥ ♥ ♥ ♥ ♥ ♥ ♥ ♥

From the desk of Sarah McKerrigan

In KNIGHT'S PRIZE (on sale now), the final chapter in my Warrior Maids of Rivenloch trilogy, Rand la Nuit, infamous mercenary and expert swordsman, hunts the elusive outlaw known as

The Shadow. But who is the mysterious, quick-as-lightning thief? And what is sweet Miriel of Rivenloch hiding from him? The quest draws Rand closer and closer to a shocking truth—that the seemingly innocent woman he's falling hopelessly in love with knows more than she's letting on about The Shadow.

Writing KNIGHT'S PRIZE presented a fascinating challenge for me—intertwining the cultures of East and West in a medieval setting. The Silk Road trade route was established at this time, so I imagined that some martial arts might have been imported along with the silk. Thus was born a very different type of damsel in shining armor—a medieval heroine who kicks butt Chinese-style!

Why martial arts? As a kid, I always thought Kato was way cooler than The Green Hornet. My guilty pleasure is Jackie Chan movies, which I watch with my teenage son. And I could watch that beautifully choreographed foyer fight scene from *The Matrix Reloaded* a hundred times.

The best thing about martial arts is that size doesn't matter. I learned that as a pint-sized girl, studying judo. It's all about momentum, strategy, grace, speed, agility, and surprise, using an attacker's own strength against him. And as you can imagine, martial arts are also the great equalizer of the sexes!

As a reader, I love surprises, so I've packed plenty of them into KNIGHT'S PRIZE. No one is who they seem to be, twists and turns abound, and the story has an explosive ending! The romance and adventure should keep you up all night. Let me know if it did at www.sarahmckerrigan.com.

Sarah McKerrigan

♥ ♥ ♥ ♥ ♥ ♥ ♥ ♥ ♥ ♥ ♥ ♥ ♥ ♥ ♥

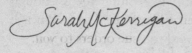

From the desk of Elizabeth Hoyt

Gentle Reader,

Whilst going through some old papers I found the pamphlet below. Although the author chose to remain anonymous, I have reason to believe that Lady Georgina Maitland, my heroine from THE LEOPARD PRINCE (on sale now), in fact wrote it.

Advice for the Landowning Lady of Means on the Hiring of Land Stewards

by an Anonymous Lady Who Knows

1. When hiring a steward the genteel lady should keep in mind that there are many Aesthetically Pleasing gentlemen who are just as much in need of work as those that are older, surlier, and not

nearly as pleasant to look upon. It is your duty to hire them.

2. The Feminine Employer should remember that it is she who is in charge. Do not be afraid to issue orders to your Male Employee, although there are times when it may be to your advantage to permit your steward to issue orders to *you*.

3. Do not under any circumstances enter into an Intimate Relationship with your land steward.

4. However, should you succumb to broad shoulders, a dry tone, and a knowing gaze, do try to be discreet.

5. Whatever you do, do not let your brothers become aware of the liaison.

6. Or your sister.

7. Or your aunt, your family, your friends, your lady's maid, or indeed any of the other servants, passing strangers, and the public in general. *Discretion* should be the watchword for the Genteel Lady desiring Further Acquaintance with her land steward.

8. It is This Author's opinion that it is of Paramount Importance that the land steward be skilled in kissing and other Intimate Arts. She cannot stress this particular point enough.

9. The Lady of Means should try to refrain from mooning about and thinking obsessively of her land steward. This behavior is apt to attract the notice of Other People (see points 5, 6, and 7 above).

10. Finally, the Genteel Lady Landowner must never, *ever*, fall in love with her land steward. That way lies disaster—or at least a very good book.

Yours Most Sincerely,

Elizabeth Hoyt

www.elizabethhoyt.com

Want to know more about romances at Grand Central Publishing and Forever? Get the scoop online!

GRAND CENTRAL PUBLISHING'S ROMANCE HOME PAGE

Visit us at www.hachettebookgroup.com/romance for all the latest news, reviews, and chapter excerpts!

NEW AND UPCOMING TITLES

Each month we feature our new titles and reader favorites.

CONTESTS AND GIVEAWAYS

We give away galleys, autographed copies, and all kinds of fun stuff.

AUTHOR INFO

You'll find bios, articles, and links to personal Web sites for all your favorite authors—and so much more!

THE BUZZ

Sign up for our monthly romance newsletter, and be the first to read all about it!